The Best Laid Plans

By

Tim Parks

Praise For The Scheme of Things

A debut coming-of-age novel about the lengths to which people will go in order to discover their true selves.

Parks' novel chronicles the story of narrator Henry Dodge, a preteen living in suburban Southern California. The book begins in 1985 with him living at his parents' home, constantly afraid of his sweet mother, athletic brother, and abusive, alcoholic father discovering his biggest secret—he's gay.

Henry spends much of his free time alone, drawing nude male figures, skimming through Playgirl, and obsessing about his all-consuming crush on his new, older neighbor, Danny Woodson. He regularly grapples with his secret and his constant feeling of being an outsider. He finally awakens to his sexuality at age 16 when he begins a physical relationship with an older male colleague at Lavar's BBQ restaurant, which inspires a series of events that ultimately leads him to come out at school—and also to his parents.

Afraid of the backlash, Henry runs away to Los Angeles, eager to find Danny Woodson. On the way, he decides to shed his identity as Henry Dodge and become a new person: Billy Collins. What "Billy" finds when he arrives in Los Angeles, however, isn't the stuff of fairy tales; he quickly gets mixed up with a rough crowd of drug dealers, pimps, and porn producers. He must then navigate through the drama of his new life.

Parks' story is an often-touching tale of a young man's self-discovery. It's long and rambling at times and packed with gratuitous sex and violence. However, the author's prose is also full of funny quips and puns: "Sooner than I knew it, the summer had flown by, the greenhouse was erected, and so was I on a nightly basis." Henry, as the narrator of the story, is also likable and tender, which makes it easy for readers to root for him.

An action-packed, if sometimes over-the-top, story about a young gay man's desire to join a community that accepts him.

-Kirkus Reviews

I have always admired Tim Parks' writings on all-things pop culture. His work for The Rage Monthly manages to add just the right amount of sass, humor, and knowledge to the "la la" land of Hollywood. Discovering he was releasing his first novel in mid-July of "faction" as he calls it... (The names have been changed to protect the not-so-innocent), I was ready to read.

The Scheme of Things is, in my estimation, The Wonder Years meets Boogie Nights. Tim Parks embodies himself in his character of "Henry." His early years of being a gay child and a hardened look at Henry's life as a teenage runaway in L.A. at 16.

Enthralling, hilarious, and suspenseful, Parks hits it out of the park with his first fictional work.

-Bill Biss, The Rage Monthly.

The writing style is fantastic. I love how the author paints rather vivid pictures with his words; it almost seems like I'm right there feeling what the main character is feeling or experiencing. Mr. Parks sets the novel in the correct time periods with reference to times and places that are right on target. His main character seems so real. This is not a fantasy book; the main character is complex, genuine, honest and very interesting. This is a very good read.

- SESCA, Amazon.com Review

I am in love with this tragic yet at times hilarious story. Tim Parks is so talented, I almost felt as if I was watching a movie. I could see the characters, hear the music and smell those amazing cookies! I laughed often and cried a few times too. I hope there's a sequel. I guarantee I'll be one of the first to buy it.

-Amazon Customer, Amazon.com

"The Scheme of Things" is a thrilling, comedic, and sometimes sad gay coming-of-age story that takes place in Southern California. The protagonist, Henry Dodge,

struggles with his sexual identity from a young age, and like many gay youth, he feels invisible to his family and close friends. Henry moves through the novel with hilarious and daring experiences which ultimately leads him to escape to LA in hopes of finding himself and his first serious crush. Most importantly, it's in LA that Henry begins to figure out who he is and isn't and also who family is and isn't. The novel has several exciting twists that keeps the reader turning the page and is chock-full of colorful characters. Tim Parks breathes life into such a relatable character with Henry that you are constantly rooting for him to succeed even when he's making questionable choices. "The Scheme of Things" is a fantastic read and I'm looking forward to the sequel!

-Alex S, Amazon.com

This Book is Dedicated To:

My Two Favorite Hags,

Past and Present...

Mariana Josimov-Goodwin, who the character of Nina is based on. And Miss Judy Taylor, a character in her right.

Foreword

This book was such a labor of love that I'm surprised I don't have stretch marks, and I expect a baby shower rather than a book launch party.

It took six years to write for various reasons. First and foremost, I wanted to make sure my first child got the amount of attention in getting recognition and shelved the sequel until that happened. Sorry, Jan.

What followed involved writer's block (the first bout with it ever), to not writing the novel in a linear fashion, as I did with The Scheme of Things. Beginning partly done, then the end spoke to me, some on the middle section and then back to the beginning and bridging it to the middle and end. Never. Doing. That. Again. Like. Ever.

A bigger reason for its delay was being sidelined by prostate cancer in 2021. Knock on wood, my next blood test will have my cancer doc proclaiming me cancer free.

However, as fortunate as I was to have my PSA levels drop from 11.7 to 1.8 at the last check-up; my nephew Jimmy Parks wasn't so lucky. He died in 2022 from this insidious disease, which also claimed the life of my mother, Mary Parks, ten years ago.

I used his strength as my own, as he never bitched, moaned, or complained about the fact that he had cancer since he was 27. He'd sum it up as it was just how his life was. I miss him a lot, as he was like a little brother to me; we were only 12 years apart.

On top of that, his sister, my favorite niece Julie Liles, lost her mother, Laura Parks, a mere six months later. She passed away in her sleep and I've known her since I was seven. The last time I saw her, we were laughing till it hurt playing Cards Against Humanity, and she told me something about me from childhood I don't remember at all.

Apparently, if there was one of my brother Fred's new girlfriends coming to our house for the first time, I would run down the stairs and say, "Who are you, and what are you doing in my house?!" She stated it was my signature catchphrase because Fred had a lot of new girlfriends.

At their dual Celebration of Life memorial, I tried to say the things that they meant to me and was so choked up that I couldn't get the words out. That's not like me at all. If you read the first book, you know why one of my hashtags was #sheswordy.

But I came away from the event with a new outlook on how fleeting life is and finished the first draft for The Best Laid Plans in three days upon my return home.

This book is also dedicated to their strength and resilience, especially my favorite niece and my brother Tommy Parks who have been through it, and like myself and Henry, emerged on the other side triumphantly.

Also, fuck cancer.

In crafting a sequel, I drew on two of my favorites, Aliens and The Empire Strikes Back for inspiration in the hope that this book will supersede the world I created for Henry and the cast of characters in the first novel. In a lot of ways, I like it better than the original.

Ultimately, it's up to you, the readers, to determine if that's an accurate statement. But just know this novelist – I have embraced that word finally - shows the first book was no one-off fluke.

On that front, I want to thank all the people who read the first misadventures of Henry Dodge for your patience. And I look forward to bringing new people into the continuing story of our intrepid hero as he returns to his quest of seeking out a tribe to call his own.

Yes, there is a third book in the works. No, there will not be as long of a gestation period.

Happy Reading,

Tim Parks (not the author of Italian Neighbors)

RED

I never knew there could be so much blood.

It really shouldn't have thrown me like it did, given all I had experienced in L.A., where it flows like wine.

Blood was at the center of why I lay in this hospital bed. Mine may be contaminated, so I decided to release it from my body. A torrent went down the bathroom sink, a swirl of plasma mixing with hot water.

I caught my reflection in the dead metal of the razor blade, a corona of light behind my head from the fluorescent lights above.

The look on my face told me three things:

Red is the color of anger. Red is the color of passion. Red is the color of fear.

Two out of the three were coursing through my veins, along with the HIV that I suspected was keeping them company; compadres in cahoots, feeding off each other in the ultimate act of internal cannibalism.

Passion was the reason for this new predicament.

It boiled down to the same old reason for the many mental skirmishes in my life; that goddamned need to be loved.

If it was possible to feel everything and nothing at the same time, then that was me. I stared at the bandages, hiding what I had tried to do. I was such a fuck-up that I couldn't even kill myself right. Being a fuck-up seemed to have been a role I had gladly assumed over the last two years, ever since…

Ever since I had run away from home after proclaiming my sexuality and blackmailing my first sex partner, Steve, who was older than me, I searched for what it meant to be gay and hoped to reconnect with my childhood crush, Danny. Unfortunately, I ran into Angel, a hooker on Santa Monica Boulevard. Angel had taken me to the palace, an innocuous apartment belonging to King George, a man mired in nefarious business dealings involving drug dealing and preying on down-and-out lost boys.

Through George, I met Nick, his partner in business and life, who was involved with turning Danny's dreams of becoming a showbiz phenomenon, which had resulted in him starring in a series of gay porn films as Miles O'Toole with a co-star, Corey Adams that bore an uncanny resemblance to yours truly.

George's son Troy arrived on the scene. His hatred for Nick, who had helped break up his not-so-happy home, was outweighed by a desire to establish a relationship with his distant father. A situation I was all too familiar with. I had spoken the words mine had always suspected but did want to hear vocalized. My mother worried that I would succumb to AIDS. The person I was most worried about rejecting me, my brother John, ended up being the one that took the news the best.

He had come to collect me during Gay Pride, after a series of revelations, like it was Danny who had taken Corey's young life and not Nick, who was obsessed with his protégé. Our family dynamic of him coming to my rescue happened after George attempted to take his own life and with Angel being shot and hospitalized. I found a real-life angel of my own in Candy, a local drag queen I met at a bar I managed to sneak into. She set me straight, so to speak, on what it could mean to be gay, a concept I was still grappling with now.

I shut my mind off walking down that particular boulevard. But there were plenty of other side streets I could traverse, and they all sprang from the sign on my bedroom door: Henry Street.

There was Anonymous Sex Avenue, the crossroad between Trusting and Not Trusting -- constantly under construction. Addiction Way was not the road less traveled.

If there had been any caution signs, I certainly did not heed them, even when the red stop signs radiated with an otherworldly glow. When I arrived home, shellshocked from my time in the trenches of the City of Devils, I developed a particular form of post-traumatic stress disorder. When pot couldn't numb me as it had once done, I hit up Jeff, a local dealer that Craig had turned me onto.

His specialty was crystal meth, and I used money from Steve to front my foray into sticking a straw up my nose for sweet relief. I entered Jeff's apartment; a territory I had sworn I would never enter. He led me to a rattan couch with a floral pattern. I sat on the middle cushion and quickly landed on the carpeted floor.

"What the fuck?!"

"Sorry, man! I was about to tell you not to sit there," Jeff said, trying to control a case of the church giggles.

He extended a clammy hand, and, despite his slight frame, he had me on my feet in seconds flat. His hand lingered a little longer on my ass, and I swatted playfully at it, not wanting to mix business with pleasure.

He withdrew it as if he'd been stung by a bee, and I was surprised he hadn't checked to see if there was a stinger lodged in it. Apparently, Craig had given him the heads up on my sexual preference, and Jeff figured we could do a little barter for the booger sugar.

I was in no mood to let him have that control over me; I was in no mood to give any man control over me again. The playground that I had discovered in a previous life was a remnant of its former glory; the metal slide now had a thin spider web to catch me should I slide down. However, the swing set was more than willing to enable the ones that governed my own mood swings.

"So, how much do I get for…" I began, trying my best not to sound like someone that had forgotten their lines on *Miami Vice*.

"Tell you what, sweet cheeks," Jeff cooed. "The first one is on me, just to see if it agrees with you."

I took the bindle and looked at it with amusement, as it was festooned with a torn magazine picture of a nude man, well, nude from the waist down.

I chuckled to myself wryly at the darker implication of this visual. The glossy image with its fine sheen looked inviting, even if a beast awaited me in its folds - poised to take me down.

"Thanks," I said, not meeting his intense gaze that was sizing me up.

"Oh, you are quite welcome," Jeff replied with a directness that made me uncomfortable. "Come back soon."

I nodded and silently made my way out the door, stepping out into a whole new world. The curtain to Jeff's window pulled back as I straddled my cherry-apple-red Honda Elite 150 scooter, and that stare was upon me again. *X: The Man with the X-ray Eyes* had nothing on Jeff, as his gaze looked right into that part of me that I was desperately trying to keep compartmentalized. With a two-finger salute from my forehead into the air, I made my way onto the bad stretch of road that lay ahead.

As soon as the door closed behind me, Jeff went to the phone like he was frantically dialing 911. He wasn't putting in a call to the authorities that his house was on fire, but he was burning up with excitement. However, what this moment of reaching out and touching someone amounted to, was a reporting of a missing person found.

"Hey! You are never going to believe who was just here. Corey Adams, the porn star!" Jeff gushed. "He says his name is Henry, but I would recognize him anywhere. Hey, you there, Danny?"

The voice on the other end of the line uttered a single "Yes" and then went silent with a click.

And where that road led me was back to the family homestead on Arroyo Street, which looked the same on the outside. A veneer of "Nope, nothing to see here; everything's normal, move along."

The inside, however, was a different story; the cogs in the machine still ran on their schedule but at a snail's pace. A year had nearly passed since I had returned home a different version of myself - changed, and not necessarily for the better.

The lime-green shag carpeting was the first thing that assaulted your eyes amid silence, as most days, I was the only one home during the afternoon.

Kate had joined Big Ed in the rat race, procuring a job as a secretary at Barrington Enterprises, a prestigious real estate firm that dealt in commercial investments and ventures. John had moved into an apartment with Jeannie a few miles away. With no one to offer me cookies or get on my case about mowing the lawn, I headed upstairs to the solitary confinement of my room.

As had become tradition, whenever I entered my Fortress of Solitude, I went over to my ghetto blaster and pressed play on Madonna's *True Blue*. The lyrics of "Live to Tell" surrounded me, enveloping me with meaning and all but threatening to take me to my past. I attempted to dig my heels into the soil, but that was fast becoming quicksand.

A man *can* tell a thousand lies, but I wasn't so sure if I had learned my lesson well. I looked at my wall at the poster of the woman. Her head was tilted upward and suggested she had the ability to change her look and sound with nary a hesitation about leaving the past behind.

I was trying my best to follow her lead, but today, I was not feeling it. My bedroom was feeling smaller somehow like the White Rabbit had slipped me a special piece of cake.

I didn't have a potion that read "Drink Me" to quell the claustrophobic feeling that had seized my day; I did, however, have a bindle in my pocket that may as well have read "Snort Me."

As I reached into my shorts, "Live to Tell" melted into "Where's The Party," and my answer was that it was up my nose, sans a rubber hose.

Being both a novice and a fan of *MacGyver*, I improvised cutting my first line with my student ID on top of the cassette housing of Duran Duran's *Arena*, which featured the telling song "New Religion." I rolled up a dollar bill as tight as I could. I was relieved that I wasn't doing this on a mirror so that I would see exactly what I was doing.

No, the mirror had been smashed many nights ago as I made my way towards what I thought freedom would be. I put the dollar bill into my right nostril and inhaled. There was a burning sensation, followed by a powerful drip that ran down my throat.

Even though no mirror was involved, I did get a fleeting glimpse of myself. The penis on the bindle looked eerily like mine.

Written underneath the phallus was the stage name Corey Adams. I couldn't crumple him up, either his photo or his memory, and throw him in the trash. There was still some crystal left in the bindle, and I folded him up and compartmentalized him in my mind, which now felt like it was on fire.

"Where's The Party" had ended, while mine was only just beginning.

I finally got to sleep two days later, with my parents being none the wiser about what had given me a bout with self-induced insomnia. I awoke from a fractured sleep to the sound of the shower running in my bathroom. The noise of the cascading water was disconcerting since I was the only one at home at 10 o'clock in the morning, save for the weekends.

Had I really slept through three days? It felt like I had slumbered for an eternity. The summer breeze was rattling the baby blue Levelor blinds on the window in a strangely calming way. Spears of light danced through the slats and then onto the floor.

I swung my feet over the bed, then shook the rocks out of my head and made my way into the hallway as the crescendo of water grew in intensity. I approached the door with trepidation, knocked once with no reply, twice.

Nothing. I turned the doorknob ever so slowly. Steam greeted me when I asked who was there, escaping into the hallway without saying goodbye.

There was a shadow of someone behind the frosted glass door.

My hand trembled slightly as I slid open the door. Standing there stark naked was King George, who turned to face me, a beauteous smile on his face.

"Morning," he said in an upbeat manner.

I snapped awake, sweat emanating from every pore, and I was breathing like I had just run a 1,000-mile marathon.

"Jesus Christ," I whispered.

Great! Now I had to go into that bathroom to drain the 'Ol main vein. Who knew who I would find in there? It could even be Patrick Duffy to let me in on why Bobby Ewing was resurrected in Victoria Principal's shower on the season finale of *Dallas*.

Since I didn't dare let anyone from the palace into my waking world, naturally, they had to haunt my dreams. One, two Georgie's coming for you.

I wanted to shut off the thoughts that bombarded my head, but I invited them in instead, and none of them bothered wiping their feet on my doormat as they barreled into the room in my brain where I hid those thoughts.

"Come out, come out wherever you are," I said in a sing-song voice.

And just like that, I was surrounded by the ghosts of love, or what I had thought love was going to be, standing there in my room.

"And you were there, and you were there, and you were there…" I pointed an accusing finger at each one of them.

George's visage faded first, followed by Nick's, leaving only Danny with his head bowed and hands resting on one another, just as they had been in court when he was being tried for Corey's death.

I was transported back to that courtroom in the County of Los Angeles last summer, sitting next to my brother, both awaiting our turns as witnesses for the prosecution. John was an eyewitness, and myself an earwitness to what Danny had "accidentally" done to Corey. The cast of supporting players on hand were Troy and Angel. Each of us told our piece to the Honorable Judge Gail Hashimoto, and she took every word intently or perhaps didn't hear us at all, given the stoic nature of her face.

I didn't want to be here, that was for sure, so like any daydreamer worth his salt, I was zoning out.

The six-man and six-woman jury didn't look like they had blood in their eyes; they exhibited an almost nonchalant air, ignoring another dead fag as adeptly as our Commander-in-Chief with the AIDS crisis.

The one person I couldn't fathom looking at was Danny, especially when he turned my way and mouthed silently, "I'm sorry." Sorriest piece of shit I've ever laid eyes on, and my mouth answered back with a silent "Fuck you!"

I looked at Troy and Angel near the back of the courtroom, whispering. Angel removed his hand from Troy's and gave me a little reassuring wave.

Hold up! Were they holding hands? Were they a couple or just showing each other moral support? Inqueeringminds wanted to know!

But before I could sneak over and ask what indeed was the fuck up, and as the judge was to make her decision known, the door to the courtroom opened. In walked a striking woman on the taller side with a short, puffy hairstyle underneath a large red hat. There was an almost animalistic way about the way she carried herself - or it was the zebra-striped print of her dress.

I'll give her props; bitch knew how to make an entrance.

The judge asked the jury foreman what verdict they had reached. Not surprisingly, in the case of Daniel James Woodson, it resulted in a hung jury. Since he posed no flight risk, the judge deemed it appropriate that he could remain out on bail until a new trial date could be set.

But what ended up happening after the court was adjourned was that Danny literally got away with murder. His lawyer arranged a plea bargain deal with the requisite probation versus time served. There was no body, no Nick, to corroborate our little band of misfits' testimony.

Outside the courtroom, the last thing I wanted to do was hang around L.A.; I was worried its taint would seep into my lungs as assuredly as the prevalent smog that hung lazily in the air. John and I were heading out to The Green Bomb when Angel called out my name, my real name, not my alias, during my own time served at the palace.

Troy hung back, standing underneath an elm tree, crisscross patterns hiding both sides of his face like he was wearing a mask. His intense eyes were on me and the exchange that was about to take place.

"Mijo," Angel said as he approached, even though I was feeling more hombre than a boy.

"John, do you mind if I talk to him alone?" I asked of my brother, not really caring if he minded at all.

"Yeah. Sure thing." John replied, not sounding convinced that it was the best of ideas given my previous track and field record of not staying put.

Trust me, the last thing I wanted to do was get sucked into more deception.

"Hey, Angel." I let my greeting hang there, unsure of what we were going to discuss. The weather? The non-verdict? He and Troy handholding? Yes, let's begin there, I decided. "So, what's up with you and Troy?"

"Oh…that," he let those two little words hang in the air.

"Yeah, *that*," I said, placing extra emphasis on the latter word.

It wasn't jealousy I was feeling or even betrayal; what we had all shared was fleeting and mired in deception. There was something else that I couldn't put my finger on.

"Well," he began trying to find the right phrasing, "He's my boyfriend, you know?"

"No, I don't know. You. Know." I punched up the last two words, so he would catch my annoyance.

"Uh, well…" he sputtered.

"Jesus, spit it out, Angel!" I chided. "Then again, that's never been your strong suit."

He gave me the kind of reproachful look that one reserves for cockroaches. I could feel a flame igniting in my mind.

"He's been there for me," he stated. "Everyone else is gone."

Yes, the palace had a thorough spring cleaning that summer, and after all the dust had settled, only Angel and Troy remained and were now as thick as thieves. If only I had known just how concentrated they were, that they had been working together covertly to take over the family business as George lay in a coma in a hospital after his self-inflicted "accident."

No, I had to go into bitch mode and drive Angel away. He had a physical scar to mark the events that had transpired, while mine was on the inside.

I was pulled out of my reverie by a flash of red. The mystery woman was walking to the parking lot. She stopped to give me the once-over, lowering her Ray-Ban's to become a living embodiment of a Patrick Nagel print.

Even though outside of the courthouse, I felt as though I were on trial by having her stare intensely at me. And just like that, she put her sunglasses back on and made her way to a cherry-red 450 SL Mercedes convertible. It looked just like the one that Bobby Ewing had driven over to Pam's the night before he was mowed down by his ex-sister-in-law Katherine Wentworth.

The car started and emitted a blast of diesel-based smog. By the time it faded away, I was back on my bed.

"Who you gonna call? Ghostbusters?" I muttered under my breath, as that was all the time, I wanted to devote to the spectral roll call I had just allowed myself to conjure. They needed to be vanquished from my mind permanently.

Everything felt in a constant state of flux, as though I had one foot in the future and one in the past, effectively pissing all over the present. Speaking of which, my bladder was starting to sing.

After I did my business, I went back into my bedroom and closed the door. I ejected Madonna out of my ghetto blaster in favor of the *Top Gun* soundtrack.

As with his title track from the *Footloose* soundtrack, I had a tough time deciphering what exactly Kenny Loggins was earnestly singing about. I knew that he could take me into the "Danger Zone," but I had no idea what was going on once I was there.

Still, one part of the lyrics spoke to me, much like the volleyball scene had. I'd never know how to get over my heartbreak, until I could get my mind as high as it could go away from the past. Or until I got a guy to blow. Again, Kenny needed to enunciate. Regardless, I wanted to take his advice to heart and take it right into the "Danger Zone," via my nostrils. I told myself only a small bump. Everything in moderation had never been my motto, but I was willing to see if I could exercise self-control.

I excavated the Duran Duran cassette tape case, then tapped out the bindle, dollar bill, and my student ID from their hiding place. Although it was a balmy summer day, there were snow flurries forecasted to go up my nostrils.

I did my best not to make eye contact with Corey's erection or name. Out of sight, out of mind. I took a snort and felt the drip. Like a gravedigger, I put all my equipment away, so the dead would not walk among the living and haunt the night.

And much like my drug use, there was also the distraction of the beach. Well, one beach in particular that I had known about for years but had never visited until a month ago.

I had parked the scooter at the Torrey Pines parking lot. My parents had purchased it two weeks ago, and I was to use the ill-gotten gains from Steve to pay them back on a monthly basis. It was some sort of barter to assure that I would be on my best behavior, wrapped up in a thinly-veiled lesson about responsibility. Gee, that's swell. I had my suspicions that Dad had relented since I had the potential to crash it. That could mean one less headache and one less stocking come Christmas.

I followed two men down the beach, unsure of where I could doff my clothes, I hadn't realized the trek to enjoy nature would be such a long one. As always, I had provided my own soundtrack, courtesy of a mixtape that featured another *Top Gun* tune. "Playin' with the Boys" poured through the orange sponges of my headphones, producing cherished memories of the homoerotic volleyball scene.

And just as I snapped back to the here and now, I watched the two men's footprints in the sand get swept away with the tide, along with their backlit figures. They made their way around a bush-covered outcropping of cliffs. I figured this locale was private enough to do my striptease to an audience of none.

Or so I thought.

As I was spreading my towel out, I noticed a mysterious stranger, completely nude and standing on the trail leading up to the bushed area. I figured that he was simply curious as to who the lone interloper was in his general vicinity. I popped open the Hawaiian Tropic suntan lotion, took in the heady aroma of its synthetic coconut smell, then began rubbing it on myself. I saw that I wasn't the only one rubbing down body parts.

He was giving me a jerky righthanded salute, waving his dick as a makeshift flag and my Spidey senses immediately began to tingle in a very localized area. He motioned for me to come closer by moving his head to the left, that I should be neighborly.

I moved my towel up closer to where the trail began, donned my bathing suit, and stuck my Walkman down the front of my swimsuit, placed the pair of Ray-Bans on the bridge of my nose when I was struck by a wave of sadness that threatened to make my hidden eyes drizzle on a gorgeous July day.

"Uh-uh, I don't think so, buddy!" I said internally to my change-on-a-dime emotions.

I let the buzzing sensation of lust run the show and moved my feet at a swift pace, until I was standing face-to-face with the average-looking man that I placed in his mid-twenties. He was a few inches taller than me, had a lithe body, a bushy brown mustache, and friendly green eyes. I waited to discover if his words matched his actions when he suddenly dropped to his knees and tugged at the Velcro on my white-and-maroon swimsuit.

Sunlight intensified the feeling of being on fire, like an ant underneath a magnifying glass, not at the threshold of death but brimming with a new verve for life. A life that I had been doing my best to erase. And as I raised my eyes towards the cloudless heavens, surrounded by azure blue on all sides with the sky bleeding into the expanse of the ocean, I felt the paint strokes filling in the gaps from the void without sex over the past year. I mean, with another person being involved.

I focused on the task at hand, well, the task in mouth technically. When all was said and done, and with nary a word spoken, this stranger had reawakened something that was stronger than the riptides lurking in the ocean, pulling me under with an invisible intensity.

I watched as he walked away, unaware of the beast that he had unleashed in me. I noted that we weren't the only souls in this setting of dusty trails and bushes in the Garden of Eden; it was crawling with a variety of serpents, all with the promise of tasting the forbidden fruit I had eliminated from my diet.

But much like a starving man at a buffet, I was back to it like no time had passed. There were no limits on my sexual appetite, save for the incorporeal voice of my mother popping into my head at inopportune moments, reminding me to be "careful." Talk about a boner-killer.

And although the numbers I was racking up were growing as the summer months moved along in a kaleidoscope of sun, sex, and sand, I still made sure I wasn't partaking in what would be considered "risky behavior."

I was cognizant of not delving too deeply into the method to my madness, that I was using sex to quell the feelings of hurt that were making my heart closed for business. While my mouth and a certain appendage were not shuttered, the organ widely associated with Valentine's Day was surrounded by the sturdiest of chains, the biggest of padlocks, and an impenetrable wall to protect its weakened state.

There was something to be said for being 17 and bitter, but it was not something that I would bring up in polite conversation. I became the living embodiment of the ad slogan "Easy, breezy, beautiful, CoverGirl." Well, minus the last part.

Honestly, I was enjoying the compartmentalizing aspect of my life now; it was like being involved in an ongoing solo game of hide-and-seek, save for the part where I would call out "Olly Olly oxen free" regarding my emotions.

And that's the interesting thing about life; you could never plan for what or who might be around the corner, as I was to find out eventually. In the interim, I was relishing my self-appointed moniker of "hard to get." I mean, technically, I was as easy as Sunday morning, free from romantic complications, motivated by my previous experiences.

But could you blame me?

My introduction to the gay world had left me lost in space; everyone except for Candy had signaled, "Danger, Will Robinson!" And I was adrift in a sea of stars with no idea when I would feel comfortable stepping foot on a still-alien world. I was waiting for the dust of Mars to settle, freeing me to explore the vastness of the empty space that was my heart.

And speaking of the place where no one could hear you scream, I had to get myself ready to meet Craig at AMC to see an afternoon matinee of *Aliens*. I was surprised when he called and suggested we see Sigourney Weaver in full kick-ass mode, laying waste to the titular creatures in the sequel.

Big Ed and my Mom had announced that they were going on a motorcycle road trip up the coast. This had been the latest wrinkle in their marriage, my mother's futile attempt to bond with him over his love for his Goldwing. I sensed that she was a not-so-easy rider.

As I piloted my own form of two-wheeled transportation and pulled into a spot in the parking lot, I spied Craig near the ticket booth.

"Hey man," he said nonchalantly. "It's good to see you. Wow! You have lost some weight."

"I believe in Crystal Light because I believe in me!" I said with an exaggerated wink.

"I see. Well, don't get too skinny, or you know, burn a hole inside of your nose," he said and then held up two tickets.

“Sir, yes, sir!” I said, echoing the story of Ripley, Newt, and the troop of space Marines in a do-or-die situation with deadly creatures.

One scene struck me in an unexpected way. When Ripley cocks her head and torches the Alien Queen’s hive, it subtly highlighted that she was facing her fear from the first film.

I actually teared up, wishing that I had the courage to face my past, or could go into a cryosleep to put my memories to rest. But I knew that I would awake with them still trailing me. At some point in time, I would need to face those demons, minus Ripley’s pulse rifle.

Afterwards, Craig and I stood by my scooter and discussed the film, deeming it a “two thumbs-up” endeavor.

“Hey, what are you doing later?” There was an electric charge to his query. “Wanna hang out?”

“Sure,” I said. “I can pick you up at 8. Sound good?”

“Most definitely.” And there was that buzzing of a Tesla coil again, and I refrained from saying, “Wear something slutty,” in case I was reading him wrong.

But I had an inkling that the words between us suggested there was a chance to feed the insatiable appetite that I had developed as of late. Suddenly obsessing over what the night might have in store for me, I raced my scooter on the short ride home with my own engine revving.

Just like the title of a Love and Rockets song I liked; I was “Haunted When the Minutes Drag.” Rather than peed them up with some nose candy, I let them pass at a snail’s pace. I killed a bit of time with my tried-and-true companion TV, then showered and primped until it was time to head out.

I almost came to a skidding halt when I saw a shadowy figure next to a familiar Honda CRX in the driveway of Craig’s parents’ house. Leave it to me to have chosen the exact time that Steve had dropped by for a little family bonding. The echoes of Craig’s confession from last year of his brother’s predatory ways almost made me turn around. I feared reprisal from Steve, the equivalent of a school bully wanting my lunch money. But it had been me who’d taken his; a price he paid for my not divulging his secret.

My hasty retreat didn’t come to fruition, and Craig emerged from the darkness. I didn’t dare bring up the subject of his sibling, so I patted the seat behind me, indicating he should come aboard.

I did not expect him to scoot up as far as he could, hugging my body. Unless he had smuggled Lavar's famous BBQ'd sausage in his pants, my gaydar had been right on the money for once.

And it kept pinging all the way home, as did the confusion of another proclamation that he had made circa 1985 right before I had made my way to…*that place*. He had delivered the news that what had transpired with his brother hadn't made him "a faggot." And although I reclaimed that bristly word with the one-two punch of a blow delivered to Scott Rainowsky's masculinity last year, I didn't agree with the chosen slur.

Both he and I had been the victims of his brother's sickness, but I didn't want to dwell on that sad tidbit from the past, as I was eager to unlock the front door to the sexual probability of the here and now.

Rather than jump his bones inside the Dodge homestead, I decided my tact would be "slow and steady wins the race." Patience had never been a virtue bestowed upon me, so I asked Craig what we should do, just to gauge where his head was at.

He let it be my choice, since it was my house and all, and I suggested a game of Quarters. His smile told me that it was an awesome idea, and I went to forage for all the accouterments to get the party started. I opted for a pitcher that Big Ed kept on hand for beer-drinking company so I didn't have to keep tapping the keg in the garage.

Big Ed had trained me to make sure the beer wasn't mostly foam with his command of "draw me one." Once when I had tired of being his Boy Friday, I returned to the backyard with a burgeoning artist's rendition of a can of Budweiser. I didn't receive praise for what I thought was my clever way of taking a stand against the man. All I got was a split-second look of amusement before the stony look returned.

And rather than become a moth to his flame of negativity, I snuffed out the foul-smelling candle of what would never be between me and him. Craig was seated on one of the two couches that John and Dad had built from scratch one summer. The matching shelving unit that they had bonded over the following fall stood guard in front of the pool table that anchored the room.

However, the why-buy-it-at-Sears-when-you-can-make-it-yourself process had been repeated on the bar shelves, which held every imaginable bottle of liquor, including the vodka that was nothing but water now, thanks to my penchant for making myself a screwdriver, most mornings before facing the drudgery of sophomore year.

It was a shame that repeatedly skipping school had gotten me a D in acting class, because there was such an ease for me to slip into what my kindergarten teacher Mrs. Treadwell had called "Let's Pretend," an exercise in stimulating our imaginations.

I placed the pitcher down, retrieved two shot glasses with a red Budweiser logo from the bar, then walked up the three stairs that led to the living room. From my days of snaking coveted quarters for an afternoon at the arcade, I knew that the piggy bank had the coin necessary for the game at hand; the pig's smile seemed to convey that it knew what I was up to.

Craig leaned back against a huge throw pillow with his legs open. The overt body language told me he was up for playing more than my favorite drinking game. But I didn't want to rush into it, figuring that making it more of a challenge was sexier, more seductive. It was sexy - until I let out a belch to end all belches, which Craig did his best to match.

I sat on the floor with the singed and varnished handmade coffee table acting as a wooden chastity belt. I couldn't help but note the slight smirk from Craig. He scooched off the couch and mirrored my sitting Indian style. Surprisingly, neither of us got into the on-two-knees position to assure a slam dunk each time.

Maybe we were subconsciously saving it for later. Suddenly, provocative words tumbled out of Craig's mouth like a lucky seven-pair of dice.

"We should make this more interesting," he said boldly. "Ever play Strip Quarters?"

"Well, I never," I said, sounding like an offended Southern belle. "What are the rules?"

"Ah, we have a virgin in our midst," he said and laughed at his own joke.

"Yeah, not so much, funny guy," I added with a smirk and eye-bat combo.

Craig explained the bylaws of this variation of this game that John had first introduced to me. This wasn't my brother's drinking game.

Soon enough, I procured two bigger glasses rather than the shot glass that was the usual target to land the quarter in. Every time you missed, another article of clothing came off. Craig was better than me, so I was soon sporting less clothing than my guest. Such was the case until I went on a winning streak. Cue a montage of a succession of quarters in slow-motion hitting the amber liquid - until the pile of clothes next to Craig was equal to mine.

But my next few attempts fell as flat as the beer was becoming. My Team Henry uniform was down to a pair of tighty-whities. But when I went for the free throw, or punt, or goal or whatever sports-ball term was applicable on a two-in-a-row streak, Craig and I were suddenly neck-and-neck. Or rather his boxers to my briefs in what would become a revealing tiebreaker.

Not surprisingly, I emerged as the loser in this adult game. I boldly stood up, then whipped them unsteadily, given my now-drunk state.

When I attempted to shoot my briefs at Craig like a rock in a slingshot, they made it only as far as the glass with the quarter resting on its bottom, signaling that the game was over. Between his laughing fit, Craig repeated Hudson's line from *Aliens* earlier that day.

"Game over, man. Game over!" he said with another uncontrollable burst of laughter before I brought that to a halt with my own quote from the film.

"They mostly come at night. Mostly," I said with a gentle tug south of my belly button. It was a burst of confidence that I wish lived inside of me always.

And, as my soldier began to give a full salute, I decided a soak in the Jacuzzi would be a good place to start getting to know Craig in a new way. Glancing nervously at each other's hard-ons and makeshift diving boards, scoring a perfect 10 from the judges, we lowered ourselves into the hot water after I had closed the blinds, then locked the door and fired up the jets.

I let the effects of the liquid courage I had consumed calm the swirling emotions in my head, which I was convinced would look like the roiling waters of the Jacuzzi as a physical manifestation. Fear went down the drain as I stared at his glistening torso, baseball-sized biceps, and the bubbles couldn't hide his taut stomach and fleeting glimpses of his impressive member.

Soon enough, we were lip-locked, as if we were underwater, and kissing was the only way to get oxygen. It made my head swim as the temperature of the water rose – but not as fast as our combined body heat from the making out and groping session.

I noted that Craig's body was similar to Steve's – but his lips meeting mine made them as different as night and day, like the lyrics to *The Patty Duke Show*. I grabbed hold of his sausage to show him that a hot dog made me lose control, eager to stop comparing and contrasting the brothers Barnes.

But then he removed my hand, and I feared that he was going to blame the beer for a momentary lapse of judgment. I braced myself for a sudden cold front in that he might change his mind and ask me to take him home as his beer buzz wore off.

"Damn, this water is really hot. It's making me a little dizzy." He took a big breath and swiped the back of his hand across his forehead, the antithesis of the song "Some Like It Hot," signaling a drop in temperature.

But like most meteorologists, my forecast was wrong, with his smile becoming brighter than the sun. He grabbed one of the white towels from a shelf on the plant bench, laid it out, and sat back, propping himself up on his elbows.

I took in the sight of him, the living embodiment of fantasies previously only provided by the stash of *Playgirl* magazines underneath the floorboards. Craig was better than a nude pictorial. His dark skin against the white backdrop of the towel made him resemble a human negative which reminded me of the dreaded question that I asked the men at Black's Beach – even when I might not even get the names.

"You're negative, right?" A turn of phrase that made me feel hypocritical, as I had never had an AIDS test, as I believed my safe-sex practices kept the dreaded disease at bay.

"So far as I know," he replied casually, but I could tell he was taken aback by it. "I mean, if you're worried, we don't have to do anything. But it's not like I do this with just anybody."

"I just had to ask." I wanted to add, "I trust you," but that illusion had been stepped upon on a boulevard of broken dreams last year. Before I took another stroll down that dangerous street, I changed course and joined Craig on the towel, my body hovering just over his. I gave him a forceful kiss to show that I wanted to finish what we had started.

When he pulled me on top of him, I let the nonverbal touching speak for me as my fingers did the walking, marching over the landscape of his body. Our once-wet bodies had begun to form pools of sweat, a byproduct of the humidity trapped within the four walls and the energy expended from our synchronized gyrating.

Soon enough, the greenhouse was more like a sauna. Rather than call 911 because my guest had passed out naked in our greenhouse, I suggested we take this inside. First, I turned off the jets and put the foam cover back on the Jacuzzi, but left the blinds down in case Gladys Kravitz had become my next-door neighbor.

Ab-nah! Ab-nah! They're going to do butt stuff!

I grabbed fresh towels, which we wrapped around our waists, unlocked the door, and headed into the den for another make-out session. I was aching to take things to the next level, making my mother surely regret not having the couch Scotch guarded.

He laid back against one of the oversized throw pillows with a look of satisfaction. But in my head, I saw his duplicitous sibling Steven again. Craig noticed the look on my face because he asked me what was wrong, breaking the erotic spell.

"Nothing, I just got lightheaded for a sec." I lied and forged ahead with my intent. "C'mon, let's take this upstairs."

Just before going up, Craig produced a condom and a travel-size bottle of lube from his jeans. I didn't have to lure him up with a promise to see my etchings. However, in the following post-coital moments, I really wanted to share my drawings - invite him into my private world. But I held back, mostly for fear of seeming too clingy and partly because I still had the mindset that equated notebooks as being a bad thing and should be kept to myself.

"That was incredible," he said, his voice slightly muffled by the pillow he was face down on.

I didn't know if I should respond with a "Why, thank you kindly," or bow, as this was uncharted territory. But now I could say that I had put my "alone time" to shame.

And that was the feeling that was welling up inside of me. I invited it in momentarily and then slammed the door shut on it, like a Jehovah's Witness with a copy of *The Watchtower*. Bye, bitch! There was nothing wrong with what we had done, although others who lived here would disagree.

"Hey, let's get cleaned up," I said, stroking his back, steering clear of my baby batter pooling at the small of his back.

"Sounds like a plan, Stan," Craig said laughingly.

"Um, my name's Henry. How quickly they forget." I chastised.

"Oh, you're very memorable," he said as he stood, cupping his hand to keep the semen from staining the carpet.

Now I did bow, making a conscious act to not curtsey.

Once each of us had cleaned off, I made a suggestion.

"I can drive you home, or you could stay over."

Craig looked indecisive for all of five seconds before he nodded. Since my bed was a twin, he curled up in the bean bag chair. Soon enough, he was softly snoring. My sleep was very uneasy. I was awakened by Dad's Goldwing motorcycle pulling into the driveway.

I was in full-blown panic mode. Craig still slumbered. But after I gave a few shakes to his naked torso, he got dressed and quickly followed me downstairs.

The only escape route was through the gate in the backyard once the coast was clear. That way, my little slumber party could remain on the qt. But as I squired him to the sliding glass door, I saw that I had left extensive evidence of our game of Strip Quarters for the eagle eyes of my mother. I quickly scooped them up and shoved them behind the throw pillow on the couch.

As Craig and I passed the greenhouse, I breathed a sigh of relief that I had the rare foresight to return it to its natural state. As soon as I heard the garage door close, I quietly unlatched the gate and shooed Craig like a fly. I gave him the thumbs-up signal, realizing that I should have mimed the "I'll call you" gesture.

I hoped he wasn't mad at me. But those chips were going to fall where they may, and I needed to get inside before suspicions were raised. As I heard the key in the front door lock, I put my game face on.

"Oh, hey. You're back early," I said from the kitchen, pretending to forage for breakfast, even though my stomach was in knots.

My mother was fussing at her much-shorter hair, rearranging it after its time underneath the motorcycle helmet. It was now gray, signaling that her longstanding relationship with Miss Clairol was a thing of the past.

"*Somebody* has to go on a business trip tomorrow, which is why I told *somebody* not to check in with work," she said with a playful jab at Big Ed's beer gut.

"Well, *somebody* has to bring home the bacon," he chided. The thought of him munching on charred pig flesh seemed nothing short of cannibalism. "Speaking of, when are you going to get off your la-, um, butt and get a job?"

He had changed his scold from my "lazy ass" to "butt" when Mom shot him a terse hard sideways look. I was sure that the look on my face equated abject horror at my parents being so lovey-dovey with each other, but it had been par for the course as of late with their shared love of hitting the road, all decked out in leather jackets that were more Heck than Hell's Angels.

Even more unsettling was Big Ed's attempts to forge some sort of understanding between us. It was somewhere in the neighborhood of "If you don't give me grief, then I won't either." The funny thing was that it was working, as I was less apt to sass him, but it didn't bridge our wide generation gap.

As much as it pained me to admit, he was right, as I tried to mentally calculate how much blackmail money I had to play with. But math is hard, so I gave him a vague guesstimate.

"Soon, Pops, soon." And I even clapped him on the shoulder. He just nodded, not wanting to ruffle mother hen's feathers.

"Did you eat yet?" Mom asked, even though I was able to add milk to cereal or scramble eggs. But it gave her pleasure, and a sense of purpose, to dote on "her boys," as she referred to John and myself. So, I let her know that I was as rumbly in my tummy as Winnie-The-Pooh seeking out honey, so she set about making me scrambled eggs and toast.

Soon enough, her nest would be empty, as John had already flown the coop and was "living in sin" with Jeannie in an apartment off Encinitas Boulevard, and I would really need gainful employment to be out from underfoot soon. I mean, it was only six months until I turned 18, so time was of the essence if I wanted to be on my own - but not in a schmaltzy Patti LaBelle-Michael McDonald duet kind of way.

As if her name was Flo, I retreated to the den to let Mom bring my meal to me. And as I leaned back against the pillow, I could have shouted out, "Kiss my grits," as my back touched the hidden evidence of last night's two-man party.

Luckily for me, Mom merely handed me a plate, napkin, and utensils with a smile and disappeared. My parents really should have raised me to be an actor/child star; I mean, I was going to end up with a drug problem anyway.

And that reminded me that I still had a bit of nose candy as dessert after breakfast. I heard them heading up the stairs, then shut their bedroom door. Soon, I heard the sound of water running through the pipes.

As I washed the three glasses and dried them in a frenzy, relieved that Mom had no idea of my entertaining a gentleman caller, I heard a noise and turned around. Big Ed was standing on the top stair.

"Ahem," he said, and I almost dropped the small shot glass.

There was nothing I could do that would get me out of this one, so I fessed up that I had a friend over last night, and we had a few beers. He gave me a knowing look, one that didn't bother to ask if it was a girl because that would have been an obvious case of ruff, ruff, you're barking up the wrong tree, Big Ed.

"You know that I don't mind if you drink, as long as it's at home," he said matter-of-factly as if this were something that Mike Brady would say to Greg. But it wasn't the end of my lecture. "However, I would appreciate it in the future if you wouldn't entertain guests with alcohol in our absence. Are we clear?"

"Cah-rystal," I said, suppressing a giggle at the double entendre. After washing my plate and utensils, then placing them in the dishwasher, I headed to my bedroom. I inhaled both lines with the efficiency of a Hoover vacuum, using the top of my dresser and an empty tape case. Suddenly, there was a cursory knock and then Mom's unwelcome entrance.

I quickly shoved the tape case, razor blade, bindle, and straw haphazardly into the top drawer. Naturally, the drips started instantaneously, making my eyes water.

I was doing my best not to snort, sniffle, or raise her suspicion with any of the tell-tale signs that she may have heard about from Nancy Reagan. And despite my best efforts, a sniffle escaped from my nose, which brought about a look of concern from her.

"Man, my allergies have really been acting up today," I moaned.

That put her mind at ease. But I suddenly remembered the discarded condom in my trashcan. I moved my body slowly, languidly, to get in her line of sight and not arouse suspicion.

"Would you do me a favor?" she queried. At this point, if she asked me to jump through a flaming hoop, I would have done so without hesitation.

"Of course!" I exclaimed, too enthusiastically.

"Can you go to the store later?"

Just at that moment, another drip slid down my throat, so I merely nodded.

"I appreciate it, hon."

"No problemo, Mamacita."

She offered a genuine smile, which denoted she hadn't a clue about either my drug use or sexcapade under her roof.

Even though I felt as wet as a cake left out in the rain, I figured a shower couldn't hurt. After that, I did another rail, this time without a surprise visit from Mom. Taking the pencil in my hand, grabbing a halfway-finished sketchbook, and positioning myself at my drafting table, I made a conscious effort not to cover up the word freedom that I had put there a year ago.

That simple yet complicated word, depending on how you looked at it, was the impetus of my creative endeavor, brought to you by the good folks at crystal meth. I became lost in the pencil strokes, shading the image that was taking on a life of its own.

The word Freedom, writ large and in a New Wave style, took up the top of the page. The accompanying sketch was my best attempt at a self-portrait; the sun hovering to the left while its celestial twin, the moon, did the same over my head on the right. A complete shadow swallowed the right side of my face, courtesy of the moon, while the left side remained in full view.

I was 75% satisfied with the first attempt and released the pencil from the death grip that a slew of teachers had chided me about throughout the years. I stared at the school picture I had used for my first attempt at capturing my essence; it was light years from my freshman one, as I had shed that dorky look. There was now something different about my eyes, not exactly world-weary but close.

I looked like any of my other contemporaries, surrendering to conformity, yet still the antithesis of the line "one of us" from a late-night viewing of the movie *Freaks*. And then the thought of school starting up deflated my good mood.

The past year had left me very uninterested in higher education, and my junior year of book learning was at odds with the life experiences I had gone through the previous summer. I wasn't exactly streetwise and hot-dog foolish, considering my numerous scooter sojourns to Black's Beach. But I hadn't exactly emerged from L.A. unscathed and there was now a definite hardness around my heart.

I pushed back from the drafting table as if it would leave these thoughts in its vicinity, but like the vapor trails of a jet fighter, they followed. They persisted even as I inhaled more fine granules of powder that I hoped would halt distant memories.

I hoped that the requisite drips would act like a variation of Drano and unclog these thoughts and banish them. And knowing myself, I'd also need Madge, the Manicurist, and her ever-ready Palmolive, because I knew I would be soaking in it for the immediate future.

I returned to the drafting table, then saw John pulling into the driveway, the sun reflecting off the Green Bomb's windshield momentarily blinding me, but not with science. I gathered up the day's exercise in creativity and put it away in the cabinet of my entertainment center. This dossier was for my eyes only.

I silenced Bananarama's serenade from *True Confessions*, and my mind wandered to the visuals of the hot and sweaty men fawning at Keren Woodward's feet in the video for "Venus." Lucky bitch! I packed away the masturbatory thoughts the video had provided, put on my game face, and left my sanctuary.

John was trapped within the tentacled hug of our momtopus, seeing as she didn't see him as often as when he was living here.

The eye roll he gave me signaled he was just about done with her unabashed display of affection.

"Hey, you little shit," he said casually.

"What's up, ya big turd?" I answered.

"Oh, you boys!" She turned around and faced me. "I was about to call out a search party. You haven't left your room in hours!"

"Maybe I should get a sign that says, 'Creative genius at work' or something, so you'll know when I'm working."

John took that opportunity to mimic me jerking off behind Mom's back. I struggled not to laugh. I had improved since the days when he made me spray milk out of my nose with his dinner-time shenanigans.

"Hon, I still need some things at the store. Maybe your brother can drive you."

John acted as if following orders from his higher-ups in the Navy. He did a quick salute.

"Sure thing," he teased. "We wouldn't want our delicate flower to tip his scooter over, like a rack of ribs on the Flintstone's car." He joked, but I could see his eyes assessing my weight loss.

"I prefer the term twig, thank you very much." And gave him a one-finger salute.

"Now, if you're done with your Colgate Comedy Hour," Mom said, "I'll go get my list."

John gave me a hug, asking if I was anorexic or something.

"Not at all. Just gotta keep it right and tight, you know, just the way the guys like me."

Rather than recoil in horror, he playfully punched me in the arm.

Mom returned with her list, written from a pad supplied by local realtor Ken Cartwright, one that had escaped my bored doodles of blackened teeth and eyes. Mom's neat penmanship had mapped out tonight's dinner. It did not take Betty Crocker to figure out that we were having what was affectionately known as Tuna Gunk, which required the binding powers of Velveeta cheese, to ensnare the tuna and seashell pasta in its gooey, melted clutches.

The thought turned my stomach a bit while the other three Dodges ate it up like someone was going to steal it out of their bowls.

Still, it was light years away from her casserole that included melted Velveeta, crumbled Jimmy Dean sausage patties, canned spinach, hard-boiled eggs, and white rice. There was more than one occasion as a kid when I had purposely done something to get Big Ed mad, ensuring that I was sent to my room without dinner.

"Let's motor," John said.

We headed to Alpha Beta, where John was a celebrity, as he had worked there until enlisting in the Navy. While it wasn't like trying to shop with Madonna, it did prove tiresome to wait on John while he answered neighbors' and staff's questions about how the military was treating him. Much like my sex life, I looked at the grocery store as an in-and-out experience, not one to dawdle and get on with my day and did just that.

In fact, it took so long for him to field questions and regale them with his naval adventures that I found myself waiting outside after I paid the bill. There was a girl standing near the exit with a cardboard box. I steeled myself to lie that I was diabetic and couldn't buy her Girl Scout cookies.

But what she uttered was more appetizing than my favorite peanut butter cookies.

"Free puppy, mister? She's the last one left," she asked John, who had silently joined me. He shook his head no, but I peered into the box.

A little black dot of a canine laid on the pitiful look, meeting my gaze. My heart melted, turning to mush as effectively as an ice cream cone on the sidewalk.

Before my brother could corral me, I picked her up. My reward was a face full of puppy kisses. John turned stern, a younger version of Big Ed.

"No. Absolutely not."

But I knew the puppy would emerge triumphant in swaying his resolve.

"Dude, Dad's gonna kill you." John hissed, causing me to hatch a plan that even the most hard-hearted person would accept.

I suggested that we tell the folks we had almost run her over along a foggy stretch of road. Naturally, this meant we would have to keep her hidden until nightfall.

"Now, what do we do with her in the meantime?" John asked.

"Good question. Can we take her to your place until later?"

"I guess so, but Jeannie isn't a fan of dogs. No matter how cute they are."

It bought us about two hours.

After we brought home the groceries and ate dinner, Jeannie called. John played it off like there was some sort of plumbing emergency, which wasn't entirely untrue since a certain little lady had peed on the carpet.

"Hey, Henry, think you can give me a hand?" I steadied myself to have our cover blown, as my parents knew my disdain for any mechanical work. But I dug into whatever acting chops I had and answered with a resigned "I guess so."

"You can't keep her here!" Jeannie squealed as soon as John entered as if she had been left in charge of Cujo.

"Ok, babe. Sorry she's been so much trouble."

"Maybe that's what you should name her!" she said.

"Nah, her name is Shadow," I announced. I had read a John Saul book called *Nathaniel*, and that was the name of the main character's dog. It was a fitting name for this bundle of joy.

"Hey, I like that," John said gently, to not raise his girlfriend's ire further. "Listen babe, how about if I make it up to you? Let's go see a movie tonight. *Stand by Me*. Henry, you in?"

"Totally." But I wondered how we were going to smuggle a puppy into the movies.

"Don't worry, little brother. There's no way they'll even know she's there."

However, when he dropped me off after the movie, I wished John had been there to help me look for the puppy. Improvising, I left her curled up on a towel in my room. She wasn't anywhere, not under the bed, not in the hall, nowhere. I was still looking around my room when the sound of Mom's voice made me jump out of my skin.

"Lose something?" she asked, walking in with Shadow squirming in the crook of her arm.

The audible gulp that caused my Adam's apple to physically hurt had to be in full view of Mom. And the look in her eyes proved that she was relishing the fact that she had stone-cold busted me, so I launched into the sob story I had concocted. Her icy look melted, and I knew that I had her hook, line, and sinker.

"Oh no, the poor baby!" she said with the tenderness reserved for when I used to skin my knee from falling off my bike.

"I know!" I said with genuine concern as the puppy added the finishing touches by licking Mom's face within an inch of its life.

"Well, she certainly is a love bug," she said affectionally, the door of her heart swinging wide open. "However, whether we keep her or not is entirely up to your father."

She handed Shadow over to me, who focused her kisses on me, as Mom exited my room. Whether it was the effects of the meth, intermittent checking on the slumbering Shadow, or the thought of the monster having the final say in our having a pet, I slept for shit that night.

The next morning's exchange with my dad turned out to be something that I hadn't expected and made me suspect a giant seed pod had duplicated him while he slumbered.

"I'm fine with it, as long as you are the one to take care of her," he said after a sip of coffee. It might teach you some responsibility. God knows you need that."

I decided to ignore his little dig, lest a nasty reply change his mind.

What I ended up ignoring, however, was keeping in touch with Craig while juggling my newfound fatherhood to a furry baby. Shadow was slowly but surely winning over my mom with her comical ways, which included living up to her name by following her everywhere.

She was my main focus, and as we began to become acquainted, I became attuned to the signs that she had to "do her business" – which sounded less barbaric than, "Do you have to take a shit?"

There was a downside to her dark blue eyes, though. They seemed to plead, "Daddy don't!" whenever I dipped into my dwindling stash of Tina. It was this fact that made me reach out to Craig, as there was something about Jeff that creeped me out. And I didn't want to be alone with him for fear that I may be added to an imagined head collection in his freezer. Not surprisingly, his tone was brusque and devoid of the musicality that had filled the night air a few weeks prior.

"Oh. Hey man. What's up?" he said in answering the phone like I was a telemarketer that had interrupted a family dinner. I knew I had to swiftly quash any hard feelings from my soft approach in making our connection a one-night stand.

"I just wanted to call and say I was thinking about you." I tried not to sound like some lovesick schoolgirl.

"Oh yeah?" Craig said with a spark of the fire that had guided our mutual ships to shore.

I did my impression of Yello's "Oh Yeah," which was featured in *Ferris Bueller's Day Off*, another of my favorite movies that summer. When he laughed, I knew the shaky ground that I had been on with him was having a plate tectonic shift back to one that supported solid footing.

We started shooting the shit, with me trying to figure out a subtle way to ask him to score for me. I mean, how do you casually slip that into a conversation? But when the direction of the exchange took a detour down a lustful road, I decided to risk the possibility of ending up in a pothole with him.

"You know what makes me really horny?"

"The answer better be me!"

"Well, mister, that's a given," I answered enthusiastically before I dropped my octave to a conspirator's tone. "Have you ever fucked around after, uh, having a chemical reaction?"

"Like a physical attraction?" he mocked and paraphrased Madonna in the same breath, which instantaneously made him swoon-worthy.

"Like from Jeff's product." I tried not to sound illicit. Like a TV commercial – Jeff's meth – now with flavor crystals!

"I can't say that I have," he answered honestly and slightly intrigued. "I'll assume that you have, since you brought it up."

"I've done it solo, but I have been wanting to try it with someone else. Unfortunately, I'm almost out. And to be honest, Jeff is a bit, well, intense whenever I go over there. Any chance you go with me?"

"Are you asking me out on a date?" he joked. "You are a true romantic, Henry. No dinner, eh?"

"I thought it would be fun to just skip to dessert."

"And when were you thinking of sweeping me off my feet?"

"You busy later?"

"Let me consult my social engagement calendar." He paused as if he really were checking his availability. "As it so happens, I do have an opening."

"Trust me, I remember it very well."

"Such a charmer."

"I try."

We decided on 4 o'clock, not wanting to see if Jeff was as odd during nighttime hours. If I didn't receive a call from Craig, that meant it was a go. But my plans were also contingent on Mom serving as Shadow's caretaker for the evening. Luckily, she didn't mind, but inquired about my plans.

"Just gonna hang out with Craig and see what's on cable." I figured I wasn't really lying since cable involved wires - and meth also made me wired.

"Just don't stay out too late."

I promised and tried to wear Shadow out with an endless game of fetch so that she wouldn't be too much of a burden for Mom. It did the trick, as she had a puppy power down. So, I got ready for my "date."

I still hadn't figured out where we could go to try out the secret powder.

I figured that we could discuss that after our evening plans with Tina. There was no way that I wanted to risk running into Steve. Unless it was with my scooter. I still felt that vehicular manslaughter seemed an appropriate comeuppance for the man who had robbed me of my naivete.

Granted, I wasn't entirely innocent. Besides, there were Craig's parents to contend with, and it was highly doubtful that they condoned homosexual acts under their roof.

Sometimes the truth doesn't set you free; you just learn to build your own version of a cage to hold it in.

Luckily, Craig decided to meet me down the block from the cul-de-sac, where plotlines ran darker than the ones on *Knot's Landing*.

"Howdy, sexy," he cooed into my ear after he had straddled the scooter and planted himself firmly as humanly possible without being inside of me. I smiled at the insistent push of his projectile, poking me just above the top of my pants.

I patted his hands that were wrapped around me, and he gave mine a squeeze, and we were off. I felt a pang of guilt that I wasn't being as transparent with my feelings as Craig was, hoping that he wouldn't see through my gay façade, so to speak. I pushed the thought away, as if it were on fire, not wanting our friendship to become a burned bridge.

I knew at some juncture I would have to risk letting him know that I wasn't capable of the romance on display in the movies, music, and books we liked, sprinkled with sex here and there. It sounded like nothing short of a recipe for disaster. I steered in the direction of Jeff's apartment and pushed away the idea.

We pulled up in front of what had been a nice apartment building twenty years ago. I was tempted to keep going, to race away from my ability to bend the truth, the invisible hitchhiker that was always riding with me. But Craig got off the scooter first, and I placed my foot on the asphalt. With no hesitation, I walked up the stairs to the second floor with him.

After ringing the doorbell twice with no answer, I thought I was off the hook. Just as I was about to say that we should go, a bedraggled Jeff answered the door, his brown hair standing up in corkscrews.

"Oh, hey guys. Sorry, I must have dozed off. Come on in." His molasses voice was thick with sleep.

"If it's a bad time, we can come back," I said.

"It's all good in the hood. Entre vous," he said, fumbling the French term for come in.

I let Craig take the lead, and I made sure that I didn't sit in the middle of the couch, lest I wanted to be swallowed by some furniture version of the Sarlacc pit in *Return of the Jedi*.

I settled for the floor with its bong water-stained carpet, which had either been bright yellow at one point or had soaked up the nicotine from the Tareyton cigarettes that Jeff smoked and was now in the process of lighting.

A cloud of smoke enveloped his head and obscured his face momentarily. He remained silent, as if we were here on a social call rather than doing a drug deal. Soon he got to the business at hand and generously asked if we'd like to sample his wares.

"Sure, why not?" Craig said with a breeziness.

"Cool, be right back."

He made his way to the kitchen, lifted the lid of a '70s "Have a Nice Day" smiley face cookie jar, and snagged a prepackaged bindle. The Cheshire cat grin was signaling that we were about to enter Wonderland. He drew out three lines that could only be described as massive and handed the rolled-up one-hundred-dollar bill to Craig first.

As Craig bent forward to the glass coffee table, Jeff snuffed out his cigarette and shot me a look that was both lustful and knowing. I ignored it, but when I took another glance in his direction, it was still affixed on his face, a permanent tattoo. I made my focus the fat line on the table when Craig handed the straw to me.

Both of us gagged on the super-strength drip. Jeff went to the kitchen for two beers.

"This oughta quench your thirst."

We simply nodded as the drips caused temporary speech paralysis. I usually tried to compartmentalize my poisons: crystal to boost my brain and beer to help me sleep when I needed to come down. But beggars couldn't be choosers in this scenario.

I took a hearty swig off the Heineken, as did Craig, neither offering a cheers. Jeff took a smaller sip, the creepy, sly smile persisting.

My suspicious mind wondered what he had on his. After Jeff did his line, he said something – and it didn't surprise me.

"You guys should hang out for a while," he said while clearing his throat. "I mean, if you want to," he added casually.

I hoped that my look conveyed to Craig that this might be a case of "Danger, Will Robinson!" But he nodded and said it was ok with him, so I didn't want to be the odd man out. I agreed to hang out - for a bit.

"Awesome! I like spontaneity in my men," Jeff said a little menacingly for my taste.

One of the offshoots of...*that place* located North of here was that I had been completely gullible, and I had been working on honing my bullshit detector.

Jeff remained the perfect host, drawing out heapin' helpin's of nose candy, adding beer chasers. Soon, we played the card game 21. I found myself having fun. The beer and crystal combo nicely kept me evenly moderated.

The only problem with drinking beer was its effect on my thimble-sized bladder. After my twenty-eighth trip to drain the dragon, I worried that I would come back to a different vibe in the room. One that would make me feel like a third wheel and want to sing the Clash song "Should I Stay or

Should I Go," the two of them naked, with mouths and hands being used in tandem.

I splashed cold water on my face, shaking my head like a dog getting a bath to get the visual out of my head, hoping it wasn't some sort of premonition of what I would see when I returned.

Alas, this was thankfully not the case. Jeff had decided it was time for an impromptu concert for an audience of two, his electric guitar plugged into an amp, Van Halen's *5150* on the turntable, and he tried to match the bravado of Eddie Van Halen's guitar virtuosity on the first cut, "Good Enough."

When the song changed to "Why Can't This Be Love," he shot Craig and me a quizzical look as if to ask why we hadn't given a thunderous round of applause. Since he was being very hospitable, I mustered up an assessment of "That was good, real real good."

He bowed as though he had just knocked the socks off concertgoers at Madison Square Garden.

"You're really good with your hands –well, I guess your fingers, really." Craig offered.

"You ain't seen nothin' yet," Jeff answered with a wink, which I took as foreplay for the scenario I had imagined in the bathroom. Rather than fuel any form of flirtation, I checked my watch and commented that it almost was nearing nine o'clock, not necessarily the witching hour, but I didn't want Craig or myself falling under his spell.

The terse look from Craig all but cemented the fact that I was the party-pooper. He seemed to have forgotten that we had made plans for just the two of us. He seemed happy to include Jeff as the third wheel - and I didn't want to be the squeaky one getting the grease or lube, as the case may be.

When Jeff took his shirt off, proclaiming that it "sure was hot in here and for us to make ourselves more comfortable," my discomfort level suddenly skyrocketed. Ignoring the panic on my face, Craig decided to strip all the way down to his underwear, his compass pointing due north, signaling he wanted to explore the uncharted territory I saw fraught with danger.

This was all the provocation that Jeff needed as they began a makeout session that looked like they were trying to steal one another's oxygen. When they came up for air, Jeff made a breathless request.

"C'mon Henry, you, of all people, shouldn't be shy."

I stood resolute, not taking the bait, especially since I was unclear of what he meant.

"Don't get all shy," Craig chided good-naturedly.

"I think I did too much, Tina," I responded. "I probably look like a two-year-old in cold water right now."

"I've got the remedy for that," Jeff said. He popped a video into the VCR.

The porn was cued to a certain alleyway with a certain former crush that had pulverized me, being attended to orally by Corey Adams.

"Yeah, I gotta go," I said feebly, feeling the walls of the past closing in around me.

"Aww, c'mon, this is my favorite." Jeff held my gaze, the creepiness factor set at 10. "Besides, I really like your work in this one."

Although my feet were commanding me to beat a hasty retreat, it was my ears that I was concentrating on. Had he really just said that? By the look on Craig's face that was staring at me, I took it at face value that Jeff had spoken those words.

"That's not me," I said barely above a whisper.

"Oh really? If not, you have a twin brother, then."

If I did have a twin, he would be of the evil variety that allowed actors to portray both ends of the right and wrong spectrum in soap operas. Besides, mine would sport an eye patch and a mustache.

"Yeah, really," I said haughtily.

"You've got to admit that the resemblance is uncanny," Craig suggested, and I didn't dare glance at the screen in order to avoid Miles O'Toole practicing his chosen craft.

"Whatever," I muttered. "So, stupid question, but are you coming or not?"

"The night's still young," Jeff said, and I instantly felt like an old fuddy-duddy. "It's cool if you want to hang out; no hard feelings."

No, I wasn't having any of those at present. The boner kind, I mean.

"Would you be mad if I wanted to stay?" Craig asked innocently.

"Not at all," I said, knowing I would end up furious. But this was a case of you reap what you sow; I had used Craig under false pretenses – so who was I to say what he should or should not do? And from the way he was pawing at Jeff, it was clear what he was going to do.

Jeff took his hand and led him to the bedroom and told me I was more than welcome to join in. He left the door open, then lit a candle that gave the room a spectral glow. The moans coming from the porn on the TV set were haunting me more than any ghostly entity. The cogs in my brain began to turn, debating if it wouldn't be so bad to participate. But when Danny's voice instructed my doppelganger, "Don't bite it, just suck it," my mind was made up. But not the way either of them expected.

I hovered in the doorway to discern if they were busy. Jeff was on top of Craig, rubbing up and down, and Craig's eyes were closed.

There was no chance I would be caught with my hand in the cookie jar. I slipped into the kitchen, lifted the lid carefully, a pig sniffing out truffles, then grabbed a handful of bindles. I put them in my pockets and returned to the bedroom.

"I'm out, but thanks for everything. You boys have fun."

Jeff removed his hand from Craig's cock and gave a small wave.

As I drove home, I was trying to combat the emotional potholes. I wanted to avoid the open trenches that ran through my heart.

Again, my mind drifted to that hateful image on the TV, now seared into my retinas. Of all the porn Jeff could have put on, it had to be *Up Your Alley* - and weirder yet, even if I had been a co-star in it, why would I want to watch? I now considered it a snuff film since a man had killed his co-star and gotten away with it.

There had been a fragile veneer of civility about Jeff that had made me believe for a few hours that I had him all wrong, that he wasn't that bad. But I was not one that could throw stones at his glass house, well, his crystal one. I was trying not to feel bad for taking what wasn't mine when a song from first grade came out of thin air.

"Who stole the cookie from the cookie jar? Henry stole the cookie from the cookie jar. Who, me? Yes, you! Couldn't be! Then who?"

"Henry," I said to myself. "Duh."

Mom was watching TV in the living room and looked surprised I was home at a decent hour. I made small talk, then carried Shadow, who gave me several sleepy kisses, upstairs to my room.

I placed her on the bed because it was likely that I wouldn't be sleeping tonight. I hid the bindles in the cassette case that had once housed the Pet Shop Boys' *Please*.

I drew myself up a generous line. Then I got lost in the tape's synth beats, listening through the headphones. The orange sponges buffered any sounds that might tip Mom off that I was a creature of the night.

And wouldn't you know it? Mom materialized in my doorway. I slipped them off to see what she wanted.

"Don't stay up too late, hon."

"I'm just gonna listen to some tunes, draw some." I kept it brief, despite my mouth wanting to talk a mile a minute.

"Goodnight then."

"Night."

I replaced the headphones, grabbed my sketchbook and pencils, and set about getting lost in music and creativity. Before I knew it, side two of the tape had ended, and I had a decent outline of an image, one born of desire.

It was a man shrouded in shadow and darkness. His hand was outstretched with a single word on the open palm: Mine. A phantom image, begging someone to step into the world of love that seemed elusive, a million miles away in the great unobtainable atmosphere of what could be.

"Someday," I said aloud to myself, but the word not only woke Shadow up but also caused a spark of yearning in me. I wouldn't term myself as a hopeless romantic, more of the hopeful variety, but a straight and narrow path towards love was not to be for me.

Given the day and age, I still had to be wary of not leaving a trail of discarded flings behind me. I guess you could call me a vigilant slut, even though the men I had relations with were of the safe-sex variety.

The clock on my nightstand read 1 a.m. I felt frozen in the moment, standing on a dark precipice, seized in the clutches of the night outside and the total eclipse of the heart within me. I didn't know when I might be ready to open up and trust again.

The mental back-and-forth between what had been and what I wanted was exhausting. Luckily, I had a well-spring of energy and drew up another line. For a second, I contemplated not doing it. This couldn't be good for me in the long run, but the short-term solution for sorting through endless emotions was up my nostril and down my throat before I could make a healthier choice.

I plopped into my bean bag chair, turned on the TV, and lowered the volume. It didn't matter what was on, as I was lost in thought. I hadn't imagined on that forever ago night that I'd be blindsided by love. Or whatever it was that I thought I'd ever had with *him*. They called it a crush for a reason.

There was a stoniness within my heart, my arteries pumping disappointment into my bloodstream. I didn't want to be 17 and jaded, left bitter by unusual circumstances, leaving me a dented can in the damaged goods section in the grocery store of life.

Adversity is a funny thing; it toughens you up whether you want it to or not, but can only be viewed in the rearview mirror of life, where objects were further away than they appeared.

The only thing I knew for sure was that I didn't know anything, but I was willing to learn and not give up on myself. And as the sky lightened behind the Levelor blinds, I became determined not to let the darkness of my being overtake the potential that lived in me, to find a way to let my light shine again.

For now, I needed to get some semblance of sleep. Somewhere, somehow, I did manage to drift off, finally roused by a canine alarm clock that needed to empty her bladder.

I passed my mother, sitting in the kitchen as she had throughout my life, nursing a cup of coffee.

"Good morning, sleepy head."

"Morning." As I headed toward the sliding door in the den, Shadow in my arms, I glanced at the homemade clock that Big Ed had fashioned in burned, shellacked wood. It was a half-hour before noon.

I let Shadow out to do her business, went into the downstairs bathroom, and did the same. As I washed my hands, I caught sight of myself in the mirror, hair standing on end as if I had been electrocuted in my sleep. The bags under my eyes were more of a carry-on and less than suitcases filled with emotional baggage that needed to be checked.

I ran a handful of cool water through my hair and a second on my face. It was temporarily soothing, pushing back on the semi-slimy feeling my skin took on the day after doing meth.

Shadow was waiting outside the bathroom door, tail wagging a mile a minute as if I had just returned from a two-week vacation. I clapped my hands on my right thigh to cue her to climb the stairs, but she resembled a teen girl in high heels for the first time. But she managed it and was rewarded with kibble, along with a side dish of praise.

"What are your plans for the day?" Mom asked. Then she went in for the kill. "Might be a good day to look for a job."

"Oh, would it?" I said in my head. Outwardly, I responded without sarcasm, "I read you loud and clear."

"Good, because you and your father are getting along better, and it would keep things that way."

Yes, rather than being like oil and water, we had found a way to tread H20 that hadn't led to any tidal waves lately. He had admitted to me one night, after his usual six-pack of Budweiser, that he was going to get off my case. In that one-sided conversation, something broke free in me, loosening my obsession with being a problem child.

So, for the sake of false family unity, I figured it couldn't hurt to seek gainful employment. Rather than consult the help wanted section in the Coast Dispatch, I figured hopping on my scooter was the better option.

After I took a *Silkwood* shower to scrub away the slimy feeling of the previous night, I dressed in business casual, ideal for a Southern California summer day. A pair of jeans and the white button-up shirt I had worn for my senior picture the previous month.

"Well, don't you look nice! Very sharp, Henry!" Mom exclaimed.

"Aww shucks, ma'am," I replied, tipping an invisible cowboy hat in her direction.

"Good luck, hon."

I drove past some of the places that I liked to frequent, the local AMC movie theater, the Wherehouse, and Licorice Pizza, not spying any help wanted signs. Not even Alpha Beta was taking on new staff, but I was secretly relieved as it would be another case of "Aren't you John Dodge's little brother?"

There was a job opening as a bag boy at Gemco, another grocery store.

I was directed to Customer Service, where a bored twenty-something girl with blonde hair and black roots handed me an application, clipboard, and pen without making eye contact, then returned to the *Daytime Digest* in her hand and smacked her gum.

Filling out my personal information was easy, but when I got to my previous employment, I froze up. I couldn't put Steve as the contact, certain that he wouldn't give me a glowing review, so I put Craig's name instead. When asked about my duties performed at Lavar's, I put down buzzwords like "hard worker" and "team player," which weren't untrue, especially when describing my efforts to give head.

I handed the clipboard back to Cindy, who was engrossed in an article on *One Life to Live*'s Viki Buchanan and her multiple personalities.

"I like when she's Niki," I said. Cindy responded with a withering look.

"Yeah, just take a seat, and Javier will look this over."

"Cool." I hoped she wouldn't tell Javier that I was a suspected soap opera fan. That wouldn't fly for boys at Gemco.

Cindy plopped down with a heavy sigh and a loud gum smack. Javier emerged from his office and came over. My heart began to pump at full capacity.

He resembled Alejandro Rey on *The Flying Nun*, handsome, tan, and suave - but minus the kicky neckerchief Carlos Ramirez always wore. He shook my hand with a strong grip, offered me both a seat - and after mere minutes, a job. It helped that I looked like a mild-mannered, nice guy.

He explained that I needed to come in for orientation in two days' time, what I was supposed to wear, etc. When he asked if I had any questions, I offered a simple "no," followed by a "thank you" for the job. I held back from saying, "You must be desperate."

When I passed Cindy's station and let her know I would be working with her, she offered up a tepid "Thrillsville." So, I decided against asking her if she was a Pisces that liked chihuahuas and Chinese noodles to gain back points by quoting my favorite B-52's song.

I didn't know why I felt the need to bend over backwards to try to win Cindy over. She was already an annoying twat. Why it was so important for me to embody Sally Field's "Right now, you like me!" Oscar speech?

Somewhere between being as buoyant as a helium balloon and wearing a pair of lead shoes, I gunned my scooter, still shell-shocked that I had procured a job so effortlessly. It felt like cause for celebration, and I knew that my best girl Tina would be up for a night on the town - well, a night in my room anyway.

After praising me about the Gemco job, Mom let me know that my friend Jeff had called twice. I prayed she couldn't hear the massive gulp in my throat, like Snoopy slinking away from the piano in "A Charlie Brown Christmas."

When she handed me the paper scrap with his phone number, I felt it was my death warrant. Jeff was not the most stable of people. How would he take revenge on someone making off with some of his livelihood?

I mean, it wasn't as if he could call the police. But I had seen *Scarface*, and you don't want to mess with a drug dealer. Besides, there was the fact that I hadn't let him say hello to my not-so-little friend in my pants.

The only way to find out what was on his unstable mind was to call. Just as I reached for it, the phone came alive with a jangle that did the same to my nerves.

"Hello?" I answered timidly.

"Oh hey, Henry," the voice said, sounding both alien and familiar. "It's Jeff."

"What's up?" That sounded casual – right?

"I want to talk about last night. But not on the phone. Can you meet me?"

Oh fuck! I most certainly didn't want to return to the scene of the crime.

"Um, sure," I said and then decided to lay the ground rules for our rendezvous. "How about Moonlight Beach in 30 minutes?"

"Yeah, that works. See you then."

"K." And I hung up the phone, still feeling like the call was coming from inside the house, and I had to beat a hasty retreat to stay alive.

I decided to err on the side of caution and wait in the parking lot so I could scout out any potential danger, like a surprise group of thugs that Jeff had summoned like the Wicked Witch's flying monkeys.

As I pulled into the parking lot overlooking the beach, I checked the sky for a smoky warning of "Surrender Henry." But there wasn't even a cloud in sight. I saw a figure backlit by the sun approaching me at a fast pace. The shadow man's identity soon became apparent. It was Jeff.

As sweat began to bead on my forehead and pool in my armpits, I knew that I could forget pulling off looking cool, calm, and collected. I was more along the lines of freaked out, fearful, and fucked when I saw his scowling face come into view.

"Hey, Jeff," I said, not sure if I should just admit guilt and hope to defuse the situation.

"Henry," he stated simply. "Unless you'd rather I call you Corey. But that's up to you."

I needed to disconnect his misguided notion that I was somehow the resurrection of Corey. Granted, I was a dead ringer for him, but he was just dead, to put it callously.

"Henry is fine," I said with conviction. "But let's be clear: I've never been in porn."

"Not yet," he responded with a detached malice.

"And what exactly...?"

"If we're gonna do this dance, I hope you aren't expecting dinner and drinks first. I don't consort with thieves."

"No, only with lowlifes." I could feel my blood boil, and was surprised that there wasn't steam rising from the asphalt around me, like the sun hitting it after a fresh rain.

"Including yourself."

While I didn't put myself in the same category as drug addicts, Jeff stung me with his accuracy. And the truth did hurt.

"What exactly do you want?" I asked it, even though I suspected what he had in mind.

"Let's just say that the people I work for wouldn't take too kindly to you sticking your hand in their cookie jar." He took a deep breath, expelling it slowly to create tension. "You do a modeling session for me, and we'll call it even."

I suddenly felt back in LA in the palace of King George, getting roped into filming *Chicken Hawk: The Return of Corey Adams.*

"And if I don't?" I bluffed.

"That's not really an option," Jeff replied with a shit-eating grin. "Your mom sounds like a nice lady. She wouldn't take the news too well about her baby boy liking nose candy, would she?"

"And how about if I tell the cops who's supplying our town with drugs?"

"Listen up smart-ass. You don't fuck with me."

"And I didn't last night." I could see that remark got to him.

"We will be remedying that lapse of judgment on your part."

"Whether I like it or not, huh?"

"Trust me, you'll like it as much as your boyfriend last night."

"He's not my boyfriend."

"Not after the fun I showed him, he isn't."

"You definitely have a type - jailbait," I emphasized *jail* in hopes that it would snap him out of his plan.

"'Hi, Mrs. Dodge? I really need to talk to you about Henry…'" He mimed into an invisible phone and had me by the balls.

"I take it we're not doing this at Glamour Shots," I quipped.

"Look at you, wising up. I always knew you were a smart guy, even if you do stupid things."

This could be my epitaph: *Here Lies Henry. A Smart Guy Who Did Stupid Things.*

"When and where?" I sighed.

"My place, tomorrow at two," he smirked triumphantly, adding, "Be there or be square."

Jeff walked away, eventually fading away like the sun dipping into the ocean. I looked out towards the sunset, like Luke Skywalker gazing at the twin suns of Tatooine in *Star Wars*, wishing it were a long time ago, in a galaxy far, far away. Hopefully, I could figure out a way to stop Jeff's Death Star from blowing up my world as I knew it without instructions from Obi-Wan Kenobi to simply trust in The Force. I was flying Han Solo on this one.

Once I got home, I began thinking of a way to turn the tables on Jeff. I frantically thought of an idea. It was born of desperation in mere hours.

Still, the next day, I was nervous as hell as I knocked on Jeff's apartment door.

"Look at you, right on time," he said, tapping his Casio watch like a spokesman for the company.

"I'm nothing if not punctual," I said, as if applying for a job – not caving in to blackmail for my meth habit.

"You're a lot of things, mister. But promptness is not the focus today." He ushered me in. "Wanna drink, Henry? It might relax you."

I gave myself a mental pat on the back since he was playing into my scheme. I muttered a casual "sure."

The fly has become the spider, and as I surveyed the parlor I was standing in, I saw a Polaroid camera sitting on his kitchen table. This caused me to gulp. Jeff returned with two beers in hand. I put mine up to my lips, letting its liquid courage pour down my throat.

"Now, now. There's no reason to be nervous," he said in a mockingly soothing tone. "It's not your first time at the rodeo, cowboy."

Rather than debate his misguided notion that I was Henry Dodge, high school student by day, and Corey Adams Hollywood hooker by night, I kept my trap shut. I downed my beer in three gulps, so he brought out two more.

Soon enough, there was a Stonehenge of empty bottles littering his coffee table, only a fraction of the "99 Bottles of Beer" song that we weirdly sang on the school bus in grade school. The dealer's total had now surpassed mine by two. When he offered another one, I declined, but he got himself another, stumbling slightly into the kitchen. Then my blackmailer was ready to get down to brass taxes.

"Let's get comfortable in the bedroom," he said with a slight slur, going for the camera, an attempt that took him two times to complete.

He had the bedroom staged as a makeshift photo studio. The lampshades were removed. A pair of Speedos lay in the middle of a bed with red silk sheets on it. Well, Jeff had his specific idea of sexiness, like something seen in a bad TV movie.

He instructed me to put on the Speedo, revealing a dopey grin on his face. The slurring was getting stronger, which meant my chances of pulling this off were as well.

I turned away for my outfit change, prompting my captor to compliment my ass. I felt like puking, but I had to stay focused. I turned to face him.

"Mmm-hmm. Come over here, I wanna see if it fits right."

I shivered inside as he fumbled with the crotch. I was so grossed out; I knew I wouldn't have an accidental boner.

"You know, I could go for a drink," I said to interrupt his fondling. "But something stiffer than a beer." I placed a big emphasis on the word stiffer. "And I like my drinks strong, like my men."

Jeff's eyes widened to see how I was no longer fighting him.

"Don't go anywhere," he practically purred.

I sat down on the bed and made a big show of smiling and wiggling my crotch, suggesting there was no place in the world that I'd rather be. Truth be told, a root canal without the benefit of Novocain would be better than this.

Jeff returned with a Jack and Coke. I made a show of taking a big gulp but was faking it, and he didn't notice. I set it on the nightstand while Jeff knocked his back, drinking it like a man lost in a desert and discovering an oasis. He clumsily picked up the camera, and I was ready for my close-up, Mr. DeMille.

Jeff began to snap a series of warm-up shots meant to help me lose my inhibitions. The only thing being lost was Jeff's control over the situation as he drunkenly gave me commands.

As I pretended to take a huge sip of Jack and Coke, I lied and delivered it innocently, "Wow, this is strong. I can't finish it. Do you want it?"

"Sure!" Jeff exclaimed, adding a few more s's and r's to the word.

There came a point when the Speedos were shucked. But I didn't want the creep to see the area that my bathing suit covered, so I used the satin sheets as a barrier. He got frustrated quickly.

"Ok, time to see the goods."

"Alright."

And as I exposed myself, I didn't feel vulnerable. There was a feeling of empowerment humming through my body because Jeff got nervous. He tripped while trying to capture the image.

"Whew, I need to sit down. Scooch over," he said. I could smell the Jack and Coke oozing through his pores.

"And I have to use the bathroom. Be right back."

I took my time, splashing my face, hoping my plan had worked.

It had. Jeff, without a stitch of clothing on, was sprawled on the bed and passed out, lightly snoring.

Take that, you fucker!

Bingo! I quickly got into my clothes and gathered up the Polaroids. Then, as I imagined doing, I left the lowlife dealer and blackmailer a friendly note on his coffee table.

"Dear Jeff,

I hope this note finds you well. If you ever bother me again, the pictures that you took of me, a minor of 17, will be taken to the police. Have a nice day.

Yours in Christ,

Henry

When I went home, I stashed them away in my underwear drawer in case Jeff ever called my bluff.

Months passed. Jeff never called again, and I completely forgot they were there.

That is, until the following September.

One Saturday afternoon, I was watching TV in the den when Mom called me up from a rerun of a rerun to my bedroom.

When I entered, she was standing in front of my dresser with a basket of clean laundry and my underwear drawer open. She was looking in the drawer with a mouth twisted by shock.

Suddenly, I remembered. *The photos! Shit!*

"Care to explain this?" she asked.

I had a few seconds to find the perfect alibi. *Think, Henry, think!* The mouth of the open drawer looked as though it was laughing, the secrets within it being excavated like rotted teeth. Then I saw she had something in her hand. The *Playgirl* magazine had been discovered. Not the Jeff photos.

"What is *this* doing in my house?" Her voice quivered with disgust and anger.

"Oh, that." I began and searched my database of plausible lies.

"Yes, *that*."

"I use it..." I said and then came up with a doozy. "It's my reference point for drawings. You know, when I do sketches of men."

The look on her face was stone-cold.

"Well, I'd rather you find some books on the subject instead of bringing pornography into this house."

While I did my best not to flaunt my sexuality at home, the slow burn of unfairness ignited within. My brother had his secret *Playboy* stash, which he kept hidden in a long-abandoned game called "Chopper Strike," which would have merely been considered a case of "boys being boys" upon discovery. My magazine was just a painful reminder that she was saddled with a gay son. Luckily, she hadn't rooted through the drawer above it and added drug user to her list of disappointments.

"Gotcha." I replied, wanting to put the matter to rest right away.

"Good, I'm glad we understand each other."

But to understand each other, I thought, we would need to have an honest conversation. But Mom still pretended that one day I would shed the gay stuff and wake up as a perfectly normal person; one that was going to get married and produce grandchildren for her and Big Ed.

I offered up a quiet, half-hearted smile. And as she made her exit, closing the door behind her, I went straight for the meth. I needed it now.

To show my rebelliousness, I chopped the crystal into a fine powder on the tape case and then lined it up into two big fat rails on the cover of the *Playgirl* - inhaling forcefully.

I immediately felt better. Instead of discarding the *Playgirl* into the garbage, as she expected, I hid it in my entertainment center's shelving.

I sat at the drafting table and produced a series of portraitures, all wearing their birthday suits, when I became flooded with reverie about what I could accomplish by pursuing my dreams of being a full-time artist. I didn't want the term "starving artist" to apply to my vocation; I wanted to succeed and prove to my family that I had amounted to something, somebody worthwhile.

And in the back of my mind, I wondered if my artistic endeavors would always be tangled up with my drug use? Were the two intrinsically linked? If I stopped snorting, would I stop drawing? The thought was terrifying.

Still, I had no idea what was heading my way. But a lot of things came and went that fall. My gainful employment was terminated after I absentmindedly put a carton of eggs on the bottom of a customer's grocery bag, crushed by canned goods.

However, I had saved up enough money to get by for a bit, due in part to not having to buy my drugs like a commoner. I was able to cruise by for several weeks on the stolen supply.

Besides, I had started my senior year at San Dieguito, and I really had to concentrate on my studies if I wanted to graduate. Speaking of which, I had grown weary of the whispers and the stares that followed me down the hallways. So much so I pleaded with Mom to let me switch to a continuation school that would allow me to do my work from home.

And since the one constant companion that I had at that time was always by my side, and up my nose, it made getting through my subjects amazingly easy. I would usually take about a three-hour break in the afternoons so that I could enjoy a little mother/son bonding time, courtesy of the residents of Pine Valley, Llanview, and Port Charles.

Similar to the *One Life to Live* storyline involving a pregnant Tina Lord Roberts going over a waterfall in Argentina, there was a surprise in store for me one afternoon that had nothing to do with Erica Kane, Viki Buchanan, or Bobbi Spencer.

No, it had to do with something I discovered when I was around another person when high; not surprisingly, I became very chatty, asking questions, digging for whatever truths my mother would willingly unearth.

They ran the gamut - from her childhood with her overbearing mother to the confession that she didn't quite know what to do with herself now that John and I were grown. She hadn't landed on what that would be exactly, as she had only worked as a counter girl at Macy's decades before. I had inherited my indecision from her, both of us in the same boat on a sea of doubt.

The disclosure of her marriage threw me for the biggest loop.

"We were set up on a blind date, if you can believe it," she said with a deep look of reverie in her aqua eyes. "My first impression of your father was that he was a stuck-up 16-year-old, some version of Elvis. I almost didn't accept a second date, but something told me that he was aloof because he was as nervous as I was. The rest, as they say, is history."

I had always had difficulty reconciling my parents as ever having been my age, until I saw *Back to the Future* the previous year.

Grandmother had been opposed to her daughter marrying Big Ed, so the newlyweds moved west from the East Coast. There, under the endless sunshine, they built a life; one where my father attended college to study mechanical engineering. He also began to practice a clandestine life, as if he'd switched roles from King of Rock and Roll to Agent 007.

He found time during his studies to partake in extracurricular activities, namely, a blonde co-ed named Barbara. He came home one night reeking of her perfume.

"It was the first time that he cheated on me," she said with a stoic face that melted into sorrow. "But it wasn't the last."

Saying that he was sorry and it wouldn't happen again became a well-worn record, like her scratchy copy of *Engelbert Humperdinck's Greatest Hits*. But she always forgave him.

"And then I got pregnant, and he swore he would change his ways. This was in 1962."

"But John was born in 1964…" I said and let it hang there in the air.

"I had a miscarriage and another one the next year."

"Oh my God, Mom! I'm sorry."

Even though what I was saying came from the heart, the fact that I was buzzing on meth made the words feel insincere as they tumbled out of my mouth.

"Thanks, hon."

I was reeling, thinking of what type of siblings they may have been.

"And then we had John, and things were actually really good for a while, until…"

And just like a Friday cliffhanger on our beloved soap opera, the phone rang. Had Jeff decided to call my bluff? Did I mention that meth makes you paranoid?

She picked up the phone in her room, issuing a standard greeting of "Hello?"

She listened to the anonymous voice and didn't say anything for a good minute that felt like an eternity.

"Yes, I see." She said. "Thank you for calling."

"Who was it?" I asked, steeling myself for her answer.

"It was the vet. It's time for Shadow's next round of shots, next Thursday at 10."

I felt like I had dodged a bullet. Not Jeff – this time. I focused my attention back on making my heart beat again.

Before I could ask, "Now, where were we?" Mom picked up where she left off.

"Your father's next indiscretion resulted in his secretary getting pregnant."

"Shit!" I said, waiting for her to chastise me for using the "brown word."

"My sentiments exactly."

"What did you do?" I asked cautiously, briefly wishing I had some popcorn to munch on.

"I took your brother and went home to my mother," she said with a sigh.

While I had never thought of her as a strong woman, my point of view began to shift. I only knew we did not discuss things of a personal nature. Well, until the night when I told them that I was gay.

Who knew that The Dodge Family could have their own daytime drama series? I bounced a couple of potential titles around, something like *Dodge City* when she continued.

"Your father called me incessantly, to the point that good 'Ol Christine threatened to have her number changed. Yeah, she seemed plenty pleased that she'd been right on the money about your father."

I knew she had finally come back; otherwise, I wouldn't have been sitting on her beige carpet, unconsciously gripping it.

"So, what happened?" I asked.

"I came back when your father told me that, uh, the problem had been taken care of and that his secretary had been transferred to Northern California."

Damn, this was some heavy stuff. But then she said she needed to lie down for a while because a migraine crept up on her as she detailed Big Ed's misdeeds.

The whole thing had left my head spinning like a world shifting on its axis, an invisible finger suddenly stopped the globe, and the centrifugal force of Mom's confession would most definitely affect the nature of the Dodge world and its inhabitants.

A few years before, The Go-Gos had lyrically asked, *"Can't stop the world, why let it stop you?"* This musical question banged around in my head, coupled with the information Mom had vocalized.

Even though she hadn't said anything like "Don't say anything," I knew how to keep a secret. But how to prevent myself from calling Big Ed out on his bullshit?

It wasn't as though I was seeing him through brand-new eyes; my vision had merely been made better, like getting a new prescription for glasses. These ones were not rose-colored, and the eye chart spelled out

M

OT

HER

FUCK

ER

Mom never brought it up again, and I didn't pry any further, not wanting to cause her any further headaches from dwelling in the past. I bit my tongue on more than one occasion when in his presence.

The only other thing that she let me in on was the unabridged story of my namesake, her younger brother Henry. He had died when he was in his teens. And she told me something that both broke my heart and chilled me to the bone.

"He was very sensitive," she said quietly. "The other kids called him horrible names."

"Sounds familiar." I offered, astonished at the parallels.

"You remind me of him in a lot of ways," she professed. "Times change, even if people don't."

"What do you mean?"

"He was, well, different. I'm sure you can figure out what I mean by that."

"Yeah," I said simply.

"We never talked about it, but the silence spoke volumes. I did my best to protect him, but I failed. He took his own life when he was 15."

"Oh my God!"

"God had nothing to do with it," she hissed.

I gulped at her undisguised anger at religion.

"All the useless praying that my mother did in church afterwards would never bring him back. And when I began to see those qualities in you, I didn't know what to do. It's why I reacted the way I did when you told us you are the way you are. I'm sorry."

There were tears streaming down her face as she asked me to forgive her. I gave my answer in the form of a hug so fierce that it could have broken her in half had I not been verging on meth-induced emaciation.

She hugged me back, patting me on the back to signal the affection was at its conclusion. And rather than retreat to her bed, giving in to another massive migraine, she announced that she needed to run an errand.

The next night at dinner, she told an audience of two that she had something to tell us. In my heart of hearts, I hoped that she was going to divorce Dad.

"I got a job today."

Two plates of food almost dropped as quickly as our jaws did. Big Ed barraged her with questions about the who, what, and where of said job. Wisely, he omitted the why, as that would open a Pandora's Box of her dissatisfaction with their marriage.

The who was Barrington Enterprises, and the next sentence made Big Ed choke on the roast.

"I'm going to be his secretary," she said with a smirk. "Now, there may be times when I may need a bit of help around the house in case I work late."

Oh, how I wanted to stand up and cheer. I was liking this 2.0 version of Kate Dodge.

"Sure thing, Mom," I said, knowing this hadn't been directed at Dad. "I'm proud of you."

Big Ed grumbled something that may have been praise, but he drowned the words in an enormous swig of beer.

I had gotten an A in Cooking class in junior high, so I was confident that I could pull off a few recipes. Besides, there were times that I didn't feel like drawing and would spend hours cleaning my room with the aid of Tina. So, tending to housework would not be an issue.

Rather than chastise her for not discussing it with him first or informing us that he'd have his dinner upstairs, which was his way of pouting, Big Ed remained tightlipped.

As it turned out, once she began work, I kept up the tradition of watching our "stories" and would fill Mom in on the ABC's soapy lineup.

That is, except for the beautiful November afternoon when I went to Black's. Little did I know what was in store for me.

I walked along the shoreline, letting the icy water wash over my feet, giving me a shock to the system. It was just a typical Southern California day, nothing out of the ordinary.

I was merely looking forward to having some male companionship. As I left the sand for the dusty trails, I saw that it was a little slim for the pickings, then remembered it was both a weekday and a November one.

There were two figures staffing lookout posts on the hills that populated the stretch of trails. The shorter of the two moved from his watchtower, making his descent in my direction. As he approached and his features became clearer, I could see that he was a few inches shorter than me in stature, but bigger in other ways, given the expanding crotch of his Speedo.

He had short dark hair, sparkling blue eyes, full lips, and a nice, tight body, complete with a thatch of chest hair. Without a word, he walked by, eyeing me. I watched him retreat, smelling a whiff of Drakkar Noir that he left in his wake, noting that he looked back three times to see if I was paying attention.

He ducked into one of the many alcoves within the bushes, this one underneath a tree. I followed in his footsteps and peeked into the makeshift love nest, seeing that my arrival was expected. Either that or he was like the pens sold at Spencer's – ones you turned upside down to remove the bathing suit on a miniaturized man.

He was already fully erect. In turn, I felt my blood flow from one head to the other. I loved the tingling sensation, what I called brain fire, whenever I knew I was going to get laid.

I entered his domain, stripped off my bathing suit, and he was on me like a jungle cat, touching me all over. He planted a sensual kiss on me.

I stroked the pelt between his pectorals, as if to say, "That's a good kitty" and traced my finger down his treasure trail until I struck gold with his veiny member. Even though I had wanted to be the star of the show today, I happily dropped to my knees and adopted a co-starring role. It must have been a standout performance because I had a salty surprise in my mouth in no time flat.

I silently freaked out because I had vowed to engage in safer sex practices. He lifted me up, and we traded positions. But my release took longer as my brain was on HIV fear overload. I took matters into my own hands, soon changing the color of his chest hair to a snowy white.

"Wow, you're a little hottie. Got a name, sexy?" he asked.

"Henry. Nice to meet you."

"I'm Tony, and the pleasure is all mine," he said with a wink.

"Well, it was mine, too," I said assuredly.

"Yes, I can see that," he said, looking down at his chest. "I need to rinse this off," he laughed, "or it'll look like I put mousse in the wrong place."

"Enjoy the rest of your day," I said, pulling up my bathing suit.

"That's it?" he queried as I picked up my backpack.

"Is there supposed to be more?"

"Come hang out with me. Don't worry; I don't bite."

"Sure, why not?"

"That's the spirit." And that smile returned to his face as he put on his Speedos.

He led me to his beach towel and his own backpack like we were nomads wandering through the sands of time. He excused himself to "clean up" in the whitewash of the winter ocean, squatting on his haunches, splashing water onto his chest.

"Damn. that water is butt-cold!"

"Says the guy with the hot ass."

"Oh, a wise guy, huh?" he said, sounding like one of The Three Stooges.

"Soitenly," I replied, momentarily channeling Curly.

"You're funny," he said. "I like that."

I found myself enjoying the unexpected shift from my usual wham-bam-thank-you-man mission. I learned Tony was a 20-year-old Italian, was the middle child with four siblings who still lived in Colorado and had come to San Diego to join the Navy. Our conversation flowed easily.

I gave an abbreviated version of my life story, omitting the events of last year. Before I knew it, I had a slip of the tongue and revealed my true age. If the subject came up at Black's Beach, I was officially 18.

"Ooh, he's chicken," Tony teased.

"Ugh, I hate that term. Besides, that makes you a child molester."

"Ouch. But I can tell that you are all man."

"Damn straight. Well, you know..."

"Oh, honey, I've had plenty of straight guys in the service. A couple drinks, and it's straight to bed."

As the sun dipped into the horizon, Tony lit me up with a question.

"Can I give you my number? I'd like to take you out on a proper date."

I was stymied, unsure if he was being sincere. But my head was nodding up and down.

"Cool!" He rifled through his backpack and came up empty. "You don't have something so I can write down my digits, do you?"

Digging through my backpack proved just as unfruitful.

"That's a negatory, sailor."

"I have one up in my truck. Did you park up on the hill?"

"Fuck no! I'm afraid of heights." I stopped before I could add my atypical retort of "That's why God made me short," given the fact that he was shorter than me. "I parked down at Torrey Pines."

"Mind if I walk with you and catch a ride?"

I weighed the options in my mind. Do I have a bonafide date, or should I just call it a wash? I thought of the GTR song "When the Heart Rules the Mind" and conceded.

We continued our talk, which had now shifted to music, and by the time we reached my scooter, I was inwardly swooning over the many commonalities we shared.

"Here we are," I said.

"Aww, she's cute!" Tony exclaimed. "What's her name?"

I had never thought of naming my scooter, as I had been scared by Stephen King's *Christine*. And look how that had worked out for her owner, Arnie Cunningham! Besides, it was my grandmother's name.

"To be honest, I never thought to do that. But, let me see…" I racked my brain to come up with something clever. But I was stuck.

"I call my truck Bessie," he offered.

"Let me introduce you to L'il Red."

"Please to meet you, ma'am," he said and even bowed towards my newly-christened scooter.

"Hop on," I said.

"Are we talking about L'il Red or…" Tony smirked.

"Play your cards right, sailor."

Dropping him off at Bessie facilitated a game of strip poker sans playing cards. As the temperature dropped outside, we were steaming up the windows of his Toyota truck. Before I knew it, both of us were leaning back, panting like dogs.

"Damn. Just. Damn," I said between breaths.

"My sentiments exactly."

Once our clothes were back on our bodies, Tony turned on the defroster to defog the truck's windows. He reached across my body to get to the glove box, generously grazing the crotch of my bathing suit. I began to stiffen again. But I knew if we went for round three, it would mean trouble at home. I hated the prospect of getting grounded.

He wrote down his phone number, checking it to make sure it was legible. I put it in my backpack, double-checking that the zipper was firmly secured lest it fly out on my ride home, carrying the promise of a date on the wind.

We kissed before I exited the cab. As I straddled the newly minted L'il Red, I smiled despite my best efforts not to. I watched his taillights evaporate before I started the engine, just as assuredly as he had started mine.

I called Tony the next day - well, I called him three times the next day, in all honesty. I got his machine twice. Even though Mom and I had a breakthrough regarding my sexuality, I was still hesitant to give out my number.

The third time was the charm, and we slid into the conversational easiness that had marked our first meeting. As our chatting got close to the 90-minute mark, he finally broached the issue I had been dancing around.

"So. What would you like to do on our date?"

My brain went through a thousand different sexual scenarios.

I hadn't been on a real date, so I had no ideas. Tony said he would think of something, and I agreed to meet him at his place near SDSU College, getting directions.

Because one way or another, I was gonna get him to paraphrase Blondie. But my brain conjured a highway sign that read "Danger Heartbreak Dead Ahead." Given my track record, I couldn't afford to begin this race before the starting gun had even gone off, so I cast such notions from my mind.

I primped and prepared to make a lasting visual impact on Tony, hopped on L'il Red after memorizing the route to his house, and then consulted Dad's Thomas Brothers Guide. It meant arriving about 20 minutes later. I knew my hair-sprayed coif was mussed by the wind. But as Tony opened the door, he gave me the reaction I had been craving.

"You look good enough to eat."

"And my, what a big package you have, Grandma," I said as I eyed him up and down.

"Speaking of eating," he said, blushing, "What are you in the mood for?"

My gutter mind went to thoughts of sampling the Italian sausage on his menu.

"Well, what's good around here?" I asked.

"You like pizza?"

"Why yes, I like anything Italian."

"Oh, you're good."

"You ain't seen nothing yet."

"Duly noted." And he pulled me in for a big kiss that escalated to making out for a good ten minutes.

We ended up at a hole-in-the-wall pizza joint called Mario's, complete with checkered tablecloths splattered with candle wax that dripped from the wine bottle.

"Best pizza," Tony stated and suggested a pepperoni and sausage combo.

"I love meat," I said innocently, causing him to leer and grope my thigh under the table, only stopping when the waiter came to take our order.

I set the land speed record for devouring half of a pizza, and Tony matched me. And he risked a speeding ticket during the drive back to his place. As soon as the door was closed, he was all over me like the proverbial cheap suit.

We were both down to our underwear when we heard a throat clearing from the living room. I silently cursed myself that we had been stone-cold busted by his lover.

"Are you going to introduce your little friend?" the voice asked as he came into view. He had close-cropped red hair, blue eyes, and a medium build underneath the white Navy uniform he was wearing. He also had a lecherous grin on his face.

"Joe, this is Henry. Henry, this is my roommate, who wasn't supposed to be home tonight."

“Well, if my trick hadn’t stood me up, I would be engaged in what you boys are. Please, don’t stop on my account.”

“Let’s take this to a more private location,” Tony said as he began to collect our clothes.

“Nice to meet you.” I said.

“You too. Hope to see more of you.” That lecherous grin again.

We retreated to Tony’s bedroom, which had white walls, blue carpet, a couple of dressers, and a bed to comfortably fit two.

“Now. Where were we?” he said, planting a kiss on me that threatened to remove my tonsils while maneuvering me onto the bed. This began us getting together every few days. I had to stop pinching myself when we were not together. If this wasn’t real, I didn’t want to know. And I tried my best at home not to let on to my newfound giddiness, as my parents could burst this bubble. It had become easier to maintain my private life now that Mom and Dad, both working, were on parent duty only on weekends.

I found myself whistling the Jo Boxers’ “Just Got Lucky” in the kitchen, a song I usually listened to after my conquests on the trails of Black Beach.

“Someone certainly is chipper today,” Mom said as she entered, yearning for the caffeinated elixir that gave her life.

“And someone looks like she belongs on *Dynasty*!” I said with a low whistle, aimed at her clothing for the office.

“Oh, it’s not too much?” she said, tugging at the silky blouse, making the left shoulder pad momentarily look as if it was trying to free itself from the garment.

“Nah, you look great.”

She smiled, and it was a remarkable sight, an actual ear-to-ear grin.

“Thanks, hon. And what is making you so happy these days?”

For a split-second, I almost spilled my guts to her. But I considered that magic spoken is magic broken.

“Geez, can’t a guy whistle?”

“You can do anything you want if you put your mind to it.”

“Alright, Positive Patty,” I said snarkily.

“Better than being a Negative Nancy,” She replied, a grin detectable over the lip of her coffee mug. “Seriously though, you seem a lot happier lately.”

I shrugged it off. So, she left it alone for the duration of our time in the kitchen, me with my bowl of Honey Nut Cheerios and she with her coffee and bagel. Then Kate Dodge, career gal, left for work.

I emerged from the shower, and my first stop was to my dresser for a little bit of Vitamin C up my nostrils. And since I didn't have Mom to gab with, I gave Tony a call. He quickly asked what I was doing that day.

"Well, technically, that would be schoolwork. But…"

"Can you come down? There's something I need to talk to you about."

I knocked twice on his door. When he answered, Tony looked disheveled, and his eyes were red-rimmed. I highly doubted, given his military service, that he was high.

There was no hug, no kiss. He limply ushered me in. He gestured to a recliner as he took a seat on the navy-blue couch.

Something was most definitely up, yet he remained oddly quiet.

"What's the matter?" I asked gently as if I was speaking to someone fashioned out of porcelain rather than skin and bone.

"Well, uh," he sputtered, and I could see on his face that he was trying to conjure up the words, a magician with something up his sleeve. "Jesus, I don't even know how to tell you this."

"I've found the best way is to just say it. It works amazingly well." This came out a little more tersely than I had planned, but I imagined that I had somehow fucked things up.

"I tested positive," he said somewhere above a whisper, but to my ears, it sounded like he was shouting it.

I could feel all the color drain from my face, and I felt sick to my stomach. But as he cradled his head in his hands, I steadied myself enough to get up, sit next to him, and put my arms around him. But I couldn't feel the action; it was as though my entire body had gone numb.

"It's ok. It will be ok," I said, wanting to believe my words of comfort, but this was uncharted territory. AIDS had haunted me ever since I had come out the solo Greek chorus comprised of my mother entered my mind.

"*I don't want you to get AIDS*."

"You need to get tested," Tony stressed. "Even though we were careful, I would rather be safe than sorry. And that's what I am. Sorry that you have to deal with this."

"But what about you?" I said, meaning that it was more for him to deal with.

"Yeah, what about me?" he spat out. "I get to be a social pariah, waiting to die."

"That's not what I meant."

"Well, what exactly did you mean, Henry? Sometimes I forget how young you are."

"Look, I know you're upset."

"Upset? Really? I am way beyond that!"

"Why are you taking this out on me?" I could feel the blood returning to my face; my temper was trying to emerge. "This isn't my fault, ya know."

"Right! This happened because I deserved it!"

"Again, you're missing the point, Tony."

"No, I get the point; you want to play the blame game."

"I want to be here for you, but you being an asshole doesn't help the situation."

"So, are you going to be my nurse while I wither away to nothing? It's not like we were in a real relationship; we were just fucking."

I took my arms off him, sat back, and looked at him with wounded eyes.

"You should write cards for Hallmark."

"And you should fuck right off."

"OK, but let me tell you something," I said. "I had feelings for you, whether you had them for me or not. I wish I'd never gone to the beach that day."

"Yeah, then you wouldn't have to deal with the real world. Henry, it's not all sunshine and rainbows."

"Listen, I don't know what you want me to say."

"There's nothing that you could say that would make this magically disappear - but that's what I think you should do. Just disappear, forget you ever met me."

"Fine!" I said with a roar. "If that's the way you want it, that's the way you'll get it, you prick!"

"You're a fucking moron."

"Well, at least I've been a careful moron." I instantly regretted it.

"Yes, and I'm just some idiot that's going to die!" he shrieked at the top of his lungs. "This doesn't make me dirty! Now get the fuck out of my house!"

I left without a word, knowing full well that he was lashing out at me. It was understandable, but it didn't make the sting of his words any less painful.

I tore off on the scooter. I sure as fuck knew that I didn't want to go home. Not right now. I was half-tempted to just ride off into the sunset like Erik Estrada and let the chips fall where they may. But where had that gotten me before? To quote The Supremes, "Nothing but heartaches," and here I had thought that my heart would be able to sing but was now silent, except for the air escaping it from its newest puncture wound.

I drove into nothingness on autopilot. L'il Red did her best to keep me from smashing into the back of any cars. I ended up pulling into the parking lot at Torrey Pines Glider Port, which could also be known as the scene of the crime.

I did feel as though my innocence had been murdered for the second time in the span of a year, that my parole of returning home from Los Angeles had somehow left me marked, a target for further hurt caused by men. I was unable to break free from the shackles of the past, a prisoner of my own making.

And my cage had been rattled today.

I parked close to "the goat trail," a precarious hike down the steep cliff. I thought of how easy it would be to rev the engine instead and go flying out, free-falling into the void that my life had become.

"What the fuck am I going to do?" I said aloud.

The obvious answer was to get tested, get the results, and go from there. But I was petrified to think that my life would be cut short. There was so much that I wanted to experience; I hadn't even reached the age to be considered an adult.

I had spent my adolescence wishing I were older. Now, I was wishing I could go back to being a kid - to return to complete innocence.

Wish in one hand, then shit in the other. See which one fills up first.

I wasn't sure where I had heard that bit of sage advice, but it certainly applied. Instead of filling one hand with empty air and the other with my own excrement, I covered my eyes as if that would hold back the flood of tears.

I must have looked like a crazy person, talking to myself one minute and crying the next. The tears fell in uniform rivulets down my cheeks, and just when I was convinced that any more could be left, the dam burst, accompanied by snot from my nostrils.

I wiped both my eyes and the mucus pooling on my upper lip with the sleeve of my shirt, catching my image in the rearview mirror, and what I saw staring back made me hate reflections. In fact, I wished for a sudden case of blindness, the type that soap opera characters recovered from a few episodes later. I closed my eyes, opened them, and said *shit* aloud. No such luck on losing my sight, as I was one.

My hair was a mess from the wind, and my eyes looked redder than Christopher Lee's version of *Dracula*. My nostrils looked like I had been fighting a nasty cold. But it was another virus that was causing this, and just like that, the waterworks recommenced.

I detected a car pulling up next to me. I mopped my tears up for a second time. I heard the car door open and slam, then the crunch of rocks underneath shoes, marking the stranger's progress towards me. I was getting cruised! Now?

The sound of footsteps stopped near me. A voice said, "Hi, how are you?"

I turned slowly towards him, letting my traumatized face answer that question. He gasped, and his overweight body became lithe like that of a ballet dancer as he sprang back to his car and drove away.

I decided that was my cue to make my exit. Besides, the sun was making its way west with a few hours until it sank into the ocean, like the feeling in the pit of my stomach. I still had time to get home, freshen up, and try to put on a cheery façade for my parents before they came home.

I was greeted at home by Shadow, who began licking my face. Despite the depths of despair I was feeling, I smiled.

"Alright, girl, calm down. I'm glad to see you, too."

She returned to a sitting position, and I knelt and hugged her close to me, reminding me of the cover of the Peanuts book *Happiness is a Warm Puppy*.

Shadow wriggled out of my grasp, ran down the den stairs and barked insistently at the sliding door. It didn't take Angela Lansbury to figure out that she needed to do her business.

Indeed, she did, and I took the army shovel used for getting rid of her land mines and flung it up on the hill covered with ice plant. If only the events of the day were as easily discarded. Hopefully, some of the stain I felt could be washed down the drain with a nice, hot shower.

One-quarter of what made our family whole was sitting in the living room watching TV after I had showered and put on fresh clothes that carried no stink of a shit day on them.

"Damn, you sure do take a long time in the bathroom. Jeannie takes less time to get ready," John said.

"Well, look who she has to impress." I figured some good-natured brotherly ribbing wouldn't tip him off that I felt broken inside.

"Ouch," he said and then laughed. "And who are you trying to impress? Got a hot date?" It was still weird for me that he truly accepted my lifestyle, and for a split-second, I flashed on Tony and just as quickly pushed him to the back of my brain.

"I would have just washed my hand for that."

"Gross. Sorry, I asked," he said and returned his attention to a rerun of *F Troop*.

"So, what brings you over here? I mean, aside from giving me grief?"

"I have to talk to you guys about something."

"Oh, you're putting yourself up for adoption?" It felt good to be jovial even though it was forced.

"Damn, dude, you're going in for the kill today."

"Seriously, what do you want to talk to us about?"

"With as much TV as you watch, I'm sure you're familiar with the term 'stay tuned.'"

"Aww, you're no fun."

"On the contrary, little brother, I'm a blast and a half, as Jeannie puts it."

"Proof positive," I began, momentarily choking on the latter word and spitting out the rest of my thought via a mental Heimlich maneuver. "There is certainly no accounting for good taste. You would think somebody that was surrounded by books all day would be smarter in her choice in men."

"Speaking of good taste," he said, totally brushing off my wry observation, "I brought over some steaks for dinner to barbeque."

"Just make sure that Big Ed hasn't downed too many beers; otherwise, he might burn them. Again."

"Yeah, the charcoal should be left in the barbeque and not end up on our plates. Remember the time he got so shitfaced when he cooked dinner for the neighbors? They were supposed to be ribs. I think."

"Naturally, he blamed it on there not being enough daylight for him to see how done they were getting."

"Stevie Wonder could have seen how burned they were. Or smelled them at the very least."

"I should have been sent to my room without dinner that night. We're lucky we didn't have Shadow then. Feeding that to her would be animal cruelty."

"To avoid any charred remains passing as dinner, I'm going to cook them."

"Who are you, and what have you done with my brother?"

"Eat me; I can cook."

"Interesting way to put it."

"And besides, I'll have you to help me."

"Oh, really? And what does this apprenticeship consist of? Will I be given 15-minute breaks, as per my union contract?"

"No, but you'll avoid an ass-kicking."

"How about a cute chef's hat?"

"Maybe Mom will let you borrow her 'Kiss the Cook' apron."

"I'll pass; red isn't really my color."

"Too bad it isn't pink with some frills."

"But then you'd want to wear it, and we all know I can take you in a slap fight."

As it turned out, my sous-chef duties entailed making a salad, and I was very tempted to not include the tomatoes John had bought. I hated the texture of sliced and chopped tomatoes. I made sure I avoided cutting myself with the knife. You know, just in case.

I was also in charge of making another Dodge family staple, white rice, and John even barked out, "Kate, what's the ETA on that rice?!" doing a perfect impression of Big Ed's inquiry to make sure the meal was perfectly timed.

And it turned out to be perfectly timed to our parents' arrival.

"To what do we owe this honor?" Mom said with a mixture of surprise and gratitude by not having to prepare a meal after a long day at work.

"It seems that Johnny boy has something to tell us," I wanted to add "Maybe he's gay, too," but refrained as I didn't want to spoil the moment.

"I hope it's good news." Mom chirped.

Yes, we could all use some of that about now, especially me.

"Well, let's not let this food get cold. I'm hungry," I heard myself say, even though my stomach was still in knots that even Houdini couldn't wriggle out of.

Big Ed plopped down in front of his plate, putting down his beer to grab his knife and fork. He made short time in telling John that his steak was good.

"A chip off the old block," he said with pride, which made John and I exchange a smirk. Our steaks were not charred within an inch of their former lives.

"Mmm, delicious hon!" Mom exclaimed.

I took a bite and saw my brother eyeing me to give my assessment.

"It's no Sizzler, but it's not bad. How about this salad and rice, though?"

He muttered "dick" under his breath.

"So, um, yeah," he started and then took a deep breath. "I do have something to tell you guys."

Big Ed put down his fork and knife. At first, I thought it was to give John his undivided attention, but he ended up grabbing his Budweiser can and draining it.

"Hold that thought. Henry, draw me one," he told me. He cracked it open as soon as I put it in front of him.

"Proceed," he said and issued a small burp.

"Eddie," Mom jokingly chastised him for his table manners or lack thereof. At least it wasn't from the other end, which he loved to blame on Shadow.

"Go ahead John," Mom pressed. "I'm on pins and needles."

The word needles made me internally bristle. Needles, like the ones they draw blood with. The thought almost made me choke on my salad.

"So, yeah, um," he said again, this time with a nervous smile.

"You said that already; get down to it, son," Big Ed interrupted.

"Yeah, what gives?" I added. This was more excruciating than Christmas morning.

"Let him talk, and maybe we'll find out," Mom said. "It's not bad news, is it?"

"I'm having a hard time because you three won't quit interrupting. It's a good news/bad news situation."

Mom's face was crestfallen, and Dad set his beer on the table while I held my piece of steak on the fork in midair. It hung there like the anticipation of what the bad news might be.

"I asked Jeannie to marry me."

"And she said no? Is that the bad news? Sorry, go ahead," Mom said quickly.

"If she was smart, she would," I muttered low enough for only John to hear.

"No, she said yes. That's your good news."

"And what's the bad news? She's not knocked up, is she?" Dad barked out.

"Ed, please!" Mom was on the verge of being frantic.

"She's not pregnant."

"Not for lack of trying," I said under my breath, but not as quietly as I would have liked.

"Henry David!" Mom chided.

"Jesus creep," Big Ed said with a sigh.

John must have thought it was funny, giving me a look that said, "Good one."

"Ok, onto the bad news portion. I'm shipping out after Christmas on a Westpac, and we want to get married before I go."

"Yup, she's preggers," I said, and this time, Big Ed laughed and did a salute with his beer can. Budweiser, when you care enough to send the very best.

"For Chrissakes, she's not pregnant! I don't want to wait until I get back to get married."

"Afraid of getting the clap?" I said with glee.

"Better than getting AIDS," he said carelessly. I felt as if the chair suddenly was going to slide out from under me, and I would end up on the floor. I didn't want to let on to what I was feeling, so I decided to let it slide.

"Damn, harsh." I mustered up, while my parents' faces resembled how The Little Rascals would react to some sort of surprise with eyes blinking and their mouths formed into perfect o's. "Sorry, I'll shut up now."

"No, I'm sorry. I shouldn't have said that at all."

"No, you shouldn't have," Mom agreed. "Back to the topic at hand. Let me get this straight: You want to get married in five weeks? How? By eloping?"

"No Vegas chapel will be involved. I want friends and family there. We're hoping that you and Jeannie's mom could pull this off."

"Honey," she said without sweetness behind the word. "I am working now, which would give me only nights and weekends to coordinate with Mrs. Carson."

"I mean, I can ask Mrs. Carson if she wouldn't mind doing it all herself," John said with a hangdog expression.

"Shouldn't you start calling her mom now?" I said, hoping it would be the twist of the knife that would snap Mom back to her maternal instincts.

"He only has one mom, and that is me. We will make it work. Count me in." Her smile was like watching a Stepford Wife, compliant and ready to serve. It was disconcerting.

"Thanks, Mom, I really appreciate it, and Jeannie will, too. Between us, I think her mother's taste is in her mouth."

"Well, I volunteer to spearhead your bachelor party," I joked, shooting my hand up like Arnold Horshack, adding his trademark "ooh-ooh."

"Sorry, Horshack; my Navy buddies have that covered."

"Maybe I could be the flower girl then?"

That was a step too far for Big Ed, who removed himself from the kitchen, retrieved two more beers from the fridge in the garage, and headed upstairs.

"Something I said?"

"It usually is," John said.

"You boys," Mom said, but her eyes were misting up, recognizing that we were men, and now one was getting married.

"I'm really happy for you, John," I said. "I know I bust your chops about your relationship because you have somebody you want to spend the rest of your life with."

"Thanks," he said, and I saw the gleam in his eye was his own restrained version of crying. "Spaz."

John was the human equivalent of the Sears Toughskins product; he was built tougher than I was. But somewhere in the fabric, there's a small tear, which exposed a softer side, while I pretty much was busted at the seams, made of Gossamer fabric, sheer but not entirely see-through.

"You'll find someone special, Henry," she said with a sniffle. "You're young and have all the time in the world to find a person that's right for you."

While it was a nice sentiment, it cut me to the quick. My time could be ticking away, a countdown with a set end date.

And even though life wasn't a game, Milton Bradley's version of it hadn't prepared me for this scenario; I felt as though I had been saddled with the thimble in Monopoly, and I might not be able to pass go or collect $200.

Instead, I decided to sit in jail for the next few weeks, subscribed to replace my bread and water diet with one of meth and denial, hoping that I could roll the dice eventually and see if my life would land on Park Place or with my luck only able to buy Baltic Avenue on borrowed time. If life had taught me anything thus far, it was that only time would tell, and I hoped it would enlighten me before it ran out, like sands through the hourglass, so were the gays of our lives.

Three years prior to my birth, Timothy Leary had coined the counterculture phrase “Turn on, tune in, drop out” and I was giving it my own twist in the weeks following Tony’s disclosure. I would tune into TV reruns that I could do the dialogue verbatim on, falling like Alice into a rabbit hole of nostalgia for the good old days that weren’t so ancient. There was no Wonderland to land in, I wasn’t late for a very important date, but the Queen of Hearts wardrobe was stained crimson with blood. If only she would decree that if was off with his head for me.

I was following the third part of Leary’s mantra, having dropped off reality’s map, preferring the company of treasured companions like Gilligan marooned on an island just as I had shipwrecked myself. Meanwhile, Sister Bertrille was able to fly away from her life, and the robot from *Lost in Space* mirrored my traumatized robotic motions on my ten-inch Zenith TV.

Yet, my real life, when it crept in stealthily, was projected on a Cinerama screen in my mind.

Each movie was a combination of a drama and a horror movie, each featuring me as its star attraction. I was either fated for a live-fast, die-young career like James Dean or would have the longevity of Elizabeth Taylor. More than likely, I’d be the first one killed in the next *Friday the 13th* movie or just end up on the cutting room floor.

I knew the way to edit this movie down from its *Gone with the Wind* running time was to schedule an appointment with Dr. Baker, my doctor, since I was a kid. But that idea would go up in flames faster than Atlanta had. Firstly, I didn’t know if he could give me an HIV test, and secondly, since I was 17, would he contact Mom about it?

Perhaps it was time for Billy Collins to come out of retirement and try to keep my identity a secret if I could figure out if there was somewhere I could go and remain anonymous. It was times like these that I wished I had someone from LA to reach out to, to teach me in a different style than George’s basic tutelage on Gay 101.

What was I supposed to do? Call 411 and ask the operator for the number of my savior in high heels, Candy. I didn’t bother to ask what her non-performance name was. And would she remember me even if I’d never forgetten her kindness and words of wisdom? I had pushed back all thoughts of that summer into the dustiest corner of my memory.

I really didn’t know how much more of this charade I could keep up: feeling freaked-the- fuck-out inside and trying to look fine on the outside. It was exhausting putting on airs. So, I picked up the phone to schedule an appointment with Dr. Baker.

Then I remembered it wasn't a number that I knew by heart, and it seemed like such a hassle to go downstairs and look it up in the Kate Dodge version of a Rolodex. She utilized a recipe card holder to keep the important digits in alphabetical order. Besides, I didn't know if it would be under B or G for Reaper, Grim.

I just wanted to melt into my beanbag chair, shrinking myself to the size of the foam beads that gave it shape. Yet I remained unmovable and resolute in being shell-shocked.

An unfortunate side-effect of my PTSD was that I wasn't utilizing a more beneficial form of distraction in taking pencil to paper. I needed to unload some of my fears onto the blank pages of my sketchbook. I imagined that it was disappointed in my neglect of it, the dust collecting on its cover.

I started to walk over to where I kept it on my drafting table. My logic dictated that it didn't really matter if Mom flipped through it. If she saw the most recent images I had attempted to draw, when I decided creative pursuits were trivial, all she would see were seeds of ideas that I hadn't nurtured, withering on the vine.

I plopped my butt back into the beanbag chair and half-paid attention to Beaver climbing up on a billboard to see if the soup being advertised was real or not, only to end up trapped and getting rescued by firefighters.

Leave it to me to desire a life that was so idyllic. I wished that Mom would call us to dinner just as sweetly as June Cleaver. I half-expected to find her dressed to the nines in a pretty dress, a pearl necklace anchored around her neck, and high heels click-clacking across the kitchen floor as she presented a perfectly cooked roast.

But she was still in today's work outfit, a sensible pair of black slacks paired with a pinstriped blouse with shoulder pads so big that it looked like she may be trying out for the Chargers after dinner. I could tell it had been a busy day at work as she handed me a tuna sandwich and potato chips.

Big Ed was seated with his beverage of choice death-gripped in his right hand, his brow furrowed as the plate descended onto the floral placemat.

"Gee Katie, you shouldn't have gone to all this trouble," he grumbled, then took a swig of beer. He offered a laugh that made it clear that he was none-too-pleased about tonight's dinner. "Where do you find the time?"

"Somewhere between working all day, planning John's wedding, and doing your laundry," she practically snarled. "It wouldn't kill you to - oh, I don't know - help out a little bit around here."

"I thought that's why we had kids?" he said, deflecting his lack of housekeeping prowess onto me. "Why don't you help out instead of sitting like a bump on a log in your room?"

"I have been meaning to ask you if there's something bothering you lately," Mom said. "You haven't been yourself."

"Well, acting weird is pretty normal for him," Dad said. "His middle name should have been lazy, in my opinion."

"And you are still the front-runner for Father of the Year," I countered. "In my opinion."

"You better watch that smart mouth of yours."

"If you stop saying dumb things with yours, then it's a deal."

"Maybe it would be nice if you both shut the hell up!" Mom snapped.

"You had also watch that smart mouth of yours as well, Katherine."

"How about this, Edward," she said. "Why don't you read my lips? You know what? Better yet, why don't you pucker up and kiss my ass."

We both stared at her like she was an alien visitor, but it was abundantly clear that she had grown a spine inside her human host. And just as my father was famous for, she took her sandwich upstairs, but instead, she slammed the door of the guest room.

Oh yeah, she was definitely pissed. This room sat empty save for the times that Mom had a migraine or after Dad had admonished her yearly at tax time. His raised voice and a slew of insults wrapped up in obscenities acted as an alarm clock in the early morning hours when Big Ed was the sole breadwinner and would leave for work in a huff.

Apparently, there was a new sheriff in town, and she had just fired her first shot by saying a word that had, up until now, been referred to as a "tush." It left Big Ed speechless, well, for a few seconds. He looked as though he was trying to figure out a difficult math problem.

"What the fuck has gotten into that woman?" Big Ed said, but I didn't have the answer. He would blame it on her "monthly visitor." Mercury was in retrograde, or the Moon was in the seventh house. The answer was that it was dawning of an age where she would use the voice she had kept suppressed and was now using to express her thoughts on being kept under his Aquarius thumb for years.

I wanted to yell, "You go girl" up the stairs. But Big Ed's bulky frame was ascending them, the stomping of feet discernible across the carpet. While I was ecstatic inside, it was very unsettling to see Mom go all Rambo on him, and she had drawn first blood in asserting herself in a way that she never had before.

As I sat alone in the kitchen, I looked over my shoulder to make sure that Rod Serling wasn't ready to add narration because this was some *Twilight Zone* shit! Big Ed had left his beer behind, so I did a boarding house reach with no one to admonish me about poor table manners. I felt the chill, said cheers to no one, and finished it in one long chug.

"Well, that certainly hit the spot!" I said, just as Shadow cautiously ambled into the kitchen, knowing that raised voices usually meant that she had done something naughty.

"Here girl," I said and tore off a piece of my sandwich to show her she hadn't done anything wrong, which resulted in tuna landing on the floor with an audible plop. It seemed like the funniest thing in the world, and the laugh that came out of me felt cathartic.

I recalled the adage that laughter was the best medicine, which made me calm down again. I thought of the very unfunny reason for my going to the doctor.

I had planned to eat the rest of the tuna sandwich, but I had lost my appetite. And Shadow found herself the beneficiary of that. I decided to make it a liquid dinner night and took three beers out of Big Ed's private stockpile.

The buzz that was running through my body was taking the sting out of what was now my predicament. I tried to be as quiet as possible since I really didn't want to get on Mom's newfound bad side.

Nor was I in the mood to answer any questions as to why I needed to steady myself against the wall on my third trip to the bathroom. The only answer was that I had passed buzzed and had entered *Sarah T. - Portrait of a Teenage Alcoholic* territory.

"I learned it from watching you, Dad, ok?" I whispered to Big Ed's closed door. I saw the glow of the TV visible underneath the door.

If those walls could talk, he'd be plenty pissed that in front of the TV, Mom had discussed all the broken branches of our family tree. That wasn't the Dodge way, not by a long shot, and as I finished what seemed like the longest pee in history, I wondered if things would truly change around here.

This would be the moment in the made-for-TV movie where the main character looks longingly into the mirror, wondering where it all went wrong.

"You probably deserve it," I said and gave my reflection a drunken middle finger.

I was awakened by the sound of nails scratching on my bedroom door. My first foggy thought was that it was Mom sharpening her claws in preparation for round two with Big Ed. It was Shadow looking to cuddle with me, and I gladly welcomed the opportunity.

I lay in the dark of a chilly winter night with Shadow acting as a blanket of unconditional love to stave off the cold - a shocking 59 degrees for Southern California. The dead of night was alive with fears greater than the boogeyman hiding under the bed. My mind flipped onto things that are associated with winter, as Dick Clark may have said on the *$25,000 Pyramid.*

Once the word "frost" floated across my field of vision on a flash card, the black ink turned red, and I remembered sitting morbidly enraptured in front of the TV, watching *An Early Frost* – a movie that delved into the taboo topic of AIDS.

I had hoped that the beers would fully turn my brain off. But there was an endless cord that stretched out for miles, keeping the plug in an outlet out of reach. I craved the freedom of mentally short-circuiting.

Shadow must have sensed that I was in distress because she began licking my face. Usually, I allowed her about three licks, not wanting to find how many licks it took to get to the center of my cheek, but it only took one to pierce my heart. This time, I let her keep going, hugging her tightly, a surrogate for my stuffed Curious George that had shared the bed with me years ago.

And wouldn't you know it? Rather than focus on the positives of having someone in my life who just loved me for me, even if she were a canine, I suddenly recalled a news story about how a dog's heightened sense of smell could detect cancer in people.

I could only wonder if she had detected that I was riddled with a disease.

Since I awoke at 10 a.m., I didn't know whether my parents had reached a truce over breakfast or prolonged the bitterness. But as I stretched my arms over my head with a yawn, I noticed that my sleepover guest was nowhere to be seen. Rather than re-enacting a version of *Snow White* with a lone animal to make my bed while I sang a song, I left the bed rumpled in a tangle of sheets and a noticeable dent in my pillow, no doubt my head made heavier with vivid dreams.

"Sleep: Those little slices of death, how I loathe them," I quoted Edgar Allan Poe. My English teacher, Mrs. Alley, had been big on him, and her enthusiasm had spilled onto me. So, I added onto that sentiment, "Quoth the Raven 'Nevermore.'"

I ate a bowl of Honey Nut Cheerios, standing with my butt against the sink, an act that made Mom once ask if I thought I was in New York City. I monitored the room for signs of further casualties from this morning. There were no knocked-over chairs, and all the sharp knives were in the butcher block.

The rest of the house hadn't necessarily fallen into disrepair, but it could use some sprucing up. It wouldn't kill me to pitch in, as all I had going on for the day was schoolwork. Besides, it would be a productive way to keep my mind off you-know-what and score some brownie points with both parents.

"Say! I have a great idea!" I said aloud. Shadow looked at me quizzically, hoping my words meant it was time for a W-A-L-K. When she followed me upstairs to my room, I shooed her out, not wanting her to look at me as I enlisted Tina's help in getting me in full *Hazel* mode.

"That's better, Mr. B," I said in what passed for an impression of Shirley Booth's loveable domestic. "Now, where to start?"

I figured since you only had one chance to make a first impression, I'd tackle the living room first, followed by the kitchen, den, and downstairs bathroom, nixing the sudden inclination to alphabetize all Big Ed's tools in the garage.

I managed to get the first part of the mission accomplished in a little over an hour. I skipped straightening up Mom and Dad's room, as the bed was already made. I wondered if Mom had made it or if Big Ed had straightened the white bedspread as his version of waving a flag of surrender.

The only sign that we had a special guest in the room that had nautical wallpaper was the clothes mom had worn yesterday, folded neatly on the bed.

I needed more energy and headed back to my room. For a split second, I wanted to take my Mother's Little Helper and dump it into the trash can, forever rid of it. But... I wasn't ready to give up that crutch quite yet, seeing I was limping through life right now.

Granted, I wondered if I could perform some sort of spring cleaning on my soul as effectively as I did on our house.

I returned to work, taking the feather duster to the neglected sketchbook, hoping that getting rid of the dust would miraculously free my creativity from the cobwebs it was encased in. But I ignored its pleas of "Help meeee" and put it back where it partially covered the word freedom that I had etched into the wood, a permanent reminder that concept was never free; it had its own way of making you pay the price.

I took a bottle of Pledge to my entertainment console, rag in hand, ready to dissolve the dust that earmarked where I had pulled books out and slid back into place, unable to concentrate on the written word, when phantom ones screamed into my ear.

"This doesn't make me dirty!"

I turned on the radio on my boom box, cranking the volume up on "Don't Dream It's Over," and let the lyrics "There's a battle ahead. Many battles are lost" follow me into the bathroom, where I did an abbreviated clean-up, leaving the shower alone.

I stared at my reflection in the toilet water. How fitting, as that's where I saw my life at this point - right in the crapper. I flushed it after a thorough scrubbing, wishing I could eliminate my problems as easily.

"Away go troubles, down the drain, my ass." I sighed angrily.

I returned to my sanctuary and turned the radio down to a more appropriate decibel, muffling Human League's "Human," just as Philip Oakley was singing of being made of flesh and blood. I bristled at the last word.

"Trust me, I know!"

I scooped up the copy of the almost week-old *Los Angeles Times* to scan the calendar section. They also carried syndicated columnist *Dear*

Abby, and I wondered how she would answer my letter about what was transpiring in my life, signed "Desperately Seeking Answers." It would probably be a four-word answer: "You figure it out."

And this is where pop culture betrayed me. I had already been touched by AIDS before Tony. I had mourned Ricky Wilson's death by playing The B-52's *Bouncing off the Satellites* on heavy rotation and had a Rock Hudson movie marathon upon learning of his untimely passing. I had seen the pictures in *The National Enquirer* that showed his decline, his once-handsome face now a death mask, and read the speculation that he may have given his *Dynasty* co-star Linda Evans the virus during a kissing scene.

But as far as having to deal with it in real life, I had no gay friends. I didn't know anyone who had succumbed to it. Now… Tony and I had also seen some familiar faces at Black's Beach fade away into the dwindling sunset of their time on Earth.

I had nowhere to turn. Nobody could grasp the gravity of what I was holding inside; the blood that could be corroding my insides, giving the term "rusty pipes" a whole new meaning.

It was the first time that the thought of ending my life crossed my mind, a cloud blocking out the full moon.

The next few weeks were a whirlwind of new experiences: Helping my mother out with preparation for John and Jeannie's fast-approaching wedding. But in other ways, it reflected the bumper sticker on the corkboard above my drafting table: Same shit, different day.

I'd awake after sleeping for two or three hours - if I were lucky and start the entire process of shoveling my feelings up my nostrils. Just wanting to remain as numb as possible to thoughts of my untimely demise - be it from the plague or of my own doing.

As my supply of forget-me-lots went from four bindles down to two, I began to envision myself as Dorothy Gale locked in the castle of The Wicked Witch of the West, sobbing in front of the hourglass, its red sands denoting how much time she had left.

I was becoming fully convinced that when the last of the crystal went up my nose, and I hadn't been presented with a medal for courage like a certain lion, there would be no ignoring the man behind the curtain for me.

I tried to measure it out per day, not wanting to run out on the nuptials of my brother and his bride. If I adhered to only doing three lines per day, even skipping a day or two here and there, I could be covered until early in the New Year.

I kept up my regimen during the week when I was alone in the house, the deafening silence of its interior battling with the screaming voices in my head, temporarily abated by the three-hour block of soaps. I still reported to Mom about our "stories" when Big Ed wasn't in earshot.

I would not eat all day but put up a good front at weekday dinners and on weekends to not raise suspicions as to why I was dwindling away until there was nothing left of me. Still, it did not escape Mom's keen observations.

"You sure are getting thin," she mentioned one night during a conversation about wedding plans. "Are you feeling alright?"

"Peachy keen, jellybean," I said with forced enthusiasm.

"You would tell me if something was wrong, wouldn't you?"

I could really rock the boat and confess that I was not only a drug user but, as an added bonus, that I could be dying. I was fairly sure this wasn't an area that Dr. Spock had covered in any of his books.

"Sure," I answered, deciding to keep it simple. This time, there was zero chance of absolution, no amount of Hail Marys that could save me from the purgatory that was now my life.

"Good," she said, slipping back into her trademark chipper demeanor. "I think that should do it for tonight. Thanks for your help, Henry; you are a real lifesaver."

"Cherry red, naturally." I joked, thinking of the arsenal of Lifesavers that she kept in her purse.

"I think I'm going to hit the hay." She emphasized the point by yawning and stretching in the dining room chair. "Don't stay up too late unless you're trying to compete with a raccoon to see who can have darker circles under their eyes."

She stood up and did something that she hadn't done since I was a kid. Her hand mussed my hair. While this was usually frowned upon as I worked to make my hair as stationary as possible with Aqua Net, I welcomed her gentle touch.

Besides, I hadn't exactly been looking my best during self-imposed house arrest. My forehead had an almost volcanic zit, a direct result of stress coupled with my Hoover activities. The mirror was a reminder that I could play a zombie in *Night of the Living Dead*, which John had convinced me to watch when I was ten. It created a week's worth of nightmares in which I was the victim of the undead and their appetite for flesh.

My own taste for skin had all but vanished. Sex was now taboo. Even giving myself a hand didn't hold allure. I had tried once over a *Playgirl* centerfold but ended up spilling a few tears instead. It hit me that sex may have very well been my undoing. I began to employ the most effective method of safe sex in which abstinence was cited as the course of action. Even if I was doing it ass backwards, it offered a fragment of assuagement.

I stayed holed up in my domain with my canine roommate. I was so bummed that I even ignored the siren song of temptation that was calling out to me from the vessel that had once housed INXS' *Listen Like Thieves* cassette case.

I did not need Tina's help in falling down the mountain, ending up with me kissing dirt.

Instead, I switched off the lights, hoping the dark would cradle me, putting an end to another endless day. The red glare from the digital alarm clock on my nightstand began to melt like the view through a rainy windshield as I cried myself to sleep, which eventually came around two in the morning.

After a fitful sleep, given that Shadow had moved to the floor during the night in response to my tossing and turning – I did my best impression of rising and shining.

Except that I didn't feel risen or particularly shiny. Just a shadow of myself, sleepy and dull in my mind and instantly anxious throughout my body. There was no amount of heart-healthy Honey Nut Cheerios that could heal me or put pep in my step.

How I envied Shadow's selective memory, as her wagging tail signaled that she bore no ill will that she couldn't sleep on my bed. I was jealous that she didn't have to endure the rigors of being a human. She was blissfully dependent on me to feed her, make sure she did her business, and give her plenty of love and affection.

I had learned the hard way that these qualities were missing from most people in what was essentially a dog-eat-dog world. Sure, most men were happy to throw me the proverbial bone but were unlikely to care and nurture me the way I doted on Shadow. As I followed her into the backyard and picked up the army shovel, I saw it as a proper analogy for getting rid of the shit in my life. However, it was a case of easier said than done.

Anger caused me to nearly pitch the discarded contents of Shadow's meal from yesterday over the back fence and into the Carter's yard. Instead, it hit the fence with a mild thud and disappeared into the ice plant that populated the hill. Too bad my thoughts couldn't be so easily disposed of; even amid being upset, my sense of humor didn't want things getting too serious. I wondered if I could earn a Farthest Shit Throw trophy added to the shelf that lined the upstairs hallway, one disruption to the shrine to John's sports accomplishments and illustrated my "Hey, at least you tried" attempts at being a variant of a "normal kid" with the three I got for attempting at conforming.

It made me think of the t-shirt I had bought myself with the saying "Why Be Normal?"

I had craved to be considered just a regular kid a lifetime ago. But a pang of sadness reverberated from my core. I could only hope that someday I'd have the chance to be comfortable in my own skin and not wear it inside out, nerve endings no longer exposed by a merciless life.

I thought I would be better off dead, and my pop culture knowledge tried to shut it down with lines from the John Cusack comedy.

"I want my two dollars!" The maniacal paperboy shouted to drown out any negative connotations.

"First, we have Frawnch fries and Frawnch dressing and Frawnch bread. And to drink, Ta-da! Peru," Kim Darby informed my brain.

While this had produced gales of laughter when I saw it at the movies, the thought that I was flashing back on a movie about suicide didn't strike me as funny.

"Really? You couldn't have picked *Sixteen Candles* or something?" I said aloud, to which Shadow tilted her head, wondering if I was using a code for breakfast.

I both loved and loathed my brain, which retained Hollywood trivia, song lyrics and passages from books that spoke to me. But there were times when I longed to have a lobotomy to erase bad memories and feelings, to have those deficits wiped out and no longer be held prisoner by fear.

There was no denying that I was currently serving time, one that could see me end up on death row.

I physically shook my head to loosen all thoughts of doom and or gloom. I needed to put on my game face, as John was making himself at home. I spied with my little eye something that started with the letter C, a container of Chinese food open on the counter. But rather than being microwaved, it was mixed into an omelet. He was his father's son since Big Ed was very fond of peanut butter and sardine sandwiches.

"I'm sorry, I thought you were my brother and not *The Galloping Gourmet*," I said with a surprising levity, given that I was in a downward spiral moments before. "On second thought, from the looks of your breakfast, I think it's me that should gallop away from that culinary fiasco."

"Don't knock it 'til you try it."

"I'm sure that it will taste better going down than it will coming up. You must have an iron-clad stomach."

"Well, it wouldn't kill you to, oh, I don't know, eat something. I always forget what's the difference between being anorexic and bulimic?"

"Hmm, I heard that it's like the difference between an asshole or an actual decent human being. They're in the same family but different at the same time. From the looks of that concoction, it's you who has the eating disorder."

"Eat me!"

"Oh my God! Did your omelet just talk? Get *That's Incredible* on the horn!"

When John was done rolling his eyes, he trained them on me and wondered if a proper nutrition lecture was coming. "There's something I wanted to ask you."

"Yes, I'm a total fag." I paraphrased Molly Ringwald's answer to Anthony Michael Hall's similar query in *Sixteen Candles*. Oh sure, now you show up, movie quote!

"I do have eyes, you know." He popped them open wide to illustrate the fact that jeepers creepers he did have peepers.

"Shoot, I'm all ears."

"I was wondering if you'd be in the wedding?"

"So, you couldn't you find a flower girl in time?"

"No idiot; despite my better judgment, I want you to be my best man."

"Are you serious?" I felt like I had been crowned Miss America but hoped that he wouldn't strip me of the title like Vanessa Williams had been for posing nude.

"As a heart attack," he said sincerely.

"Uh, bro - your breakfast is smoking."

He turned around and discovered it was a prime example of Henry's tomfoolery; he returned his attention to me, shaking his head.

"Well?" he asked.

"I would be honored to," I said, even though I wondered if I was up to the task. I figured it might provide a welcome relief from focusing on my 24-hour misery by celebrating his happiness. "What exactly does it entail, and will I be paid for this?"

"Your duties will be dressing up in a tux, not losing the rings, making a speech, and not turn it into a roast," he instructed. "It usually would mean that you'd take care of my bachelor party, but you're not able to drink, so my Navy buddy is spearheading that."

"Damn!"

"Probably wouldn't interest you much anyway because it'll be at a strip club."

"Yeah, no shoving money into some girl's ham wallet for this guy!"

"Where do you come up with this stuff?"

"Call it a gift."

"Hope you kept the receipt. I doubt store credit would cover it."

"Probably not. Now your breakfast is about to be a flambé, for real this time."

"Ok, Mr. Food Critic, let me eat this in peace."

"No problemo. That's a godawful smell. Please don't feed any to Shadow. Bon Appetit! That's French for good luck eating that!"

"Ok, Kate."

As I showered, I thought of the importance of my brother considering me as the best man soaked in. We had really come a long way in a short time, closeness replacing the vast distances that were impossible to traverse in our younger days. He was now an ally where there had once been an enemy.

Maybe he was leaning more towards being a mama's boy than a younger doppelganger of Big Ed, reaching the conclusion that there weren't many of my father's traits that needed to be repeated. And he didn't know the half of it!

I mean, if Darth Vader could cross over from the pull of The Dark Side in *Return of the Jedi*, there may be the chance that someday the mask he wore would be taken off, exposing a different side to him. Hopefully, Big Ed wouldn't resemble a distant cousin of Humpty Dumpty as the Sith Lord had in that ridiculous reveal moment that made me laugh and receive disapproving looks and a symphony of shushes from audience members.

Ed Dodge was always having a private duel with himself, one that could result in him being reduced to a pile of clothes and nothingness like Obi-Wan Kenobi. I suspected, given my own self-destructive tendencies, that I was more like him than I cared to admit.

I most definitely related with Luke Skywalker's efforts to not be swayed away from the light and plunged into the darkness, pitch-black and inescapable. But isn't that what death is when you get down to brass tacks? One day you're here, the next day, you're not, and there's nothing, not a goddamn thing that you can do about it. It's inevitable, unavoidable, and just a question of when.

I wanted to take the Grim Reaper's sickle and either bludgeon him to death with it or shove it up his ass, for irony's sake.

I was close to using up the hot water in our water heater. But I felt chilled to the bone, even after I was dried off and fully dressed, and I couldn't seem to shake it. Naturally, I wondered if it was a symptom of being HIV-positive.

I was relieved that my brother had dined and dashed, not wanting him to bear witness to what would surely look cuckoo for Cocoa Puffs. I got into bed, fully dressed in a sweater and a pair of corduroy jeans left over from the time I tried to pass myself off as preppy, plus wool socks from my grandmother last Christmas.

I got under the covers, pulled them up to my chin as I had when I was four and thought the Boogeyman was lurking in my room. The old monsters that had hidden under my bed were replaced by a new breed. Ones who could do more than merely scare me. It would take more than calling out for my mommy this time to be saved.

"It was the Boogeyman," I said to the emptiness, like my favorite final girl, Jamie Lee Curtis, in *Halloween* told Donald Pleasance. I showed my acting range by answering as his Dr. Loomis. "As a matter of fact, it was."

The night of John's bachelor party had arrived.

John's out-of-character decision was to assemble his goon squad at our house. It was easier than facing questions from Jeannie as to the who, what, where, when, and how elements of the evening, which was being billed as a night out with the boys.

He also explained it to Kate Dodge, who had her truth-extracting chocolate chip cookies on a plate, insisting each of them take one, as her suspicions of the depravity they would be up to were cooling like the tasty treats. He also stated that it would give me a chance to meet his other groomsmen since I was unable to partake in the evening's events.

"Gee, isn't that considerate of him?" I said, trying to channel the innocence of Beaver Cleaver, praying that I didn't come off as Eddie Haskell.

"I thought you're having three groomsmen?" Mom asked.

"I am," John said, pleased that the focus had moved towards his big day, diverting from his nocturnal activities.

"Well, I'm no mathematician, but there are only two young men eating these cookies like they are going out of style."

Porter, the dark-haired adorable one, started to put his cookie back on the plate, and chubby Johnny promptly shoved the remaining half down his gullet.

"You boys have as many as you'd like. I was just busting your chops."

It didn't take a call to Dionne Warwick's Psychic Friends Network to predict that Johnny took Mom up on her offer, while Porter remained wary as if she would slap his hand if he dared take another one.

Without repeating her question, she merely looked at John in hopes of him confessing about the missing member of the wedding party.

"Oh yeah, he said he might be a little late." Just then, the doorbell rang. "Speak of the Devil."

He opened the door, and the third groomsman of the apocalypse crossed the threshold. It was a ghost from my not-too-distant past that turned me as white as a sheet.

"Mom, Henry, this is Tony."

If this were the South and I was a refined belle, I would have certainly declared that I "had a case of the vapors" and asked for a mint julep, stat! I wasn't sure if I should pretend that we didn't know each other or let on that we weren't perfect strangers.

I waited for a cue from Tony, my twin in shock and dismay at the circumstances of an unexpected reunion.

Reunited, and it feels so good…or not.

"Good to meet you, Henry. You too, Mrs. Dodge," Tony said casually as if he'd never been inside of me.

"You too, Tony. Would you like a cookie?" She moved the plate towards him, oblivious to what his truth-telling may reveal about my recent mood.

His polite "No thank you, ma'am" might as well have been a "fuck off" to Mom.

I was trying to add up how my brother knew my latest romantic disaster. Was he aware that Tony was gay and HIV positive? My brother had turned a big corner in his acceptance of me, but I was skeptical that he was consciously collecting gay friends.

"I thought that since this one can't join in on the festivities, that we'd have a brewski here first," he said, giving an unnecessary thumbs-up gesture in my direction.

"Thank God!" I exclaimed with what ended up being my outside voice. I felt my face burn with a severe shade of red that no amount of Noxzema could soothe.

"Well, that's the spirit, I guess," John said, eyes full of suspicion, while Tony's were downcast as if our carpet was the most fascinating thing he'd ever seen.

Porter and Johnny exchanged looks that said, "Damn, Dodge's brother is a kook." Mom put the cookies away. I thought I saw her hair part ever so slightly to let her mythical third eye get a good look at me, peering into the depths of my soul.

John procured five blue plastic cups from under the bar and shepherded his friends into the garage. It wasn't exactly on par with Pacer's, where they were going to ogle women in various stages of undress, but it was sufficient for a pre-debauchery buzz.

Johnny had drawn the short straw as the designated driver for the evening. He seemed more at home at a buffet rather than drunk off his ass and staring at a woman's roast beef curtains.

I deduced from Tony's participation in John's bachelor party that he may not have revealed that he'd rather spend the evening at Hot Dog on a Stick or a male strip club, shoving dollars into the G-strings of bumping and grinding hunks.

As I accepted the beer into my greedy mitts, I almost guzzled it prematurely before my brother cleared his throat to make a toast. I hoped he was a man of few words. The cold of the cup nicely offset my nerves.

"I just want to thank you guys for being such awesome friends. I mean that you guys are awesome."

"You already said that. Pick another adjective," I critiqued.

"And little brother, even though you are a pain in the ass sometimes and a dick at other times, I'm glad you're going to be my best man. You'll be there in spirit tonight. Cheers!"

"Awesome!" I muttered into my cup, sarcastically amplified by the plastic.

Everyone raised their cups high in the air, but I started downing mine.

"Braaaaaaaaaaap!" I let the belch fly with no inhibitions.

The look of admiration from Porter and Johnny felt like I was basking in the brightest sunlight. And it quickly faded as I saw Tony looking slightly disgusted. I was half-tempted to pull him aside for a little chat.

Where in the actual fuck to begin? The possibilities were endless and then became finite in the realization that I couldn't exactly begin a line of questioning at this juncture. Besides, the obvious answer was to be found in his decision to go the stranger route. I wished they were staying longer than having a single beer, as alcohol could prove to be more effective than Mom's chocolate chip cookies.

I was about to suggest we have one more, but John decreed it was time to "Vamanos."

As Mom and I said our goodbyes and her seriously toned "be careful" at the door, I knew that I would return to the life preserver of the pony keg, each pull on its handle helping to drown my sorrows.

"Well, they all seem nice." Her tone dipped in sugar, and then it turned lemon sour. "Except that Tony. I don't know, there was something about him that I can't put my finger on."

If only she had known where his fingers had been with me.

"Oh yeah? He seemed ok to me."

"Anyone who doesn't eat one of my cookies is highly suspect in my book." She joked and then let out a serious yawn. "I am beat. Goodnight, hon."

"Night," I said and heard her footsteps over my head as I decided that watching TV in the den was the least suspicious option as to why I'd be going up and down the stairs for clandestine drinking.

I turned the volume down on our Zenith via its enormous remote control that could seriously hurt someone if you clocked them with it. I crept up the three stairs that led to the living room and peered up. There was no light from a bedside lamp or flickering TV light bleeding out from the space between the rug and the crack under the door, signaling that the coast was clear.

I made five separate trips to the white refrigerator in the garage, opening the door as slowly and as deliberately as my mission to get good and drunk.

It was trip number three that almost gave me away as Shadow sat in the small, dark hallway waiting for me. I almost let out a shriek. Worse yet, I almost spilled my beer, and I was feeling a little too buzzed to clean a spill efficiently.

"Damn girl," I whispered and stretched out my beer-free left hand and gave her a pat on the head.

I really loved this dog; my mind getting to that mushy place when you imbibe. Instead of "I love you, man," this was a case of "I love you, girl," and it wasn't just alcohol-induced. She made me feel less lonely, gave me some responsibility, and prompted my creativity in constructing our own language.

I didn't just scratch her behind the ear. I referred to it as a "skritch," which I appropriated from Charlie Brown and Snoopy.

As she joined me on the couch, I put the beer down on the coffee table and wrapped both of my arms around her. I then returned it to my drinky-poo and a season one episode of *Charlie's Angels* I had recorded a few months ago.

"It's kinda fucked up," I stated, almost expecting in my boozy frame of mind that Shadow might ask what was fucked up. "Kate Jackson was pretty, but just because she's not as traditionally pretty as the other Angels, they made her drive a Pinto. That ain't right."

Shadow's response was to move off the couch and lay on the floor.

"Whatever, just tryin' to learn ya somethin'," I said with a Southern drawl.

After I finished the contents of my fifth journey out to the garage and spying the clock hands both on twelve, I decided it was best to pass out in my own bed. I did a decent job of navigating the stairs, given that I didn't end up at the bottom of them with a broken neck.

All the efforts I made to not dwell on Tony came back in a flood. I wondered if he was enjoying himself or had blurted out drunkenly to my brother about us knowing each other.

I didn't know that four letters – AIDS - could carry a massive weight on their tiny shoulders. The gravity of its meaning for myself and those who were fighting it or had died trying to caused my emotions to come crashing back to earth.

There's nothing pretty about a drunk crying. It starts as snot bubbles and then comes out in a string like a magician's scarf.

But was Budweiser really to blame? Nope.

I felt defeated and not ready to fight for my life or my right to party.

In the dark of night, a light went off in my head. I didn't know where I had absorbed the information that if you hung your head upside down that it was possible to cause the blood to flow to your brain, effectively drowning it.

And with no lifeguard on duty, I decided to jump into the deep end to see if that theory held water.

As it turned out, ten minutes into my science experiment left me feeling dizzy and very much alive.

"Well, shit," I said, feeling the burn of anger and frustration that my blood couldn't be trusted and there was no salve to help soothe the pain. It felt like I had taken a bath in Bactine, letting fear soak into my every pore, and it stung like a motherfucker.

"The roof, the roof, the roof is on fire. We don't need no water. Let the motherfucker burn," I recited absently as I began to slide into zombie mode, which thankfully led to sleeping like the dead as my bed substituted for a coffin. I dreamt that I was wandering aimlessly among tombstones, a ground fog my only companion, as I went on some unknown search.

Eventually, I found a tombstone all by itself at the top of a hill, a gnarled tree serving as its protector, lurching forward with its branches trying to capture me. But I avoided its nightmarish entrapment.

Underneath a pale moon, I squinted at what the epitaph read and then backed away from the obelisk wild-eyed, the words branded into my retinas.

Here Lies Henry Dodge. Born February 24, 1969.

Yet it gave no expiration date as to when I had died. But the inscription underneath held a clue as to how:

"Blood was his Avatar and his seal - the madness and the horror of blood."

It paraphrased an Edgar Allan Poe quote from *The Masque of the Red Death.*

As I ran through the graveyard, desperate to find an exit point, the earth on several of the graves began to push upwards.

In typical Henry Dodge fashion, I hazarded a look backwards and saw a militia of corpses giving chase. The band of ghouls were familiar to me – it included Danny, George, Angel, Troy, and Nick. Not looking where I was going, I ran into the mouth of an open grave that readily accepted me as a tender morsel in its gullet.

And it gave the pursuers from my past the opportunity to make sure I would have no place in the future. Each one held a shovel in their withered and rotting hands and smoothly worked in tandem to bury me alive.

I sat up straight as an arrow in my bed, slapping at my face to get the invisible dirt off me. I looked at my hands to make sure they weren't dirty. I was feeling every inch a refugee from a Roger Corman Edgar Allan Poe movie starring Vincent Price. The horror movie actor's distinct voice from his rap on Michael Jackson's "Thriller" echoed in my head, and I sniffed my armpits for any tell-tale signs of emitting the funk of forty thousand years, given the fact that I was soaking wet with sweat. The only scent I could discern was that my room smelled like a brewery, one where Laverne and Shirley were placing a glove on a bottle of Shotz beer, which was waving goodbye to me. A realization dawned on me: night sweats were an indicator of HIV. I swung my legs out of bed and placed my feet on the ground, bucking the feeling of being fully subscribed to staying in bed all day with the covers pulled up over my head, as if the cocoon of fabrics could keep me safe from the reality of my waking hours. I walked over to the window and opened it. The cool air of the winter morning entered my room like a vampire I had invited in; one that would detect the anomaly in my blood and flee as surely as if I held a cross up to ward off its underworldly presence. I remained still, feet glued to the brown and yellow rug.

The cooler temperature from outside counterbalancing my body temperature which had made me a soaking mess. My reverie was broken by a scratching, and I sleepily crept towards the door.

But it wasn't Frankenstein's monster, nor the bandaged corpse of the Mummy, or even Lawrence Talbot in werewolf mode. It was simply Shadow letting me know that I had missed her usual breakfast time by a good hour, and she was none-too-pleased, even if her tail told a different story by going a million miles a minute.

I followed Shadow and entered the kitchen, where Mom and John sat deep in conversation, stopping when I arrived. They looked every inch the co-conspirators, plotting something devious, or as if they knew something. Naturally, I presumed they knew about my love affair with the bindles – or my terminal illness. So, I was either in for an intervention or a forced trip to the doctor to have a needle stuck in my arm and blood taken against my will.

"Tony called me this morning," John said solemnly. "He can't be at the wedding. He's sick."

I used to think I had all the time in the world to do what I wanted and be who I was supposed to be. But as the calendar pages got closer to the year's end, my days felt numbered, growing shorter with every moment, ticking away on what might as well be a Doomsday Clock.

The only thing that proved to be a distraction was John and Jeannie's impending nuptials, which were slated to commence this weekend without the added pressure of Tony at the altar with me.

While it was a relief, it brought forth more stress. The innocuous term of being "sick" held its own glossary; from him having a common cold or being shortlisted to not be long for this world. And I had nowhere to turn. No one I could ask which scenario was presenting itself.

I certainly wouldn't broach the subject with John, and I didn't think that Tony wanted me to slip into the impromptu role of chief of police, asking where he was on the night in question, one that I didn't really want the answer to anyhow.

They say that ignorance is bliss, but I wasn't a picture-perfect candidate to illustrate the notion. I was feeling detached on John and Jeannie's big day, standing by myself when the chance provided, away from the other members of the wedding party, which included Sharon, cousins Deenie, Bonnie, and Connie for Jeannie's side, and me, Porter, John, and Tony's replacement, simply known as Ace, for John's.

I was nothing more than an image on a strip of film, shadowy and negative, without the chance to become fully developed. The wedding photographer's flash went off, capturing my effigy.

I stood frozen, a queer stuck in the headlights, all blank mind and vacant stare, cursing myself that I hadn't taken the time to put paper to pen for a speech. I wasn't sure how well an impromptu freestyle rap of the *Family Ties* theme song would go over with the crowd. My lack of preparedness had served me well in school, always finding me doing well on reports that I had put off for weeks, only to hunker down on the night before.

But for once in my life, I was at a loss for words. I heard a small cough and pinpointed its perpetrator as Big Ed, who was glowering at me so fiercely that I was surprised his glasses weren't fogging up. He was bracing himself for another colossal Henry Dodge fuck up.

I cleared my throat, and the words tumbled out of my mouth as if I were under mind control.

"Sometimes in life, you meet someone, and they become your person if you're lucky enough. And despite all you have learned and been shown about what a relationship can be," I said, pausing to catch the eye of a visibly squirming Big Ed before continuing my thought. "You rise above what you think something should be and make it what it could be and will be. To John and Jeannie."

I saw Mom wipe away tears before she picked up her Champagne glass to toast the new Mr. and Mrs. Dodge. I tipped my glass of champagne in her direction. There was no arm around her shoulder from Dad, no token effort at consolation.

In fact, his attention wasn't even on his wife. His sights were set on Mrs. Woodson, a slight smirk on his mug that complemented her hideous ensemble that was the definition of "who shot the couch?" Floral overkill were the two words that described it to a tee. Hideous also applied as a third.

I wanted to stride up to her, all confidence and swagger, and ask, "Who invited you?"

I was completely in my cups and already knew the answer. John had thought it would be nice to bring the recently divorced shrew into the celebratory mix. I even had to write her name on the envelope of the invite; the thought of merely tossing it into the garbage had crossed my mind. Especially if she thought it would be appropriate to bring her son as her plus one.

It looked like Dad wanted to chuck his marriage right into the trash, based on the intense gaze he was throwing her way. And she was returning one that led me to suspect it was not their first time at the rodeo. Big Ed was ready to rope and ride the little filly, who looked more like a nag that needed to be sent to the glue factory. But he was the one stuck in the mire of his old ways, unable to change, and would only end up breaking another wedding vow, just mere hours after his firstborn son had said his I do's.

"Son of a bitch," I muttered, but I was still holding the mic. It didn't seem to be audible to anyone, save for one drunken reveler who began laughing. Mom was observing the eye play between Mrs. Woodson and her lawfully wedded spouse. She nudged him sharply with an elbow to his ribs, which snapped him out of whatever thoughts he was having about our neighbor.

He offered up a sheepish smile, and Mom pushed his hand away when he attempted to hold hers. She had crossed her arms, the ultimate sign to keep your distance. An armor forged from years of suffering through his infidelities now finally repelled the slings and arrows of an unhappy marriage.

Mom's focus was on the happy couple who were making their way to the dance floor for their first dance as man and wife. When the opening strains of "Every Breath You Take" by The Police began, I put the microphone down, lest anyone hear the giggle I could not suppress. John hadn't read the *Rolling Stone* interview where Sting explained the so-called love song was really about a stalker.

Just like the one that was infiltrating my immune system.

I didn't want to cry, as it could result in a full-blown meltdown. Luckily, I had brought a bit of the meth I had left, and it seemed like the perfect remedy. I went into the bathroom, which was for single occupants, with no need to worry about my covert business.

I sat backwards on the toilet lid, railed out two chunky lines on the porcelain top of the tank, and gratefully let the mood stabilizer enter my nostrils. I gathered it all up and tucked it away. I flushed the toilet and made my way to the mirror to make sure there were no albino bats in my cave. When I caught my reflection, I could see how tired I looked, yet it was nothing compared to how I felt on the inside.

I splashed some water on my face, letting it run to disguise the sound of me getting the drips to run from my nose to my throat. Just as I withdrew a paper towel from the metal box on the wall to dry my face, a knock sounded.

"Occupato," I said as if I was bilingual and had barely passed Spanish in reality. "Out in a second."

I patted my face dry and opened the door.

Doreen Woodson was waiting to relieve herself.

"Didn't you know the bathroom for skanks is down the hall," I said with a sneer.

"Well, it certainly isn't the men's room with you in it," she replied, eyeing me up and down. "What exactly is your problem with me?"

"It's not with all of you. Just that hellhole you call your vagina and what came out of it 23 years ago. Speaking of that axe wound, you'd better not get it anywhere near my dad if you know what's good for you."

"Oh, is that a threat?" she said with a laugh.

"Consider it a promise," I answered and made my way past her, my adrenaline pumping from the exchange and the meth coursing through my bloodstream.

I scanned the dance floor, and the generation gap was in full swing, with The Romantics' "What I Like About You" providing the divide as the younger guests jumped, jived, and sang along to it. When the song ended, the DJ played an oldie for those on the sidelines.

Elvis brought on the slow dance portion of the evening with "I Can't Help Falling in Love," and I saw Mom to my left, looking every inch the wallflower, as her date was nowhere to be seen.

"May I have this dance?" I yelled above the din of the King of Rock n' Roll's vocals.

She took my hand, and I did my best to slow my dance moves down a few notches.

"Thanks, hon," she said. "Have you seen your father? Or *that* woman?"

"That's a negatory on Pops," I replied. "However, I put Whoreen in her place, which was appropriately in the bathroom."

"I hope you weren't too hard on her," she chastised playfully with a gleam in her eye.

"Who me?" We both started laughing.

Doreen came into my sightline, a scowl fixed on her face, knowing the laughter was directed at her. I mouthed "Fuck you" over Mom's shoulder. Not that it mattered. Mrs. Woodson turned on her heel and stormed out of the reception hall. I saw a forlorn-looking Sharon alone at the bar and beelined it to her, buzzing along on my meth high.

"Barkeep, hit me," I said behind her, and she nearly jumped out of her poofy-shouldered pink taffeta dress.

"It's only me, your friendly neighborhood homosexual. There'll be no unwanted advances from this guy."

"Sorry, I spaced out. Besides, I know you're harmless. Well, to women anyway."

"God, I hope you're not drowning your sorrows about being the bridesmaid and not the bride. Just be thankful you didn't have to change your name to Sharonie for the occasion."

"I'm definitely the odd woman out by not having an 'ie' at the end of my name, for sure."

"Well, you're in good company," I said wistfully. "I'm the perennial odd man out."

"Since neither of us has a plus-one, we should have a spin on the dance floor."

"I'm game," I said.

"Yes, I know," she said with a slightly puzzled look on her face until I repeated it slowly. "Oh Jesus, duh!"

We both cracked up about her auditory faux pas as the bartender arrived with my beer and two tequila shots.

"He's cute," Sharon observed, her gaze fixed on the Hispanic man who returned his attention to cutting limes, oblivious to her lustful stare.

"A wise friend once told me never to go home with a bartender," I said after the tequila was done burning my throat.

"And why is that?"

"Elementary, my dear." I paused for effect. "They get more action than Sylvester Stallone in a *Rambo* movie, was the way I believe she put it."

"Sounds like your friend spent some time in the trenches."

"Probably. Do they give out The Purple Heart medal for ones that are broken?"

"Oh great. Did I get saddled with a melancholy drunk?" she asked playfully, but it made me aware that I had moved on to chugging my beer, gripping the bottle like a life preserver.

"I'll have you know that I can handle my liquor. Thank you very much."

"I can see that," she said with a giggle that denoted she was also heading to Tipsy Town.

"Probably the only thing I have in common with my old man," I mused, and a strange look popped up on her face. "Something I said?"

"More like something I saw," she muttered. "Never mind; it's not important."

I was tempted to ply her with another tequila shot to get a confession out of her. But the DJ playing Ready for the World's "Oh Sheila" derailed that train of thought.

"C'mon, let's go cut that rug up into pieces!" I exclaimed. I made a mental note to revisit the topic when she was drunker and more pliable.

The combination of Tina, alcohol, and my love of dancing felt like liberation from the darkness I had been shrouded in lately. The thoughts of reality were being shaken out of my very being, lost in the music. I let my crotch thrust in time when the lead singer sang three "Oh's" in a row, not caring if anyone at the reception would see that as scandalous.

Rather than have the scarlet letter H, as in homo, on my rented gray tux, I got a series of claps on the back.

When I began busting out moves like Kevin Bacon's dance double in *Footloose*, everybody cheered me on. Even John proudly said, "Damn, dude, you can dance!" I finally tapped out eight songs later, hair matted to my sweaty forehead, and little rivulets of sweat ran down onto my face, but not before one found my eye, obscuring my vision, as I scanned the crowd for Sharon.

I wiped the liquid away with the back of my hand, thankful that it wasn't tears. I was sick of crying myself to sleep. Sick of guessing the possible outcomes that might transpire if... I was positive. Disowned and kicked out of the house seemed likely possibilities. The salt in the wound would be Mom wagging her finger at me with an angry "I told you so!"

But hadn't we reached some sort of detente? She had made me her confidant and seemed to be coming around to the fact this is who I am: take it or leave it.

I didn't know that for certain; just as I couldn't predict what the future held for me.

"Jesus, I need a drink," I said, but no one heard me, and it was oddly comforting to shut my inner voice off by using my outer one.

The bartender saw me approach and smiled. I turned around to (a) make sure he wasn't flashing his teeth for someone behind me or (b) I was on *TV's Bloopers & Practical Jokes*. Neither Dick Clark nor Ed McMahon were waiting to tell me I was on the receiving end of a gag. He had a beer waiting for me.

As I wiped another flood of sweat from my forehead, he produced a sizeable stack of cocktail napkins to assist me. I felt a little gross, honestly, but he responded to my disheveled appearance with an unwavering gaze and impish grin.

"I'm Chris, by the way," he said, extending his hand over the bar.

"By the way, is that Dutch?" I quipped, even though he was Hispanic and a cute one at that, with a head full of thick black hair and a body that wasn't sculpted at the gym. In fact, the beginnings of a belly were pushing against the front of his crisp white shirt.

If he were sans pants and wearing a red half-shirt, he could pass as Winnie-the-Pooh's human doppelganger. I wondered if he saw me as a honey pot – or as doom-and-gloom Eeyore.

"A comedian, eh?" he countered, his grin having bloomed into a full-blown smile, with a hint of lust just beneath the surface.

"You should catch my act. There's a small cover charge and a two-drink minimum."

"I think you're about two drinks over that."

"What are you? The drink police or something?" I said, looking directly into his mud-brown eyes.

"Why? Do you want me to frisk you?" he asked pointedly, signaling there was a new sheriff in town, one that was causing me to feel uncomfortable with his attentions and a sudden hardness in my underwear.

"Now who's the comedian?" I said, wanting to steer the conversation back into a safer neighborhood. "Hey, you haven't seen my friend around, have you?"

"The one you were tearing up the dance floor with? I haven't. Too busy watching you and wondering if you're as energetic in bed."

His bold statement made me self-conscious of the fact that I looked a mess, inside and out.

Suddenly, his boss materialized.

"We need to start packing it up unless you're too busy talking," he chided, focusing his attention on Chris, which gave me a chance to hide the beer. I didn't want him to get in trouble for serving a minor.

"If you see my friend, let her know I'm looking for her. Thanks for your help."

"Sure thing, guy."

I walked away, relieved that he had broken the spell that Chris was putting on me when it was I that was cursed.

The poison apple was leeching into my bloodstream to cause permanent slumber. No Prince Charming was coming to my rescue. Disney cartoons had not prepared me for this fairy's tale.

I looked at the crowd starting to thin out and did not spy Sharon with my little eye, but I did see something that began with the letter B, as in Big Ed. He looked a bit disheveled, hair slightly mussed, suit a tad wrinkled. It may have been one of the few times we physically resembled one another.

As our eyes met, I thought I detected something sheepish, even something human.

The moment suddenly vanished, and his eyes squinted in anger. The DJ was busy getting his equipment together, which was a shame as I wanted to request the theme from *The Good, the Bad, and The Ugly* as Big Ed made a beeline for me, striding across the dance floor.

"You just can't help yourself, can you?" he spewed.

What in the hell was he accusing me of? Did he realize my energy on the dance floor was the result of illicit drugs? Or had he seen Chris trying to get me out of my tuxedo pants?

"Regarding what exactly?" I asked plainly, deciding to ditch the smart-assery.

"You know what I'm talking about. You're not that dumb, so do not play it with me," he hissed through clenched teeth.

"Well, it's a good thing you and Mom didn't name me Sonny because I'm not feeling all that bright right now. What gives?"

"What gives is my hope that you could actually stop being an asshole just for a day. But you've gone too far this time."

"How so, Daddy-O?"

"Mrs. Woodson told me what you said to her. Christ, you have a mouth on you! What the hell is wrong with you?"

"That, dear father, is a whole separate conversation. The long and the short is that she bothers me, aside from the fact that she has very questionable taste in men."

"Is there something wrong with me feeling sorry for her," he asked. "She's on her own."

"There's not a single thing wrong with compassion for another human being." Then I lowered the boom. "Just keep it in your pants."

"You little son-of-a-bitch…" he glowered, turning fire-engine red.

"More like a son-of-a-bastard." I countered heatedly. "Haven't you done enough damage in your marriage already? I know all about you, so don't think that I won't be keeping my eye on you!"

"Fucking kid," he muttered and stomped off.

"What was that all about?" Mom came up and asked.

"Just a little father and son chat," I said, trying not to sound shaky.

"Apparently. Well, we're going to head home in a bit."

"Sounds good," I replied with some semblance of cheeriness.

I turned around as if the force of my heel pivot could fling any bad notions out of my head and into the stratosphere until they reached the darkest reaches of the universe. In space, no one can hear you scream. Try telling that to the space between my ears, my goddamn overthinking cerebrum. I saw a way to dam the flood of emotions I struggled to keep at bay.

My beer was still at the bar, and better yet, Chris was nowhere to be seen. Until he popped up at the precise moment I had the Budweiser in my hot little hand. After I downed the remainder of it, I was going to admonish him for scaring me. But it wasn't like he was the Boogeyman or something; he was more like a walking hormone decked out in a white dress shirt with a bowtie anchored around his neck.

The return of his grin showed that he remained preoccupied with getting me undressed.

"Can't stay away from me, can you?"

"I'm here for the booze. Any chance I could get one more? I need it."

"You know there's a difference between needing something and wanting something. And I'll be good and goddamned as to why I want you, even though you are being such an asshole to me."

Now, it was my turn to apologize. His boss and my dad had rubbed us the wrong way tonight. But it was very apparent that both of us wanted to be rubbed the right way.

I went back to the bathroom. My bladder needed to get rid of the beer, the number one side-effect of imbibing. The second was it impaired my decision-making, and number three, with a bullet, was it made me horny. I wished that horniness were as easy to drain as taking a piss.

Granted, both began with unzipping my pants, but I needed to stay steely in my resolve to not give in to desire. Being unsure of where I stood with my status, I didn't want to kneel down or lay next to another man; no amount of absolution could forgive me for giving in to temptation.

And the corker was that it would be easy enough to make a doctor's appointment, get the test, and see if I passed or failed. Fear had me pinned to the mat and had the upper hand in this situation. The grit I needed to overcome it felt herculean in scope.

Naturally, all that analogy did was conjure up celluloid memories of Steve Reeves and Harry Hamlin. At least they were fearless warriors, able to go the distance in seeking the Golden Fleece and vanquishing Medusa.

The images of them in their Greek garb were making it difficult, if not downright hard, not to want to release The Kraken with Chris.

Where was Medusa when you really needed her to turn you to stone?

I was contemplating doing a bump, but the dwindling powder in the bindle and a knock on the door made the decision for me. This time, it wasn't Mrs. Woodson, but a very drunk Jeannie, who looked as white as her wedding dress.

"Move!" she yelled and barely made it to the toilet, retching in a very unladylike way.

"Do you need…" I began, unsure what could stop her from doing her best Linda Blair in *The Exorcist* impression. But she pushed her left hand back, signaling I should back off. I was happy to oblige because when someone blew chunks, it caused sympathy bile to rise in my throat.

When I heard the contents of Jeannie's stomach splash into the water, I took it as my cue to exit, unless I wanted to pray to the porcelain god with her.

"Welcome to the family, sis," I said as the door closed behind me. "And may the power of Christ compel you."

Now, I needed to finish my beer to silence my inner demons, but it could prove to be a trial by fire where Chris was concerned. But he was nowhere to be seen. My beer was still on the bar with a napkin bearing his number and an invitation to call him anytime.

I wadded the napkin up into a ball in my right hand, raising it in my best interpretation of someone adept at sports. I scored a two-pointer in the trash can.

"Sa-wish!!!" I said, grabbed the beer, drained it in two swallows, and went to find my parents to get a ride home.

It was the quietest ride of my life since neither parent was talking. While I found some solace in the quietude, my mind wandered back to my days as The Invisible Boy, and I yearned for someone to break the ice if only to prove that I existed.

For how long though was anyone's bet, for I was convinced the end was drawing near.

On the last night of the year, I sat by myself in my room with misery as my sole companion, glad to put 1986 behind me - to eighty-six it as it were. But I knew the same problems would just carry over into the new year.

Usually, I made lots of resolutions, but not this time, since HIV was looming larger than any want to make changes that were destined to fail.

I was tempted to throw the *Meatballs* soundtrack on the record player in the living room and listen to the reasons why David Naughton was "Makin' It." It wasn't as if Big Ed would yell to turn it down since he and Mom were at a New Year's Eve party at his co-worker Mr. Carrier's house.

I had the house to myself, but I kept the door closed, just in case I didn't hear my parents come home and catch me doling out the last of the meth.

The only sounds were from Shadow scratching at the door, which I tried to drown out with Casey Kasem's countdown of the Top 100 songs of the year, with Whitney Houston's "The Greatest Love of All" narrowly missing the Top 10 at number 11. Just like me not being able to embrace the lyrics, always missing that concept by one point, which remained lost on me.

Now seemed like a good time to break out the final bit I had "borrowed" from Jeff. There's nothing sadder than an empty bindle, but I suddenly discovered two big rocks trapped in one of the folds.

It afforded me a chance to be creative, given it was New Year's Eve and all. I formed one line into an 8, and the other became a 7.

I did a figure eight with the straw resting in my left nostril and then switched it to the right one and dosey-doed its partner up with a big double-snort. I chased down the drip with a gulp of beer in a blue plastic cup.

I placed it back on the drafting table, wiping away the water ring that had formed next to the drawing I was working on. The image that I was putting on paper birthed in my imagination, was becoming fully formed and only needed a few more touches in completing its gestation cycle.

I turned my attention to Shadow's nails scratching it. A pang of guilt hit me, knowing she only wanted to be included.

I opened the door, and she immediately jumped up and put her paws on me. While this would be frowned upon by a dog trainer, it was our version of hugging. She must have sensed that I needed one – plus a series of slobbery kisses.

"Hey, buy a guy dinner first!" I said with a rare laugh, a foreign sound as of late. "Ok, let's get you a little treat."

She devoured the chicken breast that was supposed to be my dinner. When she made short work of it, her eyes looked pleadingly into mine to convey, “Please sir, may I have some more?”

All that was left was broccoli, and I had learned the lesson about avoiding that. The first and only time, she had thanked me for her greens with a series of noxious farts that lasted all night until I was forced to shoo her out of my room.

“That’s all for you, Missy,” I said with forced enthusiasm. Just then, buzzing on meth, my brain began barraging me with questions about what would happen to her if I wasn’t around. But I cut those thoughts off at the pass.

I went into the den, opened the sliding glass door, and let her out into the chilly night. She returned just as I made my way back from the garage with a fresh beer. I placed it on the drafting table right next to the drawing that would be my last artistic endeavor - and would hopefully explain why I had decided to take my life.

I gulped down my beer and finished the drawing I bestowed with the name “Drowning Man.” From a sea of red pencil strokes rose a hand, reaching out for someone to save him. The closest help appeared in the left-hand corner, mere fingertips that would not reach him.

It was only a matter of time before I went under, never to come up for air.

Fittingly, as the clock ticked closer to another year, Casey Kasem announced the number one song of the year was “That’s What Friends Are For,” the charity single released to raise monies for AIDS research and prevention.

I turned the song off, rejecting Casey’s final sign-off pep talk to keep my feet on the ground and keep reaching for the stars. It was time for me to sign off, too. I began going over my options. Pills mixed with alcohol was out since we had no sleeping pills in the medicine cabinets.

There was the method I’d seen in the TV movie *Surviving*, in which Molly Ringwald employed the family car to unleash its deadly fumes in the garage.

I wasn’t sure how effective that would be with L’il Red’s smaller engine, and given the fact that my parents could show up soon. As soon as I looked at the razor blade that I had used to chop up the meth, I knew it was the right instrument to end my life.

It was deceptive in its deadliness; it was so lightweight to handle the heavy job of cutting into the veins of my wrists, releasing torrents of warm blood. The juxtaposition intrigued me and that a new pain would replace the old one that had consumed me. It was oddly exciting in some strange fashion.

Before I made the final exit from my room, I snatched up the bindle and licked it for any residue. Then I returned all the accouterments to their hiding place. But I left the cassette case where it was, a challenge to finally make my family look beyond the surface of things. Maybe they would ask themselves why I had done it and look through my personal effects for clues.

Before heading to the bathroom, I stood in the doorway, looking wistfully into the room I retreated to, found solace in, and began my creative journey. Like any good sitcom character worth their salt, I even turned off the light, like Mary Tyler Moore, Bonnie Franklin, and Linda Lavin had done for their final episodes.

But there was nothing funny about what I was going to do. I turned on the bathroom lights, and it felt like I was in the spotlight.

But it was my turn to plunge into the darkness of nothingness.

RENEWAL

Flashes of light, bright and persistent, cause my eyes to flutter open, everything out of focus. Is this Heaven, and the Almighty is chucking lightning bolts at me to stop me from entering the pearly gates for my transgressions? Or am I in the fiery pits of Hell, flames licking at me, ensnaring me in eternal damnation for said peccadillos?

Was my checklist of wrongdoings on par with being a murderer? Nah. The only thing I was guilty of killing were brain cells. This is my brain, this is my brain on drugs, to paraphrase that PSA that always just made me want eggs after they used the cracking of one into a hot frying pan as the penultimate example of drug abuse.

Yeah. Not so much.

The light is moving back and forth between my left and right eyes. Perhaps I've been abducted by aliens. If there was an anal probe involved, it obviously wouldn't be my first time at that rodeo.

"Do you know where you are?" a disembodied male voice asked.

As I stared up, my vision brought things into a sharper focus. This was not a Close Encounter of the Third, Fourth, or any kind. I was in the emergency room at Scripps, and my doctor resembled James Brolin as Dr. Steven Kiley on *Marcus Welby, M.D.*, but with the bearded look he had on *Hotel*. Who was the attending nurse, Connie Sellecca?

I attempted to sit up, and the doctor gently put his hand on my chest, keeping me down.

"You've lost a lot of blood and have a pretty nasty bump on your forehead," he said. "Can you tell me what happened?"

Did I go for the star pupil route of underscoring the seriousness of what I had done, of what I was afraid of? Leave it to my brain – and not Beaver – to be riddled with nothing but questions.

I let the tears explode from my eyes, much like the blood that had gushed out of my wrists, do the talking for me.

When I was beginning to border on hysterics and hyperventilating, he told me to focus on my breathing and gave me a short, guided meditation.

I muttered that it was fine, and I got the sense that he was the opposite of what I had been making him out to be.

I took a few breaths before gathering strength to utter the words I had kept to myself. Maybe I could highlight my emotions and worry about being HIV positive. I could explain being addicted to crystal in an interpretive dance to Lisa Lisa and The Cult Jam's "All Cried Out?"

Or I could stop hiding behind my pop culture defense mechanisms. Wow, I was finally self-aware. Amazing.

"I need to get an AIDS test," I said quietly.

He had a stricken look on his face as he had been near my blood, stitching up the physical wounds now underneath gauze and bandages. The mental ones would require more than a field dressing to help them heal. Just as quickly as the look had shown on his face, it passed like a lunar eclipse, and he was once again open and inviting.

"We can certainly do that," he said. "But I'd like to do so in a day or so when you are a better candidate. Are you familiar with a 5150?"

Naturally, my brain went right to the last Van Halen album, with Sammy Hagar taking the lead singer reigns from David Lee Roth. But I didn't think he was looking for an album review. In fact, I was sure that the term meant crazy. And I was nowhere near the poster boy for sanity.

I just nodded no.

"Well, when someone is a harm to themselves, they are placed on a 72-hour hold for observation in a, uh, facility."

A "facility" was just a nicer way to say mental hospital.

Even though his face was neutral, I thought I detected an inkling of judgment in Dr. Kiley. And just like that, I began to rage at him. I was truly Big Ed's son.

"Fuuuuuuck you! You don't know me! You're not better than me!"

He stepped back from the flying spittle out of my mouth containing concentrated acid in it; the words carried the threat of venom. I quickly went from molten-hot anger to dissolved into tears. You could practically see the steam rising off my body from the shift in temperature.

"I understand that you're upset," he meekly said, his bedside manner for shit. "We'll get you a little something to calm you down and then we'll take you over to the facility." He did not stammer on the last word this time around, as clearly, I was a prime candidate for a padded cell and a form-fitting jacket with "Have You Hugged Yourself Today?" written across the front.

He called a nurse in, instructed her to prepare a mild sedative in shot form, then gave me a weary look and pretended to look thoughtfully at my chart.

"Would you like me to call your parents and let them know where you are?"

I gave him a very intense look as he backed away from me as if I were about to flip shit out again.

"They didn't bring me here?"

"No, you were brought in by ambulance," he said and continued warily. "A call was placed to 9-1-1, but there was no one there when the EMTs showed up."

Just then, the nurse re-entered, needle at the ready, a medicinal gunslinger to put me out of my misery. Hopefully, she would have better luck than I had. It totally hadn't sunk in that I was still here, of this Earth, in this mortal coil.

But that wasn't what was troubling me the most.

The last thing that I was thinking before I got caught in the undertow of drowsiness was: "Who the fuck was in my house?"

I awoke to a stream of sunlight encouraging me to rise and shine to what I assumed was the next day. I briefly thought that I was safe in my own bed. The suicide attempt and the emergency room had not happened, just like events in the ninth season of *Dallas* being all a dream.

Sadly, that was not the case.

I was in a bed, yes, albeit it wasn't mine. It faced a non-descript windowless wooden door, oak, and an ocean of white linoleum covered the floor. To my right was a bathroom, and all around me were off-white color walls sat still, sentinels safeguarding me from the outside world. I was lying on my right side and saw bandages wrapped around my wrists. I wondered how the scars would look eventually.

How did it come to this, and why did I let it happen?

And just like clockwork, the tears commenced, pooling in my eyes at first, salty reservoirs building to the inevitable dam bursting. But I will be good and goddamned if I didn't stop them in their tracks. Frankly, I was sick to death of crying.

I snorted up a sizeable phlegm globber into my throat. I headed towards the bathroom to spit it out. I stood at the sink and flashed upon a sequence from Stephen King's massive novel *It*. I imagined that fountains of blood would erupt from the drain. The crimson tide mirroring what I had tried to extract from my wrists, body, and my mind.

As I spat into the toilet, I had a ghostly twinge of the drip that only Tina had provided. Oh Jesus! Was I going to get the shakes and or see spiders crawling out of the wall, like the PSA drug scare films shown in school?

"And how are we this morning?" A male voice asked from the doorway.

Out of force of habit, I did the soap opera spin and looked boldly at his face. Standing there, sexy in his stance, was the definition of a real man.

"I'm Pete," he stated in a mix of sweetness and strength.

One muscular arm crooked above his hair in the doorway, a head of brown hair, jawline, and chin lined with stubble, piercing blue eyes, and the face of a Roman soldier.

Rather than being dressed in battle armor, the blue scrubs he wore didn't need to have his musculature fortified with metal impressions of the body beneath; it was there for the eye to soak up: well-defined pecs, biceps, triceps, and undoubtedly a six-pack underneath it all.

I just stood there staring, like Cindy Brady staring at the TV camera's red light when she went on a kids' quiz show. God, I hoped I wasn't drooling!

"You alright there, Henry?" he said without consulting a clipboard. Meaning he already knew my name. Swoon.

"Um, yeah, great," I winced.

A smile revealed the only chink in his perfect armor. Pete had a dead front tooth that was graying. But I shut down that bitchy, judgmental part of myself. Who was I to look down on anyone? The poor little fag who tried to kill himself because he might have the plague, that's who. Ouch! Pointing that high-powered weapon at myself felt like it split me down the middle, reducing me to mere particles.

"I'm here to take you down to your session with Dr. Chan," he instructed ever-so-gently. He'd undoubtedly heard about my flip-shit episode with James Brolin.

"Sounds like fun," I said sarcastically.

"A sense of humor; that's good," he smiled. "You're gonna need it in here."

We didn't chat about the weather, movies we'd seen, and thankfully not about what sports ball team he was following; we traveled in silence. Dead man walking. The irony of that term almost made me giggle, but there was zero funny about the situation. That's my fucked-up sense of humor for ya.

We reached another windowless, brown door, which he opened for me like a gentleman, and gave me a knowing wink. I accidentally on purpose, brushed up against him as I walked in.

Look at me! Flirtin' in the loony bin!

Maybe Pete played for my team after all. Well, batter up! I flashed back to those hours sitting in the dugout when I tried playing Little League. "What position are you playing?" Big Ed would ask and not let me answer, providing his own. "Left out!" It never failed to make him and John laugh.

Sitting behind a wooden desk, without a nameplate, was a pleasant-looking Asian man, mid-thirties with a crew cut and slender build. He rose and shook my hand but introduced himself as David rather than Dr. Chan, which put me at ease.

"Please, have a seat."

I waited as he extracted something from his desk drawer. He produced a small stack of white cards, and I thought we were going to play an impromptu game of *Password* to get to the root of my problems.

"Are you familiar with the Rorschach Test, Henry?" All I had to do was tell him what the inkblot images reminded me of. I had seen enough movies to know about this. He was trying to see how crazy I was, and my smart-ass nature kicked into gear.

He held the first one up, a side-by-side black smear image touching and resembled a pointy hat.

"Two gnomes playing patty-cake."

The next one looked like a bat in midflight.

"Na na na na na na na, Batman!" I answered in a singsong voice.

He put it down, and I heard a low sigh escape from him. I was getting under his skin.

The next card had a moth-like creature.

"Looks like the demon that comes to me at night and invites me to rule by his side," I said with bored nonchalance. "But he's worried I would just take over Hell, so..."

"If you aren't going to take this seriously…"

"What? You don't believe me?" I responded with feigned dismay, absently clutching pearls that had never been around my neck. "His name is Bill. Well, Bill the Demon technically, but we're tight."

"I know what you're trying to do, Henry."

"Well, I should certainly hope so! You are a shrink, David."

"You might want to consider that you tried to open up your wrists to celebrate the new year," he said with a deadpan delivery.

I just sat there, not blinking. He was calling me out on my shit. "*How dare you sir! If that is your real name!*" My mind silently countered while my mouth remained quiet as a church mouse.

"Now, if you're done wasting our time – shall we continue?"

He held up the remaining cards, and I answered in succession without sarcasm.

"Puzzle pieces. Two rabbits. A man in a tuxedo. Bigfoot. John Lennon with crabs around his head. Two bears playing Ring around the Rosie. A woman with a crazy beehive hairstyle."

He wrote notes down on his legal pad while I weighed the concept of doing something of Rorschach Tests as artwork might be interesting. Considering that the only art I had done lately was my visual suicide note, my renewed desire to create gave me a spark of hope.

"Ok, that was better, even if you seem to be mocking the process. Listen, I get it. You are hurting, you want to lash out, but I am here to help you get through this. But you must work past this unless you want your mother to identify you on a morgue slab."

I nodded sullenly at the scolding.

"I see that you want to get an AIDS test. Tell me about that."

Oh, this guy was smooth, the human antithesis of a jar of JIF chunky peanut butter. But maybe releasing all the mind poison, a polluted stream of consciousness always in my brain, could lead to understanding why the fuck I did the things I did.

Instead of asking myself endless questions and getting obvious answers that I mostly chose to ignore, I should pull out a pair of tweezers and mentally excise the sliver.

"How much time do you have?"

As it turned out, he had about an hour before he signaled that it was time to end the session. Although it was the tip of the proverbial iceberg of what I needed to say, I felt as lucky as being among the women and children first on the sinking Titanic.

I was feeling more instant gratification than my multitude of vices provided. It was like being on a really good first date when there was a good rapport. Something I had only seen in TV and movies but hadn't really experienced firsthand - except with Tony and, to a lesser degree, *HIM*.

And, yes, that was one of the subjects I needed to get into. That would encompass more than an hour. Several sessions, probably. Like a mini-series on par with *Lace* or *Hollywood Wives*. I'd explain my deadly dance with Tina - frenetic and melancholy.

I was living the lyrics from The English Beat song "I Confess," in that I had survived my suicide attempt, and being dead would have halted the hurt in my soul. Also, it was a definite case of cards on the table time. All the queens were smiling benevolently, no aces up my sleeve, while the jokers were face down and silent for once. And the subject of kings, or just one in particular, would be reserved for a later date.

"There, now," David asked me, a slight smile on his face. "Doesn't it feel better than keeping all of that bottled up?"

Of course, Barbara Eden's animated title sequence from *I Dream of Jeannie* danced across my mind.

The genie was out of the bottle, and there was no putting it back in. Living on the surface for so long had taken a strange toll on me. I was hopeful the defense mechanisms that I had set up for myself could finally blast down the walls that held me inside.

"It does. Thank you." And I meant it.

"OK, we will regroup in a bit," he said.

There was a knock at the door, and hunky Pete poked his head in.

"Henry, your parents are here to see you. Come with me."

A pit, more like a pit and a pendulum, opened in both my stomach and my brain, which was vacillating on how this reunion would go down.

Either it would be a love fest or a stern lecture.

It was time to get out of this chair, walk with Pete, and face the music, although I expected it to be the same old song and dance. I could name this tune in one note: tears from mom and disapproval from Big Ed.

I got up and silently followed Pete to a seating area – allowing myself the distraction of watching his meaty glutes shift in his scrubs as he strutted. But then I saw Big Ed, his arms typically folded, scowl affixed on his mug. And Mom was red-eyed from crying. Neat!

"Oh, Henry," she exclaimed and hugged me fiercely. "Why would you do this?! Are you all right?"

I didn't respond to her questions. The answers were self-evident. We were at a mental hospital, and I had tried to end my life. It was abundantly clear that all was not ok, and I didn't want to get into it with them about why I was here. Not yet, not now, maybe never.

She broke down in tears and continued to hug me tightly.

"Jesus Christ, Kate! You have always coddled him; probably why he's gay."

"No, sucking dick made me gay," I barked out.

Bam! Take that Big Ed.

That shut him up, so I decided to continue with that tact, laying it on thicker.

"Studies of gays suggest an 'absent father' is really to blame. No matter which way you slice it, I was always going to be a fruit cake - and I wouldn't have it any other way."

"Yes, you seem really happy with your choice of being a gay who doesn't want to live." Big Ed had found his voice again. Still snide, still dismissive, still selfish.

"Shut up. Just. Shut. Up," I growled, fighting fire with a flame.

"Too bad you'll never be man enough to make me," he said with the petulant nature of a bully. But when you broke it down, that is what he really was and had always been to me.

"Oh, so now I'm not a real man. Well, it takes a real man to take it up the ass."

"You disgust me."

"Trust me, the feeling's more than mutual."

"Stop it, just stop it!" my mother said with admirable ferociousness. Just then, Big Ed stormed off.

"I would say that I was sorry, but I'm not," I told her.

"I understand, Henry. I really do."

Of course, she did, as she was primarily the prime target for his anger. Albeit it was more verbal than physical abuse like that was a consolation prize. But she had always been in my corner, and I was proud of myself that I had taken the kid gloves off with my father.

In the span of a few minutes, I had unloaded substantial emotional baggage. I felt lighter, but taking on Big Ed filled me with a buzz better than anything I'd snorted up my nose.

Pete approached cautiously and asked if everything was "copacetic."

"No, but it will be," I answered with a unique air of confidence.

"Mrs. Dodge, I need to talk to you about Henry's stay here. I assume you have insurance?"

She simply nodded.

"Do you mind coming with me?"

Again, she answered with a nod and followed him down the hallway.

I figured the best course of action was to retreat to my room. Reaching one of the many wooden doors, I opened what I thought was mine. And it turned out not to be the case.

Sitting on her bed reading a book was a girl with a shock of magenta hair, a plain black tee and red and black plaid pants. I had seen her in the hallways of school and was trying to remember her name when she spoke.

"Are you the welcome wagon or just have a staring problem?"

Despite the tone of her voice, I felt some sort of kinship with her because I could sniff out a fellow smart-ass a mile away.

"Sorry, wrong room." But rather than leave, I peered at the tome she was holding. It was John Irving's *The Hotel New Hampshire*. "I love that book; he's one of my favorite authors."

"Thrilling," she said and returned to the story of the eccentric Berry family.

"They all die at the end," I said and made my exit.

I had just encountered the Marlena Dietrich of San Luis Rey, and she most definitely wanted to be alone.

"Hey, hey you!" she called out and made a beeline for me. "I saw the movie, butthole, so nice try."

"You want a medal or something?"

"Your name will suffice," she said, offering up a smile.

"Ms. Jackson if you're nasty. Or Henry. Your choice."

"Nice to make your acquaintance, Ms. Jackson."

I let a genuine laugh escape from me.

"And for the record, I'm Nina." She curtsied.

I responded with a bow.

"It's nice to meet you now. Before? Not so much."

It was her turn to laugh. Her gaze went to my bandaged wrists.

"I'd ask you what you're in for, but…"

I could feel the walls starting to rebuild themselves, but I halted their construction.

"You must be here for the ambiance, I take it."

"Not exactly."

She looked momentarily forlorn but switched to an impressive Yoda impression.

"Soon will I rest, yes, forever sleep. Earned it, I have. Just not today. Sleeping pills and vodka did not do the trick. Oh well, what are ya gonna do, right?"

I wanted to say that I was sorry, but it's highly doubtful she wanted pity from someone else who had failed at suicide. I was relieved she didn't end her sentence with, "if at first you don't succeed, try, try again."

Nina was already gaining points with me for her taste in books and movies. Before we could continue our tête-à-tête, I saw Mom and Pete coming towards us.

"Looks like the jig is up. I'll see you later," I said with an eye roll.

"Not if I see you first."

My mother said a wary hello to Nina, as if she might catch crazy, and was off to the sitting area again. This time, minus Big Ed, who hadn't returned. He was probably in the parking lot, wondering if he'd made me gay or at a nearby bar drowning his sorrows.

"So, and I know that it's a boring topic," Pete said, "but I spoke with your mother about your insurance. With the plan that your parents have, you can stay here for one week, then we can figure out some after-care. Sound good?"

What was I supposed to do, yell out with a "Yippee?" And add a midair kick for good measure to express my enthusiasm? Insurance only gave me a week in paradise. More like a truncated prison sentence.

"Sure," I said with feigned enthusiasm.

"Awesome!" Pete exclaimed and lit up with a smile. And there it was again, that dead tooth.

I was staring, and Pete quickly closed his mouth.

"I just want you to get better, Henry," Mom said softly. "I know you can do it, son. You're stronger than you think you are."

My mind wandered to Candy in the not-so-forgotten-past and her telling me that my coming out was an act of bravery. Now, my mother was championing me. I hoped at some point that worn-out record of self-hatred would stop playing. The day that music died could not come soon enough for me. Bye, bye Miss American Pie, you bitch!

And I knew there was arduous work for me to begin to get at the root of not only myself but the rotted ones of my family tree. It played into who I was but not who I could be.

I wanted to say that I was raring to go, but that would be a lie. Yesterday, I wanted to be dead, and that feeling wouldn't vanish with the flick of a magic wand. Presto change-o.

But I felt an odd sense of openness to exploring this avenue. I mean, it couldn't hurt, right?

Pete excused himself, and I felt a twinge of regret for being judgmental. Pete was a lovely person invested in seeing me get better, and I was just a bitch taking him at face value. Well, at mouth value was more like it. I made a mental note to give him a sincere compliment later.

"Well, I suppose I should see if your father waited for me or not," Mom said with a sigh.

"How have you put up with him for all these years? How can you still take his shit?"

"Henry! Language! Besides," she smiled wryly, "that would take me some time to figure out."

And she strode off. Her words echoed, just like her high heels on the linoleum.

I went to the nurse's station for directions to my room. I was three doors down from Nina. They should really put some sort of markers on the door, not some cutesy shit like a puppy and a kitten to denote the difference between the male and female populace. Or a Band-Aid for people in my situation and a pill bottle for people in Nina's.

Maybe they had a suggestion box.

I was lying on my bed, staring at the ceiling, overthinking, when David came to visit.

"Alright, there's a couple of things that I want to go over with you." With clipboard in hand, he spoke slowly and deliberately, as if I were a child with a learning disability. "We actually have a class which is like arts and crafts. Sometimes, it helps to get out some pent-up emotions."

I was hoping it meant drawing and or painting - not having to learn needlepoint. However, that was probably frowned upon, given the general populace's desire to harm themselves or others.

"Ok."

"Breakfast is at 8 am, so you need to shower and dress first. Lunch is at 12. Since you missed breakfast, you're probably on the hungry side. Dinner is at 6."

I felt like I was on *The Love Boat* with such a structured itinerary; it was doubtful that I would be dining with Captain Stubbing, more likely Lauren Tewes, who played the perky Julie McCoy.

David handed me a pamphlet with the blaring headline of, "What is an addict?" I tossed it on the bed as if it were on fire, set alight by a match to petrol.

"I honestly think that you can benefit from our meetings. Unless you just want to answer that question by looking in the mirror."

Words that hurt, David. Words. That. Hurt. I couldn't respond with a "How dare you!" The proof was in the pudding, just as assuredly as the straw had been up my nose to numb the pain.

"I'll think about it," I replied sourly. I wasn't used to people not sugarcoating things in my life.

"Good. Now go shower up, and don't get your bandages wet."

How the in the actual fuck was I going to manage that? I headed for the bathroom. I wasn't sure how David's suggestion of looking at an addict in the mirror was possible, as it didn't have any actual glass, only some sort of murky distant cousin.

The better not to cut you with dear, it seemed to mock.

There was a little basket with a toothbrush, floss, comb, and deodorant. Noticeably absent were any type of shaving accouterments.

Yes, let's give the guy who slashed his wrists open with a razor, albeit one that couldn't repeat my attempt - but why risk it?

I sniffed my armpits, and they reminded me of the smell of the cumin-heavy hamburger when Mom would make tacos.

I tossed the hospital gown on the floor, and then my underwear followed suit. Damn, I should have asked my mom to bring me some from home. I wondered if this prison allowed one phone call so I could ask her about clean tighty-whities.

Double damn, I hadn't thought to ask her, just who had called 9-1-1. It would keep. But I wanted to delve into the mystery of my savior.

I turned on the shower and got it to my desired temperature, just below scalding. Some like it hot when the heat is on indeed.

I positioned the shower head as far down as it would point to not get those reminders of my suicide attempt wet. Besides, I couldn't stomach seeing the results of my desperation. I stepped into the smallish shower and leaned forward to wet my hair with either hand on the wall in front of me, resembling someone being frisked by the police. I stepped out from the radius of the water and shampooed my hair from a hotel-size bottle.

No amount of that and the tiny bar of soap would wash away my sins.

I dried myself off and reluctantly put on my twice-worn underwear and oh-so-fashionable hospital gown.

I didn't know if I should go out into the strange world outside of my door or just stay put. I opted for the latter. A few minutes later, Pete was once again in my doorway.

"Well, you clean up nicely," he said, setting off a ping on my gaydar - or was he just being kind?

"Why, thank you, sir. You're not too bad yourself." I responded flirtatiously.

He merely smiled with his lips, so I didn't push it further. Pete was hot, but I wasn't sure of his sexual proclivities. I stopped the thought immediately, as I did not want to pitch a tent. Well, pitch a tarp was more like it with my current ensemble.

"Ready to eat?"

"I'm famished," I said, adding a hint of sex to the statement.

He cocked one eyebrow, and I detected the beginnings of a blush coloring his cheeks. Ping! Well, that answered that question.

"Come on; let's get a little meat on those bones. And I'll introduce you to everybody."

Trepidation crept into my feet, and a lump rose in my throat, but I decided to put on a brave face.

"I'm ready."

"I have a feeling that's never a problem for you." And there was flirting in his voice. Ping! Ping!

I felt a crowding in my underwear. I was going to meet everyone while sporting wood. Talk about a memorable first impression.

Pete glanced down and gave me a Cheshire cat grin. "Uh oh, did I do that?"

Ping! Ping! Ping! We have ourselves a winner.

"Well, it wasn't Mother Teresa."

But it was marching right along, steady in its outward trek. I couldn't use the heterosexual trick of slowing things down by envisioning baseball. All that brought up was images of their butts in jockstraps underneath their uniforms.

Luckily, Pete responded with a laugh that led to a smile. Again, that dead tooth was a boner-killer. But it took a hot second to deflate like a helium birthday balloon that had seen the last of its days, indicating the party was over.

My caretaker was still looking south.

"My eyes are up here, Pete."

He broke himself out of his reverie and met my eyes impishly. I didn't dare look down to see if I had the same effect on him.

Hopefully, they added saltpeter to the food here, like John had told me that they used to do in the Navy to keep raging hormones at bay. I was assaulted with the reminder that I couldn't do anything with Pete until I found out my HIV status.

"*This doesn't make me dirty!*" Tony's spectral voice shouted into my brain.

"Alright, sweet cheeks; let's get a move on." And I wasn't too surprised when he pinched my ass heading out the door.

This was certainly uncharted territory, given the setting, as was what awaited me at lunch.

I stood outside the dining area, the breath catching in my chest, first at the ¾ level, then ½ until it had that familiar feeling of the airflow being turned into cement, as it continued to rise. Pete noted my anxiety and simply patted me on the shoulder and not on the ass. Yeah, put me in coach, I'm ready to play. I'm sure that my body language conveyed the opposite.

And I hoped my first meal with fellow inmates, err, patients, wouldn't resemble the wedding dinner party in Tod Browning's *Freaks,* with the group crying out to me with a chant of "One of us, one of us. Gooble-gobble, gooble-gobble."

This nightmare was akin to the first day of high school, times infinity. Still experiencing nerves so frayed that they felt threadbare, I turned the corner. That's when I realized my San Dieguito comparison had been spot-on. Sitting at the table were five kids from my school.

There was Heather, a pretty, blonde cheerleader type who shot me sharpened daggers. Carlos now didn't look as tough as he did strutting down the hallway; he was defeated by the private battles he was waging. There was Tiffany, one of the only ginger kids at school, and another anomaly, Reuben, regarding his ethnicity, the only black kid at school, aside from Craig. He sat across from Nina, arms folded and the same scowl he wore to school, like a jock sporting a letterman jacket.

The Dream Warriors that I had read about in Fangoria magazine and were set to make their screen debut later in the month in the third *A Nightmare on Elm Street*, we were not, even if we were keeping our respective demons at bay. As it stood, we looked like the cast of *The Breakfast Club*, except we were all vying for Ally Sheedy's role as Allison, the basket case.

"Sorry, I think I underdressed for dinner," I said, only garnering a laugh from Nina, so I took a seat next to her.

"Tough crowd," I whispered to her. "I'll be here all week. Try the veal."

She stifled her laugh by pretending to cough. Now I was finding it hard to suppress my own laugh and made a weird snort noise that caused Nina to laugh harder.

"What's so funny?" Heather inquired in a haughty manner.

"Notttthiiiing," we both answered in unison, and that set us over the absolute edge. So to speak.

"Kooks!" Heather said and folded her arms across her chest. That's when I saw how thin her arms were. And she noticed that I noticed and tucked her arms away.

Right then, a severe-looking Hispanic woman approached the table. She wore a world-weary face, her hair in a ponytail, and blue scrubs to separate them from us.

"What, exactly, is so funny over here?" she asked, echoing Heather.

Rather than fire off a smart-ass comment, Nina stayed quiet, as did everyone else. I decided that it might be in my best interest to follow suit.

"Well, isn't that better?" she asked, sounding like The Church Lady.

I think I could answer Dana Carvey's never-ending question of, "Could it be SATAN?"

Yes. Yes, it could be, whereas she was concerned.

Her 5'4" belied that she clearly stood seven feet tall in her mind. Her mouth was in a permanent frown, with a deeply furrowed brow and brown eyes that could be mistaken as black, made even darker under the unflattering fluorescent lights.

"You Henry?"

"Yes." But I couldn't control my outside voice; self-important people were high up on my pet peeves list. So, I added: "Yes, sir. I mean, yes, ma'am."

The other five members of The Dinner Club opened their mouths wide in shock. And Nina kicked my shin underneath the table. I had made a misstep, but this bitch was walking with steel-toed boots on my very last nerve.

"Oh, we have a little comedian in our midst? She eyed my bandages. "Yes, being here will be nothing short of a laugh riot, I'm sure."

I refused to break her gaze while the others pretended to say Grace, heads bowed.

"I'm sure it will be an absolute delight," I said.

"Oh, I'll make sure of that." And although no one threw a bucket of water on her, The Wicked Witch of the West disappeared.

Reuben whistled low and shook his head, while Heather and Tiffany looked at me with a mix of respect and shock, Carlos cocked an eyebrow, and Nina was looking at me with undisguised adoration.

"Just exactly who in the hell was that?" I asked.

"Nurse Ramirez, but we call her Nurse Wretched," Nina said, not needing to explain the *One Flew Over the Cuckoo's Nest* reference.

"Dude, you are definitely on the top of her shit list," Carlos said.

"Like I care," I said defiantly.

"Oh, you will. You will," Reuben responded ominously.

Heather and Tiffany nodded in unison, and Nina gave a weird downturn to her mouth, looking like she had a stroke.

"Groovy." This was going to be a long week.

The mediocre food arrived, consisting of meatloaf, mashed potatoes and broccoli, which everybody ate with tepid enthusiasm. Heather mostly pushed it back and forth with her fork.

I was hardly a Clean Plate Club member lately and honestly could not remember the last time that I had eaten a full meal. I would save my appetite for when my mom would make her crunchy pork roast and matching crunchy potatoes - the best things in Kate Dodge's cooking wheelhouse, if only because there was no Velveeta added.

After dinner, I wanted to call my mom. But, wouldn't you know it, Ol' Wretched was the only one at the nurse's desk. I planned to walk right up, look her square in the eye, and tell her of my intentions. But I had enough drama for the day.

In my room, with the door shut behind me, I let out a huge sigh. I turned off the lights, took off my gown, and got underneath the covers.

Within an hour, my light was switched back on.

"Did I interrupt your slumber, Sleeping Beauty?" Maleficent asked.

Hovering over my bed was Nurse Wretched, and trust me, that is not the first thing that you want to see when you wake up.

"What time is it?" I asked groggily.

"Time for you to face the music," she said gleefully as she picked up my "What is an Addict?" pamphlet and tapped it ominously. "Now put your gown on, Cinderella; it's time to go to the ball."

I didn't have it in me to banter back, and for once, I just did as I was told in the face of this evil Disney Queen.

She escorted me to a plain room, folding chairs in a circle, with two posters promoting the Twelve Steps and Twelve Traditions of Alcoholics Anonymous. I took momentary umbrage. I wasn't a hopeless drunk; I was a hopeless drug addict.

There was a difference, after all, in my eyes.

As people started to file in, the average age group shifted upward as people from the adult ward took their seats. And it was a packed house. I wasn't the only one who fell into the category of Generation X. Carlos was seated across from me. His sullen look made me realize we were compadres in not wanting to be here.

A tall, baldheaded man, roughly 60, sat down and spoke.

"Hi, my name is Larry, and I'm an alcoholic."

Everyone but Carlos and I responded with a robotic "Hi Larry."

A woman picked up a laminated piece of hard stock paper and read the AA preamble, adding, "I'm Miriam, and I'm an alcoholic."

She read eloquently from the words put before her, and the forty-something lady looked pretty put together – not my notion of an alkie. It was as if Sue Ellen Ewing was playing hooky from *Dallas* to slum it up with us peasants. She was at least dressed to the sixes, with nicely coiffed brown hair. I felt more out-of-place in my gown and twice-worn undies.

Next up were more readings and admittance of people's battle with the bottle. After that was done, Larry spoke about the topic of gratitude and asked volunteers to speak about their experience, strength, and hope on the subject. All of the Baby Boomers were more than happy to drone on about how this program was changing their life, receiving applause for their honesty.

"Would one of our new faces like to share?" Larry asked earnestly.

Oh fuck. He was focusing his attention on me.

"Henry, is it?"

Really, bitch? And I could feel my eyes roll up into my skull so far that they must have seen my brain.

"Hi, I'm Henry," I began, refusing to add the "and I'm an alcoholic" part. "And I'm just here because the shrink here thought it would be good for me. But the jury is still out on that one. That's pretty much all I have to say."

There was a smattering of polite laughter and a golf clap usually reserved for uptight cocktail parties, ironically.

Larry gave me a knowing look and a benevolent smile.

"Thank you for sharing, Henry. Hope to see you back here." There was no mistaking the sincerity in his voice, but all I wanted to do was cocoon myself until this week was over. Would I emerge as a butterfly or just the same version of myself?

"Carlos?"

With a very loud sigh, Carlos fell back on his tough-guy façade. He shook his head and refused to give his two cents worth on being grateful. I had much respect for him that he hadn't felt pressured to do so and firmly stood his ground.

"Well, then, that is all of the time we have for tonight. Brenda, will you lead us in the serenity prayer?"

Again, a mechanical recital from the adults, all looking at the floor with heads bowed. I wondered if there would be a Kool-Aid meet-and-greet afterwards.

Nurse Wretched quickly came to collect the junior crazies. All three of us walked in silence. My mind was still trying to process what I had just been "encouraged" to do.

As we rounded the corner, I saw Nina and sat next to her. "Lights out in an hour," Wretched growled.

"Let me guess," Nina said. "You were spending time with Jim Jones?"

"Good guess. It was, uh, "'interesting.'"

"They tried to make me go twice. You can still see the scuff marks from where I dug my heels in. Definitely not for me. Like at all," saying the last part like a Valley Girl.

"Like, oh my God. Like gag me with a spork," I said, channeling one of my favorite movies. "This SOOO not tripendicular."

"What was up with Nicolas Cage's chest hair in that movie? It was like an upside triangle, so dumb."

"I still would have banged him, though," I said. "But not in *Peggy Sue Got Married*."

"Why is that?" she asked sincerely.

"I wouldn't want them teeth anywhere near my junk!"

"Oh my God!" she squealed and started to laugh.

"It's me, Margaret."

I was the only boy in sixth grade who read all about Margaret Simon and her period since all the girls in Mr. Granville's class were passing it around. I guess I had always enjoyed the company of girls; the long-ago friendship with Kelley may resurrect itself with Nina. She and I spoke the same language, so I wasn't feeling entirely like a freak of nature.

"OK, enough fun and games," I said once our collective laughter dissipated. "What's the lowdown on our colleagues here?"

Nina was deeply knowledgeable in all things San Luis Rey. Tiffany was a cutter, Heather had an eating disorder, Reuben had some anger issues and trashed his parents' house – but Carlos she hadn't been able to pin down.

"Well then, Jessica Fletcher, I suggest we find out."

"Why would anyone hang out with that lady? Someone gets killed in her town every week. I mean, it's a numbers game, really."

Nurse Wretched's voice soon came over the PA system, announcing lights out. I expected her to add Elvira's signature farewell of "unpleasant dreams" on *Movie Macabre*.

Nina hugged me after our little gossip session. I was a little bit taken aback at first by being shown affection. It was like a pair of ill-fitting pants. With time, I would get used to it.

What I wouldn't get used to was the way life would zig when I wanted to zag, as a special guest star would visit me tomorrow. But for now, I turned in and slept the sleep of the dead.

I awoke feeling something strange; it was called being well-rested. What a novel concept after the last few several years, no longer watching the darkness of night bleed into the pink of dawn.

I didn't remember having any dreams, but that wasn't surprising given the day that I had, my mind wanted to shut down from the overload.

Before I was ordered to take a shower, I decided that I would show up and sparkle on my own. And then I would call Mom because three days in the same underwear did not constitute good hygiene.

As I stood there waiting for the water to warm, I saw that my bandages needed changing. I dreaded the thought of looking at the physical evidence of that New Year's Eve.

It was odd; it was as if the act itself had set me free from the notion that I was not worthy to walk the Earth among the living, with my lifeblood flowing out of me. I was certainly still circling the drain, still haunted by ghosts – but the cobwebs that ensnared me felt less likely to keep me trapped.

Of course, there were the results of my HIV test. The two-week turnaround time would seem an eternity, and I was dreading the prospect of being in limbo that long.

The voice of Doris Day reminded me that it would be a case of "Que Sera, Sera," whatever will be, will be. And while the future was not mine to see, I did finally want to live and might end up dying in the process.

"Que Sera Sera, motherfucker," I said to myself and decided it was a much more positive mantra than "Same Shit, Different Day." Stepping into the shower, I made a mental note to ask Mom if she could track down any remaining Wham! Choose Life shirts that had been all the rage a few years back as part of my hospital ensemble. I again stood like a wanted felon. Arms outstretched, as if being frisked. The jig's up, Henry! And it most certainly was.

I was toweling off when I realized that I was not alone.

There stood all 6'2" of Pete, silently watching me. I was tempted for a hot second to not wrap the towel around myself so that he could drink it all in. But I knew that wouldn't be such a great idea.

I returned his leer. Pete filled his shirt out very nicely, the result of a steady workout regimen assuring it would hug his body, much in the way that I was considering hugging it. But there was a two-week moratorium on that.

"Good morning," I said, walking to the permanently foggy mirror.

"It is now," he cooed. "Damn baby, you are fine."

"Thanks," was all that I could muster.

"No, no. Thank you." Then he shifted gears and covered his lust with professionalism. "I came, um, stopped by to see if you were ready for breakfast. It's pancake day."

I hoped that they were stocked up on syrup, as I was notorious in my family for using nearly all the sweet stuff in the Log Cabin container to drown either pancakes, French toast, and or fill every waffle square.

"Cool, I'll be there in a minute. Just have to get dressed."

"That's a damn shame," Pete said, winking at me before he left.

I put on the overripe underwear, then the not-much-better gown, tying it in the back before pulling on the non-stick socks that served as makeshift shoes.

Breakfast was a tad uneventful as Nurse Wretched was absent. Just as last night, Heather mostly pushed her pancakes, cut into bite-size portions, around on her plate. Reuben seemed half-zonked by meds that they were trying out on him to see if it could abate his rage. Tiffany would take a bite and then look wistfully at her plastic knife, Carlos seemed a little less agitated, and Nina was studying him for some sign of why he was here.

As for me, I could not get enough pancakes, and Mrs. Butterworth's down my gullet. Officially stuffed, I made my way to the nurse's desk, relieved that Nurse Wretched didn't work a double shift that day.

"I need to call my mom," I said.

Nurse Susan was the polar opposite of Nurse Wretched, both pleasant and concerned about everyone's general well-being.

"Sure hon, what's the number?"

I gave her the phone number I first memorized in kindergarten. She dialed and handed me the receiver.

"Hello," Big Ed grunted.

"Is Mom there?" The last thing I wanted was a repeat of yesterday's ugliness.

His response was him yelling that the phone was for her, not saying who was calling like I didn't exist in his eyes or ears.

"Hello?" She sounded skeptical, like I may be a salesman peddling a time-share condo.

"Hi Mom. It's me." I figured that she knew which of her two me's it might be, given that John wrote home recently from his WestPac aircraft carrier. I questioned if my parents would ever tell him about what was happening with him a month away from his home Port of Call.

"Good morning, Henry." She sounded distant.

"I need fresh clothes. Can you bring some, please?" I made sure to add the magic word she had taught me as a child.

"Of course. I took the day off today. Your father did, too." She didn't sound thrilled at spending more time with Big Ed than was necessary.

"Can you not bring him with you?" I whispered as if he might hear me.

"I don't think that will be a problem."

I was relieved but also saddened. On some pathetic level, I still wanted his approval, but I didn't see that happening any time soon. I was never going to be the Golden Boy that he had wished that I would be. I was too tarnished now.

"Thanks."

"I'll see you soon, hon."

I thanked Nurse Susan and was walking back down the hall when Tiffany came running, lifting her shirt up and screaming at the top of her lungs. Jamie Lee Curtis had some fierce competition for the title of Scream Queen from the sounds of it. Switching back to one of my other senses, I saw that there were almost tribal markings along her torso. The lunatics had taken over the asylum, if only on a temporary basis.

Heather was standing there in shock and dismay, covering her ears, before she added her own war cry. "Cover up, Tiffany! Nobody wants to see your C-section scars!"

Tiffany had gotten pregnant, and her parents made her get an abortion. She alleviated her pain with the act of cutting herself.

Heather's outburst made Tiffany stop dead in her tracks and focus her unbridled rage onto Heather. Ooh, girl fight! But it didn't get any traction, as Pete came up behind Tiffany and restrained her. Nurse Susan appeared, and Pete calmly requested 25 milligrams of Thorazine.

Neither Heather nor myself could seem to look away from the car wreck.

Once Tiffany was sedated and began to slump against Pete, he picked her up like a rag doll and carried her into her room. Was it weird that I was hoping he would someday sweep me off my feet and carry me into his bedroom? I mean, minus being drugged and all. But that was just the way my brain was hardwired. There was comfort in the absurd.

Nurse Susan remained composed and told Heather and me it was time for art class like it was the most natural thing to say after Tiffany's psychotic episode.

The art class resembled a schoolroom. I spied something from my grade school days: a poster of a kitten hanging from a tree branch with the slogan "Hang in there" written in childish script below it.

Hey thanks, kitty; I'm cured! It was a Christmas miracle about a month late.

On each desk was the only medium students could use to illustrate their pain; a pad of paper and colored pencils. Noticeably absent was red. I sat next to Nina in the middle row. Carlos was in the back row, another scowl on his face. Reuben seemed a bit dazed and confused at the desk adjacent to Carlos. Heather chose a desk in the front row.

"Girl, you're not going to get an A in this class," I stage-whispered to Nina.

"Yeah, she can't blow this teacher for a good grade," Nina whispered back, resurrecting the rumor about Heather's attempt at a perfect GPA in school.

"Somebody drank their Snapple this morning. Remind me to stay on your good side, k?"

The smile she unleashed was sunny and devoid of storm clouds. However, the look on Heather's face told me that she had heard us dissing her.

"Eat shit," she hissed.

"Clever. Did you come up with that on your own, blondie? Must have been hard - like Mr. Jensen's dick," Nina said.

Heather appeared ready for more girl-on-girl action when the teacher entered the room. It was Larry, Styrofoam cup of coffee in hand, sitting down and taking in the sight of his temporary student body.

Heather shot us a death glare.

"Good morning," he said.

Were we supposed to respond with a "Good morning, Larry?" A variation of the AA routine?

Did he have a secret penchant for repeating people's names with a "Hi" in front of it? I would just take my cue from the failed McLean Stevenson sitcom and give him a resounding "Hello Larry!"

We all remained silent. I hoped he wouldn't assign a project that saw us writing out new posters of the 12 steps. I looked at the kitten poster again in the hopes that it might somehow take with its simplistic message. It didn't.

Larry sipped his coffee after blowing on it. Hopefully, Heather didn't take that as some cue to stay after class. He instructed us, in a monotone delivery, to draw whatever we'd like, share our work, and leave it on our desks when class was done.

I knew my own Rorschach Test concept wouldn't fly here, so I began searching somewhere in the depths of my brain for a spark of creativity. Meanwhile, Nina was zoned out and drawing a series of circles within a circle, some offshoot of a Spirograph.

I honed onto the kernel of an idea.

I looked at the colors that had been provided. I didn't think turquoise or hot pink would do for what I had in mind, but as luck would have it, there was a black pencil, and I began drawing, shading, and filling the outline of an idea that was taking on a life of its own. Before I knew it, Larry announced that it was time to put our pencils down. Our version of the San Luis Rey SATs was done, and now it was time for Show and Tell. Larry chose his first victim, Reuben, who may have dozed off during our assignment.

He held up a blank piece of paper, save for the word "Life" scrawled in the upper right corner.

"And what does that represent for you?"

"Life ain't nothing but a blank space." He didn't elaborate any further.

"Ok then. Carlos, what about you?"

He grabbed his paper between his thumb and index finger like he had changed a diaper that stunk to high hell. He had produced a good rendition of a bottle of beer with the slogan "This Bud's for you, Larry." Larry's critique was a grimace.

I saw Heather practically squirming in her seat for Larry to call on her next, but he chose Nina instead.

"Circles, because you know, circles," she explained vaguely.

"Interesting," Larry said with a sigh.

More squirming from Heather, but it was my turn. I held up a lone gravestone on a pitch-black night. Its inscription was *Henry Dodge. We Hardly Knew Ye. Born 1969.*

The death date was just a question mark.

"Hmm," Larry muttered.

"I don't get it," Heather said.

"That's not what I've heard," Nina taunted.

"And lastly, Heather."

"Well, I want to go to design school for fashion, so I did this."

She held her picture defiantly like Sally Field had her UNION sign in *Norma Rae*. I actually liked what she had produced; it had nice, clean lines.

"I hope that you achieve that goal," Larry stated and said the class was dismissed.

I was proud that my creative slump was gone and felt cathartic in doing the work that I had completed, even if no one got my art.

I was used to being misunderstood, perpetually marching to the beat of my own drummer. This made me think of a poem that Mrs. Alley in English class shared one spring morning. The promise of renewal hung in the air, pregnant with the possibilities of new growth as she spoke the words of Henry David Thoreau – and they resonated with another Henry David.

"If a man does not keep pace with his companions, perhaps it is because he hears a different drummer. Let him step to the music which he hears, however measured or far away."

Even though I was on the precipice on becoming a quote-unquote man at the far edge of seventeen, I still had to figure out my way into adulthood, which would mean there would be baby steps, tumbles, and falls.

"For the record," Nina said, breaking my inner reverie, "I liked your picture. I got it. Your work is a lot deeper than you talk."

It was one of the weirdest compliments about my artwork, but I knew that it wasn't meant to be backhanded.

"Well, that's me," I said. "Mr. Keep-It-Light."

"I am really glad that we met," she said. "You're a cool cat."

"Thanks Chicky Baby," I added in my perfected Pee-wee Herman voice.

"Wow! That is spot-on."

And then she broke into one of my favorite scenes during his *Big Adventure*. When he finally arrives at The Alamo and joins the tour group led by Jan Hook's Tina character, who then introduces everyone to mannequin residents Pedro and Inez and points out that the clay pot that Inez seems very proud of was made from PAAAINT and GLAAAZE.

"There's no basement in The Alamo!" We both said in unison.

Nina was proving more effective than shrinks in pulling me out of myself, proving to be the embodiment of the saying that "laughter is the best medicine." Finding someone who speaks your language, the banter of pop culture, when you thought you had always been communicating in an alien tongue, was refreshing.

While we walked past the sitting area, I saw Jeff parking his ass there, leaning forward and looking every bit a candidate for a scoliosis test,

What in the actual fuck was he doing here?

Nina noticed I stopped and asked what was wrong.

"I have an unexpected visitor. Can you give me a minute?"

"Sure."

I approached him cautiously like he might be here to drop off Tina, and I didn't want to be within a thousand-mile radius of that bitch.

"What are you doing here?"

"I heard what happened. Wanted to see how you were."

I felt the heat start to rise in my body, like Charlie McGee from *Firestarter*. I guess my parents hadn't gotten the memo that this was not something that I wanted to be public fodder, more or less like a real-life game of *Don't Spill the Beans*.

"Who in the hell told you?"

"Your dad let me know. I hadn't seen you for a few weeks, so I called."

Yeah, more like he wanted to reach out and touch someone who had something over him yet still wanted me still under his thumb, beholden to him. I didn't know why he couldn't get it into his thick skull that I wasn't interested in him. Like. At. All.

"That son of a bitch," I muttered. "I'm just fine and dandy, as you can see."

"Well, if you need *anything*," he stated, "you know how to get a hold of me."

"To be honest, Jeff, I won't be seeing you for a while. If at all. My life is kind of a mess, thanks to Tina. She and I aren't a good match anymore."

"Oh."

He looked slightly hurt.

"Sorry man. I just have to get my life back on track. This train's been derailed for too long."

"Offer still stands," he reiterated. "And that doesn't include Tina."

"Cool. Well, I'll see you around."

A slight smile and a small wave indicated he was making his exit. Well, fuck me, Amadeus! There was a chink in the family motto of "Nothing to see here. Move along." And from Dad, no less. I may or may not have stomped down my room. Oh, who was I kidding? I totally did. I plopped down on the bed, wishing that I had something to distract me from this new fury towards Big Ed.

Before I knew it, I had dozed off, awakening in a pool of drool.

I went into the bathroom, splashed water on my face, checked my breath by breathing into my hand, and then decided a teeth brushing couldn't hurt. I heard my door open. Nurse Susan said my mom was here.

I walked back to the guest area where I'd had my heart-to-heartless chat with Jeff. Kate Dodge sat statue-still, clutching a large brown paper bag.

"Damn, that's one big lunch!" I said, checking to see if she had drawn a smiley face on it like when I was in grade school.

The smile she gave was terse.

"So, did you do anything with all of your underwear?"

"Say what now?" I looked at her, puzzled.

"Well, I looked under your bed, in the laundry, and in your drawers. They were nowhere to be found. I had to buy you some."

"That is beyond weird," I said, followed by whistling *The Twilight Zone* theme.

"I don't know, hon. And weirder still, the sliding door was wide open when we got home. That Shadow, she's quite the guard dog."

Yes, we both know that she would roll over on her back for a tummy scritch for anyone, including a thief after Big Ed's new stereo or my underwear, apparently. But all my underwear was gone? And nothing else. Hmm, that's queer.

I was not only going to enlist Jessica Fletcher, The Hardy Boys, and Nancy Drew, but I'd have to involve the entire roster of *Charlie's Angels*, past and present, except for Shelley Hack, my least favorite employee from The Charles Townsend Agency. I would even include Jonathan and Jennifer Hart for good measure.

Another mystery! Was it connected to the anonymous call to 9-1-1?

"So, I wanted to tell you something. I had a visitor, a 'friend' who called the house, and Dad told him I was here. Can you tell him not to tell people about this?"

"Wait, what? He did that? Well, he was plenty p.o.'d at you after that argument. I will let him know. If he's still talking to me, that is."

I felt culpable immediately. Kate Dodge had the uncanny ability of booking you on your very own guilt trip.

"That bad, huh? I'm sorry for all of this, Mom."

"Well, our marriage doesn't need any more stress than it has. Nothing you should worry about. Your father is just a difficult person."

"No duh," I said, and despite the brevity of the situation, we both snickered. "I'm going to do my best to get better. I promise."

"I believe you and in you, I hope you know that."

I nodded, just like I would do as a boy when she would have me talk to my grandmother on the phone. Mom would remind me that she could not see me nodding and to speak to her, when it was pulling teeth to have her even call her own mother, usually at the behest of Big Ed.

I had never asked her about the physical and mental distance between daughter and mother during my meth-induced conversations during *General Hospital* viewings.

I could count the times that I had met my maternal grandmother on one hand and how she didn't appear to be remotely parental. In a word, she was scary and insistent that we attended church at St. John's Catholic Church on Sundays during her visit. Luckily, I had never been struck by lightning upon entering and didn't fall asleep during services. That cardinal sin would have raised her Irish temper and resulted in a thump on the head with a Bible.

"I need to go home and take a nap; I didn't sleep so well last night."

"Thanks for bringing this to me." I couldn't wait to get to my room and change out of this outfit that would make Mr. Blackwell's worst-dressed list.

We hugged, and she made her exit. This time, she wore more sensible Keds rather than her dressed up high-heeled footwear yesterday, sporting her "it's all good" uniform for whoever cared to notice.

When I unpacked my makeshift suitcase, five packaged pairs of colored Jockey bikini briefs fell out first. This was certainly a far cry from the usual tighty-whities that she would buy. Had she read in *Good Housekeeping* about how to properly dress your gay son? As it was, I was touched by the thought that she was becoming more subscribed that my homosexuality was not a phase after all.

But the next discovery from the treasure trove told me that she wasn't too keen on me having added attempted suicide to my resume. All of the shirts were long-sleeved – perfect for hiding razor-blade scars. No fun graphic tees whatsoever, not a Le Tigre polo to be found.

I put the socks, shirts, and underwear into a dresser drawer, then took off the gown and seen-better-days underwear, relishing the feel of clean clothes.

Nurse Susan came by to look at my bump.

"Oh, Henry," she said, "I was coming to collect you for blood work."

"Blood work" - a kinder, gentler way of saying AIDS test. Whatever pep may have been in my step drained out of me like the blood that they were going to take. Fun fact: Henry Dodge does not like needles. It would take three nurses to restrain him for getting shots as a child.

While I didn't mind referring to myself in the third person, I was starting to bristle at the idea of a needle in my arm; my palms instantly got sweaty. I wasn't sure Nurse Susan could contain me if I went spider monkey on her ass, with Pete being the literal muscle to hold me down.

I felt raw and vulnerable as Nurse Susan escorted me to a torture chamber, an innocuous room with a chair with an arm rest that I sat in. I found a spot on the ceiling and focused all my energy on it, forcing myself to become dead inside.

She swabbed my arm with rubbing alcohol. "Ok, this is going to pinch for a second."

"I've heard that one before," I said, figuring that my knack for adding levity would prove beneficial in keeping my mind occupied.

And just like that, it evaporated as Nurse Susan's hand on my arm felt strange to the touch. I saw that she had donned rubber gloves to prevent my blood from getting on her. A standard medical precaution, but it made me imagine that just one spilled drop could eat through the floor like the defense mechanism of *Alien*, like mine also contained concentrated acid, as Dr. Kiley had also feared. Well, in my mind anyway.

I felt the needle enter the skin as I looked back at the dead zone on the ceiling.

"There, now that wasn't so bad, was it?" Nurse Susan asked. "We'll have the results in two weeks. But in the meantime, I would like you to read this."

I saw the pamphlet in her hand. I half-expected it to have a small bird on its cover with the tagline: "You're a whore, and that makes me sad." But it was all about safe sex, and like a weird version of a Cracker Jack box, the prize inside was a condom. I think I'd rather have a decoder ring to figure out how to get through the next two weeks. *Que Sera, Sera*.

There was a lot of sameness over the next five days.

Breakfasts, lunches, dinners, art classes, and cults, I mean, AA meetings that weren't hitting their intended target audience with me; I was trying to pass the time with Nina before she left the hospital a day before me.

We were both using the mystery surrounding Carlos as a distraction. Did we really care once we were sprung from the joint about him at all? My vote was for no, but it was a way to circumvent the mind-numbing day-in and day-out operations at San Luis Rey. But I took comfort in knowing that Nina and I would stay in touch after our forced sojourn.

One day, as we debated the merits of Mary Ann versus Ginger, Nurse Wretched broke up the great pop culture debate, informing me that I would come with her. For the record, I was making a compelling case for Mary Ann Summers since she was sexy but approachable, unlike Ginger Grant's honey-trap ability to snare men.

"Do you need a written invitation? Move it!" Wretched barked, further illustrating that she was not made of sugar, spice or anything that remotely resembled nice.

She led me to the same room where I had taken my blood test. Rather than wait for her to snap at me to take a seat, I did so on my own accord. She removed a roll of gauze and medical tape from a drawer and moved as efficiently as a Cyberdyne Systems Model 101 Series 800 over to where I was sitting. She silently unwrapped the bandages. I found that dead zone on the ceiling again, not wanting to see the damage.

"That's a deep cut," she said, adding a whistle for effect. "You really must hate yourself."

It was as if they had put Hitler in charge of a daycare center, and instead of issuing building blocks to play with, she was handing out live grenades with her words. Like with any bully, it was best to pretend like I hadn't heard. At least for now. However, "now" lasted about a nanosecond.

"I have a question," I said. "Don't you have to like people in your profession? I mean, if this is your bedside manner, I feel really, really bad for your husband. But there's probably nothing for me to worry about there."

I looked at her ring finger, empty as expected.

Wretched's eyes filled with hate, and she muttered "Puto gilipollas," under her breath.

I had gotten under her skin and found her Achilles Heel. Bingo! I would share these glad tidings with Nina.

Wretched pulled the bandages tightly over my wrists and then instructed me to leave the room. I doubted that she would dissolve into a puddle of tears because crying had to be a threat for the Wicked Witch of the West.

As I made my way down the Yellowed Linoleum Floor, I saw tough guy Carlos, sitting by himself, the antithesis of The Tin Man. A heartless look was on his face, and I approached him every inch the Cowardly Lion. But I still had the adrenaline pumping from my verbal confrontation with Wretched surging in my veins.

"Mind if I sit down?"

He looked at me warily, like I was going to put the moves on him. In other circumstances I may have tried, as he was handsome, athletic, and confident.

"What are you in for?" I asked. Given his slight resemblance to Elvis with jet-black hair, half-lidded eyes, and pouty lips, perhaps he'd bust out with *Jailhouse Rock.*

"It's kinda complicated," he said.

"Complicated like Calculus?" I said.

"Pretty much," he replied and actually smiled. "More like Home Ec. Can you keep a secret?"

"Does a bear shit in the woods?"

He began telling me, in a quiet voice, about high school. He and a fellow football player got in the habit of experimenting, several times, usually after a night of partying.

One time, they had both passed out after the lovin' - as one of my mom's favorite singer's, Engelbert Humperdinck, had sung about - and Carlos's dad found them the following day. They were both buck nekkid in bed, and the jar of Vaseline sat on the nightstand may have also been a tip-off.

I couldn't help but wonder: Where in the hell were all of these questioning guys when I had felt like an Eskimo living alone on an icy tundra for all of these years? I mean, they were practically crawling out of the woodwork now. Then again, I could blame my faulty gaydar.

"Oh shit! What happened?"

"What do you think? My dad flip-shitted out on me. My mom cursed me up and down in Spanish. I had to look up what maricón meant."

While I also was unfamiliar with that terminology, I did remember seventh-grade gym class when a group of Hispanic boys would try to pull down my gym shorts and call me joto - akin to fag in English.

"I almost got kicked out of the house," Carlos confessed. "I told my parents that it was a one-time, drunken mistake. They made me swear that I wouldn't ever have him over to the house again and that I was not to 'associate with that boy.'"

It was all very *West Side Story*, minus the singing and dancing. And I wondered if he was a Jet all the way? From his first pole smoking to his last dyin' day? His next statement put him at a three on The Kinsey Scale.

"And then I met Missy, and everything seemed fine until she got pregnant, and her parents sent her away, and she put the baby up for adoption. And now she won't even talk to me."

Carlos explained that he couldn't squelch his taste for men forever. He returned to it right after graduation. He drove to the viewpoint that overlooked Cardiff and was a cruising spot for men who lived the undercover life.

He found a kindred spirit and let him get in his car, bypassing the option of going into the bushes.

I made a mental note of this previously unknown homosexual territory that I had yet to stake a claim in, as Carlos continued in just above a whisper tone.

"I was unbuttoning his pants," Carlos continued, "When I looked out the window. There was my dad's car. I panicked and thought he had followed me. But he was leaning back in his seat, and, well, that definitely wasn't my mom's head that popped up from his lap."

Well, everybody Wang Chung tonight!

"Oh shit,"

"Oh shit is right! Because, lo and behold, that head belonged to none other than *him*."

"No way!"

Turned out the Mustang's tight end was more of a wide receiver.

"He spotted me and freaked, getting out of the car with his pants around his ankles. And Dad backed out of his spot faster than any station wagon. Last thing I heard, my friend moved to Arizona."

Carlos's dad drove like a bat out of hell – ashamed of the paradise found and lost by the dashboard lights. He was suddenly sideswiped by a semi-truck while exiting the on-ramp. In the hospital, his father slipped into a coma from which he never came out of, and Carlos put the blame squarely on himself. This, coupled with his uncertainty about which team to play for, had landed him here.

I couldn't imagine Big Ed being in the same boat as Carlos's dad. Then again, he did ask me to rent the movie *Lust in the Dust* with Divine and Tab Hunter. And he did have a few Judy Garland records in his collection. I pushed the thought so hard out of my mind that it almost gave me a concussion.

"You have to promise not to tell anyone!"

I gave him my solemn word, and he produced a smile of relief. I saw Nina emerge from her room, mouth wide as she saw who I was talking to. I knew that I couldn't repeat what he had confided. Carlos saw her and walked away with nary an utterance of "Good talk, bro."

"What did you find out?!!"

"Nothing much, really." I hated lying to her, especially when her face took on a crestfallen look. "We were just bitching about Larry and Nurse Wretched. You won't believe what that bitch said to me!" I recounted the bandage changing.

"That bitch! What the hell is wrong with her?"

"That, my dear, is a question for the ages."

"I'd really like to fix her wagon! Wait a minute..." She took on a Blair Warner tone when she got another one of her brilliant ideas. But it would have to be hatched before she left tomorrow.

She only had a few hours to prep before Nurse Wretched's shift was over. The plan would take place at high noon. I was told my part. I watched the remaining hour slowly pass by in a series of seconds and minutes, until the clock was pointing straight up with both hands.

I went to Nina's room to "let her know" that it was time for lunch. I was so grossed out by the fare that I hungered for a Kate Dodge Velveeta concoction. I was light years away from my strict Tina diet and had an appetite again. I was honestly glad to be getting free of her iron grip on me, Fay Wray trapped in the clutches of King Kong.

I entered Nina's room, and she was lying face down, in case it hadn't been me.

"You ready, girl?"

Her answer was a thumbs-up. Operation Takedown was ready to be activated, even though the operative resembled someone playing the rainy-day game of "Head's Up 7-Up" that we played in Miss Hooker's fifth-grade class. The game we were embarking on was akin to chess. The goal was a case of "Checkmate, bitch" where Nurse Wretched was concerned.

I walked at a steady clip out of her room, my heart beating at the idea that this would work.

"There's something wrong with Nina!" I called out. "She's not moving!" I added a tremble to my voice.

I saw an actual look of concern on Nurse Wretched's face, who dashed down the hallway.

Thirty seconds after Nurse Wretched entered Nina's room, I heard a bloodcurdling scream, followed by "Get the fuck off of me!"

An orderly named Max, the polar opposite of Pete, waddled quickly to Nina's room on two legs resembling elongated ham hocks and managed to pull Nurse Wretched out, removing her from the crime scene.

David was running down the hall as the rest of the patients were milling about, reminiscent of the scene in *Halloween* when Dr. Loomis and Nurse Marion Chambers arrive at Smith's Grove Sanitarium to find the charges moving zombie-like in the pouring rain, a danse macabre.

"Get back to your station," David commanded Nurse Wretched.

"But that little bitch…" she hissed, a rattlesnake coiled and ready to strike.

"I will deal with you later! Go!"

Max released his tenuous grasp on her. Perhaps if she had been a meatball sub, which he ate daily, then he would have been able to corral her better with his meaty hands. Nurse Wretched shot me the crustiest of looks and retreated in defeat. Max and David entered Nina's room and closed the door. They emerged with Nina a few minutes later, and she had a hand over the eye that would blacken later, a victim of her own clenched fist.

David escorted her to the adult ward so the nurse on duty could assess the damage and file a report.

"Alright, show's over," David said sternly. "Everyone to lunch!"

Still walking slowly down the hallway, Nina leaned against David for support as she feigned the post-traumatic effects of Nurse Wretched's "attack."

We all ate our lunch silently. Well, except for Heather.

"Little slag got what she deserved," she huffed, still stinging from Nina's pointed words from days before.

"Didn't anyone tell you not to play with your food, Heather?" I said this as if addressing a four-year-old.

This immediately shut her down. She didn't eat her ham sandwich or potato chips, either. Later, I sat outside of David's office, awaiting our therapy session. Inside, I could hear as he dressed Nurse Wretched down.

"I didn't do it!" she yelled.

"Well, that young lady's eye would beg to differ!" David retorted. "You're suspended indefinitely."

Nurse Wretched suddenly emerged, and I jumped. She slammed his office door and noticed me there. She stopped to glare at me, daring me to respond.

I took her challenge happily.

"Bye, bitch. You should take this time to reflect on how you treat people. Now, be gone before somebody drops a house on you, too!"

She stomped off so forcefully it was surprising there wasn't a burst of flames to denote her exit. A moment later, David summoned me into his chambers, fitting given the fact that I had played my part in being judge, jury, and executioner to Nurse Wretched's employment.

"I'm sorry that you had to hear all of that."

I certainly wasn't. But I couldn't let on. It had been gratifying beyond words to have played a part in halting her reign of terror, even if temporarily. I wouldn't have to see her mug for the rest of my stay.

And that's what David wanted to discuss: my aftercare treatment. I shuddered that he might make me attend more Alcoholics Anonymous meetings. I had nothing against people trying to better themselves and change their lives, but it just was not for me.

I wasn't even 21 yet and only wanted to be done with meth. No mas for me. It didn't hold any allure for me now. But I wasn't ruling out the prospect that I could still smoke pot or sneak a beer out of the fridge in the garage.

"I would like you to continue with our sessions, as well. Your mother thinks that it would be for the best. What are your thoughts?"

And there was the hiccup. I wasn't sure if I wanted someone else in my head; the committee already in there took up too much space as it was. I knew I should choose the only door offered to me in this version of *Let's Make a Deal*. Perhaps David's straight talk was just what this gay guy needed.

"OK, I guess so," I muttered.

"Well, don't be so enthusiastic! It will be beneficial, I promise."

The next day couldn't come fast enough, especially since Nina was ready to go, but not before her mother threatened a lawsuit against the hospital. David managed to talk her off that particular ledge.

We said our goodbyes in the hall, knowing this wasn't the end, and we solidified that pact by exchanging phone numbers and fierce hugs.

"You're a really good hugger," she said, and I noticed a small tear.

"That's what all the boys say."

She laughed and said she'd see me later.

"Not if I see you first."

"Oh my god, I love *Stand by Me*!"

"Color me surprised."

I watched her leave, feeling really alone – but now hopeful since I had a new friend.

I went through the motions of my final day, waiting to be checked out before I was released back into the wild. My paper bag was packed hours ago.

I was pouting that I wouldn't be able to say goodbye to Pete, given he had mentioned that he would be off today. Just then, I heard my door open. Apparently, he had picked up an extra shift. Hmm, I wonder why.

"Hey you. Your mom is here to get you." He looked behind him, carefully closed the door, and made his way over. "This is generally frowned upon here, but can I give you a hug?"

Before I had a chance to answer, his massive, muscular body was pressed against mine. I detected Drakkar Noir clinging to his body as I was now. It felt good to be held in a non-sexual way. But this was Pete we're talking about.

"I'll miss you, sweet cheeks," he cooed and cupped my ass. "See you around sometime."

"You never know, Pete."

And that was a perfect statement to be made in this uncertain moment of what I would face at home for the remaining days until I got my test results and for whatever the future held in store for me.

The overjoyed exuberance of my return and how it would relate to Shadow was a no-brainer as she let her tongue convey how much she had missed me. But the silent treatment I was expecting from Big Ed upon my homecoming didn't surface. In fact, he was more talkative than, well, ever. Maybe Mom had taken him to task for narcing on me to Jeff. Or maybe my big mouth going off on him in the hospital forced him to respect me more, seeing me as a person. Who knows?

I opted for the latter, not knowing that she didn't want to rock the boat with his uncharacteristic spilling of family secrets, especially to a stranger, and hadn't broached the subject.

Mom really missed her calling as a tightrope walker in the circus, just as I could moonlight as a professional eggshell dancer. One-two-cha cha cha. Right now, the spotlight was on me as Big Ed laid out some ground rules.

"Ok, Henry, some simple requests," he emphasized the last word as if I were slow on the draw. "You need to get a job. You've had quite a bit of, uh, free time lately. Best to occupy your mind with more positive things. And earn your keep around here."

I was wondering if he had any idea of what the word "positive" could mean to me. I also questioned if he had ponied up the money to take a class on how to deal with your suicidal gay son. But that would mean he had sought outside help in how best to address me, and you could file that one under "N" for both "Nope" and "Never Going to Happen."

Big Ed was a staunch advocate for "If you can't solve your own problems, then don't look for someone else to." Mom disagreed; that's why she told me we would keep my appointments with David a secret. She would pay for it out of her own paycheck from Barrington Enterprises.

"Second new rule," Big Ed said, a familiar scowl on his face. "You've been using the keg in the fridge."

Uh-oh busted.

"I know you are going to drink. Hell, I used to nick vodka from your grandpa. So, do me a favor. Just do it at home."

I just nodded, not wanting my smart-ass nature to mess up a rare tender moment with the old man. Maybe he was going to Assholes Anonymous. "Hi, I'm Big Ed, and I'm an asshole." Doubtful, but stranger things have happened.

I didn't know how long this nice spell was going to last. I was going to ride the wave all the way to shore, still looking out for the rocks that had defined our relationship. I would never be the golden boy, or "bronze god," that John was apt to proclaim himself as at the height of his envy-inducing summer tan.

I felt a pang of sadness. I was missing John; we had turned a corner when he came to rescue me from the boulevard, and he had not wavered in his support of his little tag-along brother. More like little fag-along brother. I would be seeing him soon, but it could not be soon enough.

I think, somehow, he had always known. Like that night after his shift at Alpha Beta and how he had bagged groceries for two gay guys shopping. He never made it a joke. He just let it hang there, like when he told me about a gay character on *Dynasty*.

I secretly began watching the campy drama every Wednesday night, even though Steven's character was sort of a wishy-washy gay, even though he had a boyfriend last season. Sadly, Billy Campbell's character Luke didn't survive The Moldavian Massacre and thankfully, neither did Ali McGraw's Lady Ashley. Perhaps if the guns that the men who stormed the wedding had been loaded with acting abilities rather than bullets, then her survival would have been welcome.

Since it was Wednesday, I knew what I would be doing at 9 p.m. Last week, Krystle was finally rescued from her captivity, and her double, Rita, and her cohort Joel had been in a car accident. I was hoping that my road to recovering from crystal meth wouldn't end up in an emotional ditch.

"You still with me, Henry?" Big Ed said, snapping me out of my trance.

"Yes," I said, and then did something out of the ordinary. I added "sir" to the end of that sentence.

He looked shocked, as was I. At this point, Mom popped her head out of the kitchen.

"Hon, you look tired. Go lie down for a bit. We're having your favorite for dinner, fried chicken."

Kate Dodge knew her way around a chicken. So, this was the epitome of good news.

"Awesome. Thanks, Mom." And I started the ascent up the stairs, Shadow trotting behind me, and headed to my room. First, I took a right and observed the pitch-black interior of the bathroom, like a coffin.

The scene of the crime. I had to face that fear of going in there because there wasn't a way around not using the bathroom or showering.

I closed the door behind me, flipped on the lights, and looked over at the sink on the right-hand side of the counter. It was whiter than virgin snow. My poor mother had to scrub away the dried blood. I decided to use the left sink to splash some water on my face.

I dried it on the towel behind me, hanging on the shower towel rack, when I heard a phantom voice coming from behind me.

"*We all float down here.*" While he was Pennywise, I was not hotdog foolish enough to believe that a clown who lived in the sewers was speaking to me at that moment. Kudos to my overactive imagination for providing a temporary distraction.

I went back to the sink and gave myself a good, hard look in the mirror. While my skin had cleared up, and the circles under my eyes weren't entirely as black, there were traces of the damage that I had let Tina inflict.

I remembered I still had the apparatus in my room. I had to throw them away – but where? Upon rifling through my drawer, I could not find the bindle, straw, or razor blade. She had ended up leaving me without so much as a Dear Henry letter. And though it was sunny outside, a bolt of lightning struck me. I hadn't returned my drug paraphernalia to its proper hiding place that night.

"So, did you do anything with all of your underwear?"

And there it was, a voice scarier than any fictional dancing clown. In her search for clothes to bring me, Kate Dodge discovered I was the poster boy for my anti-D.A.R.E. campaign.

"Groovy," I said, sounding a bit like Jan Brady. But there hadn't been any special episodes revolving around the perpetually troubled middle child getting caught with drugs.

But then I turned that frown upside down. There would be no dramatic flushing of Tina down the toilet or Mom addressing what she had found. Then again, she might.

Whatever the case, the siren call of my bed, expertly made courtesy of Kate Dodge and with Shadow on top of the bedspread, was irresistible. I undressed down to my underwear, a colorful shade of blue, and got under the covers after scooching Shadow over a bit, which reignited her licks, telling me how much I was missed. While this was not an uncommon occurrence, it wouldn't surprise me if my suicide attempt had placed me in a parallel universe. Up was down, left was right. I had an actual friend. Mom finally seemed accepting of who I was. And Big Ed gave a shit about me.

This was the last thought I had as sweet slumber overtook me. It was dark out, and Mom was sitting on my bed, saying dinner was prepared.

"I'll be down in a minute."

Maybe now she'd discuss her discovery.

"Sounds good, hon." She said, nothing else came out of her mouth, not another single, solitary word.

Nope, I had skirted that bullet.

I dressed hurriedly. While I wanted to rush to the dinner table, I opted for a slower pace to avoid another goose egg on my head.

My father was already at the table, a can of Budweiser at his side. Mom brought over the heaping plate of fried chicken, which took her hours to cook. She dished up mashed potatoes and steamed broccoli on our plates, always serving herself last.

I grabbed two drumsticks and a thigh, while Big Ed opted for a single breast. Mom speared a thigh. There was zero conversation; we were laser-focused on devouring Kate Dodge's delicious poultry bounty.

I was half-tempted to snag another drumstick, but I made myself resist and pushed myself back from the table. "Accidentally," dropping a chunk of thigh meat on the floor for Shadow and her unwavering gaze and whimper routine during dinner.

"I'm going to go to my room for a while," I said.

"Oh, but *Wheel of Fortune* is almost on," she said.

While I usually liked watching Pat Sajak and Vanna White, especially when Mom would shout out part of the puzzle, and I would steal home with the answer, I wasn't in the mood for games. But her crestfallen face caused me to amend my train of thought.

"I'll come down and watch *Jeopardy*."

While *Jeopardy* was a bit like our time-honored watching of *Hollywood Squares* in the past, with Big Ed now questioning me about the school system in Encinitas failing to teach me the main export from Columbia. What is cocaine? I may have answered in another time and place, but for now, I was going to mind my p's and or q's.

I left the door open in case Shadow decided to visit rather than try to procure more table scraps. Mainly, I didn't want to cause my mother extra worry as to what I may be up to. It wouldn't be a case of the same ol,' same ol' that was for sure. But this was the problem with the rinse-and-repeat life that I had been living. I needed to find a way to occupy my time differently.

I reached into my pocket and procured the piece of paper with Nina's number. Just as I grabbed the receiver, the phone rang.

"Hello?"

"Hi, is Henry there?" Nina asked timidly.

"Leave a message at the beep," I said.

"Um, hi, I was calling for Henry..." she began.

"Thanks for calling Psychic Friends Network. How may I help you?"

"Well, if you were a psychic, you'd know that now wouldn't you, smart-ass."

"Busted. How's the shiner, slugger?"

"A little sore, but totally worth it!"

"Well, she definitely had a comeuppance due."

"So, how are you doing? Everything good at home?"

"Well, it's weird. My dad is being nice to me."

After light conversations regarding TV shows, music, and movies we liked, I told her a smidge about my home life.

I was tempted to whisper, but just then, I heard my mother yell out some of the puzzle on *Wheel of Fortune*, to which my father chimed in with the answer. I knew I'd be left alone. So, I told her about Pete standing in my doorway – and his one-sided game of grab ass.

"Wow! That's crazy!"

"Well, we oughta know."

When she didn't respond with a laugh or a pithy reply, I knew I had struck a nerve.

"Sorry," I said.

"Well, now that we are out of *there*, I have an aversion to *that* word. I don't know about you, but I am not going to be telling anyone about it. Mom told my siblings that I was visiting our grandmother. It's what I am going to be telling my friends, too."

"You steppin' out on me?" I was suddenly jealous that she had other friends. But I was glad I was counted among them.

"No, baby. I mean, I am a hot property, what with this black eye and all. And I want you to meet them. You are gonna love them, I promise. What are you doing tomorrow?"

"Well, there's the little matter of finding gainful employment."

"The movie theater is hiring. You could work with me!"

"That would be amazing! I'm not sure if you know this about me, but I love movies."

"For a minute there, I thought you were going to tell me that you're a notorious homosexual."

"No, no, notorious," I said, and she responded with the precise gasp that followed in the song by the now trio of Duran Duran.

"Alright, call me after your job hunt tomorrow. Maybe we can hang out?"

"I'd like that."

We both hung up after saying goodbye. There was nothing along the lines of "No, you hang up." "No, you hang up first." I was surprised, as we both seemed smitten with each other. The smitten kitten and the cool cat were now officially an item - and it felt amazing and uncomfortable.

I mean, Craig was still in my life, but he now held a slight negative connotation of hooking me up with Jeff. But I really shouldn't hold it against him; I was not an innocent bystander in the scenario. I made a mental note to reach out and see how he was doing.

"Hon, *Jeopardy*'s on!" my mother called out gaily.

I sat on the beige couch with her, and Shadow was asleep at my feet in the living room, which was a neutral beige rather than the colorful orange and green striped thing that had been our spot when she would read *Curious George* to me when I was four. I could have read it to her, as I had memorized every line of that book and had been picking out words from books at two, according to Mom. Big Ed sat in "his chair," a matching beige recliner, another Budweiser on a coaster on the teakwood end table that had survived the great '70s purge when the house decor was freshened up.

Here we sat, minus one key player in the Dodge Family, looking every inch the normal family to people walking down the street who may glance at the seemingly picture-perfectness of it all through the living room window.

As the categories came up, I was hoping for cartoons rather than a math category. No such luck on any kind of pop culture category that I could sweep, but there was nothing Algebra-related, so I did my best to come out ahead on Potpourri.

The only Double Jeopardy Big Ed seemed to care about was downing two beers during the first round. He didn't chastise me or the public school system when I answered wrong. This kinder, gentler version of Big Ed was nothing short of unsettling, and I suspected that it wouldn't last too long, dissipating quicker than the scars on my wrist that would become less pronounced over time, even though the words he would wound me with would always remain.

Fortunately, redemption came in the form of Final Jeopardy, which was about Greek mythology. I had been fascinated with a book by Edith Hamilton in sixth grade because of the movie *Clash of the Titans*.

"Rivers leading into this place include Cocytus, Phlegethon, Acheron and Styx," Alex Trebek asked contestants.

"Hades," I answered immediately.

Of course, the underworld, where souls went upon death, would be something that I should know about. I looked down and saw the bandages poking out slightly from my long-sleeved Quicksilver shirt. Would I now lead a life of never wearing short sleeves or my favorite summertime tank tops again?

All I had to go on as to how my wrists looked was based on Nurse Wretched's nasty remark to me, so it might not be as bad as what that twat said. I would see the next day when I had to change the bandages. I also had to follow up with my primary doctor, Dr. Baker. He would deliver the results of my HIV test, a far cry from the times that I had come with a case of strep throat.

I almost missed Dad nodding at me in approval for knowing the correct answer due to my deep thoughts. I wanted to shout out that it was freaking me the fuck out how he was trying to be a father to me. I figured whatever spell that practical joker Uncle Arthur had conjured up outside of his *Bewitched* day job was better left unbroken.

The half-hour of family bonding ended with Dad and I retreating to the winds of familiarity within the confines of our rooms, except for Mom, who went into the kitchen to clean up the results of her culinary triumph.

I turned on my TV but couldn't really focus on Balki and Cousin Larry on *Perfect Strangers*. The pile of notebooks and drawing pads were in my field of vision. They were encouraging me to do a little drawing.

I got out of my well-worn beanbag chair and rifled through the stack, procuring the one that I had done most of my late-night art class for, and grabbed the plastic case of pencils.

I flipped through the pages, struck by the imagery, mostly angry-looking creatures, charcoal drawings of dead trees, or waves crashing against rocky shores. My artwork had taken on a time and place element - but what did I want to express in this fragile moment of uncertainty?

I steered away from the darkness that charcoal provided both in context and feeling and instead chose an array of colors for my impromptu project. I was so immersed that I almost missed the opening strains of Bill Conti's *Dynasty* theme.

The aftermath and whereabouts of Rita and Joel weren't really resolved. There were smoking corpses pulled from the fiery wreckage. But their misdeeds against Krystle were brought about by scheming Sammy Jo. She was my favorite character on the show, aside from Alexis. Damaged goods recognized damaged goods.

When the show ended, I looked down at the notebook. A marked difference from the long-ago notebook that had held a secret that I couldn't really name. It was also a 180-degree shift from the sketches done on meth. A serene ocean led to a cliffside with a tree sprouting new, green leaves full of oxygen and colorful birds nesting in its strong branches.

I wrote "Renewal" at the bottom and decided that it was time for bed.

I awoke the next morning feeling like the name of my drawing. Another full night of sleep had not eluded me, and I felt refreshed, ready to take on the day.

First was the draining of the dragon. I flipped on the light, and there was another creature awaiting me, this one I had to slay with whatever bravery I had in my heart and soul. A mild-mannered roll of adhesive tape sat smack dab in the middle of the counter, left there by Mom as a subtle reminder to change my bandages. I closed the door, peed, and turned around to face the music.

Slowly, I undid my bandages, without the manic glee of Claude Raines in *The Invisible Man*; unlike his strip tease, there was something to be seen once these bandages were removed. I did not look down as I did this, not wanting to sully the big reveal. Once both were done, I threw the discarded bandages in the trash, went over to the left-hand sink, and looked.

"That fucking bitch!" I said to my wrists.

Not-so-surprisingly, Nurse Wretched had just wanted to get her dig in because the work that James Brolin had done on my stitches was genius. Nothing like the massacre I had anticipated.

I prayed the scars would be light. But there'd still be a reminder of my self-loathing, be it physically or mentally.

I covered up another secret, this time with bandages, and pulled my sleeves over them. I went downstairs to an empty house, save for a certain canine companion. She leapt up and began her friendly assault with a barrage of kisses.

"Did you miss me, girl?" Her answer was more kisses.

A thought percolated up again: Who had she allowed to come into our house - and why had they taken only my underwear? I pushed it into a box reserved for evidence that UFOs really existed and were being piloted by Bigfoot.

I leaned down and gave her a pat on her hind quarters, and she expressed her gratitude by looking at me with her soulful brown puppy dog eyes. I promised to put a walk on my agenda for the day and made my way into the kitchen. It was still a strange sensation to be meth-free and hungry. While I was tempted to chow down on leftover fried chicken, I opted for the healthier choice of Honey Nut Cheerios.

It was most definitely a honey of an O and filled my empty stomach. Now it was time to shower, shave and shine. I had to look presentable for my job hunt. I emerged from the shower as a butterfly fresh out its chrysalis.

I had brought my ghetto blaster into the bathroom, set the volume to just under its loudest setting, and put on "Venus" by Bananarama. I mouthed the words, as singing was not my strong suit. I looked in the mirror. For once, I was not appalled at what I saw staring back.

Yeah baby, he's got it!

The phone rang, and I hoped it was Nina.

As it turned out, Mom was checking up on me.

"What are you going to do today, hon?"

"Heading out to look for a job, actually."

"That's great!" she exclaimed before her tone turned a bit stern. "Make sure you wear a sweater or a jacket."

"Um, ok," I said as I looked outside. The sun was shining bright, temperatures in the upper sixties. Welcome to winter in San Diego. But the only dark cloud in the forecast was the reminder by Mom. I knew why she was asking me to do this: extra coverage for my bandages for applying for the job at AMC.

"I need to get back to work. Good luck today."

"See you tonight."

I put on my favorite purple and black patterned sweater, careful not to mess up my perfectly gelled hair, then went out to the garage, backed L'il Red up, and got her purring like a kitten. I checked the combination lock for the garage door twice to make sure it wouldn't pop open for anyone who wanted to steal my socks, and I was off to Weigand Plaza.

I parked and walked to the box office with an air of confidence like I had the job already.

I was familiar with Diane at the box office since I was one of their best customers. I mean, I had seen so many movies here, they ought to have a reserved seat for me.

We exchanged pleasantries, and I asked for an application. She smiled and handed it to me on a clipboard and pen. I walked over to one of the wooden benches that flanked the theater, sat down, and began filling out the pertinent information. And then it asked for my former employer.

I winced, recalling blackmailing my former superior and not-quite-boyfriend, wondering if that was grounds for a harsh critique? Probably. Like my Gemco application, I again put Craig down as the point of contact.

Better safe than sorry. I decided to not include my time as a bag boy, re-writing that not-so-illustrious chapter of gainful employment with a case of temporary amnesia.

I returned the application to Diane. As I did, she picked up the phone and then held one finger up to signal that I should stay put.

"You have time to talk to the manager?"

"Sure thing," I said, playing the paragon of cool, calm, and collective. The sweat on my palms begged to differ. Diane - no pun intended - ushered me into the theater.

The door next to the concession stand opened, and a giant of a man strode across the lobby. I discreetly wiped the sweat off my right hand just in time as he enveloped his huge hand into mine with a handshake. Diane handed him my application, which he scanned briefly.

"I'm Erik; nice to meet you, Henry."

"Thanks, you too." I craned my neck up and met his pale blue eyes. He had Nordic in his DNA, as was evidenced by his blond hair. I followed this long-lost Viking to his office.

"Have a seat. I see you worked at Lavar's. Yvonne works here as a supervisor, a nice gal. So, tell me why you'd be a good fit for us."

I went into my love of movies, and he seemed impressed by my lifelong affair with pop culture. I talked up my hardworking abilities, believing the words that were spilling forth in a nervous stream of my strengths. I added that I knew Nina.

"I need to confer with my managers, but I have a feeling you'd be right for the job. I'll give you a call."

He rose, towering over me, and I was escorted out. I could have skipped all the way to L'il Red but decided against it, as I would have looked like some sort of loon. Well, I had just gotten out of the looney bin, but each step I took was creating a distance from that place. I was feeling damn good, like a new man.

I went home and took Shadow for a walk to the place that John and I called The Dump, which housed no landfill material but was full of bushes and arroyos. This was fitting since it was located down the block from my street.

I let Shadow off her leash, free to chase birds in her own personal playground. Watching her romp and play in the bushes recalled my own recreation area in the trails of Black's Beach. Which led to Tony, which led to if my HIV status would change. And that brought me back down to Earth.

Tick tock, t-minus one week and counting. My appointment with Dr. Baker was an early morning slot. I did not want to sit around that day, awaiting my fate, punishment or whatever the religious right was calling it on the evening news.

I decided it was time for a more structured form of fun and games for Shadow, specifically Hide and Go Seek. I made her sit and went off and hid, called out, “Shadow, Shadow, Shadow!” I awaited her inevitable finding of me and repeated the exercise several times before calling it a day.

I put her leash on, and we returned home to the sound of the phone ringing. I practically ran into the kitchen, hoping that the other higher-ups at AMC had deemed me worthy of working there.

I only heard the sound of heavy breathing. I hung up forcefully. I had seen enough horror movies to know that this was never a good thing, usually leading to a “the call is coming from inside the house” scenario from *When a Stranger Calls*.

And here I was, all alone with the world’s worst guard dog. I locked the front door and double-checked the sliding glass door as if that would protect me from Jason Voorhees shattering it with his brute strength. But I was being a good teenager, no drugs, no sex for the near future. And although I was no virgin, I thought my chances of survival were solid.

And when the phone rang again, sending an actual shiver down my spine, I let the answering machine field that call. It turned out not to be some psycho wearing a hockey mask, but Nina, so I picked up.

“Whatcha doin’?”

“Just got home from walking my dog, and I applied at AMC, so if they ask you, as far as you know, I’m an upstanding citizen.”

“So, lie then?”

“Yes, please.”

“Wanna meet up?”

Why not? What did I have to do, aside from waiting for more strange phone calls or a machete to the midsection?

“Sure. What do you have in mind?”

I didn’t know that I was on the precipice of something new as I made my exit from the house. And this date with destiny, one that I long dreamed of, was to take place somewhere more innocuous than I would have imagined. But it contained magic, nonetheless, no ruby slippers were needed on this journey to Oz, no Yellow Brick Road to guide me towards my destination, and guiding me along my journey. Plain old asphalt and a red scooter were the only way to get there.

I pulled into the Gemco shopping center and parked in front of Aaron Brother's Art Mart. And standing out front, like The Guardian of the Gates minus an all-green ensemble, was Nina, dressed all in black, her hair now iridescent blue.

I expected her to say, "Nobody gets in to see the Wizard, not nobody, not nohow." Instead, she greeted me with a knowing smile resembling a Goth version of the Mona Lisa, and gave me an enormous hug. A pair of Ray-Bans covered the results of her Flyweight solo boxing match. When she took them off, her black eye was pretty much gone.

"Alright, I'm here," I said.

"Yes. Yes, I can see that." She was every bit the smart-ass that I was. And I loved it.

"Ok, sassy pants. Why have you summoned me?"

"Well, my dear boy, there's some people that I want you to meet."

She must be introducing me to who she had lovingly had referred to as "the boys" before. It was doubtful that Neil Tennant and Chris Lowe were inside to serenade me with my favorite Pet Shop Boys song, "Opportunities (Let's Make Lots of Money)." Because that should obviously happen at the pet store across the street.

She opened the door and led the way. Standing behind the counter was a tall redhead that I recognized from the drudgery of San Dieguito; he had graduated two years before I was supposed to. He sported a black apron that hung off his lanky frame, and his name tag informed customers that his name was Michael.

"Henry, this is Michael."

"Yes, girl, I can read. Nice to meet you."

"Ooh, we've got ourselves a little firecracker! It's a pleasure to make your acquaintance, Henry." He did a little bow.

"Yeah. He's somethin' all right," Nina said.

"So, how do you two kids know each other?"

An "oh shit" look covered Nina's face, so I jumped in.

"Oh, we met at summer camp. Camp Crystal Lake, wasn't it, doll? We had a good time until some kid drowned."

Nina nudged me with her elbow straight to my ribs.

"No, no. We met at interpretive dance class," she said and swayed back and forth like a sapling in a strong wind, her wrists limp and dangling. "I call that one The Homo Hurricane."

"Well, wasn't that money well-spent…" Michael said with an eye roll.

"If you say so," I added, bouncing off his sarcasm that had dripped from his tongue like the bitterest of honeys, made with salt rather than sugar. "Well, let me give you a taste of my skills. Can you guys hum the theme from *Dallas*?"

Michael began, and Nina followed suit as I went into my routine, made up on the spot. When I was done, Michael gave me a strange look while Nina offered a golf clap.

"I live to dansch and dansch to live," I said with a German accent.

"Well, the judges gave me tens across the board, so suck on that!" Nina put her hands over her eyes dramatically as if she were offended that her dance skills were in question.

"Oh honey, that's hard to swallow, even for me," Michael stated. "And don't be such a drama queen - that's my department."

"As it should be," she responded. "Besides, a crown would mess up my hair!"

It was Aqua-Netted within an inch of its life, crunchy to the touch.

"Girl, if you teased that hair any more than you already do, it would be abuse."

I was surprised at how easily I slid into this ribbing that outsiders might consider borderline hateful. Previously, we had all been high school misfits, freaks of nature, outsiders. Stay gold, Ponyboy.

"Daaaaamn!" Michael proclaimed; a girlish laugh escaped him.

"I think I'll keep him around," Nina said and looked at me, batting her eyes.

"You better; he's easy on the eyes." Michael cooed.

I silently wondered if the gay mecca of Hillcrest had been relocated to Encinitas. There were more gays here than I could shake a stick at lately. Hopefully, Michael didn't think I was going to beat him off with one.

"Aww, shucks." It was my go-to when confronted with a compliment.

"You remind me of someone. But I can't think who?" He said, his fingers and thumb stroking an invisible beard.

"Must be Tom Cruise; I get that all the time."

"Well, you are a little bit taller than him," Nina smirked. "But not by much."

"Bitch." A jackknife smile highlighting the intent.

"Well, love, it's definitely a case of takes one to know one," she bantered back. "Now, where's the other member of the gruesome twosome?"

"He's restocking and in a pissy mood. He broke up with you-know-who," Michael said.

"Forewarned is forearmed, as they say, though I have no idea who *they* are," Nina retorted.

"I believe *they* were the great philosopher Popeye," I said and offered my version of Popeye's laugh.

"We've got us a regular Rich Little over here," Nina teased.

"Better than looking like Phyllis Diller."

"Damn, dude," Nina said.

"Whaaat?" I feigned innocence.

"Move it along," she commanded.

"Sir, yes, sir!"

And we met her other "boy," angrily stuffing fan paint brushes into a round wooden display container like he was trying to fit the fabled square peg into a round hole.

"What did that brush ever do to you?" Nina chastised.

"Oh. Hey," he said, not looking up from his task. "What's up? I'm kind of busy if you haven't noticed."

"Trust me, I can see that. I just wanted you to meet somebody."

"Oh, for fuck's sake!" he said, then tossed the brushes forcefully on the floor as if they had caught on fire.

He turned and stared at me, no howdy do, greeting and or salutation. Just the slow burn of anger dancing across his eyes.

Nina and I both unconsciously took a step backward, and I wanted to grab her hand for safety. He stood up, chin up, chest out, signaling he was the cock of the walk in Nina's life.

"This is Henry. And this guy who is likely to go nuclear is Derek," Nina joked.

But Derek didn't seem like he was ready to play the same tennis game that she, Michael, and I had just participated in.

"Henry," he said. It was neither a statement nor a welcome. It just hung there in the air, like humidity prior to a thunderstorm.

I wanted to say that it was nice to meet him, but I wasn't sure I was.

"Well, while it's been a stimulating conversation, we'll let you get back to it." Nina said, rushing me back to Michael, who was still standing behind the counter.

"Hey! Time to lean, time to clean," Nina teased.

"I really wish that I had never told you about *that*!" Michael sighed. He explained that it was an annoying slogan by Karen, the store manager, and said during every shift."Well, wish in one hand and crap in the other and see which one piles up first. Ta-ta."

I gave Michael a little wave, and I followed Nina.

"Sorry about Derek; he's not usually such a cooze. He's better off without that annoying boyfriend. Scott was just bad news all around and wishy-washy about being gay."

"Sounds like a real treasure; someone should bury him."

"Trust me, I've wanted to invite him over for tea and hit him in the back of the head with a shovel a time or two and offer him a sammich." She mimed a "bam, bam, bam" for added effect.

"Norman," I said ala Mrs. Bates in *Psycho II*, knowing the scene that she was referencing from the movie.

"Do you wanna come over to my house?"

"So long as you don't offer me tea."

"You're safe," she said, waiting a beat. "For now."

"If this is your good side, I'd hate to see what your bad side looks like."

She lived at the apartments off Encinitas Boulevard at the top of the hill. I had driven past them many times, never knowing that they housed someone who was fast becoming my friend.

As we walked into her mom's apartment, her long-gone dad a few years late to witness our entrance, three kids rushed up and hugged her: two younger girls and a pre-teen boy. They sized me up a bit warily. I got the same reaction from the gray Maine Coon cat lounging on a love seat. Slivers of shadows from the Levolor blinds gave it the impression that it had stripes on its coat.

"This is Susie, Nadia, and Dimitri - and that lazy cat is Mrs. Bernstein. Guys, this is my friend Henry. Be nice to him, or it's curtains for you, ya see," she said like Edward G. Robinson and the girls giggled.

"Top of the world, Ma!" I said like Cagney, having watched *White Heat* because Madonna's song of the same name included snatches of the movie's dialogue.

"Well, get up, stand tall, put your back against the wall." She countered.

I was now officially her friend, *AND* she could quote Madonna songs? Pinch me; I must be dreaming.

"You guys are weird-o-rama!" Susie said, stating the obvious.

"He'd have to be to be friends with her," Dimitri chimed in.

"What's the matter, Dimi? You got your period?" Nina asked with motherly concern. "Tampons are under the bathroom sink."

"Shove it!" He cried.

"Dimi, why you do this to me, Dimi?" The voice of Damien Karras's dead mother from *The Exorcist* took over Nina with a haunting quality that I remembered from the few times I had watched the watered-down version on Channel 13.

"I told you to stop doing that!" he shrieked.

"Letting him watch *The Exorcist* at five may not have been my finest hour," Nina confessed in a stage whisper to me.

"You should have waited until he was six." I did the shame-shame finger gesture.

"Alrighty, enough with this nonsense," Nina said, adopting an air of authority. "You guys do your homework?"

"I did!" Nadia exclaimed, raising her hand in the air as if being called on in class.

"Very good, Nadia. You may watch TV."

Nadia ran over to the cream-colored couch, plopped herself down, and picked up the remote, selecting *Gumby* as her reward.

The little green slab of clay who could walk into any book with his pony pal Pokey, too, was a happy memory for me. I would watch him after pre-school and then followed with a rather bizarre choice for a four-year-old, *The Galloping Gourmet*. I felt a pang of jealousy; to be that young and innocent again was now a foreign concept.

"What about you two?"

Dimitri looked at the floor, and Susie began searching for something on the ceiling, counting the number of cottage cheese-looking pieces on the popcorn ceiling or hoping an answer would fall onto her head.

"Yeah, I didn't think so. What's on your docket, mister?"

"I have to write a dumb book report," he mumbled.

"Don't you have to know how to read to do that? Better get hoppin' on that pronto. No watching scrambled porn until you're done." Dimitri turned a very noticeable shade of red and exited.

"And you, Susie Q?"

"We have a spelling test tomorrow." She said, her eyes on Nina and no longer the ceiling.

"How do you spell go?"

"G-O." She answered without hesitation.

"Then that's what you should do, now, isn't it? If you get stuck, let me know."

She took a seat at the kitchen table and went over a list that her teacher sent her home with. She silently mouthed the words, then squinted at the descriptions of what each word meant.

"Sorry you had to see that ugliness," Nina smirked.

"It's cool. Besides, I don't even know the number for Child Protective Services."

While I wanted to sit with Nadia and watch Gumby thwart The Blockheads, I followed Nina to her room.

There were posters of The Cure, The Smiths, Depeche Mode, and I'll be damned if there wasn't the same poster that had been in Larry's classroom: that cat clinging to the tree branch for dear life was a sharp contrast to the moody music that she liked.

She caught me staring at the Hang in There cat.

"A little welcome-home gift from my mother. I don't have the heart to take it down and burn it."

"You'd have to have an actual heart."

"Ouch." She gave me a little sock on my arm.

She put on a record, The Smiths' *Meat is Murder*, and I was getting caught up in the lyrics of "How Soon is Now" because I, too, was human and just wanted to be loved. She started telling me about her family dynamic.

Her mother was working two jobs, sometimes three, which left Nina responsible for the younger kids. It also allowed her total freedom. When she had to work or needed a break, a kindly neighbor lady would look after them.

"Nadia's the best behaved. Susie has her bratty moments but knows how to work the cuteness factor." She paused and told me about her brother. "I feel bad for Dimitri, surrounded by all this estrogen. I really bust his chops, but I'm trying to toughen him up."

While she had a tough exterior, you could tell that she also had a marshmallow center.

"Yeah, he got pretty embarrassed about that porn comment," I said.

"Oh my god, I was the one who was embarrassed first. I caught him on the couch with his pants around his ankles. Kids, they grow up so fast. He sleeps in the living room while Nadia and Susie share a room. It's tight quarters around here for five people. Not that it would be any better if my deadbeat father were in the picture."

She launched into how her father, a Russian immigrant, had never pulled his weight in any capacity and had launched a Cold War against her mother with words meant to undermine her at every turn.

"Sounds like our dads should play golf," I said to break the tension.

"Or they could start The Bastards Club. I'd have to care about mine to actually hate him."

"Mine's no walk in the park, for sure." And I detailed how it was growing up the least favorite child of two.

"Damn, he sounds like a real dick!"

"Well, lately, he's mellowed. He's treating me with kid gloves, so I don't pull a repeat of... you know."

"I don't think I'll be trying my impression of Sleeping Beauty any time soon. If I'm not being too personal, why did you do it?"

"How much time do you have?"

I offered a CliffsNotes version of what had transpired, emphasizing the truth behind the lies that I had been telling myself. I did omit the part about Los Angeles, lest our conversation turn into a miniseries called "The Henry Dodge Story."

"I never tried meth," she said without judgment. "I'm hyper enough as it is. I like to slow down with a joint.'

"That is definitely in my wheelhouse," I confessed.

"Well, my friend, you are in luck." And she opened a childhood music box. A ballet dancer popped up with a joint in her outstretched arms while a refrain from Tchaikovsky's "Swan Lake" played.

"Well, that gets a P for presentation."

She grabbed the joint, bowed, opened a window, stuffed a towel under the door, and we sat on the floor. Since she loved to smoke clove cigarettes, she removed a lighter from her pocket and lit the joint so that we could get lit in turn.

She and I were no first-timers, so neither of us coughed. This didn't stop Dimitri from saying loudly in front of her bedroom door that it "smells like you're burning rope." Nina merely suppressed a giggle from becoming a full laugh.

"Helps me from getting to the end of my rope. Sister's little helper."

I felt an unfamiliar calm and trust. I had bared most of my soul for Nina, and she hadn't rejected me like Kevin had when I attempted to come out to him. We had been a surface friendship until I dug the grave for our time together with a shovel fortified with truth, exposing what I had been burying deep.

With Nina, I could be myself with no fear of repercussions.

"Man, this is strong stuff, I said, the beginnings of cotton mouth creeping over my tongue.

"Yeah, Jeff has the best shit."

I swiveled my head like the ventriloquist dummy that came to life in *Magic* and stared at her.

"What's with the one-man staring contest?"

"Jeff, that lives in Leucadia? The guy with the messed-up couch?"

"Oh damn, I fell down on my ass on that couch!"

"Ever think he's a little on the creepy side?"

"He's always nice to me. Never gave the 'ass, gas or grass' spiel, probably because he likes the dick and all."

I gave her the lowdown on him, including our encounter at San Luis Rey.

"Well, he's not the only game in town. I'm going to get my mean green from someone else."

Hopefully, Nina hadn't made the same mistake that I had in giving him my phone number once for him to let me know when a new shipment of Tina was available. I'm sure the last thing that she needed was her mother giving her a Nancy Reagan "Just Say No" speech. We were more of the "Just Say Yo" mindset.

"Let's go check on the hellspawn, err, my delightful family and see what's what." She stood and was the definition of being able to maintain.

I, on the other hand, felt like it might take a crane to extract me from my position on the floor. My legs had fallen asleep from sitting Indian style, and I did my best to scale up her bed to right myself. Once I sat upon her vacated bed, I met her raised eyebrow sheepishly.

"Lightweight."

"Hardly. Oh, and thanks for the help."

"If I've learned anything from our little chat, Henry Dodge, it is that you can fall down and get up again. Now shake it off."

I always found it interesting how people could see something in you that you couldn't see in yourself.

"Yes, ma'am!" I saluted her for full effect.

Once I could feel my legs again, with the echo of "It's a Christmas miracle!" pinballing in my brain, we headed to the living room. Nadia was transfixed by the adventures of *He-Man and The Masters of the Universe*; Susie was still poring over spelling words, and Dimitri was sequestered in his mother's room.

"Scooch over," Nina said to Nadia, who slid over in a zombie-like state.

I took the middle cushion, putting my hand down to avoid repeating what Nina and I had experienced at Jeff's. I was flanked by two out of three Sokolov females.

I looked at Nadia and hoped that Nina and my eyes weren't as glazed over as hers, being entranced by the boob tube. Currently, He-Man was Prince Adam, he of a slightly high-pitched voice, purple tights, matching quasi-Speedo, pink shirt, and a bowl cut.

"What queen came up with Prince Adam?" Nina whispered to me.

"Yes, he is definitely a little light in the boots. Fabulous secret powers, indeed!"

"He should live in Castle Gayskull!"

This cracked Nina and I up. Nadia, not so much, as she shushed us.

"Don't get me started on Fisto. Hello!" And this caused more eruptions of laughter and a bigger shush from Nadia.

"I'm trying to watch my show!"

"Sorry, we'll be quiet," Nina promised.

And that assurance only lasted momentarily. This time, Nadia got up, gave us both a death stare, and stormed off to her room.

"Something I said?" Nina called after her.

"Well, there goes her Miss Congeniality title!"

"Works every time," she whispered.

"You're so bad."

"So bad I'm good." She cooed ala Mae West. "Ok, enough of this kid's stuff."

She grabbed the remote from Nadia's vacated seat, reaching across my lap in a "boarding house reach" as my mom called it.

She flipped the channels until it landed, or shipwrecked, on *Gilligan's Island*. It was one of the early black-and-white episodes, and The Castaways were, as always, trying to get off the island. If I were them, I would be happy to live there.

"It's so stupid that they didn't add the Professor and Mary Ann to the theme song," I said.

"I know, like it was so difficult to do!"

"And the rest, my ass. Like without The Professor, they wouldn't have any chance of surviving, even if he couldn't fix a hole in a boat."

"And who can make a coconut cream pie without flour or even an oven?"

"Gee, I never thought of it that way. And don't you think that they would have banished Gilligan to the other side of the island after the first twenty times that he screwed up them being rescued?"

After two episodes of the survivors of the S.S. Minnow, it was time to head home. I had an hour to get my stoned wits about me before the parental units would be home, plus Shadow would need to be let out to do her business.

She walked me out to L'il Red and told me she had a blast, and I reciprocated the sentiment.

"I'm off like a dirty shirt."

"Blaine? His name is Blaine? That's not a name! It's a major appliance!"

Obviously, we also shared a love of John Hughes movies, amongst so many other things. If my love life had taught me anything, I had to be careful not to be a lesbian in this given situation. There would be no mix tapes to express feelings that I was at a loss for. I didn't want to scare her off.

I directed L'il Red towards home, with the words of the Pet Shop Boys echoing in my ear from memory and not my ever-trusty Walkman, as I took a ride to "Suburbia" to run with the dogs tonight. Or walk mine in the afternoon, if I could shake off this lazy haze.

While I was not currently feeling like I was living in this suburban hell, as their lyrics described, I had felt the fires of loneliness lapping at my heels, fueled by the powder keg that Tina provided. I really hoped that I was strong enough to resist her, but imagined her slow-burn method to feed my addiction was never going to have a good outcome. Still.

"You like the flames, Henry, don't cha?" I asked myself as I pulled onto Arroyo Street.

Well, if I played with fire, I was going to get burned.

I pulled my scooter into the garage next to my Dad's Goldwing. Big Ed was home early. Damn. I went inside, each step taken with trepidation.

Shadow, a greeting committee of one, was extremely excited that I was home, jumping up on me, and then ran towards the sliding glass door. I was half-expecting it to be wide open, signaling more underwear would need to be replaced. Screen door slashed beyond recognition, but it remained intact. I joined Shadow outside, deciding in my stoner state that a rousing game of soccer was a better option than a stumble, I mean, a walk.

Shadow would stop the ball with her nose and then edge it towards me and run back to her spot. And the game would continue like this until I usually tired of it before she would.

Crouching on the back lawn was the sweetest girl ever. I found it sad that most people thought pit bulls were killers. She would never hurt anyone. It was a case of training, but I detected distrustful looks from people when I walked her. I really wanted to get some toothpaste, brush her teeth, and make it appear that she was foaming at the mouth. Just for shits and giggles.

"Let's go inside, sweet girl."

Her answer was to nudge the ball a little further. I patted my thigh and told her to come, and she obeyed, albeit defiantly. I went upstairs and checked the answering machine. The red light was blinking off and on.

I stood in the doorway in a moment of indecision that seemed to last forever. Eventually, I crossed the blue and green rug in what had once been John's room and pressed the button, which alerted me that there was just a single message.

"Hi Henry, this is Erik. Good news: We want you on board here. Give me a call so we can discuss details."

Amazed, I played the message back several times to make sure that I heard correctly because I didn't believe it. Also, I was that high.

I called, and Erik asked if I could start on Monday. I answered as though I was having an out-of-body experience, and he said I should pick up my uniform beforehand.

But my sweaty palms told me that I occupied Henry Dodge's body and was not some sort of interloper. This time, I skipped all the way to my room and then stopped mid-skip. I hoped that I didn't sound wasted, but he didn't question my sobriety, so I was in the clear. I went to my window, sure that the skies would be as blue as my mother's eyes and that there would be a thousand birds singing my praises.

What I also saw was Big Ed crossing the street from the Woodson house. It had been a few months since Mr. Woodson had called Arroyo Street home, leaving Doreen Woodson to fend for herself.

He strode across the street and made his way to the house, and I decided to tell him of my good news. As I hit the last stair, I saw a strange sight: the man, usually not vain, was fixing his hair in the mirror. He tugged at his white t-shirt, like it was ill-fitting, but was looking down at it like he was searching for the meaning of life. He began smoothing out a road map of wrinkles on his after-work uniform when he detected my presence.

"Oh. Hey. You're. Home," he said, in a monosyllabic delivery, affirming my belief that he must be descended from Neanderthals.

"In the flesh."

"Uh, how was your day?" he asked tenuously.

"I got a job at AMC!"

I suddenly noticed that not only was his shirt on backwards, but there was a red smudge on it.

"You get dressed in the dark?" I asked innocently, though my bullshit detector was set on high.

He looked very uneasy, which quickly went into something that looked like terror.

"Mrs. Woodson needed some help. Guess I wasn't paying attention."

"Were you painting something for her?"

He looked at me quizzically. That may as well have been him saying, "Beg your pardon?" He pulled the back of his shirt so that he could get a better look at it, a smudge that looked suspiciously like lipstick.

"Good eye. She asked if, uh, I would paint a red accent wall in her living room."

"Red. Huh, that's an interesting choice. Remember when mom told us the story about how grandfather told her she couldn't wear red shoes because only *whores* wore those?"

"So, you got a job in one day? See what happens when you apply yourself?" He was happy to change the topic.

"It's amazing what a person can get done in a day," I shot back with a brazen sneer. "Well, this has been ultra-stimulating, but I'm going to work on some drawings. Maybe something in red. Thanks for the inspiration, Pops."

He stood silently, knowing I had the upper hand, and it would be curtains for him if I told Mom about what I suspected had happened across the street at The Worst Little Whorehouse in California.

To quote PSA-based ventriloquist Willie Tyler via his partner-in-crime, Lester. "I may be a dummy, but I ain't no fool!" Even if I hadn't said "Nope to dope and ugh to drugs" today.

I sat on my bed, seeing red over the lipstick. Rather than stew about it, I decided to distract myself by practicing my craft. However, I decided against red, opting for black, the color I figured was in synchronicity with his heart and soul.

I was mid-pencil stroke when a noise in the hall distracted me. Big Ed was carrying a basket of laundry down to the garage, a sight I'd never witnessed in almost 18 years on this planet. Oh yeah, motherfucker was guilty as sin. I wanted to call him out on it while he was Shouting out the lipstick smear, but I wanted him to twist in the wind, just like the knife that would be plunged into Mom's heart if she found out.

I closed my door and went back to the task at hand until I heard the Dodge Ram van outside. The engine turned off with a little bit of a cough and the sound of the driver's side door slamming.

I soon heard a raised voice coming from downstairs. When I opened my door, I heard my mother going to town about what a piece of "sugar" the van had become. It was abundantly clear that she was standing firm in her convictions about wanting a new car.

"It died on me at the stoplight on Encinitas Boulevard, Ed. People were honking at me and using their middle fingers to tell me what they thought of that *van* holding them up!"

"Now, Katie, calm down. I'll look at it this weekend."

Visions of 9/16th wrenches danced through my head. Perhaps if I pulled out my best Faye Dunaway in *Mommie Dearest* and defiantly proclaimed, there would be "No 9/16th's ever!" that it would somehow get me out of helping Big Ed. Doubtful. But it would be worth a try, at least. My own mother was having a very Joan Crawford moment, putting the kibosh on the threat of that dreaded chore.

"While you do, I'll be looking for a new car. Do whatever floats your boat, Ed. But I am done with that *thing*. It was fine when the boys were younger, but we don't need it now."

"Yeah, you're right," he said, surprising us both with his out-of-character caving in.

"Damn straight, I'm right!"

Ooh, she said the D-word!

"Alright, we'll go and look for something new on Saturday," said the man who knew all about finding something new.

"Good!"

Ever since she'd gone to work, there had been a slight shift in the balance of power in our house. Subtle things at best, she was always going to be that worrywart that cared a little too much about other people rather than for herself. But she was different, too.

She ascended the stairs and went into her room, unaware that I had been eavesdropping. But he followed her, saw me standing in the doorway, and I gave him a raised eyebrow as a greeting.

He didn't react; just looked right through me, and I, in turn, saw right through him.

Dinner was tense at best; the only person who spoke was Big Ed, peppering the silence with praise for the bland meal of macaroni and cheese with hamburger.

Mom gave a curt smile that signaled she wasn't buying his big bag of bullshit. When we were done, and Big Ed went to watch the news, I told her

I would clean up. Then my plan was to cheer her up with news of the new job. But she turned in early.

I had my chance the next morning before she went to work at 10. My news was met with the joy and acclaim that I would not have received the night before, making me feel good that I had given her less reason to stress about me.

"Don't forget to call and make an appointment with your doctor," she said before leaving for work.

Hold up! Did she know about my HIV test? No, she had meant an appointment with David.

"I left his card by your phone. Make sure you put it away."

"Sure thing, Mom," I said, knowing it was highly doubtful Big Ed would go into my room.

My thoughts turned to the work that lay ahead for me. David and I had started to scratch the surface of what drove me to my self-destructive patterns. I was filled with trepidation about diving deeper into my soul, getting to the heart of the matter. What awaited me at those murky depths?

I decided to act on this right away, skirting my usual procrastination ways. The card had two different numbers: one for San Luis Rey and the other for his private practice.

I opted to try to reach him at my former stomping grounds first. The unmistakable sourpuss tone of Nurse Wretched was on the other end, and I was tempted to just hang up. But I hadn't backed down from her in person - so why now via Ma Bell?

"Dr. Chan, please," I said with an air of authority that frightened me.

"May I ask who is calling?"

"First name, Nunya. Last name, Business."

"Oh, it's *you*," she snarled. "He's not available. He's helping another pathetic homosexual at present. May I take a message?"

"Well, here's a message for you, but it's hard for you to see. But here's a hint. Guess how many fingers I'm holding up?"

She slammed the phone receiver in my ear, a clear sign that I had gotten under her skin again. Eat it bitch! But how in the hell was she back? What happened to her suspension? I shuddered at the thought that she was free to terrorize again.

I didn't want to spend any time thinking about it or her. I went over to my ghetto blaster and pushed play on Janet Jackson's *Control* – because, according to the title track, it was all about that. And I needed to fortify myself with having lots of it.

Ms. Jackson had encapsulated what I was feeling perfectly. A lack of self-control had shipwrecked me on my own secluded island. Once the music erased the sourness of Nurse Wretched from my system, I dialed David's other number.

I got his answering machine and left the pertinent information of who I was and what my phone number was, deciding to move my one-man dance party into the bathroom and take a shower. I was toweling off when I heard the phone ringing over "The Pleasure Principal."

David was on the line, informing me that he had a last-minute cancellation, which equaled an opening at 1. As I really didn't have anything better to do, I answered in the affirmative, leaving me with literal time on my hands until my appointment.

I could watch TV or read a book, but Shadow came into view, nudging me with her head. I decided we could both benefit from some fresh air.

The day was cloudy and cool, with little shafts of sunlight poking through the clouds here and there, as if God was keeping a watchful eye on me. Doubtful. I tried to focus on playing our usual game of Hide and Seek, but I was half-hearted compared to Shadow's unencumbered enthusiasm. On our way home, I was lost in a million thoughts. It was no surprise that I didn't notice the car that had followed us to our playground. Nor did I know that the driver sitting behind the wheel had parked near where we had entered and were now making our exit.

Once we got to the front door and I unlocked it, I made an omelet. While it cooked, I called Nina, her number already committed to memory.

"Whatcha doin'?"

"Going to work in a bit."

"Speaking of, I'll be working with you! I start Monday."

"That's awesome!"

"And on the not-so-awesome front, I have my first session with David today. I feel like I'm crawling out of my skin."

"Why's that?"

"I feel like opening up may have the opposite effect, and I'll shut down," I confessed.

"I'm a good listener. Hit me with your best shot. Fire away."

"Thanks, Pat," I chuckled. But where to start? I didn't want to unload all my baggage on Nina for fear of scaring her off. However, after turning down the flame cooking my breakfast; I told it true about the trepidation of finding out the why behind my behavior. The next sticky wicket, I informed her, was my date with medical destiny next week.

"I'll go with you if you want."

"You'd do that?"

"Psyche! Of course, I will. You're my friend. There's something about you, Henry."

"Why, that's mighty Level 42 of you."

"Consider it my lesson in love, friend. Ok, I've gotta go. But you can talk to me about anything."

Dammit, if she didn't pull me out of my funk. It gave me hope that the session with David may prove fruitful, as the things that I held onto inside with a death grip could be released. I had forgotten to tell her about Nurse Wretched, but I'd keep that to myself as our friendship was moving away from how we had met.

Surprisingly, the omelet turned out perfectly. Slow and low was the key to it not burning; perhaps I could apply that own mantra to my life.

"Slow and low, Henry. Slow and low." I said aloud to an audience of one.

My mistake...make that an audience of two, as Shadow sat watching me eat my late breakfast, hoping for a bite, as perusual. Her eyes watching every bite I took, and I would emphasize each one with an over-the-top "Mmm," like I was auditioning for a commercial. She would shift her body a little bit, edging closer to me by scooching her butt on the floor, faux-shaking the whole time as if she hadn't had her own breakfast.

"Man, am I stuffed!" I exclaimed when there was just a single bite left. "Sure wish I knew a cute girl I could give this to. Do you know who would like this?"

I addressed Shadow as if she could answer back. A slight whimper emphasized her communication skills, as did a small strand of drool that landed on the white patch on her chest.

"Oh well, I can't think of anyone either." I stabbed the last bit of egg and cheese and started to guide it towards my mouth until Miss Shadow nuzzled up to me, summoning every ounce of cuteness.

"Oh? Would *you* like some?"

Her answer was to take the food from the fork and lick her lips after she finished, her version of "my compliments to the chef."

I gave her a skritch behind the ears, then saw that it was time to get going, as David's office was in Carlsbad. Time may fly when you're having fun, but I didn't think that the person who coined that phrase had thought about the opposite of that sentiment in that time drags like a motherfucker when you have to wait. Should I branch out creatively into coming up with greeting cards for Hallmark?

Well, that imagined endeavor would have to wait. I had the all-too-real task of first cleaning the omelet pan, to not leave a mess for Mom, and then "ride like the wind, to be free again" on 'Lil Red.

"Be a good girl," I said to Shadow. "I'll be back in a bit."

Rather than take the freeway, which meant I'd have to wear my helmet, I opted for the more scenic drive. The office building where David practiced what he preached loomed large just past the Army/Navy Academy that Big Ed had threatened to make me attend when he learned I was ditching school.

A group of cadets were running around the track. Although it was January and a "chilly" 68 today, they were glistening with sweat. I was overcome with a feeling that seemed like a distant memory, being horny. I still hadn't taken care of any personal business since leaving San Luis Rey; that was highly unusual behavior for me, and grounds for me being re-committed to the mental health equivalent of being shipped off to Shady Pines, Ma.

I looked down at my appropriately named "Tutti Frutti" white Swatch watch. The purple, what appeared to be a melon slice, informed me that I had a good ten minutes until my session. I pulled off to the side of the road, across the street from what could have been my alma mater.

I suspected that if I just sat there and stared, I would be akin to the guy in the white, windowless van offering free candy. Although I wouldn't need a sugary treat, as I felt like a kid that was already set loose in a confectionery store. I feigned checking the tires of the scooter while the mental strains of Madonna's "Physical Attraction" played in the jukebox of my mind.

Aside from the guys running track, there were others doing push-ups, jumping jacks, and a shirts/skins game of football while the beefy drill sergeants barked orders. Damn! Why had I not taken Big Ed up on his bluff of making me attend here again?

Oh, that's right. It would be like sending me into the lion's den wearing a suit made of pork chops, always at the ready to be torn to shreds. As I took one final look at the backfield in motion, I let out a big sigh and drove off.

I supposed it wouldn't hurt to relieve some tension when I got home, fire up the jets on the Jacuzzi, then see if I still had some weed squired away in one of the dozen places it could be in my room. Never hide weed when you're stoned, kids.

Now I just had to get through the next hour, parking L'il Red, and then looking for Suite G. I found it by using the alphabet that *Sesame Street* had helped me learn. TV was the definitive babysitter in the Dodge home. I was raised on Mike Brady's life lessons, learned about being gay from *Soap*, and how to channel my uber-bitch from Alexis Morrell-Carrington-Colby-Dexter. It was as if I had embodied Malcolm McDowell's Alex character in *A Clockwork Orange* when his eyes are clamped open, but my TV watching hadn't been forced, it was a way to while away the hours until my next disappointment.

I stood outside of Suite G as though it were a crossroads. If there was ever a case for something being now or never, this was certainly it. And if I didn't venture into what made me tick, I may never do it, and an actual shiver ran down my spine.

It was akin to what John referred to as a "pee shiver," meaning it was his body's way of telling him he had to take a piss before his bladder informed him of it. It felt like all the liquid had dried up in my body, most certainly in my mouth. I wished that he were here to help me navigate all these landmines, personal traps laid by yours truly, along with the bomb that my dad's secret behavior had dropped on me yesterday.

I decided it was time to stop the mental back-and-forth by walking through the door. There was a small waiting room and a middle-aged receptionist with cat-eye glasses and gray hair swept into an up-do – a character right out of Gary Larson's *Far Side* comic strip.

"May I help you?" Her glasses sliding down the bridge of her nose, giving the impression she was sizing me up, determining what brand of crazy I was bringing in with me.

"Damn glasses!" She muttered and pushed them back into place.

"I have an appointment with David."

"One moment." She even held up her finger as if I were just grasping the English language, speaking slowly, and picked up the phone. "Your one o'clock is here."

I was resigned to being a designated time slot and not a flesh-and-blood person.

"Have a seat, young man. He will be right with you."

David soon emerged and approached me.

"You ready Henry?"

And that was the question of the hour. I rose from the chair and simply nodded. I followed him, looking for the couch I was probably supposed to lie down on and spill my deepest, darkest secrets. Instead, there were two chairs below the psychology diploma he received five years ago.

He extended his hand, and I sat down as if sentenced to the electric chair.

"So, how are you doing today?"

My need to be a people pleaser, the not-so-straight A student, was kicking into overdrive. I wanted to answer that everything was never better and have him excuse me from the session because I was obviously cured.

"If I said 'great,' would you buy it?"

"Not even for a penny. You looked stressed out."

"Yeah, that's the understatement of the century."

"What's on your mind?"

"It feels like a ton of bricks are on me, honestly."

"Care to elaborate?"

I filled in the outlines of what was troubling me, a barrage of information concerning the uncertainty of what my HIV test would reveal. He would jot things down on his ever-present yellow notepad.

"Naturally, fear of the unknown can weigh you down. Do you have any outlets to keep you preoccupied?"

"I guess." But my typical escape routes would not serve my needs. I obviously didn't want to have sex with anyone, my concentration was certainly not all there for artwork, and I didn't want to go anywhere near Jeff's apartment to score.

"Hang on one second." David went over to his desk, rifled through a folder, and came back with a familiar-looking piece of paper.

"Larry showed this to me, and I have to say that you have some talent inside of you. Why not let it out? Get those thoughts and feelings down on paper. Also, have you considered keeping a journal?"

I could just see it now.

"Dear Diary,

You'll never believe what happened today!!! Biff asked me to the sock hop!!! I said yes. Which poodle skirt says I'm not putting out on the first date? Well, maybe I'll let him get to second base. He's dreamy!!!"

"Not really. Sounds kind of gay."

"Well, then it should be right up your alley."

Oof, I didn't ever want to think of anything alley-related again, for the obvious reasons being Danny and Angel.

"Look out! Robin Williams has some stiff competition."

"But seriously. I think that you could have a two-fold way of dealing with the things that you want to express but don't verbally."

This was absolutely true. There were things that I didn't want to address for sure, even with myself. Creativity could prove to be the conduit that linked my heart and mind together in a cleansing burst of synchronicity.

"I suppose I could try it," I said this in a monotone voice, looking at my Nikes.

"Try to cap that enthusiasm, Henry. I think you will be surprised."

"It would have been easier to do when I was on meth," I accidentally said.

Fuck!

I raised my head and met his eyes, sure mine read as "The jig's up, Dodge." I couldn't believe I had turned my little brother propensity for ratting someone out on myself.

"Oh really? Do tell," he said evenly.

I gave him the abridged version of the Tina Chronicles, not explaining how this was my self-prescribed medicine to deal with the memories of LA, giving me a way to circumvent those post-traumatic feelings, protecting me from the nightmares when I closed my eyes.

"Are you still using?"

"I haven't since…you know."

"Before you got your new fashion accessories?" He directed his eyes at my bandages, partially peeking out from my sleeves that I wished were longer.

"You certainly have a way with words. You should keep a journal." I said the last word with venom.

"I do, actually."

"It's not just for fucked-up people? Duly noted."

"You are not fucked up, Henry. Everyone goes through rough times. It's how you cope with those times that defines who you are. If you have good coping mechanisms in your arsenal, you can fight those wars being waged inside. Make sense?"

As much as I hated to admit it, it made perfect sense. This guy was good. He could have helped Norman Bates with his unhealthy mother fixation. I was feeling less psycho and more hopeful. The trouble was I couldn't move in here and have David at my disposal 24/7. There was a great big scary world lurking outside of Suite G, and I was going to try my best to navigate it.

"Do me a favor. If you do want to use again, play the tape all the way through and get to the outcome of how it makes you feel. You had a lot of resistance to meetings at the hospital. You should reconsider attending one. It would do you a world of good."

He went back to his desk and procured an AA meeting schedule pamphlet. What was it with him and the pamphlets? Like something written inside of a folded piece of card stock held the solutions to all of life's problems. I resentfully stuffed it into my pocket, making a mental note to toss it out before Mom found it while doing laundry.

"Our time is up. But you have homework."

"*Please don't let it be math problems!*" I shouted in my head. Besides, I didn't know the square root of crazy.

"OK," I said skeptically.

"Bring me one drawing each week, along with a little writing on what it means to you."

"Will I be graded on this?"

"That is for me to know and for you to find out. I would like to see you once a week. Can you do Thursdays?"

"I have to see if I'm going to be working those days."

"Wait, you got a job? That's wonderful! You should have led with that."

"Well, I don't like to brag." I brushed my chest like I was shining an apple.

"You can schedule an appointment with Karen. I will see you next week."

As I left, I ran into his next patient.

"Why, if it isn't Heather. How's tricks, hooker?"

I really needed to cap the unique brand of Tourette's Syndrome I suffered from.

"Sorry, that was bitchy." I offered sincerely.

"I wouldn't expect anything less from a rotten queer," she huffed and stormed off to David's office.

I would catch shit from David the next time that I saw him. I imagined there would be a sign in the waiting room the next time, alerting patients to "Please don't disturb the crazies."

I turned to say goodbye to Karen, but the disapproving look on her face told me I should beat a hasty retreat.

Admittedly, I did drive slowly by the Army Navy Academy, watching a few shirtless runners making their way around the dirt track, planting the seed that I should spill mine when I got home. Naturally, I hit every red light between Carlsbad and Encinitas, and despite that, I managed to remain upbeat, humming Michael Jackson's "Beat It."

Driving up Arroyo Street, I saw Mrs. Woodson at her mailbox with black letters declaring that the Woodsons lived there, although it was just her now. Her son scot-free, in his old West Hollywood haunts, which had proven to be a nightmare for me and a husband who had now been replaced by my mother's. At least in the bedroom. I shook that visual out of my head immediately, lest it get stuck in there and ruin my designs for the afternoon.

She offered a mild wave, knowing full well that I couldn't stand her. I was tempted to give a one-finger salute but didn't want her to get any ideas in that empty head of hers that I may be onto her and my father's duplicitous affair.

I pretended like I didn't see her, even though I saw right through that bitch.

With L'il Red in her designated parking spot and Shadow released to the yard, I went upstairs and changed into my bathing suit. It was just in case Big Ed came home unexpectedly early again. I really wished that I could return to those halcyon days of being The Invisible Boy, remaining undetected by him, quickly disappearing into a vapor of smoke in his sightline.

The thought of smoke made me crave the last remaining bit of the mean green that I had gotten from Craig a lifetime ago. The dilemma was that I couldn't quite remember where I had stashed it - damn, short-term memory loss!

I went through every tape I had, including the very first one that I had saved up for, Bryan Adams' *Cuts Like a Knife*. And this search was cutting me to the quick, slicing me open, exposing my addictive personality.

I began checking behind the books on the bookshelf when it came to me. It was stashed in a miniature treasure chest from childhood and it contained the booty I was craving.

"There you are you little minx."

I was very glad that Craig had given me a joint, as rolling one was never something that I could master. If it had been a bud, then I would have had to fashion a makeshift pipe out of a Pepsi can. So gauche! But it came in handy when my apparatus had mysteriously disappeared after one of Mom's sweeps on my room.

"Aar Katie, ya didn't think to look here." I sounded less Blackbeard and more like Tommy O'Doyle Shanahan, as I named my Irish impression.

All I needed was what Jim Morrison had sung about, an implement to "Light My Fire," or to light my joint in this case. The house was devoid of lighters since Mom quit smoking when I was seven. Big Ed still had the occasional stinky-ass cigar, but I couldn't track down a book of matches. I could light it on the stove, but the smell might linger in the kitchen.

"Damn. Double damn!"

I heard Shadow barking out back. My eyes fell upon the box of big matches on the fireplace. I took the box of huge matches outside, and Shadow began edging the soccer ball to me.

"Not now, girl. Daddy needs his medicine."

Toking in the back of the greenhouse was just what the doctor ordered. An immediate sense of calm overcame me. I didn't care if the smoke signals I was putting out into the air of Arroyo Street spelled out that a stoner resided at 532.

I snuffed the joint and returned the matches to their appointed spot, even moving them several times to make sure that I got them back correctly, lest it raise suspicions with my parents. I went back out to the yard and stopped; I had forgotten a towel in my quest for cannabis.

I grabbed one, then got just as far as before when I realized that a cup of water from the dispenser on our newfangled refrigerator would certainly hit the spot.

I entered the greenhouse, locked the door, drew the blinds, pulled off the blue foam Jacuzzi cover, turned on the jets, and checked the temperature. It wasn't as warm as I had hoped it would be, given the fact that Big Ed had installed solar panels on the greenhouse roof and it wasn't the warmest of days.

I stripped off my clothes and threw them on the floor, hot and bothered. I dropped on all fours, flattened myself, becoming one with the floor, and shimmied between the floorboards and the bottom step leading up to the healing waters.

The smell of earth filled my nostrils, and it was a strangely comforting scent that I would forever associate with my hidden stash of *Playgirl* magazines. I had a narrow escape once when the jets wouldn't work, and Big Ed pulled up the floorboards right above my cache. Fortunately, I had placed them all face-down, and his only comment was, "John better not let your mother find these." I did not say anything because I wasn't in my body at that precise moment.

But I was in it now, as a stirring started in my gut and spread all through the rest of my body until it reached the area referred to as a "groin" in medical terms. I laid my towel down dropped to my knees, and that's when the boner killer happened. I was naked except for the bandages over my wrists. I didn't want to take them off, nor have the sight of what they represented detract me from what I wanted to do.

The solution came in moving the magazine to the top edge of the towel, avoiding a gaze downward, and then all would be right in my private world. And it felt good to get in touch with myself, to let everything go for a bit. Especially with the nude visage of Sam Jones, AKA Flash Gordon, encouraging me. The celebrity nude issue was a definite favorite. And before I knew it, I suddenly released every pent-up frustration all over the towel.

I calmed my breathing.

"Remember to focus on your breathing. It's the first thing we do when we enter the world and the last thing we do as we exit," the spectral voice of David said. It brought reality crashing down all around me.

"Motherfucker."

I tried to stop the tears that wanted to spill from me more forcefully than my orgasm.

When I opened my eyes, I saw a 17-year-old version of Danny sitting in the Jacuzzi, the summer my crush on him hadn't yet achieved crushed status.

"Come on in; the water's fine."

My jaw dropped, my heart raced, and my eyes closed firmly. When I gathered the courage to open them peepers of mine, he was gone.

Jeepers creepers, this was some good pot.

And then I heard a hand on the greenhouse doorknob.

Oh shit! Dad must have come home early, and I was going to be caught red-handed. Well, red-palmed was a more appropriate assessment.

"Occupato," I called out in solidarity with the tiled sign that hung outside above the door that let people know that the greenhouse was a case of "Mi casa, es su casa."

Another attempt on the knob made me throw the magazine into the space between, fold my towel, and put my bathing suit on.

I opened the door and found no one there.

Well, almost nobody.

Shadow was lying on the winter brown grass, gnawing happily on a soup bone. It wasn't like my dad to give her treats like that. Maybe Mom had begged off work and returned early, courtesy of one of the migraines that plagued her from time to time? They usually surfaced after she and Big Ed argued.

The sliding door was open, and given my current state of mind, I couldn't remember if I had closed it, even though my buzz was fading fast. Something didn't feel quite right, especially after I called out to her, not for a drink of water in the middle of the night as I had been apt to do as a child.

I switched gears and called out with a "Hello?" But I quickly quashed doing that, as that was usually the time when movie psychopaths popped out and plunged a knife, machete or finger knives into the person wondering who was in their vicinity.

Well, I figured I'd take a page out of the final girl's playbook and go into the kitchen and grab a butcher knife. A final girl could never be too careful.

I slowly made my way through the house, remaining as stealthy as possible so as not to give out my position to the intruder. As I broached the stairs, I was careful to stay in the middle, lest Mrs. Bates come out of hiding either in my parent's bedroom on the left or the hallway on the right.

The handle of the knife was slick with sweat due to my undiagnosed hyperhidrosis, but I didn't want to pause and wipe my hands on my bathing suit. I reached the top of the landing, and much like crossing the street, I looked left, then right, the left again as I had been taught.

In Mom and Dad's room, there was nothing amiss. I went around to the right side of their bed and checked under it. Nope, nothing to see there.

The bathroom and the closet door were open.The closet was as dark as the midnight hour, and I totally expected the *Friday the 13th* theme of "kill

kill kill ma ma ma" to start as I walked over to it and flipped the light switch. I checked under the clothes hung on hangers and led down to pairs of shoes, searching for an unfamiliar pair attached to a lunatic.

I gave the closet the all-clear and went to the much brighter bathroom when my overactive imagination decided to grace me with its presence with the intro from my Saturday night staple, *Tales from the Darkside*. "Man lives in the sunlit world of what he believes to be reality. But there is, unseen by most, an underworld, a place just as real, but not as brightly lit…a darkside."

But the realm of the bathroom held nothing within its four walls, be it man, beast, or deranged lunatic.

It was time to walk the hallway, something I had done countless times but never in full Jamie Lee Curtis mode. My pitch-black bathroom was fraught with endless possibilities of what could be lying in wait for me. Flipping on the light illuminated the fact that I may be on a wild goose chase. So did checking John's bedroom, mine, and the extra room designated for visitors. None of them contained an interloper.

"What in the actual fuck?" I said and clamped my left hand over my mouth. The bandages briefly gave me a butterfly kiss, gentle in nature but coarse to the touch. I may have given myself up, just like Danny's ghost in the Jacuzzi had disappeared.

My hours of watching *Scooby-Doo* caught up with me in hunting a spooky specter. But who would be the person underneath the sheet? Certainly not old man Withers, given the fact that I knew no one with that surname.

I did a clean sweep of the kitchen, living room, and dining rooms. Nada. I was going down the three steps into the den when I heard the gate slam shut. I ran out back and heard the sound of shoes running down the breezeway between our house and our next-door neighbors. I caught a brief glance of a shadow figure getting into a car.

I broke into a gallop, then realized I was running onto the driveway with a knife in my hand. I tossed it aside and made my way down the driveway. My mother's spectral question of "What would the neighbors think?" being the deciding factor in forsaking a final girl's ultimate rule: Do not get rid of your weapon! Oh, and don't die was up there, too!

I usually didn't give a fuck, not a single solitary one, but this went a little beyond the norm of being "that gay kid," as I had heard Mrs. Bentley say to Mrs. Delacruz when I was walking Shadow.

But it was all for naught. I had been outrun as a white Honda Civic tore off down the street.

The brave side of me wanted to jump on L'il Red and give chase. The usually absent logical side pointed out that by the time I got my scooter into gear, I wouldn't know if the car had turned left or right onto Encinitas Boulevard.

This sounded like a remarkable story for Robert Stack and the team at *Unsolved Mysteries*. I let out a huge sigh, which matched the deflated feeling I had in the pit of my stomach. Would this stranger be back for a return engagement? What if it was just my mother at home alone when that occurred? The conundrum of whether I should make mention of it to the parentals was at odds with the dichotomy of being a truth seeker and truth hider.

I didn't want to cause her any undue stress. As for him, well, that was another quandary. Even though I was onto his strange behavior as of late and was more of the mindset of he didn't really care about me - then why should I care about him? Still, I didn't want anything bad to happen to him. Even if he was just as capable with his fists as he was with his words that hurt, which had left me as a wounded child, a broken thing.

I retraced my steps, picked up the knife, closed the gate, and turned off the closet and then the bathroom lights. When I returned the knife to the drawer, a thought struck me, a bolt of lightning that seared into my brain.

I ran out to the backyard and took the bone away from Shadow. If someone was ballsy enough not to break in, they might give her a bone slathered with poison. She thought we were engaging in a game of Tug-O-War, but I was not playing around.

I tossed it out in the trash can on the side of the house, burying it underneath an existing bag of garbage, an act that was hauntingly familiar. I was surprised to not find my long-ago sketchbook in there, held in Danny's holographic hand.

"Who you gonna call? Ghostbusters, bitch!"

I wanted to be done with the boys of the summer of '85 and their lasting grasp on me. David was going to get his money's worth when I put him through the paces of trying to fix me.

Shadow was lying on the grass, the lackluster wagging of her tail informing me she was upset with me.

"Come here, girl."

She stayed put.

"Who's a good girl?" My voice was sugary sweet. This time she answered with a medium wag and then nuzzled my outstretched hand as if to say, "Aww, I can't stay mad at you."

I thought that if she had anything bad in her system, then the symptoms would be immediate. I had to be vigilant and watch her closely. How would I explain it to the vet?

I walked into the greenhouse when I saw my towel was missing. This thief had a strange penchant for taking things that only belonged to me. He must have doubled back and retrieved it. As I crawled into my own cave of wonders, there was another visual surprise in store for me.

On top of the *Playgirl* were two pieces of rope and a scrunched-up strip of duct tape. I shoved them way under the floorboards. I was spooked now. How could I ever come back out here and perform my ritual again? I gathered up my instruments of pleasure, making quick work of tossing the rope and duct tape under the floorboards. I hoped they rotted, disintegrated beyond recognition, and wished the same for the person who intended to make me a kidnapping victim.

But who would want to do that?

I was numb inside, going through the motions of turning off the jets, covering the Jacuzzi, and raising the blinds. I had shaky hands and an utter feeling of fear and dread. I closed and locked the sliding glass door, placing the dowel Dad had fashioned to keep it secure. But how safe was I really? Glass could shatter just as surely as my sense of security.

Big Ed did own a gun that I had been coaxed into firing during a few trips out to the desert to do away with an army of Budweiser cans that he would down beforehand. But that was locked away in a small safe in the garage.

I certainly couldn't ask him for the combination, even if I slid into conversation at the dinner table.

"Pass the broccoli. Oh, and what's the combination for the safe?"

Who did I think I was going to be anyway, Dirty Harry? Even though I was no Clint Eastwood in being a dead aim, shockingly having not missed all intended targets in the dry oasis, I could certainly point it at this unknown asshole and give him a solid, "Go ahead, make my gay!"

But there was one positive upswing: the scattered nature of my brain had been replaced with a singular theme of figuring out who had it out for me.

Naturally, my mind went into the dark corners of my past. Was Danny back in the neighborhood, angry about my testimony during his botched trial?

Going down the list of could-be abductors, I couldn't have upset Angel enough to warrant this type of retaliation. Doubtful. George was out of the picture. His son was done with me once he got what he wanted in the name of pleasure. That left Nick, who was conspicuously absent from the legal proceedings. Had he been off stewing in his own juices, cursing me for unintentionally crumbling an empire he had a stake in? Somehow, I doubted that he had turned in his boat of a car for something less luxurious. Besides, that would be akin to him purchasing a clown car, given his girth.

He had only tried to help me before, so I was at a loss; I had to gain insight into the five journalistic cornerstones. But only who, what, and why remained. The how had been obvious, as was the where.

In my mind's eye, I put the contents of Los Angeles memories in a box marked "hazardous" away into a dusty corner among the spiders. I wanted to fortify them with something stronger than an arachnid's silky filament. The thought of using rope caused me to utter "Godammit" before landing on using a lock and chains fortified from steel to secure this Pandora's Box. The lid threatened to pop open like a maniacal Jack-in-the-Box, but I secured it with more chains and dual padlocks. How long it would hold was solely up to me. The haven of my room sounded mighty inviting. As did the solace of immersing myself in my art; that seemed like a positive to counterbalance the negativity of…Nope, wasn't going to go down that road, especially after a field of stop signs rose to stop those thoughts.

I stashed the *Playgirl*s in a better hiding place among the multitude of magazines in a wooden rack next to my bookshelf. I would find a better Kate-Dodge-proof spot for them later.

Right now, inspiration had a hold of me, and I didn't want it to let go. Grabbing a pencil and my notebook, I plopped down into my bean bag chair. When I heard the garage door open, my heart stopped, but the familiar sound of Big Ed's Goldwing was oddly reassuring.

I had been working on my sketch for nearly two hours without even noticing the time. I was definitely in a zone with the image I was creating. But I made sure that Shadow was above board. She didn't show any signs that there was anything wrong with her health, and I was relieved.

Big Ed was at my door. He was home on time, so he hadn't stopped in to "help" Doreen.

"How's your day been?" he asked nicely – as if I were John.

Knowing the honest answer would knock his socks off, I just shrugged. And I certainly couldn't tell him about my session with David.

"It was OK. I'm kind of busy. Something you wanted?"

He looked like he wanted to say something, most likely to ask me not to say anything to my mother but walked off to his room.

I looked down at what had flowed from my head into my right hand. I wasn't sure it would be something that I would show David as a homework assignment. I would present him with something a little lighter. More than likely, I draw something on par with the images I did as a kid, pre-sketchbook, something cheery with the sun firmly anchored on the left side of the page.

Big Ed's full figure dominated my doorway.

"Can you come with me? There's something I found, and I'd like to get your take on it."

I detected cigar smoke clinging to his white T-shirt. Could it be that I hadn't placed the matches back in their proper spot, and he wanted to have a heart-to-heart about the dangers of being a pyromaniac? Fire bad!

Shadow at our heels, he started towards the spa, and I nearly crapped my pants. How in the hell had he managed to get his beer gut into my hiding spot? And what could I say about his discovery?

Luckily, he veered left and made his way to the back of the greenhouse, the scene of a crime against no one except for my brain cells. Plucking the joint out of the ashtray, he stared at me, and his look reminded me I was every inch the fuck-up that he thought I was.

"And what do we have here?"

"Looks like a joint to me? You branching out there, Big Ed?"

"Don't get smart with me! You're lucky your mother didn't find this!"

"You never cared about what I did, or about me, for that matter. So why start now? Guilty conscience, perhaps?"

His face lost a few shades of pigment, and he began to sputter like a motorboat, the captain of sinking his marriage.

Schoolhouse Rock had instilled the virtue that "knowledge is power," and I liked the newfound leverage I had on him.

"Just take this shit and find a better spot for it, little creep."

This had been his absolute favorite term of non-endearment for years. It was probably lost on him that if I was a little creep, that made him a big one.

"Yes, sir!" I said without any respect.

I sauntered off, a gunslinger who had won this round of high noon. Well, a high afternoon was more like it.

The mean green tended to make me feel a tad paranoid when I smoked it. But there were reasons to be paranoid now, like Rockwell's one-hit wonder "Somebody's Watching Me." I would stay frosty regarding noticing my surroundings. But I didn't want to spend the rest of my life looking over my shoulder, a prisoner of fear.

And I should most definitely train Shadow about stranger danger. Even if it didn't take, it was still worth a try.

I sat back down in the beanbag chair and looked down at what I had created. A large hand took up the bulk of the drawing, a smaller skeletal hand reaching out to it, a darker version of Michelangelo's *The Creation of Adam*, but their fingers did not touch. Both hung suspended in my trademark black background. Yeah, not homework material to present to David.

Echoes of my seventh and eighth grade English teacher – and huge crush – Mr. Tyler asking if I owned a knife because I did so many oral book reports with a much darker subject matter than my contemporaries giving their take on *Rumble Fish* or the *Sweet Valley High* series. The adage of: "It's the quiet ones that you have to watch out for" must have played into it.

I had more to say now, as I hadn't found my voice then. I was stronger than I gave myself credit for. There could be bright skies ahead. I suspected that I had it within me to weather the storm, although a few thunderstorms were in the immediate future.

I wanted next week to just hurry up and get here and for my would-be-kidnapper to get a case of instant karma, a solo car crash as he sped away. Dead on arrival, just like Jimmy in the Shangri-La's "Leader of the Pack," which I cracked myself up with my take on it when I sang it into the bathroom mirror.

Jimmy didn't fall into the category of being a sick son of a bitch to Betty; they met at a candy store, for chrissakes, and he didn't want to kidnap her!

I finished shading my drawing, although, like any creative type, I wasn't fully satisfied with it, but grateful for the outlet to plug my imagination into.

I heard the van pulling into the driveway, the reverberation of my mother's slamming of the door, signaling that it would be another tense dinner. Neat!

I greeted Mom with a hug and suggested that I cook dinner. The strongest dish in my limited culinary arsenal was fried rice with whatever leftover meat that could be served up as more than just a retread of the meal it had been days ago.

She received the offer with a slight tear in her eye, freed from the shackles of her servitude in the kitchen, even if it was only for one night. She slid Andrew Jackson's paper doppelganger into my hand with no request for the receipt. This had been routine during my time spent at the local arcade, and I pocketed the quarters. Backing L'il Red out of the driveway and bringing her to life with the purr of a kitten rather than a lion's roar, off I went.

I constantly checked my rearview mirror to make sure that a certain white Honda was not closer than it appeared. I sought out soy sauce, celery, and green onions for my recipe, knowing that we always had a steady supply of eggs and rice. During barbeque season, Big Ed would always bark out to Mom, "KATE! What's the ETA on that rice?" Often, depending on how far into his cans he was, the given meat would have a blackened outer coating akin to the charcoal he used to ruin dinner. Much like the rest of his life, his timing sucked.

I walked into Alpha Beta, which was swarming with people trying to forage for food under the fluorescent lights, a far cry from the hunter-gatherers of the past. It was doubtful that a group of Neanderthals had been armed with double coupons. I was about halfway to the produce aisle when I stopped dead in my tracks.

Whoever was in my house today could very well be in here, silently stalking me. I looked behind me; a gaggle of hausfraus were ogling the signs announcing *Buy One, Get One Free Hamburger Helper*.

Ahead of me was a mother and her five sons, ranging in age from sullen teenager to spastic youngest, who kept leaving the cart with a box of Kix, running down the cereal aisle with it, and would return with a box of Cap'n Crunch with Crunch Berries. On his third attempt, she clearly had enough.

"Timmy! Knock it off! You can't have any sugar. Go put it back. NOW!" Timmy stomped all the way down the aisle and threw the box down. There was a colorful rainbow explosion of Crunch Berries.

"Tommy, Freddy, Andy, Mike…go help your little brother! NOW!"

Each one gave her a forlorn look but obeyed. I looked down the aisle at Timmy standing there with a petrified look on his face as his four brothers descended upon him and the mess he had made. It looked like they were going to clean up his mess and then clean the floor with him.

I saw a lot of myself in that kid at that moment; he was afraid and unsure of what to do. His answer was to run down the aisle away from the trouble, a quality that had proven not-so-beneficial for me in the past. As I watched the events unfold, their mother focused her attention on me.

"Something I can help you with?"

"Doubtful."

"Well, that's no surprise," she said, eyeing me up and down.

"Oh, I see you're getting Kix. Kid despised; mother insisted." I said, giving my own spin on the cereal's tagline. "How's that going for you? Not so well, I see."

Her response was a shaking of her head. Hopefully, young Timmy could develop a shield for himself, otherwise, that family was going to chew him up as quickly as he wanted to devour a box of Cap'n Crunch. As I moved along, I heard a pair of feet behind me.

Then, a male voice said my name from right over my shoulder. I turned around quickly, electrified by fear, and was confronted by the kindly face of the store manager, Mr. McGee, my brother's old boss.

"Sorry, I didn't mean to startle you."

"It's ok. How are you?"

"All good in the neighborhood. Say, when does your brother get back?"

"A few weeks."

We made some other niceties, and I made it home without incident. In the time I had been gone, the door to my parents' room had been shut. This usually meant they were at odds with each other or they were on each other.

I focused on cutting the vegetables, my least favorite part of making fried rice, as it would keep my mind off what they were doing. Can I get an eww and an ick?

I opened the knife drawer, opting not to utilize the butcher knife for a second time today, selecting a smaller one. About a half-hour later, Mom and Big Ed made their way downstairs, each freshly showered and chummy.

"Smells delicious! Doesn't it, Fuzzy?" She practically cooed, calling him her pet name. I grimaced as I gave a final stir to the green wok.

"It sure does! I'm starved." There was an alien enthusiasm in his voice.

I shot him a crusty look, knowing he was stringing my mother along with his pretense, both of us knowing that she was playing second fiddle in his duplicitous orchestration.

"You even set the table? Thank you, Henry!" Mom said.

Big Ed was already sitting at the table, and I was surprised that he wasn't pounding his fork on the table, demanding he be fed first. I dished up three bowls and served him last, showing him where he stood with me. He looked at me with disdain, which I returned with a raised eyebrow and a fake smile that read as "Bon Appetit, fucker."

After all was said and devoured, I cleaned up the kitchen, both my mother's sanctuary and prison. They went to watch Vanna White deftly turn those letters, with Dad solving Mom's half-guessed answer.

I produced one in my mind. B _ G ED _'S A D_CK. C'mon, Mom, buy a vowel! As it was, Big Ed finished the Place hints for Hawaiian Paradise.

"Oh shoot!" She said, partially defeated but still in her afterglow.

"That's the way the cookie crumbles, Katie."

Just like the foundation of their marriage vows was collapsing all around our family unit, fissures threatening to swallow the Dodge homestead whole or see it evaporate into thin air like the Freeling family's had in *Poltergeist*.

This house was most definitely not clean! And it didn't take Tangina Barrons to proclaim it unfit, not that it had been a fully formed structure to begin with, the negative energy creating tiny ghost-like puffs of dust lazily hanging in the air, ready to strike.

Good thing I had never been sucked into the TV like Carol Anne; chances are I would have been stuck on the other side for eternity. There was no way that Big Ed would risk life and limb to get me back; he'd just chalk it up to a loss and call it a day. Besides, living inside a TV sounded like a dream come true.

"You're gonna die in there!" I whispered to myself as Reverend Kane from the sequel, as I put the last plate into the dishwasher.

"*Jeopardy* time!" Mom called out, unaware of how that phrase could apply to her own life. I needed to say something that subtly informed her that Big Ed was a no-good cheating son-of-a-bitch. Again.

I took my spot on the couch, as they were both very cozy in matching his-and-her recliners. Every now and again, she would look at him with the kind of gaze he reserved for his cans of Budweiser, of which he was about three deep.

Since I had an hour till *Dallas* started, I excused myself to finish the final shading touches to my drawing.

An hour passed before I proclaimed it a complete work of art, one that I was proud of, too. As I was heading downstairs, Big Ed was heading up. We were the living embodiment of the old saying: "Oh, East is East, and West is West, and never the twain shall meet." In simple terms, the divide between us couldn't be closed because we were mere inches from each other. I suppressed the desire to hiss at him.

Mom was sitting on the couch in the den, so I chose the spot of being right in the middle, sitting back in the rocking chair in front of the fireplace, giving off the vibe nothing was amiss.

After a preview of what to expect on this exciting episode of the Texas-based drama, now in its tenth season, we both settled into the show. I looked for a way to broach the subject of Big Ed's infidelity.

I had an idea: J.R. would be my in. He was currently wooing April Stevens to get her share of Ewing Oil, as she was the ex-wife of the tasty Jack Ewing, who was missing from recent episodes.

"You know who J.R. reminds me of?" I said, looking straight ahead at the TV. "Big Ed."

I could feel her eyes on me, and I turned to meet them.

"Why's that?"

"Well, for starters, he loves to drink."

"Everyone on this show drinks, even in the daytime." She brushed away the suggestion like an annoying gnat.

"And the way he treats Sue Ellen, disgraceful. Talking down to her, cheating on her."

I let that one dangle in the air, an invisible carrot for her to take a bite of, leaving nothing but a bitter aftertaste in her mouth. A brief, strange look snuck onto her face and then vanished just as quickly.

"Your father is really trying to change. If you haven't noticed, he's working on being better to you." She wasn't taking the bait.

"But what about you, Mom?"

"Can't this wait until the commercials?"

"Just want you to be happy. That's all."

From the look on her face, I could see I had struck a nerve and that she wished we had bonded over watching *Fantasy Island*, less cause for reality-based conversations to be had over that show.

"Why don't we worry about getting you better. I'm fine." She said absently.

As the commercials began, she softly inquired how my meeting with David went. I told her it was good and what I needed to do for extracurricular credits.

"I like that idea; getting those feelings on paper and out of your head. You've always been my daydreamer and artist. I had wanted to be a writer a long time ago."

"You could still do that. You can do anything you put your mind to." I said in a moment of role reversal. It had undoubtedly been a *Freaky Friday* type of day, and I breathed a silent sigh of relief that we had not switched bodies.

"Perhaps," she said wistfully, and then the conversation ended as the commercials faded away, just like the aspirations she had dreamed of as a young girl.

I always suspected that my right-brained tendencies had been from Mom. But my addictive persona and temper were from Big Ed's DNA.

When the show ended, we started chatting again.

"Can you go and get the things that you need for work tomorrow?" She asked as if I were five and wanted to cross the street by myself.

"Of course; I am a big boy. I can even add 2 + 2. I mean, I think it's 5? Math is hard!"

"Alright, smart aleck. Are you excited to start your job?"

While I was, I wouldn't be Henry Dodge if I didn't overthink how my first day would and, in my mind, should go.

"Yes. Oh, I need to get a journal, too. I'll pay you back once I get my paycheck."

"It's my treat." She really had faith that I had changed my fucked-up ways.

I was hopeful that it would be the case - but what would Charlie Brown have been if he didn't have the blind belief that he could kick the football out of Lucy's grasp? He still tried, and it was the best that I could do: dust myself off and try, try again. It reminded me of that toy commercial slogan: "Weebles wobble, but they don't fall down!"

And there it was, my new mantra for life, as well as the seed of an artistic notion.

She decried it was her bedtime, and I decided to utilize this new brainstorm of creativity, lest it slip away like a thief in the night. But the stagnant swamp that had been any artistic endeavors had sprung a lone flower, and the bloom was staying on the white rose, luminescent, glowing in the light of renewal.

I made myself stop before the alarm clock's red numbers signaled a new day had begun. I gladly crawled under the sheets, very ready to put yesterday to bed, knowing that while tomorrow was just another day, it held promise upon its arrival.

But that was not to be the case. I awoke to the shrill ringing of the phone - just when my sex dream about Tom Cruise was just starting to get good. His flight suit from *Top Gun* was down around his ankles, and he was about to do a fly-by, not near the air control tower, but my manhood into my mouth. Maverick!

"Godammit," I complained sleepily.

The clock said 9:30. It better be a fucking emergency!

"Hello?" I snarled.

I only heard the faint sound of breathing, which led me to believe that the driver of the white Honda wanted to see if I was at home.

"This call is being traced. I went to the cops yesterday, so you better knock it off!" I even believed myself as the words tumbled out of my mouth.

But the creep stayed on the line, so I slammed down the receiver. Well, rise and fucking shine, indeed! I was hoping that yesterday would be an isolated incident, and I didn't want to give him the leverage that he held anything over me and wanted to convey that I wasn't afraid to act against him. There was a sliver of hope in the tactic of using brains rather than the brawn I didn't have.

Once I had double-checked all the locked doors, I felt better but still uneasy. My stomach was in knots, so I skipped breakfast but gave Shadow her kibble and fresh water.

Once I had finished showering behind a locked door, I opened it warily. When I wasn't cut in half by a machete-wielding, hockey-mask-wearing psychopath, it was safe to go to my room.

Still, I closed the door behind me. The prospect of being locked away in self-made exile for the day crossed my mind. The prospect of forgoing my errands with the 40 dollars from Mom seemed the safer bet. But I hadn't ever been one not to take risks.

"Fuck that noise," I spoke directly to the chorus of voices in my head.

At Miller's Outpost, I focused on what I needed and chose a black pair of 30/32 pants, as they never had my actual 30/30 size, which meant I'd have to cuff my work pants. Good times!

Then it came down to deciding on a long-sleeved or short-sleeved white shirt. I tried to imagine what kind of impression bandaged wrists would make. I doubted that I could claim that the post-suicide look was all the rage that year.

With clothes in hand, I was busy fumbling for the cash in my pocket, so I wasn't paying attention to who was staffing the register.

Why, if it wasn't my sworn enemy, Scott Rainowsky.

"Hey man," I offered nonchalantly.

"What's up, Henry?

I wondered if he thought I was going to haul off and punch him again. Craig said he had moved to Arizona to live with his older sister after being teased for getting "beat up by a fag," as I had put it at the time.

"Just getting some clothes for my new job at AMC."

"That would be a cool place to work," he said, adding, "I hate it here."

"Boring, huh?"

"You could definitely say that." He paused, then whispered, "I want to say sorry for all the shit I gave you. My New Year's resolution is to be less of a dick."

Doubtful. As Bono had sung, "Nothing changes on New Year's Day." But who was I to judge? Mine had been to not be alive in 1987, so there was that. Besides, if I could change, there might be hope he could ditch his jock douche ways.

"That's all in the past, so don't worry about it."

"Maybe I'll see you around sometime."

Was he flirting with me?

"Yeah, sure, whatever."

"It was nice to see you."

When stripped of all his bullying jock pretense, he was the type of guy that I could go for. But even if he were flirting with me, I would avoid that imaginary scenario.

I made my way over to Aaron Brothers to check on their journal selection. Today, Michael was not present, but Derek was.

"Oh, hey," he said cheerfully, a change from his foul mood first impression.

And just as Scott had done moments before, he, too, apologized for his actions. And my answer was that he shouldn't worry about it.

"Do you guys have journals?"

"Just stuff for drawing. Hey, are you going with us to *Rocky Horror* tonight?"

"I haven't talked to Nina today."

And then we launched into our mutual admiration club of all things that made Nina rad. When we said our goodbyes, I went to check for a journal at Crown Books.

Fortunately, Jeannie wasn't working, and even though it was doubtful that this would constitute something she would write to John about, I was relieved. Sharon was busy unloading books off a cart and putting them on the shelves.

I hadn't seen her since the wedding and my visit to San Luis Rey. I wondered if Jeannie had filled her in on my "shenanigans."

"Well, looky what the cat dragged in," she teased.

"Did you just call me a pussy?" I countered.

"I calls 'em like I sees 'em."

"Oh, is that why you wear glasses?"

She pulled them down to the bridge of her nose and gave me a look that said, "Touché."

"What can I do you for?"

"Well, bookkeep. I need a journal. You have them in these here parts?"

"Mosey this way."

She led me to the selection, but most of them had floral designs. Journals, strong enough for a man, yet made for a woman.

"Miss, can you ring me up?" A staunch-looking woman inquired.

"Be right there, ma'am." She hurried away, her black hair jetting behind her, trying to catch up with her swift gait.

I perused the selection and discovered a plain black one under another with a garden that said: "From the smallest seeds come the biggest ideas" on its cover. I pulled the remainder of the money in my pocket and decided that this one might get the long-dormant creative juices flowing for my mom.

Sharon was putting the money from Ms. C.U. Next Tuesday into the drawer.

The woman told her she was going to report her to the manager for the "language" that she had overheard. To which Sharon tapped her nametag that bore her job title of manager. She added a sarcastic "have the best day ever" and mumbled "miserable bitch" under her breath as the door closed behind the uptight woman, who looked like she referred to her womanhood as the place her bathing suit covers.

"Why the journal? Are you going to a girl's birthday party? Or need to write down your secret desires?"

"Nah, I'm making a shit list. Guess who's at the very tippy-top?"

She put her hands to her chest and mouthed, "Who? Me?"

"Not that it is any of your business. But this one is for my mom, she used to write, so I thought she would like it. The other one is for me, Miss Noseybody."

"Aww. That's really nice of you."

"I try, Sharon. Lawd knows I try."

"Sounds like you succeed," she said.

"Catch ya on the flipside," I said and gave her a little two-finger salute after I made my purchase.

"See you, sweetie."

At home, the answering machine's red light was beeping. It was highly unlikely that my stalker, who may or may not have asthma, left me a message with his phone number in some breathing morse code. It was Nina inviting yours truly to join in on the fun at the *Rocky Horror Picture Show* at the La Paloma Theatre.

"The show starts at 10. We'll be meeting up outside at 9:30, be there or be square, Daddy-O." She repeated in my second playing of the message, in case I had heard wrong the first time.

John and he-that-I-didn't-want-to-think-about talked about the movie, its audience participation, and how I would be what they called a "virgin" for my first viewing. Oh honey, that ship had sailed, capsized, and left me stranded on the sands of Black's Beach for a year now.

I called her back, getting her answering machine, and told her I'd see her tonight. With two journals in one hand and my Miller's Outpost bag in the other, I went to my room. Shadow was sleeping on my bed on her back with her legs splayed.

"Get up, lazy bones. You were supposed to look for a job today."

Her response was to remain in that position, open her eyes, and close them immediately.

I was glad that I hadn't gone with the parentals to pick out a new car for Mom; it would have driven me to the brink of boredom. A nap at noon seemed a little decadent, so I decided to tune in and tune out with a bit of TV. An hour of *The Munsters* and an episode of *Lost in Space* bled into two back-to-back episodes of The Castaways there on *Gilligan's Island.*

The song "Reminiscing" by the Little River Band alerted me that it was time for *The Family Film Festival*, hosted by a man who had shown me the joys of drawing on the Sunday morning show *Popeye and Friends*. Tom Hatten was a surrogate father of sorts who fed both the creative and pop culture side of me; he always had some fun facts about the movies that he would screen. And I was all about fun facts!

Today's offering was one of my favorites, *Mad Monster Party*, a stop-motion animated flick that had all the Universal ghouls plus a King Kong-type ape. It was made by Rankin and Bass, the minds behind the perennial Christmas classic *Rudolph the Red-Nosed Reindeer*. I always thought Hermey was a little light in the elf shoe department, and his desire to be a dentist really came across as a thinly-veiled desire to be a card-carrying homo.

I figured without the folks around that, it would be ok to take a toke or two and just blow the smoke out the window. Then I sprayed the air with Lysol and settled into my bean bag chair.

About 15 minutes in, I felt that all-too-familiar stirring in my loins. Pot usually made me hungry or horny, and both fed an appetite.

I was trying to concentrate on Felix Flankin's Jimmy Stewart-sounding voice, hoping that it would draw me in and steer me away from giving myself a hand. The steady stretching of my Jockey shorts told me that I was unsuccessful in that endeavor.

I did have that stash of *Playgirl* magazines in my room, but they have been paged through ad infinitum. But there was the prospect of using my imagination to jump back into my interrupted Tom Cruise dream.

Or…I remembered a beach buddy telling me about a phone sex line: 976-Meet, I had told him that was clever marketing for finding cock. He had corrected me on my assumption that it was spelled meat. My bad.

I scooted Shadow out of my room and closed the Levelor blinds and my door. My gut did a little jump, just as it did when I was about to have sex in the bushes at Black's. Even though my HIV status remained unclear, this was the definition of safe sex. I'd just be a voice on the phone with no plans to get together. I could revel in the freedom of being someone else if I wanted to.

I kept the TV on but turned the sound down. I picked up the receiver and dialed the number. It felt like an eternity until a recorded, and quite friendly, voice told me that I was going to be connected with a real live guy, and I could bypass those I deemed undesirable by pushing the pound button.

A doorbell sound almost stopped my heart, thinking someone was at the front door, but it was on the phone and signaled a caller looking for some backdoor action.

"Hi, who's this?" The person sounded a bit into his AARP card years.

I had forgotten to choose my fake name. I didn't want to go in my Wayback Machine and say that I was Billy Collins, especially since I wasn't sure what the weight limit on emotional carry-on baggage was. I looked at the TV, and the animated version of Boris Karloff was onscreen.

"Boris. Who's this?" And dammit, if I wasn't using a Russian accent.

"Morty." Yup, he was in an age range that I wasn't interested in. "What are you into?"

"Hunting moose and squirrel," I answered as I pushed the pound button. This time, I landed on the name Charlie, as Mom used to call me Charlie Brown.

"Hey, what's up?" the next person said, as smooth as buttering toast.

"Three guesses."

"What do I get if I guess right?"

"Probably a mess to clean up."

He sounded much younger than Morty.

"Where do you live?" he asked.

"North County." I decided to keep it general. I already had enough trouble with my exact locale being pinpointed by a certain unknown creep.

"Awesome. Me too! Where?" he pressed.

"Cardiff." There, that should throw him off the scent.

"Encinitas here."

Of course, I would have to find someone who lived in my town. He would want to 976- Meet me, for fuck's sake. I almost pressed the pound button again, but my curiosity got the better of me as I wondered if I knew him.

"I'm Charlie," I said casually.

"Seth. Nice to meet you. Well, on the phone and all."

"How old are you? I'm 19."

"18."

"What are you working with there, Seth?"

"Excuse me?" His question revealed that he hadn't gotten around the block like I had, thankfully not having to work a corner almost two years ago.

"How big is your dick?"

"I have never measured it. Big enough to get the job done."

"How about you?"

"Let's just say that I've never had any complaints."

"Are you playing with it?"

In fact, I was, an unconscious effort that I hadn't been aware of.

"Yes."

"Is it hard?"

"As a rock, stud. What about you?"

"Yeah. Feels good, but I wish it were in your mouth."

"Oh yeah, I love to suck dick." I couldn't believe what a natural I was at this, like a fish to water, even if this salmon had no intention of spawning in person.

"You swallow?"

"Spitters are quitters."

"You're funny. I like that."

"Thanks, Seth. I'm also really good at sex."

"You sound like boyfriend material." When I didn't answer, he nervously asked if he had said something wrong.

"No, I'm just not sure how you'd feel about having a boyfriend with three eyes. I'm still a good person, but I have to wear two pairs of sunglasses at once. Gets expensive."

"Well, I'm ugly on the inside, so it sounds like a perfect match!"

If only. He could volley what I served, and that was my ideal. Damn the timing of all of this.

"So, Charlie, what are the chances of us going on a date?"

Right now, it was slim to none until I went to the doctor next week.

"Well, I'm a little busy right now, starting a new job at AMC on Monday…"

Fuck and double fuck – did I really divulge that information?

"Oh, I see." His voice took on a strange quality. "Is your name really Charlie?"

"Uh-huh." I felt like I had been caught with my hand in the cookie jar rather than down my pants. "Why do you ask?"

"Just a weird coincidence. Anyways, what if we talk here at the same time next Saturday?"

"I don't know when I'll be working yet."

"Hey, if you don't want to hang out, just tell me."

"It's not that. Life is a little bit complicated right now. How about this: Let's connect here next Friday at 10 in the morning."

"Perfect! It's a date."

I figured that by Friday, I would know where I stood, good or bad.

"Cool. Talk to you then."

"Alright, Henry."

The doorbell sounded again, but I hung up the phone, stunned.

Oh, what fresh hell is this? Was it possible that the stranger had gone from breathing to being conversational? If this motherfucker wanted a date, he was going to have one with destiny and get his comeuppance in the process. The hunter was about to get captured by the game, as The Marvelettes had sung about twenty years ago.

"Checkmate, bitch!"

Two sounds interrupted my thoughts of revenge. One was Shadow scratching at the door, and the other was a horn honking in the driveway. I opened the door, and Shadow jumped up on me, ran downstairs, and was at the sliding glass door, meaning she had to relieve herself.

I let her out and rushed out the front door to a beaming Kate Dodge standing next to her convertible VW Cabriolet. She was beside herself with joy. The white car glistened in the sunlight, a bright spot in her otherwise drab life.

"Isn't it beautiful?"

"That's awesome, Mom; you deserve it!"

"And it's brand-new. Your father wore the salesman down and even got us a good deal on the trade-in."

No surprise there; he had been wearing me down my entire life.

"Speaking of, where's the old man?"

"Oh, Mrs. Woodson had a plumbing problem and asked if he could help her out. Isn't that nice of him?"

"He's such a giver, that one. Say, I should see if he needs any help."

The look on her face was saying, "You?"

So off I went like the dutiful son.

I rang the doorbell, and when nobody came to the door, I thought that it may be as broken as my father's marriage vows. I knocked on it, then pounded on it like I was the police coming to raid her house. Mrs. Woodson finally opened the door a crack and peeked around it, not looking like someone who had been getting her drain snaked. Well, maybe she had.

"Hello, Henry." Her voice was ice-cold, but her face looked flushed and hot.

"Is it safe to come in? You look like you're coming down with something!"

"I was trying to help your father."

Yes, right out of a long-term marriage.

"Well, you are in luck! I'm here to offer my services." But only as a junior detective.

"Oh, I think your father has it under control."

"Huh."

"Huh what, young man?"

"That's a weird shade of red. Looks white to me. Must need my eyes checked," I said, staring into her living room and the alleged painting Dad had done.

"What are you talking...?"

"Oh well, I would just get in the old man's way. He's probably got his hands full." I stared directly at her midsection, which had taken on an alcohol bloat after her husband abandoned her.

I turned on my heel, smugly knowing that she would report my behavior to Big Ed.

Mom had parked her new baby in the cradle of the garage. When I asked what was for dinner, she suggested pizza from Round Table and offered to pick it up.

"Sounds good." I smiled internally, wondering if Big Ed would be full from the crow I had made him eat.

"Did Dad not need your help?"

Before I could answer, Big Ed walked through the front door, and I could see the internal struggle of him trying not to glare at me so as not to tip his hat that there was something wrong.

"Hey Dad, we're having pizza! I bet you worked up quite an appetite servicing Mrs. Woodson's rusty old pipes."

"Oh, it was an easy fix."

Emphasis on easy.

"Gee, that's swell," I said in full *Leave it to Beaver* mode.

My mother just stared at the two of us, sharing this Bizarro World version of our usual selves. Still perplexed, she went to phone in our order.

Big Ed approached me, the anger now popping out on his features like the cystic acne he had as a teenager.

"You little shit. Keep it up, and I'll make your life miserable," he whispered ferociously.

"Try me, dickhead. Hey, Mom!"

If his jaw could have dropped any further, it would have gone through the floor.

"Yes, hon?"

"Can we get sausage and mushroom?"

"Of course, hon."

My father, a whiter shade of pale, went upstairs and closed his bedroom door. When we got back from our joy ride, he was still up there.

She called out to him that dinner was here. He didn't answer, so she went up, then returned with a concerned look.

"He has a headache and wants his pizza upstairs."

This was not an uncommon occurrence, though it was usually reserved for John's birthday parties and getting away from the gaggle of kids that would show up bearing gifts for my popular brother. He'd always have his cake upstairs.

Now, he thought he could have his cake and eat it, too.

Always the dutiful wife, she took him his dinner and two beers. Then we sat down to mack out on my favorite pizza on the planet.

"I'm going to go to the movies tonight with Nina."

"Oh, that girl from the *hospital*."

"One and the same. There's a few more people going."

I thought that Mom would be glad that I had a friend. She seemed to not relish the idea of still being in communication with someone who had been a patient at San Luis Rey.

"I suppose it's OK." She missed the point that I wasn't asking for her permission, just informing her about my plans for the evening.

"I like her, and she works at the movie theater, too."

"Did you get your uniform?"

"Yes, and I picked up something else, too. Hold, please."

I came back to the table with the journal, and either she was taken aback that I got it for her, albeit with her own money, or that I had paid attention to something that she had told me.

"That's very sweet of you, Henry." She reached over to tousle my hair, stiff with hairspray.

"Watch the hair!" I said in my best John Travolta as Tony Manero voice.

"Pardon me, pretty boy."

"I'll let it slide," I said laughingly.

When she laughed, there was a little piece of mushroom on her tooth, and my mind immediately went to Pete and his dead tooth.

The hour drew nigh when I was to venture out and meet up with everyone, who turned out to be Nina and Derek. Michael was set to arrive but always did so at the last minute, according to Nina, who was puffing on a clove cigarette, dressed in a mini skirt and Day-Glo top.

The Sixties revival was alive and well in her closet while I was wearing my favorite purple sweater and a pair of white Levi's. Derek had on ripped jeans and a Keith Haring t-shirt with an earless Mickey Mouse and two of the outlined men he was known for.

"Cool shirt," I remarked.

"Got it in New York last summer."

"Hey, what about me?" Nina asked.

"Far out, mama," Derek said.

"Groovy," I added.

She did a little curtsey, pulling the edges of her miniskirt dangerously close to exposing her lady parts housed in pink panties.

"Hey, I didn't order fish! Hike that skirt down," I teased.

"Yes, we get it; you're strictly dickly."

"You're outnumbered in that arena tonight, girl," Derek said.

"I can suck the chrome off a trailer hitch, thank you very much," she sassed.

"You been looking for dates at the trailer park again?" I added. She flipped me the bird.

"Enough with this small talk. Come with me if you want to live," Nina commanded.

I had never felt more alive, electrified to be with her posse.

We walked over to a brown station wagon that she referred to as Lulu. Nina pulled out four orange-flavored California Coolers.

"One for each of us, except for Michael. That bitch's concept of time is truly awful. His loss is our gain."

I took a bottle, looking suspiciously at the pulp that sat at the bottom like sediment from a sewage plant.

"Bottom's up, unless you're a top, Henry," Derek said.

"He has Boner Garage tattooed on his ass with an arrow pointing to his butthole," Nina sniped.

Derek had taken a swig and was trying not to spray it all over the front seat. Luckily, I was still twisting the cap off.

"Bitch," he said once he had gotten it from his mouth into his throat.

"Alright, chug-a-lug."

Like seasoned pros, we downed our bottles in no time flat and then passed Michael's between us. The warmth of a buzz had taken hold of me. Nina handed us a Wintergreen Certs out of her purse, a younger and hipper version of Kate Dodge.

"Thanks, Mom!" I said with a slur. I didn't think of myself as a lightweight, but I had only followed my father's footsteps in drinking Budweiser.

Derek emitted a voluminous burp and laughed.

"Classy, ain't cha?" Nina chided. "Alright, let's blow this Popsicle stand."

"Is that like sucking the chrome off a trailer hitch?" I inquired.

"Ask your uncle."

"I'll show *you* on the doll where the bad man touched me!" I said, pointing to my crotch.

We exited with peals of laughter escorting us to the box office, plunked down our money, and found our seats, saving one for Michael. He showed up with minutes to spare before showtime, no apology, a shit-eating grin on his face.

"I know that look," Nina whispered. "Somebody was at the viewpoint."

"I'll never tell," Michael said.

"You don't have to. The cum stain on your pants is a dead giveaway," Derek said and then broke into song. "Sex shooter, shooting love in your direction."

Michael looked down at the stained spot on his pants and sank down into his seat, putting his box of popcorn over the mark. When he got up, I thought it was too early for "The Time Warp." He was heading to the bathroom. He returned moments later, his crotch even wetter, but the stain eradicated, just as the lights went down.

Speaking of liquids, when revelers used squirt guns during a rain scene, in my buzzed state, it felt like people were spitting on me. Or that I was getting doused in pig's blood at my prom. Visions of my newfound tribe pointing and laughing at me, their friendship nothing but a clever rouse to humiliate me, danced in my head in a circular motion, like the dizzying scene with William Katt and Sissy Spacek at the ill-fated prom in *Carrie*.

But I eventually got over that feeling and settled in for the new experience, which had elements of being old hat for me.

Talking back to the screen was something I did at home to the TV by myself, but I wasn't very well-versed in the mechanics of this, given it was my first time. My only contribution was to tell Nina that I thought Rocky and Brad were hot. That counted for something, I suppose.

As the lights rose and we made our way out of the theater, I saw a familiar face in the crowd. Scott Rainowsky was up ahead, escorting one of those cookie-cutter blondes from school. Megan? Kelly? Stacy! That was her name. Well, there went the suspicion that he had been flirting with me until he turned around and winked at me.

But I wasn't the intended target of his wink.

"Piece of shit," Derek said.

"Choose a team, asshole," Nina said at full volume.

Scott's right arm was around Stacy's shoulder, and he flipped our group off sideways, unbeknownst to her.

"Wait. I'm confused," I stammered.

"Not as confused as him!" Derek said, ready to spit tacks. "That's my ex-boyfriend."

"Say what now?"

All three of them said "what," and I regretted my choice of words.

"Come on, you guys! I'm being serious. He tormented me in high school. I finally clocked him when I got fed up with it."

"Bravo! Bravo!" Derek said, giving a restrained golf clap.

"Look at you! Bitch got what he deserved," Nina said with admiration.

"Don't fuck with a seasoned fag," I said. "Who knew he wanted a different kind of pounding."

"Henry, you are so over the top!" Michael said.

"You make it sound like it's a bad thing."

I wanted to explain how my gaydar had pinged at Miller's Outpost today.

"Tick-tock," I said, tapping my Swatch watch that covered the top part of my bandages.

"We'll go to Denny's, have some coffee, and give you the deets? Capisce?" Nina said, every inch a mob boss.

Speaking of tick-tocks, the hands on my watch were almost straight up. While I wasn't particularly worried about this thing other kids called a curfew, I didn't want to push Mom's good-natured, albeit blind, trust in me.

I wasn't a coffee drinker, but the three of them certainly were and were putting the acceptable amount of how many cigarettes were appropriate in the smoking section to the test. Our waitress, Arlene, seemed none-too-pleased that we appeared to be on a liquid diet. All they were having was coffee, while I opted for a Diet Coke to maintain my girlish figure.

"He was a lot more than inconsistent with me," Derek explained. "One day, he was all about me. The next he might not be. It went on like this for months and months. But I was so flattered that The Big Man on Campus was into me that I fell for him."

"OK, I'm curious. How did you guys even meet?" I asked earnestly.

"Ever hear of 976-Meet?"

Holy shit!

"I should have known he was no good. He gave me a fake name; said he was Seth. If he was going for another name that began with S, he should have picked Satan!"

"Well, he's still at it," I confessed.

"What do you mean, jellybean?" Nina asked.

"We had ourselves a nice little chat today, and we're supposed to talk next Friday. But fuck him!"

"No, don't fuck him, but we can fuck with him," Michael offered.

"Do tell," Derek said, his mouth curling into an evil grin that suggested a maniacal version of Dennis the Menace with the freckles that flanked either side of his pug nose.

Michael laid out his plan, which saw me keeping my appointed date with the bonus of a not-so-nice surprise for when we met.

"Remind me not to get on your bad side," Nina whistled.

"Everyone knows what to do?"

We all nodded, signaling that "Operation Take Down Closet Boy" would be set into motion prior to Friday with the stroke of a Sharpie pen, some well-placed calls, and the power of the press.

It would be a welcome relief from worrying about Thursday. Even though it hadn't been the creep on the other end, I was still pissed that he was interloping on the great time I had tonight. He would be another assignment for our hit squad in the future.

I received zero flak from either parent about my late night, save for my mom's observation that I looked tired. But no further questions as to why aside from rolling in after 1a.m. It meant she still trusted me.

I spent the day with more mindless TV and some worry about starting my job the next day. I gladly welcomed some structure in my life. A routine. The sweet slumber of sleep happening at 10 o'clock and the beeping of my alarm clock telling me it was time to embrace the newness of the day.

Mom had hung up my freshly ironed uniform in the closet, and when I tried on the pants, I saw she had hemmed them. She figured it would save her from letting me know that the complaint department was closed, along with her little chastising song of: "Poor Henry, it's sad for him. He moans and groans all the livelong day." Quite the self-esteem builder there, Katie.

I wondered how I would fit in with the people at work. All I could be was myself, and that was starting to feel as comfortable to me as the hemmed pants that fit as they should. I changed out my bandages, knowing that soon they would be gone. They were undetectable beneath my smelling-of-bleach white shirt. I did a final check in the mirror. Not a hair out of place, no stress break-outs, nothing in my teeth.

So, with a spring in my step, I hopped on L'il Red and drove off.

A different girl was at the box office, prepping her booth to receive whatever people go to a movie on Monday afternoon. She was a blonde, and a familiar one at that. It was Stacy, and she let me into the empty theater lobby.

Although she said it was nice to meet me, there was something in her voice. It made me suspect that Scott may have pegged me as part of the assembly of misfits who had been mouthy to him.

Erik's gigantic frame was soon in front of me, and I was soon in his office again. He handed me a black vest, a matching clip-on black bowtie, and a name tag. I had a little trouble with the bowtie, so he bent down like a father helping his toddler son.

My first day would consist of shadowing my supervisor during the first four hours of my part-time shift. He explained and then asked if there were any days that I couldn't work. I did say that I needed this Thursday off, and if I could get a later shift on Friday, it would be greatly appreciated.

"Other than that, I can work whenever you need me to."

"Well, whatever doesn't interfere with school."

"Oh, I graduated early." The lie felt like the truth, as I wasn't currently enrolled but planned to get my G.E.D. at some point. I had spent the last year learning the kind of life lessons that couldn't be learned from a chalkboard, microfiche, or textbook.

"The earlier shifts are usually harder to fill on the weekdays. I will work you into the schedule for the rest of the week. Now, let's get you familiar with your duties here."

We went behind the counter and my supervisor turned out to be none other than Steve's sister, Yvonne. Erik left me alone with her, which I'm sure would be an altogether different experience of alone time with her sibling in the hallway at Lavar's.

"Nice to see you again, Henry. Ready to get started?"

"Yup."

She went over the opening steps of melting the lard-looking butter, heating the nacho cheese, putting the hot dogs on the tiny rotating grill, and placing the buns into a heater. Then it was to the back, where she produced a black trash bag full of last night's leftover popcorn. She stood in front of the popcorn machine and dumped it in, using a scoop to layer it evenly. Next, she showed me how to turn on the oil and poured the exact amount of popcorn kernels into a metal kettle.

The popping began in earnest after a moment, and after it stopped falling into the machine like a more solid version of snowflakes, she dumped it. Then, it was my turn to perform the task, amid her warning of the dangers of burning it. I repeated her actions in a perfect mimic of her expertise.

"Someone's a quick study. That's good. Just follow my lead, and you'll do fine."

"Thanks," I said as the first patrons approached my workstation.

"Medium popcorn. Two small Cokes."

"For 25 cents more, you could get a medium Coke."

They elected to take her up on her offer, ponying up an extra 50 cents for the upgrade, which was called "up-selling," according to Yvonne after they were out of earshot and off to see *Outrageous Fortune* with Bette Midler and Shelley Long. I steered the conversation to the benefits of working at the theater.

"Yes, you get to see free movies. But usually not on weekend nights because that's when we have sell-out shows, especially in the summer. There is a probation period here; if we keep you on after a month, then it's free flicks and snacks."

A small queue of people was forming, mostly seniors looking to beat boredom with six movie choices at the Cineplex. I watched her use her gentle form of persuasion in play with each one of them. When the movies had started, the handsome usher with short blond curly hair who had been tearing tickets in two came over and introduced himself as Matt.

We exchanged our "nice to meet you's" and he grabbed his broom and long-handled dustpan combo to sweep up popcorn that patrons had spilled. I watched Matt bend over, taking note of how well his pants fit.

"You like that, eh?" Yvonne smirked.

"Huh?" I said, feigning innocence.

"It's OK; I know," she said. "My brother told me."

I thought she meant Steve for a split second, but realized she meant Craig.

"Oh, that. Guilty as charged," I said, trying to sound nonchalant.

"Well, Matty is a tit man through and through," she said in a conspiratorial tone. "And don't worry about it; no judgment here if you like hot dogs. Speaking of wieners, go make sure they're not overdone."

The rest of my shift involved checking the syrup levels on the soda boxes for the dispensers, restocking candy, and learning the cash register. It was a lot to take in. I let her confidence in the job spill over me like the hot butter that dressed up the popcorn.

I was clocking out when Erik brought over my copy of the weekly schedule in his gigantic hands. I saw that I was working on Wednesday night, which meant recording *Dynasty*, and the next two shifts on Saturday night included working with Nina.

"I'm a working girl with income now." I said as I straddled L'il Red.

I pulled into the same spot on Wednesday. This time there was a Hispanic girl working the ticket booth. She was patting the sides of her Aqua-Netted, Lisa Lisa -sans Cult Jam- style hair. She reached out a slightly sticky hand from her primping.

"I'm Carmella. Welcome aboard," she said warmly.

Matt was at the ticket stand, said hello with a little wave, and I went to clock in. At the door of the concession stand stock room, I found Nina with a cache of Junior Mints in her arms, cradling them like a newborn. There were traces of chocolate on the corner of her lip.

"New lipstick?" I said as I wiped it off with my hand.

"I had to make sure they didn't have razor blades in them!"

"Girl, you're so bad."

"So bad I'm good. We better get out there."

My job tonight was popcorn and soda fetcher. Nina would bark out, "Adam and Eve on a raft and wreck 'em" if someone ordered a hot dog. My shift with her was breezier than the learning curve with Yvonne. But she did fill me in on some things in between the two waves of moviegoers.

"And after each movie breaks," Nina explained, "a technical term the ushers use for a movie ending, they blow the theaters."

"Beg pardon?"

"You perv. They have leaf blowers that moves all the trash to the bottom of the theater, and they sweep it up."

"There goes my movie theater orgy fantasy."

"Orgy? You're looking for a little one-on-one scenario. I see how you look at Matt."

"Well, he's hot."

"Uh, duh. I have eyes. But you should get yours checked; he's as straight as they get."

"I'm just window-shopping, not shoplifting."

Then the conversation turned off in a direction that was not on any Thomas Brothers map or something I wanted to discuss at work.

"How are you feeling about tomorrow?"

"I don't know."

"You want me to go with you?"

"Nah, but I appreciate it."

"Let me know what happens."

"You'll be my first call. Witches honor." I said and repeated the gesture from *Bewitched.*

"Hmm, that's queer. I didn't think you knew the international sign for eatin' pussy."

I responded by showing her the universal sign for what a middle finger meant.

Nina showed me the closing procedures, then it was time to clock out and put the schedule that had been paperclipped to my timecard in my pocket. Before I made my exit, I received a bear hug from Nina.

Back home, I answered the barrage of questions from Mom while Dad stayed quiet. I changed clothes that reeked of popcorn and butter and went to the den to watch the latest doings in the luxurious world of a certain

Denver-based family. But what I found was nothing short of a nightmare for me. The record button was slid to the off position, meaning it was access denied.

"Hey, did you guys mess with the VCR?"

My mother hadn't, but Big Ed's pointed look told me who the culprit had been. He was playing a dangerous game, considering that he knew all it took was for me to tell, an older version of my tattletale days that had been honed on John.

"You probably forgot to set it up," Big Ed snapped. "It wouldn't be the first time that you made a mistake with that machine." He was referring to the time I cut off the conclusion to *The Winds of War*, which he didn't know was on purpose for another baseless grounding.

I didn't need a nighttime soap to watch; I was living in one. Granted, our power struggle wasn't as glamorous as the one between Blake and Alexis.

"Well, guess it's bed for me, then."

"Sleep tight," Mom said, not knowing that I expected to toss and turn most of the night in anticipation of tomorrow.

Like the worst version of Christmas morning, I came downstairs in the morning to an empty house, and not a pine tree, sparkling with festive lights and strands of tinsel, presents underneath its lowest branches. There would be no gifts today except for the knowledge of if I would be adding a plus or minus sign to my HIV status.

I stood in the kitchen as a single ray of sunlight streaming into the window found me in its path, becoming a spotlight. I looked towards the world outside the kitchen window, my gaze looking skyward, the sunlight highlighting the little gold flecks in the muddy brown of my eyes.

I was struck by the need to recite a prayer, but I really didn't know any aside from "Now I lay me down to sleep." Then I found myself humming the Dionne Warwick classic, "I Say a Little Prayer."

Preach Dionne, sing out Sister Warwick!

I wiped tears from my eyes and decided I had to wear a brave face today.

I was not hungry in the least, so breakfast was out. The clock on the microwave mocked me with the fact that 10 o'clock was an hour and a half away. It wouldn't hurt to get ready now and take a ride beforehand.

I had proclaimed it a "say something hat day," so I'd sport one of John's old baseball hats, brim pulled low to put my face to put it in the shadows. After a quick shower, I threw on my black jeans and a black long-sleeved shirt. I felt like Nina, dressed in constant mourning. I scrounged through John's closet for a dark blue hat with a tattered "Keep on Truckin'" patch on its front.

An appropriate message for the day.

I put the hat on the left-hand side of L'il Red's handlebar, as it would have blown off my head on my ride. I headed for Moonlight Beach and sat and watched the ocean until it was time to head off and find out my fate.

Sitting in the waiting room, I wanted to go back to a simpler time when I merely had a curable sore throat, flipping through a *Highlights* magazine and get life lessons from Goofus and Gallant. Instead, I sat with my hands in my lap. Looking down, I saw that I was doing inverted prayer hands and left them that way, figuring that it couldn't hurt.

"Henry Dodge," Dr. Baker's nurse and wife, Maggie, called out.

I rose steadier than I imagined, given the shaky vibrations running through every inch of my body.

We made our pleasantries of how my mom was, the weather, the results of my weigh-in, and she led me to a sterile white room. I hopped up on the crinkly paper covering the medical exam table. My temperature was normal on a day that was anything but. She said the doctor would be with me shortly, but it stretched into an eternity of five minutes, then ten. I was about to open the door and ask what the holdup was when Dr. Baker opened the door.

"You ready for your results, Henry?"

The air was sucked out of the room, all four walls closing in like the inside of a coffin. I saw his mouth forming words, but it was coming out in slow-motion, sounding like when I would slow my 78 records down to 33 1/3 speed as a kid to mix up my listening experience from something I had heard the same way, ad infinitum.

What was Dr. Ike Baker, M.D., saying? He could have been reciting the lyrics to "Da Doo Ron Ron" for all I could discern.

I asked him to repeat it.

"Negative. You're negative, Henry."

Negative!

I wanted to hug him, but I held back. He gave me a quick spiel about safe sex practices, thankfully without an accompanying pamphlet, then gave me a tepid handshake. In response, I gave him the most vigorous one I could muster. Before his exit, he informed me that Maggie would be in to remove my bandages as he tried to discreetly wipe his hand on his slacks from my slick handshake.

I didn't know if I should laugh, cry, or do a jaunty jig. Before I could decide, Maggie came in. She went about the task at wrist of removing the bandages too slowly for my taste.

"Not bad at all. Hardly noticeable."

"Do you think so?"

"Absolutely."

I looked down at her medical opinion. They were a little more prevalent than I would have liked. So, it would be long sleeves and sweaters for the foreseeable future. Thankfully, it wasn't summertime.

I was tempted to ask her to have me step on the scale again because I felt pounds lighter. The weeks of agonizing worry evaporated just as the deep breath I exhaled went into the air of the now good day. I was surprised that L'il Red did not take off into the sky, like Greased Lightning at the end of *Grease*.

As I let the engine idle, I looked at the building that I had called my temporary home for a week. Acting on spontaneity, I walked through the glass door at San Luis Rey slowly to see if Nurse Wretched was at the nurse's station. Thankfully, it was Nurse Susan, busy with paperwork.

I cleared my throat, and she looked up startled, and then smiled.

"Hello, Henry. How are you?"

"Much better, thanks. I was wondering if I could leave a message for Pete."

"Oh," she said, looking crestfallen. "He doesn't work here anymore."

"He doesn't?"

She leaned in closer and took on a confidant's lowered voice.

"Nurse Ramirez had him fired. She caught him with one of the patients."

"Damn," I said this, feeling like he had cheated on me. "Well, thanks. Nice to see you."

"You too, glad you're better."

"You and me both, sister."

I arrived home and went about the ritual of locking the door behind me, opening the sliding door for Shadow, closing it, and locking it when she had done her business. I went upstairs and the red button was blinking on the answering machine. It was David who asked why I hadn't scheduled my next appointment in a stern tone.

This week had been fraught with newness and uncertainty, and I had honestly forgotten. I called the office and got the monotone voice of Karen, guardian of Suite G, who informed me that David was currently in session. I gave her my name, and she responded with an "oh, you" and asked me to repeat my phone number.

I hung up, dialed Nina's number, and got her answering machine. Rather than blurt out the news of my clean bill of health, I just asked her robotic message retriever to have her call me back. Then, a new line of thinking went through the live wire of my brain. I found Tony's phone number on the piece of paper that he had written it down on.

My finger was a little shaky as I punched the number into the phone. I also got his answering machine and was secretly relieved, as I didn't think that I could say what I wanted with his voice on the other end.

"Hey, it's Henry. I'm sorry about everything. Uh, hope you're well and all."

I didn't feel the need to share my good news with him, as it would be akin to rubbing salt into his wound. Hopefully, my recorded apology will suffice. I may never know, but I felt better for having done it.

When the phone rang an hour later, it was David. I wanted to chastise him, saying I was gainfully employed and couldn't be bothered with such trivial matters as my mental well-being. In a perfect world, I would have said that, but I listened to him berating me about keeping on track with our sessions. I promised to call on Monday when I got next week's work schedule, which appeased the psychiatric gods.

It was another two hours before Nina called me back.

"Gurl, where have you been?" I would have made a great Jewish mother because my concern level for those I cared about was a shade below smothering. I had imagined any number of situations that could have prevented her from giving me a jingle back, from lying dead in a ditch to a fire in her apartment.

"I was initiating Phase One," she said slyly.

"How'd that go?"

"I was just the wheelman. But Michael did the dirty work. We will know more tomorrow. It's hard to hold the phone and rub your hands together like a Bond villain."

"Well, Pussy Galore, I can't wait to see the look on his face."

"Enough about that douche nozzle. What's the verdict?"

"Negative."

"Fuckin' A! We need to celebrate!"

"Whatcha got in mind?"

Her mother was taking the younger kids to visit her sister for the weekend, and that meant that Nina could throw a party Saturday night.

"A small gathering of the cream of the crop of society, little sandwiches with the crust cut off, Dom Perignon. Or just the usual gang of misfits, Doritos, and whatever is in the old lady's liquor cabinet.'

"Sounds top-drawer, old bean," I said as Thurston Howell III.

"What does one wear for such an auspicious occasion?" she asked as Lovey Howell.

"Well, my guess is going to be black for you."

"Brilliant deduction. But I mix it up from time to time!"

We chatted more about the downfall of Scott. I admitted that I had butterflies the size of Mothra in my stomach about our plan.

"Bring back the egg; you must bring back the egg," she said, like the twin faeries who protected the gigantic creature.

I laughed as she told me it would be "aces," and I believed her.

It was time for her to go to work. I promised to call her tomorrow after my telephone rendezvous with "Seth." to let her know that all systems were go. Then, she was to set her part of the plan into motion during her shift.

My mother noticed I was in a good mood as we sat down to pork chops and applesauce - gee that's swell! Big Ed remained silent, sullen, and on his way to being drunk. Just your typical day ending with Y at the Dodge home.

I went to bed earlier than usual, tired from the lack of sleep last night, and the adrenaline rush of the day was wearing off.

I woke up earlier than usual the next day, which meant Mom was still home.

She scrambled my eggs, asking what I was doing that day. Oh, just your typical Friday. Nothing to see here. Certainly not getting revenge on an old nemesis.

"Nothing much. Haven't really decided."

"When do you work again?"

"Tomorrow afternoon."

"Are you liking your job?"

"So far, so good."

Smiling, she sat as I ate my eggs, sitting with me for a few minutes, polishing off her cup of coffee, and then headed off to her own job.

Before I knew it, the time had arrived to call 976-Meet, a few minutes ahead of when I was to connect with a certain somebody. As I was hoping, the first person that I was connected with was Mort. This time, I gave my name as Seth, gave him Scott's description, and told him where I would be that afternoon. I did this with two more horndogs, really playing up the angle my friends and I had decided upon in a group consensus.

On the next doorbell ring, I was chatting with "Seth" again.

"Good morning, sunshine," he said, as slick as a wolf in sheep's clothing.

"Hey you." I was hoping that my jangly nerves weren't audible. "So, I'm curious. How did you know who I was?"

"Just deductive logic. Is that a problem?"

"None whatsoever. I just wish I could place you."

"See for yourself. I mean, if you want to meet up."

"Sure. Do you know the Pannikin in Leucadia?"

"Hopefully, that coffee comes with cream," he practically purred.

"Play your cards right."

I suggested 1 o'clock because that was when the rest of his gentlemen callers were scheduled to show up. I called Nina, gave her the time, and got showered, not worrying about looking cute for a date that I had no intention of attending, except from a distance. I parked L'il Red in the parking lot near Pannikin, finally using the helmet that Big Ed had made me buy, which I never used for vanity reasons, as it flattened my hair. The absolute nerve!

I saw Nina's station wagon in the parking lot. Three familiar figures ducked down as Scott pulled up in his blue Chevy Camaro. They popped up like three groundhogs, signaling six more weeks of winter as he went inside, got his coffee, and settled into a table on the patio. I saw him check his watch, an impatient look on his face. Then, it turned into one of shock and dismay as an older gentleman approached his table.

It had to be Mort, gray Polyester pants hiked up to his round stomach, loud checkered shirt, bald head, and thick Coke bottle glasses. He was carrying red roses to a first "date."

When he sat down, Scott jumped up so forcefully that he knocked over his coffee. He swatted at the roses; red petals began to drown in the house blend remnants running off the side of the table. And as he attempted to get away from the confused Mort, he knocked into another date: Sam, in full leather regalia, as I had told me that I/Scott/Seth was into being disciplined. Sam took advantage of their proximity to twist Scott's nipples underneath his Quicksilver shirt.

As Scott pushed Sam away and tried to escape, he nearly knocked poor, clueless Stacy over.

Nina had said that there was something she needed to tell her that had to be outside of work. Hi! Your boyfriend is a big homo, Stace. This fact was further solidified by Marcus, a thin as a rail thirty-year-old with a porn stache, who planted a big sloppy kiss on Scott.

Stacy pushed past Scott, hands to her face, got into her yellow Le Car, and sped off, nearly plowing into a white Honda Civic. I was transfixed by the car as if I were hypnotized by the spinning of its hubcaps until its driver found a spot. The chances of it being driven by the creep were drastically reduced by a mother and her small child exiting it.

Now Scott's Camaro was burning rubber out of the parking lot. Phase One had been set into motion. That's when we placed a classified ad in the gay publication *The Update*, complete with Scott's home number and instructions to get him "hot and bothered" with a sexy message about what the caller would like to do to him.

Unfortunately for Scott, his little sister answered the phone and wrote down all 20 of the messages that she shared with his mother.

Weeks later, we heard that Scott was again shuttled off to his older sister in Arizona again. And there was a phone number change for the Rainowskys.

I gave Nina, Derek, and Michael the “Hang Loose” sign that signaled it was time to disperse. We planned to meet up at our appointed after-plan meeting place at Denny’s, where we had hatched the scheme.

“Oh my God! That could not have gone any better!” Derek said, tears running down his face.

“He got what he deserved, fur shure!” Nina exclaimed.

“I kind of feel bad for Stacy,” Michael said.

“Well, better to find out now and not after having 2.5 kids with that asshole,” Nina said in defense of our little chess game. I was starting to regret it myself until I started receiving platitudes from the group.

“Good going, Henry! You’re not too pure to be pink!” Derek yelled out.

A senior citizen couple sitting two booths away swiveled their heads as quickly as their ages would allow. The lady raised her finger to shush us, but that didn’t dissuade me.

“I’m not a street, so don’t cross me, bitch!” I said enthusiastically.

This was the absolute limit for the elderly duo, who tossed their napkins down, paid their bill, speaking sharply to the waitress and pointing their fingers at us, and slowly stalked out of Denny’s.

“Something I said?” I inquired innocently.

“Maybe?” Nina said in an up-talk manner, which was a statement that sounded like a question instead.

We all burst into laughter just as the waitress informed us that we needed to leave.

“We’ll have none of your foolishness in here!”

Once outside, Nina suggested a way to have our own version of Moons Over My Hammy. At the count of three, we dropped trou and pressed our ass checks against the windows.

“How about out here?” Nina shrieked, and we ran off to our respective vehicles.

We were still laughing about Denny’s the next night at the party, cackling like a bunch of hens at our previous day’s shenanigans, passing a joint amongst ourselves, waiting for the other revelers to show up, our wine coolers dripping condensation onto their appointed coasters on the kitchen table.

In my honor, Nina put on Madonna's first album, and she was currently singing about the virtues of not forgetting in the musical lesson that was "Think of Me."

"Well, I guess we'd better find a new place to haunt," Nina giggled. "We're 86-ed from Denny's!"

"We have photos of you so-called mooners!" Michael said in his best Eve Arden as Principal McGee in *Grease*. "Nice ass, by the way, Henry."

"This old thing?" I said sheepishly. I didn't want to lead him on, so I steered away from my derrière. "I think it's a safe bet that we can't hang out at the Pannikin, either."

"Ya think?" Derek asked and began choking from the toking.

"Hey, what did you tell Stacy?" I said a few decibels higher than I had intended.

"I asked her what she thought my chances with Matt were."

"And she bought it?" I asked.

"Like toilet paper that's on sale. Cuz I'm the shit!" She did a touchdown dance.

The doorbell rang. People I had only seen in the halls at San Dieguito were filling up Nina's living room. Among them was studly Matt. He looked very Emilio Estevez in *The Breakfast Club* with a blue Nike tank top hugging his muscular frame. With the double glow of pot and wine cooler coursing through my veins, I approached him.

"I have that tank top," I said this and instantly felt lame.

"Cool," he said, quickly turning back to Diane.

Well, so much for that scintillating bit of conversation. Ruff, ruff, I was barking up the wrong tree. Why did I always go after the wrong guy? I should stick to safe sex with strangers. Once the weather got nicer, I could resume my bushwhacking ways at Black's.

Just then, Michael sidled up next to me, the heavy smell of alcohol on his breath.

"Struck out, eh?"

"Yeah. He would be fun to play ball with."

"Don't you mean to play with his balls?" He put his hand over his mouth and tittered like a geisha.

"Hey batter, sa-wing batter! We want a pitcher, not a belly itcher!" I chanted like the kids I had played in Little League with.

"His tank top must be restricting the blood flow to his brain. At least to his eyes. Anyone would be lucky to be with you."

I could see the lust in his eyes as surely as I saw how red and glazed they were. He leaned in for a kiss.

"Listen, Michael. I like you. Just not that way. Let's not fuck up our friendship. Cool?"

"So, I guess a blowjob's out of the question?" he said, which made us both laugh.

"What are you ladies carrying on about?" Derek said and put an arm around each of our shoulders.

"The usual. Stupid boys," Michael said.

"Ugh," This was all that Derek offered on the subject. "I need a drink."

"Precisely," I said, and we all went into the kitchen, where Nina was holding court at the kitchen table with two guys. I thought I was seeing double, as they were San Dieguito's resident identical twins, Jeremy and Joshua Weiss. Four empty bottles stood sentry in front of her, one of them acting as an ashtray for her clove cigarette.

Derek and Michael took one for themselves out of her thinning pack in an unspoken manner that conveyed this was old hat for them. I grabbed two wine coolers from the fridge, gave them to the boys, and took two more for Nina and myself.

"Can I have one of those?" I said, looking at the cigarette pack.

"Of course, doll," Nina said with a definite slur. She lit it with her Zippo.

I convulsed with coughs.

"Smooth, like smoking asbestos."

"You should see about being their spokesperson. Go easy on that; it's not like smoking pole," Derek suggested.

"Now, where were we?" Nina slurred.

"Mary Ann or Ginger," Jeremy reminded her.

"Oh yeah. So, which one and why, you tools?"

"Mary Ann!" Jeremy proclaimed.

Joshua disagreed, stating that the movie star was the hotter of the two.

"No way!" Jeremy argued.

"Yes way!" Joshua stated, even punching his former womb mate on the shoulder for emphasis.

"Ow! What the fuck, Josh?"

"Just trying to knock some sense into you, bro."

"Ok, before you lugs get into fisticuffs about this," Nina said, "let me offer up an alternative. What about when Mary Ann thought she was Ginger? Best of both worlds, amma I riiiight?"

Both considered it for a moment and nodded their heads.

"As long as I get laid, I don't care which one," Joshua said.

"Spoken like a true gentleman." Nina chided and then waved her hands. "Now shoo, flies, shoo!"

"Jesus, that was a lot of testosterone!" Michael said.

"Yes, they are chock full of the stuff," Nina said, then launched into the story about how she had sex with them. "Not at the same time, mind you. At separate times, cuz I'mma lady."

"Lady of the evening is more like it," Derek said.

"Takes one to know one, hooker," Nina said, extending her middle finger.

"Which one was better?" I asked.

"Well, I'd have to go with Jeremy. He wasn't a two-pump chump like Joshua was. I was like, 'I took a shower for this?'"

I loved how Nina did not apologize for what she wanted to do or who she had done. I hoped that some of that would rub off on me.

As the night wore on and our buzzes increased, the crowd began to dissipate. Then it was just as it should be, the four of us. We helped Nina clean up, like any good gay friend should, until was time to head out.

But there was another destination besides home I wanted to check out.

A blanket of darkness surrounded me as I tried to adjust my eyes to the black and not get scratched by the bushes. The mental note that I had written myself when Carlos had told me about the viewpoint being a cruising spot was unfolded, a treasure map to follow, *Indiana Jones and the Temple of Cock.*

It was a nighttime version of Black's. I felt like Mr. Magoo, blind as a bat and feeling my way around, when my hand landed on a shirtless, muscular back. In front of the shadows of the night was someone on his knees and going to town of him.

"Sorry," I muttered.

"What's your hurry?"

As the moon briefly peeped out, I caught a flicker of a handsome face. Better to hedge my bets here, and this was a case of "a bird in the hand is worth two in the bush," as hands started to unzip my fly.

I was instantly hard and the guy on his knees vacillated between us, as I played with the shirtless one's well-defined chest. He began to moan and, seconds later, was zipping his pants and leaving.

I returned my attention to the man who was towering over me, who bent down and began kissing me. When he pulled back, the full moon gave me another brief clue as to the identity of who this stud was. From my vantage point and in a shaft of moonlight, I caught a glimpse of a gray tooth.

"Pete!"

He stepped back to try to assess who knew his name in this anonymous situation.

"Henry?"

"The one and only."

His response was to come closer, kissing me harder, his hands feeling everywhere and everything; I returned the favor with a skilled groping and make-out session. I could discern that he may give Danny a bit of a run for his money regarding the amount of hardness pressed against my sternum.

When I stopped, because the thought of Danny was making my skin crawl, he asked if I was ok.

"Perfect."

"You wanna come back to my place?"

"Definitely."

We dressed hurriedly and headed back up the slight incline, Pete holding my hand as he led the way. This was a game of Follow the Leader that I could get behind. He unlocked the door to his green MGB roadster and revved the engine.

I started L'il Red and followed him southbound, exiting on Villa De La Valle, then traveling a few more miles until we reached a cluster of condos.

"Home, sweet home," he said when we reached his condo and then pounced on me before I could compliment him on his place. It would have been impossible, as his tongue was jammed down my throat.

When we finally came up for air, he led me upstairs to his bedroom. He stood before me, a descendant of a Greek god, forgoing a himation in favor of an outfit purchased at Chess King.

He stripped in record time. I could see clearly now that I had not been wrong in my assessment of his manhood. He took my clothes off me with greater care than he had shown for his wardrobe, gently pulling down my bikini briefs.

"You're a sight for sore eyes," he said, looking me up and down, a lion with a piece of meat. Then it was feeding time as he scooped me up in his massive arms and plopped me down gently on his queen-sized bed. He lay down next to me, pulling me on top of him. We explored each other's bodies like an all-you-can-eat buffet. He held my head in his massive mitts and asked if I was ready for dessert.

"You want me inside of you?" he panted.

"Do you have a condom?"

He pulled open his dresser drawer, producing a gold-wrapped Magnum, Elbow Grease lube, and a small amber bottle of poppers.

"You are going to need this. If it's too much, I'll stop. OK?"

I nodded, and he uncapped the Rush, and I took two big whiffs. The euphoric rush gripped me. Before I knew it, Pete was where he wanted to be. Dammit, if it didn't hurt, but he was every inch the gentle giant.

He didn't come inside of me, pulling out just before and taking the condom off, doing a good imitation of a fountain.

"You're incredible. Damn, that was hotter than I imagined, and I have a rather good imagination," he said once his breathing had settled down.

On the inside, I was swooning and giving myself a mental high five. But outside, I was doing my best Danny Zuko, when he ran into Sandy at the pep rally.

"*I mean, you know how it is... rockin' and rollin' and whatnot.*"

And my split had been divoon, as Frenchie had put it so eloquently.

And even though I was lying side-by-side with Pete, I was beside myself with the prospects of what could be. The hopelessly devoted to you romantic in me was kicking into overdrive.

Our pillow talk consisted of nothing too substantial, just what kind of music, movies, and TV shows we liked. I was trying to butch it up, not wanting to reveal my love of *Dallas* and *Dynasty*, substituting them for more macho shows like *The A-Team* and the just-cancelled *Hardcastle and*

McCormick. I had watched because Brian Keith had played Uncle Bill on *Family Affair* and Daniel Hugh Kelly had been easy on the eyes.

We delved into *The Brady Bunch* and *The Partridge Family*, which he favored over the story of a lovely lady and a man named Brady and their six combined offspring. They were no competition for David Cassidy's shag haircut and puka shell necklace. Then, it was back to the modern-day TV lineup.

"You don't watch *The Golden Girls*, do you?" he asked, looking intently into my eyes. I was not sure if it was a trick question.

"Why? Do you want me to tell you a story about St. Olaf?" I asked innocently.

"Picture it, Sicily…" he said and laughed.

"Shady Pines, Ma!" I responded.

"Are you a Dorothy, Sophia, Rose, or Blanche?"

"Well, I can be snarky like Dorothy and a little dense at times like Rose."

"Are you like a Blanche when it comes to men?"

I gave him kudos for his roundabout way of asking if I was a slut.

"Well, I have had some gentlemen callers in the past," I said, conjuring up a slight Southern lilt. "Why do you ask?"

"Just wondering if you're a one-man type of guy," he said, lighting a cigarette.

"Why? Do you want to go steady?"

"I would like to get to know you better, Henry. And I'd most definitely like to pin you again."

"Well, there's no time like the present," I said, grabbing his cigarette from his hand and snubbing it out in the ashtray on his nightstand.

And round two was on. Afterwards, I knew two things. I would be walking funny tomorrow, and it was getting late. Even though I had the upper hand with Big Ed; I didn't want to unleash the beast and end up getting busted for coming home after streetlights, as John and I had joked about our curfew. Pete and I took a shower and dried off. I held back from touching him again as much as I wanted to.

"So, do you want to spend the night?" Pete asked.

"I really should get home."

"Ah, OK." He looked crestfallen.

"I want to. But I have to work tomorrow at AMC. Besides, I don't want to piss off the parents."

"Yeah, I've seen your Dad in action." He said with his eyebrow raised and whistled. "How about a proper date? When is your next day off?"

"My schedule comes out tomorrow," I said. "And that would be really nice."

As Pete escorted me to the front door in the buff, he stopped and wrote down his number on a yellow Post-it, shoving it into my pocket, before he bent down and planted an intense kiss on my lips.

"Now, don't lose that," he teased.

"I won't, I promise."

"Pinky swear?"

I locked my pinky into his and kissed him with the same ferocity that he had just done to me. Signed, sealed, delivered, I'm yours.

He sighed and looked at me, both angelic and devilish at the same turn. I suspected round three could be a go if I didn't leave.

"Alright, scat!" he said and slapped my ass.

"Sir, yes, sir!"

"I like the sound of that." He smiled, and there it was, that goddamned tooth. Would it be rude to take a bottle of Wite-Out to it while he slumbered?

I gave him a little salute.

"Night, sweet man," he said, closing the door.

As I drove home, the streetlights seemed extra bright, spotlighting the happiness I was experiencing. And as I pulled up and parked in the driveway, I knew I had to stay up a bit longer.

I had a mixtape to make for Pete.

I decided against any songs that had the word "love" in the lyrics and included some classic rock entries, like "Light My Fire" by The Doors and "Burnin' For You" by Blue Oyster Cult, among other selections like "The Perfect Kiss" by New Order and Duran Duran's ode to the one-night stand, "Save A Prayer."

I wrote a simple "For Pete" on the label of the multi-colored Memorex tape and put it in its case as a yawn escaped me. I was totally satisfied with how this day turned out, and provided me with dreams where I was flying high in the sky, never once plummeting to the ground.

I awoke, feeling as free as a bird, uncaged, a song escaping from my heart as I hummed "Two of Hearts" by Stacey Q. Then I switched to General Public's "Tenderness."

"Well, someone's awfully chipper for getting in at 2:38 last night," my mother said when I came down. She was cooking her version of Potatoes O'Brien.

"I helped Nina clean up after her get-together," I explained earnestly, using the euphemism for rager in the hopes that it sounded like we were having a rousing game of Monopoly that had run later than expected.

But no dice, no passing go, or collecting $200 - she wasn't buying it just as she never did when she landed on Baltic Avenue.

"Well, let me remind you that curfew is midnight. A very generous curfew at that. Are you reading me?"

"Loud and clear, lady."

Staying up to all hours of the night had never been an issue before since my social life was bathing in the comforting flicker of the television screen. I was bracing for the "while you're living under this roof" speech but circumvented it with a heartfelt sorry for making her worry. The stern look that she rarely showed subsided, replaced with her usual sunny disposition.

"Are you hungry?"

"Starving!"

If only she knew how I had worked up my appetite, it would have killed hers. I wished we had the kind of relationship where I met a guy and she'd be genuinely happy.

I knew I was chipping away at her slowly, showing her that I was an older version of the sweet little boy who would make a heart made from macaroni shells as a Valentine's Day card in kindergarten. But I had also shown her a dark side that would be hard to forget.

And she knew I was trying to change by going to David, with Big Ed still in the dark about it. Secrets in our house scattered like cockroaches when the lights were turned on.

She plated my food, which included sausage links, but before she could serve it to me, I gave her a big hug and a peck on the cheek.

"I love you, Mom."

"Now what brought that on?"

"I just felt like saying it, that's all. Now sit down."

I served her breakfast, relieving her from her indentured servitude.

"Now, if you could get your father to do this, I may die from shock."

"Where is the old man?"

"Mrs. Woodson was having trouble with her car."

I bet. That motherfucker didn't even have the decency to do it when Mom was at work.

"Hey Mom..." I started and was interrupted by the front door opening.

"Something smells good," Big Ed said, but all I could detect was the scent of a rat.

He grabbed a plate and fork, then piled the remainder of the breakfast on his plate and sat at the head of the table. His white shirt did have grease smudges on it. But so would mine when I was assigned with the dreaded task of helping him "fix" the car so that I could feel a part of the bonding time that he and John shared. The human equivalent of the Shake 'N Bake tagline, "And I helped."

Mom asked, "What were you saying?"

"This is delicious. Thanks for making it."

"Yes, Katie. Thanks."

We finished breakfast in silence, except for the dialogue in my head of what I really wanted to say. I wasn't sure how much longer I could hold back and not tell my unsuspecting mother. The time was drawing near when I had to sink his battleship, but I had to think of a gentle approach before I blew up their marriage with my atomic words. He was safe for now, as I had to be at work by noon, so I went about the three S's: shit, shower, shine.

"I'm dragging ass today," Nina said when I joined her behind the concession stand.

"Gee. I hadn't noticed." I said, ignoring the dark circles under her eyes.

"You don't look worse for wear. What's your secret?"

"Gurl, which one?"

We laughed, and before I could confide about Pete, Eddie, a lanky blond usher, opened the floodgates of people wanting to enjoy a leisurely afternoon at the movies.

As we restocked and prepped for the next wave of moviegoers, I 'fessed up.

"I went to the Viewpoint after your party. You'll never guess who I met up with."

"Not Michael!"

"Um, no. Although he tried putting the moves on me at your party. I politely declined."

"Good call; he's seen more ass than a toilet seat."

"You certainly have a way with words."

"Don't make me play Twenty Questions! Tell me!"

"Actually, that sounds like a great idea."

"Fucker. Ok, is he bigger than a bread box?"

I held up the hotdog that I was putting on the grill.

"Definitely."

"Damn! Enough with the games already."

"One more hint." I leaned in closer to her. "He's from where we met."

"Carlos?"

I shook my head.

"Dear God. Not Larry!"

"I happen to have standards."

"Pete?"

"Aaaand Bingo was his name-o."

"Wow! He is hot, except…" She stopped mid-sentence to tap at her own tooth.

"Yeah, yeah, yeah. I know. He wants to take me on a date!"

Our conversation was cut short by Yvonne inspecting our work.

Nina took her lunch at Arby's but returned quickly and out of breath.

"Oh my God, you should see your scooter!" she exclaimed.

I was expecting 'Lil Red to be utterly destroyed due to the urgency in Nina's voice, little fragments of red sprinkled across the parking lot.

But what I saw was that my cherry apple red scooter was mutating into something resembling a drivable banana. *One banana, two banana, three banana, four* came drifting up in my mind, but it was doubtful that Fleegle, Bingo, Drooper, and or Snork were behind this.

Practically every square inch was covered in yellow Post-its. For a split second, I thought that the Honda driver had struck again, and then it clicked that Pete had written his number down on the very same squares. The multitude of notes was the result of pillow talk.

One read: "Marcia! Marcia! Marcia!" Another had the entire theme of *The Golden Girls* on several squares that extended in a neat little paper trail across my dashboard. The biggest display was made by a field of yellow, with a simplistic rendering of a heart.

Sitting on the seat, secured by a piece of tape, was a single sunflower with an accompanying message that read: "Last Night Did Me Colors."

I was beaming. However, I couldn't leave my scooter like this and asked Nina to help remove them, which I stashed in the glovebox, and the sheer volume of yellow came close to the door not closing. But making big things fit into tight spaces was quickly becoming a specific skill set I was becoming adept at.

"Damn! Henry and Pete sitting in a tree, f-u-c-k-i-n-g," Nina teased.

"Jealous? Girl, green does not go with your uniform."

"And I thought lesbians moved fast!"

"And what makes you the authority on lesbians?"

"Well, dear, let's just say I've been to a clambake a time or two."

"So, you're an equal opportunity whore."

"Whores get paid. A slut gives it away for free."

"Duly noted."

I was taken aback by her mention of being bisexual, not because it was shocking, but because she was so laid-back about it. Like any gay man worth his salt, I had a soft spot for strong women who knew what they wanted and weren't afraid of going about getting it.

Yvonne was on the sidewalk with her arms folded, a frown on her face over my unsanctioned break. I snatched up my flower and approached Yvonne.

"Sorry. I will take a shorter lunch to make up for it."

A smile bloomed on her face.

"Aww, I can't stay mad at you. Just make sure it does not happen again, cutie."

There was a flirtatiousness about her reprimand - what was it about the Barnes family and me? Like sister, like brothers.

I offered up an awkward smile and returned to restocking candy. Just as I bent over and slid a few Snicker bars into place, fingers pinched my ass. I assumed it was Nina, but as I stood up and spun around, I saw that it was Yvonne.

"That is one nice butt," she said.

"My boyfriend thinks so, too."

"He gave you that precious flower? Sweet. But if things don't work out, we should hang out."

"Um, OK."

I didn't want to say no, as she reported to Erik about how I was doing, and I still had two weeks of probation to go before they determined if I was permanent popcorn-slinging material.

She issued a whiplash smile and disappeared into the back, re-emerging with a broom and dustpan to help Eddie clean the theaters. I'll be damned if she wasn't singing "Hungry Like the Wolf."

"I'm on the hunt. I'm after you," she sang.

Nina put her hand on my shoulder, and I jumped a country mile.

"Jesus! Don't do that!"

"Sorry! Why so jumpy?"

I launched into Yvonne's unwanted advances and my physical relationships with both of her brothers.

"Wow! If you sleep with her, you would have done a whole family! Are their parents hot?"

"Gurl."

"You should go for it!"

"Yes, it will look great on my resume."

"Well, it does fall under the 'being a team player' category. Besides, don't knock it till you try it, junior."

It wasn't like the prospect of sleeping with a woman disgusted me. Frankly, the situation had never presented itself – but there were times when I had wondered if my life would be easier if I was "normal." But normal meant boring with a capital B, and my life had been anything but that up until this point.

Besides, I had a date with Pete to focus on. That night, I took my schedule home and retrieved his phone number from the pants I had worn last night; I felt giddy and hopeful because what he did made my mixtape to shame.

I put the flower on the nightstand next to my bed. Thankfully, I didn't have a hope chest to put it in because my poodle skirt was at the dry cleaner's. I needed a proper vessel, so I grabbed one of the plastic 7-11 Slurpee Rock cups from the kitchen that my mother had kept for more than a decade.

I chose the KC and the Sunshine Band one over Grand Funk Railroad. I was filling it when my mother came into the kitchen.

"Somebody's thirsty."

"No. I have a flower that needs a drink."

"A flower?"

"Yes, I got it from, um, a friend," I said this, wanting to be gentle with her that I may potentially have a boyfriend. But that remained to be seen.

"Well, what a thoughtful *friend.* What is his name?"

Hold up! Was she really being ok with this?

"Peter," I said, hoping she wouldn't make the connection between my mystery man and the one she'd met at San Luis Rey.

"How did you meet him?"

I did not want to say in the bushes at the viewpoint, so I lied again and said at Nina's party.

"Well, that's nice. Make sure he treats you nicely, OK?" She cupped my chin in her hand.

"It's nothing serious. We're just getting to know each other."

"And be *careful.*" She meant to be cautious about practicing safe sex.

I shuddered but appreciated the concern at the same time.

"I'm making tuna gunk for dinner!"

Another concoction brought to you by the good folks at Velveeta with shell pasta and generous portions of Chicken of the Sea coupled with its appropriate name snapped me out of my good mood.

Back in my room, I put the flower in its makeshift vase and then dialed the number on the Post-it.

"Hello," Pete said firmly, as if I were trying to sell him a newspaper subscription. I disguised my voice with a Southern twang.

"May I speak with the man of the house?"

"What can I do for you?"

"Mah name is Jimmy Billy Bob Lee, and I was wonderin' if you are satisfied."

"Satisfied with what?"

"The hot piece of ass you had last night," I answered breathily, back to my normal speaking voice.

"Mmm. Very." He said with his normal, even-keeled demeanor. "How are you, babe?"

"A-ok in the US of A. That was quite an art project you did on my scooter."

"Huh? What are you talking about?"

Then Pete burst out with laughter.

"Very funny."

"I thought so, Jimmy Billy Bob Lee. It wasn't too much, was it?"

"To paraphrase Dirty Harry, it made my day!"

"Paraphrase, eh? Someone's cracked open a book."

"What can I say? I'm more than a pretty face." My jitters evaporated.

"I suspected as much. So, when is our date? I really want to see you."

"My social secretary says I have an opening tomorrow. What's that Miss Moneypenny? There are also slots open on Tuesday or Friday night."

"Well, the place I have in mind isn't open tomorrow."

"Uh, McDonald's is always open!"

"I'll give you a Happy Meal."

"Promises, promises."

"That is a promise I intend to keep. Friday is too long to wait, so Tuesday it is."

We decided on him picking me up at my house, as he was being cagey about where our evening would take us. I almost gave him the address next door. I did not want my mother peering through the curtains to see who I was going out with, then running down the driveway in her purple housecoat with pink piping to meet my suitor, resembling a nighttime version of Gladys Kravitz.

I hung up the phone without either of us saying, "No, you hang up first," I knew that I needed to reach out to another man tomorrow. And that would be David. Granted, that phone call wouldn't leave me with butterflies that were flapping around, looking for a way out of my stomach.

I pictured myself standing in my room on the night of my date, an explosion of Monarchs escaping from my mouth, circling around me, and once they had dissipated, I would have on the perfect date night ensemble, just like Cinderella.

"Bippity, Boppity, Boo, indeed!" I said to the butterfly-free air, snapping my finger.

Deciding to hunker down and journal, I was surprised when the words poured out of me.

Sooner than I knew it, bedtime was upon me, but I couldn't shut my head off. I imagined the opening credits to *Love American Style*, and the two stars featured in the hearts were us. Sorry Karen Valentine, you didn't make the cut! Then I realized I didn't know his last name, or that much about him for that matter.

Pete had the upper hand, having studied my chart, but those were just words, and whatever they said didn't dissuade him from wanting to get to know me on a level I hadn't experienced before.

Well, there was Tony. But that wasn't meant to be, and while I wouldn't claim to being anything close to what you would call being religious, I had the momentary notion that I should clasp my hands together, bow my head in reverence, and pray that Pete would turn out to be different.

And that was the way it felt. I had done plenty of deals with the Devil in my not-so-distant past, and my last thought before sleep overtook me was if I could fit "Send Me an Angel" onto his mixtape.

The next day, I scheduled my David appointment for Friday, not letting Karen's sourpuss nature put a damper on the electricity surging through my body. I stayed in my mental health mode and finished my drawing for show-and-tell with my shrink.

I put a call into Nina after I was done.

"Guess who has a date tomorrow night?"

"A hooker on El Cajon Boulevard?"

"Hardy-har-har. Me, dummy!"

"Same thing."

"Alright, Shecky."

"So where is Mr. Wonderful taking you?"

"He's surprising me with the where, but to dinner is the what."

"Then a midnight snack at his place?"

"A lady never tells."

"Good thing I'm not talking to one."

"I am ssso a lady! If you sssay I'm not, I'll bop you one!" I said in my best Cindy Brady lisp. It made me think of George, the last person I wanted to let into my brain.

"Oh, Thindy. Do you think they meant to write her as a special needs character?" Nina joked and replaced it with a serious question. "Are you nervous?"

"A little bit, but I'm sure it will go to a lot of bit tomorrow."

"Henry likes a boy!"

"And he likes me, bitch."

"I hope he bought stock in Post-its." I heard a voice in the background. "OK, gotta go to the grocery store to get something for dinner. Apparently, kids like to eat. Talk to you later, masturbator."

As the day bled into night and the next morning, then afternoon, and finally evening, I was schoolgirl nervous as predicted. My shaky hands made it hard to style my hair. I skipped shaving for fear of accidentally cutting my kissing lips with the wrong stroke of the razor.

I had an outfit all laid out on my bed and then went to the closet to explore other options. What did I want my outfit to convey? I didn't want to dress too provocatively. But I didn't want to be too casual, either. I decided to go with my gut feeling and chose a Periwinkle Brittanica polo shirt, white jeans, and my cleanest white Nikes. I opted against taking a jacket, hoping that he would have the top up on his convertible, so my hair wouldn't deconstruct further.

I went downstairs, using the metal railing for support, and there was my mother in the very housecoat I had hoped she wouldn't be sporting. I stood at the window and looked outside; Pete was due any minute. I turned around, and my mother was wearing a white nightgown, and her blonde hair was now brunette and curly like she had been electrified or was channeling Ted Nugent.

"That boy's not coming!"

"Stop it, Mama! I'm nervous enough!" I imagined she was channeling Piper Laurie in *Carrie*.

"I can see your dirty pillows. Everyone will!"

Before she demanded that I come to my closet and pray, a pair of headlights flashed across my field of vision and Pete's convertible was idling in front of the driveway.

"See ya, Mom."

"Have a good time. Remember your curfew."

"Gotcha."

Pete opened the passenger door for me. I wondered if Mom was peering out to get a clear view of him. What she would have seen was a gentleman decked out in a black button-down shirt and a pair of khakis that accentuated every minute he devoted to his gym regimen and her youngest son practically levitating into the car, snatched by the winds blowing him up to cloud nine. Pete had the radio set to 91X when I remembered the mixtape in my pocket.

"I made something for you," I said, handing it to him.

"Aww, sweet. Thanks. Henry."

He put it in, and The Thompson Twins began singing "Hold Me Now." When we were at the bottom of the street, he pulled over and laid one hell of a kiss on me, putting the heater to shame in getting me warm.

"I've been dreaming of doing that all day."

I began running my hands over his chest. Before either of us knew it, the windows had begun to fog up, and he switched the heat to defrost.

"So where are we going, mister?"

"How do you feel about barbeque? I know this great spot just down the road."

Say what now?

He meant my old workplace. My stomach was in knots. Almost as bad as the physical aversion to coleslaw I had developed working there when it was time to tackle dishwashing duties. The sink would often clog with the side dish, and I would have to stick my hand through the milky water to unclog it. Just the thought made my stomach jump, but not as much as stepping across the threshold there again. Damn. I did not want to come off as difficult to please on the first date. And puking on Pete would diminish my chances for a second date.

Besides, what are the odds that Steve would be working?

The odds were against me. Steve greeted us at the door, giving Pete a big smile and then reserving a scowl for me.

"How have you been, my friend?" Steve asked Pete.

"Excellent."

I remained silent, soaking up the knowledge that they knew each other.

"And how are you, *Henry*?" Steve asked, playing the congenial host who really wanted to punch me in the throat.

"Great."

"Oh, you two know each other?" Pete said, shooting me a puzzled look.

"Yeah, I used to work here."

"He worked directly *under* me," Steve replied.

"Steve taught me everything that I needed to know." I paused for effect, eliminating the word "blow" from my next statement. "It was my first *job*."

"Yvonne said you are working with her now."

"Yup." I was detecting a confused look on Pete's face, so I kept it light, not wanting to disclose my *Dallas/Dynasty* moment of blackmailing Steve. I mean, at least not on the first date and all.

A familiar looking busboy came to the table with our waters. My old buddy Kevin - who had dropped off my friendship radar after I had come out to him - said it was great to see me. There was a small part of me that thought it would be a case of turnabout is fair play that he might have to figure out what Steve had in mind for training.

Naturally, Pete chose a half-rack of ribs and coleslaw, not knowing of my physical aversion to it that started at the very spot we were dining at. Visions of the sink clogged with it almost mademe want to hurl, and I wanted to forgo my order of two pieces of chicken and sausage.

"Wow, it's like old home week for ya here." Pete offered.

"Yeah, something like that."

We made as much small talk as I would divulge being at the original scene of the crime, as I didn't want Steve to overhear anything about my personal life. Once we were done and Pete had paid the bill, I excused myself to use the bathroom to get the excess barbeque sauce off my hands that the Wet-Naps had missed.

The hallway looked the same, but it didn't give me the same excitement as I walked across the carpet I had once laid down upon, naked and entwined with a man ten years older than me, figuring out what made a man tick.

Kevin emerged from the bathroom.

"Watch out for Steve," I said curtly. "He's kind of a creep."

"He's been nice to me."

"Do not fall for it."

"OK."

"He'll put the moves on you. He did with me."

"But he knows I'm straight."

"Yeah, but he doesn't know that he is." I cautioned and then channeled my inner Kate Dodge. "Just be careful."

"Thanks for the heads-up."

"Yeah, sure thing. Just make sure his doesn't try to go down into your lap." It was the last thing I said as I went into the bathroom.

Once my hands were clean, I headed back to the dining area. Pete was gone. Steve stood behind the register as I approached.

"Lose something?" he said sarcastically.

"Just looking for my *date*."

"He's out-front smoking. You two have a good night, *fag*."

"Takes one to know one, even if that other one is a pathetic closet case."

That promptly shut him up.

"Toodles."

Pete was leaning one muscular leg back against the building, like a true Marlboro Man.

"Howdy, cowboy."

"There's my buckaroo." He gave me a half-hug. "Ready for part two?"

"Definitely," I said.

Pete hit the 101. Was he taking the scenic beach route to add some romance that had not been on show at Lavar's? He pulled off to the side of the road, parking adjacent to the rocks that lined the Cardiff shoreline. I thought it was time for another make-out session. But he directed me to exit the vehicle. He took a blanket from the trunk and led me to the beach.

We sat there, the sounds of the waves putting me at peace and the moon providing candlelight. Pete reached into his pocket for what I figured was another cigarette and produced a distant cousin instead. He held a joint up and asked if I wanted to partake.

"Yes, please."

He lit the joint and inhaled deeply. Then he held it up to my lips to take a toke. Unfortunately, I did too big of a hit and did my best to not make it sound like I was someone with TB, issuing a few little sputtering coughs.

"It's some good shit."

"Yeah, it's Maui Wowie."

"Well, say aloha to my brain cells."

"Hey, what was up back there? You were as nervous as a cat in a roomful of rocking chairs, as my granny used to say."

"I'm not the biggest fan of Steve. I didn't leave the job on the best of terms."

"You know how straight guys are around gays. They think we want to get them into bed."

"And did you?"

"Oh, hell no! Not my type, and besides, he has a black belt in karate. I didn't want him to go all Cobra Kai on me." He quipped and took another long drag from the joint.

"So, no whack-on, whack-off then."

He held the reefer up to my lips again, and I took a more sedate inhale.

"Aww, you're jealous. That's cute as fuck."

"Not really, but that's 'cute as fuck' that you think so. Alright, tell me about you."

Pete Kowalski was 24, originally from Long Island. Came here after a bad breakup to attend nursing school and then landed the job where we had met.

"So, I heard you're not working with Wretched anymore."

"And how do we know that cutie?"

"A little birdie told me when I went to leave you a note with my phone number."

"Did you now?"

I wasn't going to say I knew about Pete's dalliance with a patient, but he was willing to sing. Turned out that the patient was me – and Heather saw us hugging.

"Oh shit, I'm sorry!"

"I'm not. It all worked out. I was getting burned out, to be honest. There was a lot of sadness in that place."

"Yeah. Was I part of that sadness?"

"Well, you were going through a tough time, but I could tell you wanted to change that."

"I do, and I am."

"Good. Ok, your turn."

I completely glossed over LA and Tina. Just the surface was gleaned, nothing too deep, as I didn't want to scare him off that I was merely damaged goods.

I was actively working to exorcise those demons that had lived within me for the entirety of my life. Then, I talked about expressing myself on a sketchpad.

"I'd love to see some of your drawings sometime."

"We'll see."

I was excited at the prospect of where this could go. As it was, the immediate future saw me up against the boulders, pants dropped down to my ankles as Pete went to town on me. We finished just in time as a police car drove up, flashed a spotlight on where our blanket was, and merely drove off without further inspection.

"Well, that was a narrow escape. I should get you home. I have a job hunt tomorrow."

"You're hired because you give a mean one that begins with b, ends in w, and has two letters in between."

"There's more where that came from if you want." Pete purred.

"Well, my Mom didn't raise a dummy. So yes."

"Remind me to thank her for that."

As Pete steered us to my house, I started leaping ahead in my ideas. This guy wanted a real relationship – something that I had never experienced. Maybe it was the dawning of the age of a queerer us. Perhaps Jupiter, Mars, and all the February stars were aligning, and Pete may be "the one."

Once we were parked in my driveway, we kissed some more, and then it was back to reality and the ground, feet carrying me in a dazed motion. The Maui Wowie, combined with Pete's passionate kisses, were causing the internal marimba rhythms to make me sway. I steadied myself against the front door, digging for my key, when the door opened, and I almost fell on my face.

Big Ed stood back and took in the sight of his son who was lust-stoned, and well, just plain stoned.

"I'd appreciate it if you didn't flaunt your proclivities in front of the house." He said tersely. "The neighbors don't need to know what a disappointment you've turned out to be."

"Afraid it might scare off Mrs. Woodson? Oh wait, her treacherous son is also a dirty queer. Is that what you bonded over?"

"You little son of a bitch!"

"More like a son of a bastard. Enjoy your time with her because it's coming to a close, maybe sooner, maybe later. I'll determine that when I see fit. Now, excuse me; I simply must brush the taste of dick out of my mouth."

I left him standing there in the dust and went to bed, but not before I reveled in the fact that I had the upper hand to Big Ed's underhanded ways. I had stayed under his thumb for so many years that it felt exhilarating to come up for air.

The next day, I called Nina to give her the not-so-gory details about my night with Pete, including tearing my father a new one.

"Jesus! Is it too late to nominate him for Father of the Year?"

"Almost 18 years too late."

"That reminds me; do you have plans for your birthday?"

I was sure it would be the usual yearly ritual of a homemade lemon cake with green icing and chocolate chip ice cream, culminating with Big Ed having his cake upstairs.

"And why do you ask, pray tell?"

"Well, the boys and I want to take you out, cool?"

"Absolutely! What do you guys have in mind?"

"Well, my dear, that's the surprise."

"Otay. Is there a dress code I should know about?"

"It's casual. No top hat and tails required, love."

"Gotcha."

When we hung up, I contemplated the fact that in two weeks, I would be considered a man. It was a weird concept that I couldn't quite wrap my head around. Would there be some detectable change, a different vibration running through my being? Likely, I would be the same Henry Dodge.

However, I figured I had one more act of teenage rebellion left in me.

After taking scissors to my most tattered blue jeans, I went to work on an equally well-loved t-shirt. I entered my Mom and Dad's closet to complement and highlight my ensemble.

I passed the time until Big Ed got home by smoking some Mean Green and hazily playing soccer with Shadow. I changed into my Daisy Dukes, showing off my nice sticks, hugging me front to back, not leaving much to the imagination. A hint of ass cheek and exposed belly was a bit breezy on this February day, but the warmth of revenge was all I needed to stoke the fires of insurrection. I straddled L'il Red, wearing the red pumps I had snagged from Mom. I revved my scooter like I was the toughest Hell's Angel around and then drove her across from our house. As Big Ed pulled into the driveway, I pulled out and started my one-person Pride parade.

"Holiday! I'm so gay!" I sang at the top of my lungs. "If we took a holiday, I would still be real gaaaaaaaaay!"

I drove by our house at a slow speed and repeated my take on Madonna's plea for having a celebration all across the world and in every nation. But the only state I cared about was the shock that had stopped my father dead in his tracks. I stood up, kicking one high-heeled foot out, followed by the other, careful not to lose my balance.

Mrs. Delacruz came out of her front door to see who was causing a commotion, followed by Mr. Shaw. Suddenly, every pair of eyes in the neighborhood was on me, including that slag Mrs. Woodson.

I could see why people got addicted to stardom as I played up every ounce of gay that I had inside of me and projected it outwards, an imaginary rainbow spotlight following me as I repeated my lyrics for a few more laps.

I pulled up to our driveway, parked, hopped off L'il Red, and began to bow, and then I click clacked past Big Ed. I was waiting for him to try and hit me.

The slamming of the front door told me I had struck a nerve. I went inside, changed clothes, and stashed my revenge outfit in the closet, ironically enough. I'd put her shoes back when Big Ed wasn't holed up in their bedroom.

I called Pete and recounted the story of letting my freak flag fly, which consisted of the rainbow colors that Candy had told me what they meant.

"Damn!" He sounded impressed.

"Yeah, you won't like me when I'm angry."

"Well, I'd like to see you Hulk out of your clothes."

I was getting a chub thinking about being naked with him again.

"You better stop. You're giving me wood."

"You make it sound like a bad thing," he chuckled. "I shouldn't tell you I just got back from the gym, and all I'm wearing is a jockstrap. Oops, I just did."

I liked the playful nature of our banter, a dirtier version of Bruce Willis and Cybill Shepherd on *Moonlighting*.

"While I like the mental image, I definitely want to see that in the flesh."

"Deal." He said as my Mom called out that dinner was ready, and I told him that I had to go. "Hopefully, your Mom didn't make kielbasa for dinner."

"Hopefully, she did!"

"Atta boy. Call me tomorrow."

"Roger, roger."

"Over and out."

I went into the bathroom, praying that my evening wood would subside, and it finally did.

I sat down to see that Big Ed was three cans deep. I offered him a knowing smile, then devoured the Minute Steaks, mashed potatoes, and steamed broccoli. All types of appetites were back for me, but Big Ed pecked at his food like Heather had. He finally proclaimed that he had a headache and retreated in defeat.

I had won that battle and felt that I could do the same with the war we had been waging for years. Mom and I settled into *Who's The Boss?* Before long, it was time to call it a night.

Two days later, I was loading my homework into my backpack and headed off to my appointment with David.

"How have you been?"

"Peachy keen, jellybean."

"You seem happier. Why is that?"

I explained that I had actual friends now and had stood up to my father. I figured that since Pete was no longer employed at San Luis Rey it was OK to divulge his identity to David.

"Hmm," David offered.

"And what does that mean, exactly. Is that a psychological term?"

My defense shields were starting to rise, and I was instantly on guard.

"Well, just be careful with him. He has a bit of a reputation."

"Like he puts out on the first date kind of reputation?"

"You would know that better than me. He had several warnings about his behavior with the younger male patients before he was let go."

"And he was ratted out by Nurse Wretched about hugging me when I left. Scandalous!"

"First, Nurse Wretched is a perfect nickname for her. Second, that's not what happened. He was caught in a comprising position with Carlos."

I felt the air being let out of my tires, deflated at the notion that Pete had lied to me.

If kindergarten had taught me anything, aside from the art of the nap, it was learned from the book that Mrs. Treadwell was fond of reading to us during story time. The world was broken down into two types of people: Warm Fuzzies and Cold Pricklies. I was moving from the idea that the warm fuzzies he had been giving me were nothing but a façade of the cold pricklies that he hid underneath all those muscles.

I wondered if a new, passive aggressive, mixtape featuring The Eurhythmics "Would I Lie to You" would bring forth a confession, rather than straight out asking him about it. To justify his behavior, I wasn't blind to the fact that I hadn't been exactly forthcoming with all my baggage, either.

I would compartmentalize this bit of information, stowing it away with LA and white Hondas.

"Nobody's perfect," I stated.

"That is one way to look at it. Just thought you should know, is all."

"Got it." His words whizzed by my ears so that I didn't have to focus on them.

"Alright then. So, do you have something to show me?"

I produced the drawing from my backpack and handed it to him. I had drawn a cocoon at the bottom. A boy emerged from the chrysalis and had sprouted wings.

"Impressive. You have some real talent, Henry. I hope that you will explore it further."

"That's the plan, Stan."

"May I read what you wrote?"

"I should read it to you. My handwriting falls somewhere between a serial killer's scrawl and a doctor's handwriting. Don't read too much into that, Doc."

I began reading *Caterpillar Boy, Butterfly Man* aloud.

"I travel on the whispers of the night; my legs carry me to my destiny. Caterpillar Boy, keep moving. My fuzzy little exterior is beginning to wane, like the moon that is giving way to a brand-new day. My interior follows suit, but still feels the same until I stop, sensing a change. Am I to know, can I imagine what will transpire?

Caterpillar Boy, keep moving.

I am encased in darkness, a child in a self-imposed womb where all there can be is exile and silence. My body begins a life-altering change, brought on by time and the flow of the seasons.

Caterpillar Boy, keep moving.

I emerge from the cocoon, resilient in the newfound beauty, wings stretch outward, as fragile as fine China at first, then become as strong as a herd of elephants. Splashes of majestic orange and brown colors combine with the pink hues of the early morning sunrise.

Butterfly Man, keep flying.

Swooping, soaring, and exploring, caught up in the splendor of beauty. I spot a field of brightly colored flowers, although they are not as colorful as I. Perhaps I shall let them bask in the glow of my beauty.

Butterfly Man, keep flying."

"I'd give you an A."

"Thanks."

"You are really onto something by combining the meaning behind your works of art. It enhances the beauty."

"I wouldn't have thought of it unless you had assigned it to me."

"I look forward to the next one. Call on Monday for your next appointment, OK?"

"Aye, aye, captain."

When I got home, I used Nina as a sounding board to what I had been told about Pete.

"For lack of a better, and slightly ironic, term for it. Don't pussyfoot around with him," she said. "Who knows what else he's keeping from you?"

"Well, there's some stuff that I haven't been on the up and up about with you, either." I launched into my time in LA and my deadly dance with Tina.

"Never put anything in your body that you make in their bathtub! I did it a few times, and I didn't like it. I'll stick to the reefer and wine coolers. Thank you! But maybe you had to do it, to deal with all that LA business."

"Yeah, something like that. But the nice offshoot was that it made me hyper-focused on drawing and other stuff."

"Yes, other stuff, like your dick."

"I was trying to be a gentleman."

"Please, we're beyond that! But I'm glad you told me."

"Me too. OK, I'm out. I have to figure out this Pete thing."

"Keep me posted."

"Naturally, Toots. Bye for now."

I called Pete and got his answering machine. After the beep, I left a message. A half-hour later, he returned my call. I did my best to not let my voice give anything away.

"Hey, sweet cheeks. How's it hangin'?"

"Straight down the middle presently."

"Oh really?"

"Yes, really."

"You are such a cocktease."

"Why I never!"

"I know that's not true."

"Busted!" I said as a fun retort, as well as to myself that I was onto him. All I had really wanted to be on was him, under him, next to him. Godammit, I just wanted something normal in my life.

"When do I get to see you, mister?"

"You free later?"

"I'll make an exception and not charge you."

"That's mighty white of you."

"Yeah, why don't you come by at 7?"

"It's a date."

"See you then, cutie."

But I had a feeling I would be seeing right through him, minus the X-Ray specs advertised in the back of the Spider-Man comics I loved as a kid.

I parked L'il Red in the parking lot of his complex, and it struck me that I didn't exactly remember which one was his, as they were all the same. I walked back and forth on the sidewalk, trying to remember anything that would distinguish his place from their cookiecutter sameness.

Suddenly one door opened a crack.

"You should have chosen door number one," Pete said from the shadows.

As I entered and asked what my prize was, I saw that it was Pete nude except for his jockstrap. My plans for a confrontation were immediately altered as he scooped me up and carried me upstairs.

After all, wasn't said, and plenty had been done carnally; I re-entered my body, and that path led back to my mind. I let a few minutes pass in silence before I broke it.

"Hey, been meaning to ask you. How's the job hunt?"

"I have some prospects lined up," he said sleepily.

"That's cool." I left it at that, wondering how best to broach the subject.

"Hey," he said softly. "There's something I've been meaning to tell you."

"What's on your mind?"

"I wasn't honest with you." He reached over to his nightstand, lit a cigarette, and turned back. "I didn't get canned because of you. Wretched found me giving Carlos a mouth hug."

"Oh," I said, not wanting to tip my hat that I already knew this.

"I'm sorry. Forgive me?"

I nodded.

"Just make sure it doesn't happen again."

"I promise. I really like you, Henry. You're a cool dude."

"Thanks bro," I said with a deeper voice than God had given me.

"You're a butthole."

"Best butthole you'll ever meet."

"That's the truth, Ruth."

He took a long drag off his cigarette, inhaling the truth and exhaling the lie he had confessed to. He snubbed out its life expectancy in the ashtray. He pulled me closer and started to kiss me, tasting a little bit like the cigarette he had just finished. But round two was interrupted by the sound of a bell. The doorbell, to be exact.

"Shit! I forgot he was coming over!"

"Who?"

"My dealer. I thought we might visit Maui again."

"Wow, a dealer that delivers? That's better than Domino's!"

"Yeah." He said, putting on his silken bathrobe and jockstrap. "Dr. Feelgood makes house calls. Jeff is the best."

Pete had told me to stay put. Even if he had wanted to introduce me to someone whom I was unfortunately already familiar with, I would not have left the bed. Jesus! Were there no other drug dealers in the greater North County region?

I got up to see if I could eavesdrop on their conversation, but it wasn't loud enough to hear. I imagined it was stitched together with the thinly veiled niceties reserved for drug dealers.

"How about this weather? Give me my weed."

When I heard the front door close, I tiptoed over to the window and peeked out. Yep, the same Jeff was making a beeline to his white Honda that was parked right next to my scooter.

Holy shit did not begin to cover it!

I heard Pete's heavy footfall on the stairs, and I headed into his bathroom. I splashed icy water on my face, but I still looked shaken.

I stood at the sink, taking in the cologne inventory that Pete had on display. There was an emerald bottle of Ralph Lauren Polo, a smaller black bottle of Drakkar Noir and finally one that Jeff should have his name emblazoned on, instead of Calvin Klein, the word Obsession spotlighted by the bathroom light above the sink.

"Hey tiger. You alright in there?"

"Just dandy," I said and went back to join Pete on the bed.

He was busily rolling a joint.

"So, how well do you know Jeff?"

"Not that well. You know him?"

"He used to be my dealer, too."

"Small world."

It was shrinking every day. Pete knew both Jeff and Steve – what were the chances?

My host suggested that I root through his VHS collection and choose something. I gladly accepted the challenge and the chance to discern what he had deemed appropriate to want to watch again, which had left some sort of mark on him.

I discovered that he liked science fiction as much as I did. There were copies of *Close Encounters of the Third Kind*, the *Star Wars* trilogy, *Alien* and its sequel. I selected one for us: *The Terminator*.

We sat on his beige couch in our underwear, my head on his well-defined chest and his muscled right arm around me. When Kyle Reese told Sarah Connor to "Come with me if you want to live," I felt it was something Pete might say, that he would protect me at all costs.

I wondered if I told him about Jeff's true nature if he would whoop his ass.

Besides, a kernel, much like the one at the bottom of the bowl of popcorn we were munching, was starting to pop in my brain. I was figuring out how to show Jeff who was the boss, minus any appearances from Tony Danza and Judith Light. Of course, I was going to enlist the help of my new partner-in-crime, Nina, as she had proven invaluable in dispatching Scott Rainowsky.

I mouthed along with Linda Hamilton as she proclaimed, "You're terminated fucker!" As Sarah Connor drove off towards her destiny, Pete spoke up.

"Did you ever think it sounded slutty of her that she's essentially telling her son that he was the product of a one-night stand?"

"'Maybe it'll be enough if you know that, in the few hours we had together, we loved a lifetime's worth.' I think it's romantic."

"Potato, potahto," he joked. "But it is sweet that you find it romantic. I want the chance to romance the fuck out of you."

"Better than the other way around."

He gave me a playful punch on my arm, then started another passionate make-out session. Soon, our underwear was discarded, and we were working up a sweat.

I needed a shower before I went home. I poured a healthy dollop of Aussie shampoo into my hand, but Pete massaged it into my scalp, by far the sexiest thing he had ever done to me. Then he scrubbed my back with St. Ives Apricot Scrub and created a lather by rubbing himself on me. Then he hugged me voraciously as if I were going to slide down the shower floor into the drain, disappearing forever. Technically this could have been a worry as I was melting in his massive arms, and he was thawing the icy remnants that had surrounded my heart.

I arrived home to a darkened house. I jumped out of my freshly clean skin as Shadow emerged and began sniffing me, sensing a new scent on me from both different shower products and Pete's lingering fragrance.

Her wagging tail hit me on the leg as if she were offering her approval of him, following me to my room, signaling that we were going to have a slumber party. While we weren't going to be braiding each other's hair, we would most definitely be talking about boys via the new mixtape I had in mind for Pete. I gathered an armload of cassettes from my dresser drawer and laid them out across the carpet, creating a story written with the lyrics of others who would be informing Pete how I felt about him.

The Romantics let him know what I liked about him, the Jets that I had a crush on him, and that he could be the one courtesy of Josie Cotton. I again left off any mention of love, but who knew - by the time mixtape #3 rolled around, we could be at the point where we expressed that sentiment.

When I was finished, I pulled back the covers and patted the bed to let Shadow know that she could sleep with me tonight. Once she found her spot, we both drifted off to sleep.

Standing behind the concession stand the next day, which had become my version of a confessionial, I told Nina about Jeff.

"Son of a bitch! You should go to the police."

"The only proof I have is duct tape and pieces of rope. Not exactly a smoking gun. Besides, they'll chalk it up as a fag problem."

"But what are you going to do? He's dangerous, Henry!"

"You're preaching to the choir, sister."

"Again, what are you going to do?"

"I was kind of hoping that it might be what we are going to do…"

"What's going on in that head of yours?"

And I laid it out, the where and what, she agreed to be a who in the scenario.

When we were done for the night, I saw that Pete had struck again with just a single Post-it with a smaller picture of a heart accompanied by a lone sunflower.

In the dark of the night, my ride home was illuminated by my headlight and the yellow radiance of the sunflower. It was becoming clear to me that Pete and I were a lot alike. Both used our preferred forms of communication via Post-its and mixtapes to say what we were feeling without saying it to each other.

The look on my mother's face spoke volumes as I strutted through the front door like the cock of the walk, for lack of a better phrase, with my second flower in a week.

"Well, well, well. Someone is quite taken with you."

"Seems that way."

"I'm happy for you."

"Really?"

"Yes really! I just want you to be happy, son."

"And that's what I want for you, too."

Before going to bed, she pointed out a plate made up in the fridge for me to microwave. With a full belly and fuller heart, I headed upstairs and switched out the withering sunflower with the new one. If this keeps up, I might have to spring for a vase. I called Pete and thanked him for the lovely gesture. We stayed on the phone for an hour.

"I better let you go, it's getting late." I said, stifling a yawn.

"You better not. Let me go, that is."

"You're a smooth talker, Betty Crocker."

"I have a recipe for you. You and me, cooked at 350 degrees for a lifetime."

Jesus! He was going to say it. But I didn't want it to be over the phone. I had envisioned it at sunset, walking hand-in-hand on the beach.

"Sounds delicious," I stammered. "Well, it's bedtime for Bonzo. I'll call tomorrow."

"I'll wait with bated breath."

"There's mouthwash for that."

"Smart-ass."

"Better than being a dumb ass."

"True." And then he broke into Spandau Ballet's song.

"You should try out for *Star Search*!"

"Remind me to smack you on the ass next time I see you, which I hope is soon."

"Deal."

"Goodnight sweet prince."

I stared at the flower for a few minutes before I turned off the light. It looked like Charlie Brown was finally going to kick the football.

I dreamt I was Madonna in the *Like a Virgin* video, all dolled up in a wedding dress. Rather than a mysterious stranger in a lion's mask, Pete wore a huge Post-it with a heart drawn on it.

The next day, Nina and I welcomed a new hire, best described as tall, dark, and handsome. Darren was learning how to be a popcorn jockey from Yvonne. When Nina entered the back and Darren was on his lunch break, Yvonne moved beside me.

"I didn't know that Pete was your new boyfriend."

I answered with a pedestrian "yup," not wanting to say more for fear that my anger about Steve would come out.

"Pete's a very lucky guy," she said, putting her hand into my left pocket, and copped a feel. "Mmm, very lucky indeed."

She heard the door from the stockroom open and withdrew her hand as if my pocket had been made of molten lava. Nina walked in.

Rather than having my dick retreat into my body, a snail into its shell, I was surprised when I had to casually adjust myself.

What fresh hell is this?

"Well, I need to help clean some theaters," Yvonne said. "You guys help Darren."

"Sure thing," Nina said.

"Yup," I said, still a bit stunned.

"Everything copacetic there, Henry?" Nina asked.

"Yup."

"You're quite the conversationalist."

I was about to go into Yvonne's hands-on approach to supervising, but Darren had returned. Rather than make a big deal about it, I made no mention of it. But we did discuss what was to occur the next day after work, and Nina would be the one to set the plan in motion and carry it out, per my instructions. She wasn't my minion, doing my bidding, just an equal who wanted me to maintain my sense of security. Granted I did feel better that I knew the identity of my once mysterious stalker.

Still, if our agreed-upon strategy didn't gel, we would have to devise a backup plan. I felt secure in the fact that my friend hadn't scored an A in Drama class for nothing, as this was going to call upon her thespian training.

I ventured to her apartment at 11 in the morning to observe her pulling from a well-spring of emotions for her performance as the human namesake of her beloved feline.

"You ready, Freddy?" She asked.

"If you are, superstar."

She responded by calling the operator in character and asking for the non-emergency number for the Sheriff's office just down the road from her.

"Hello officer, my name is Irene Bernstein." She began and sounded slightly like Rhoda Morgenstern. "There is a drug dealer that has been pushing his poison on my youngest son, Elliott. He's only 15 years old, for Chrissakes!"

She listened to what the officer was saying to her and gave me the thumbs up.

"I know the creep's name is Jeff Densmore." She stated. "I made poor little Elliott show me where he lives, so I also have his address."

She gave the officer his location, again listening to what was a phantom conversation for me.

"Well, that presents a problem. I don't want my husband to know about this. Would there be a way for me to check in with you?" The stress of the faux situation was evident in her slightly trembling voice. "Oh good, thank you, Officer Diaz. Yes, I will check in with you tomorrow. I appreciate your help."

She hung up the phone, and we high-fived.

"And the Oscar goes to!" I exclaimed proudly. "Meryl Streep better watch her back!"

"Oh, that hack. It was nothing, dahlink. But no autographs, please!"

But she had just signed a pact that we would be friends for a very long time.

"I really owe you for this," I said with reverence.

"Um, no you don't. That's what friends are for."

"In good times and bad times, you'll be on my side forevermore?"

"For sure, but only if you keep smiling and keep shining."

"You, dear friend, have it made it much easier to do that."

"The feeling is mutual. Now, before we start making out, let's get to our stakeout."

We parked down the street from Jeff's apartment complex, slightly huddled down in our seats. Nina lit a clove cigarette and handed it to me without asking if I wanted one, figuring I needed something to calm my nerves.

But she was the one that kept looking at her watch and muttering, "Where the fuck are they?" Around the tenth time that she repeated the query, a lone police car pulled up to Jeff's apartment complex.

Two men in beige exited their vehicle and ascended the stairs to Jeff's humble abode. We both sat up to better see them forcefully knocking on the door. One of them was holding a piece of paper, a search warrant, no doubt. On the third pound, Jeff opened the door, looking disheveled, hair standing up in points, telling me they had woken him up this Sunday afternoon. He stepped back with a panicked look on his face, and their appearance was proving to be more effective than the world's strongest cup of coffee, he seemed wide awake now.

But I was getting jittery, like I had ingested the Big Gulp equivalent of Maxwell House, and my nerves settled down once I saw Jeff being escorted down the stairs in handcuffs by a handsome Hispanic police officer while the other had a sizeable duffel bag in his right hand.

"Busted!" I pronounced as we slid all the way down in the station wagon's front seat, not wanting to have Jeff see us.

"Oy! Such a day." Nina said, channeling Mrs. Bernstein. "This should keep him out of your hair for a while. OK, Sherlock, back to the real world. Let's go back to my place and have a celebratory doobie."

"Elementary, my dear Watson," I said, knowing my buzz would abate by my shift later.

The next two weeks passed by in what seemed like a blink of an eye and with an air of repetition. Friends, work, David, Pete, who still hadn't uttered those three little words. I was two days away from what constituted "manhood" in terms of age.

Big Ed was scheduled to travel that week, so he would not be judging my friends, whom Mom said to invite over, even including Pete. I lied and said that I would check with him. Besides, Pete planned to take me out to celebrate the next night.

Hopefully, barbeque was off the menu for this date.

Waking up on my birthday, I felt like Molly Ringwald in *Sixteen Candles*, wishing she had gotten "four inches of bod" to mark another year of teen angst on earth. My mind conjured up the final scene, where Jake Ryan was replaced by Pete, and I played the part of Samantha Baker.

We sat across from each other on Pete's kitchen table, a birthday cake between us, its 18 candles illuminating our naked bodies.

"Happy birthday, Henry. Make a wish," Pete said.

"It already came true," I answered, gushing shamelessly.

I blew out the candles just as the vision went up in smoke, due to my Mom calling me to breakfast. It was a feast fit for a king. Waffles, scrambled eggs, sausage and bacon, and more plates than were necessary for the two of us.

"What gives?"

Just then, my three amigos jumped through the other entry door to the kitchen from the dining room.

"Surprise!"

"Happy Birthday, hon!" My Mom kissed me on one cheek.

"Are you surprised?" Derek asked, and I was convinced that my face must have been the color of my white jeans.

"Totally."

"Ha ha, we gotcha!" Nina joked.

"Big time!" Michael added.

"I thought this would be nicer than the usual cake and ice cream routine," Mom said.

"It definitely is," I responded. "Does that mean I don't get a cake tonight?"

"Well…" Mom said suspiciously.

"You're coming out with us tonight," Michael explained.

"But we were going out on Saturday." I felt a little crestfallen, as I was looking forward to celebrating all week.

"We still are," Derek said. "Patience is a virtue, old man."

"Let it unfold like a lotus," Nina advised.

"Alright, dig in before it gets cold," Mom instructed.

Between bites, I caught my Mom smiling, happy to see her son surrounded by actual friends. My gang of three earned brownie points by insisting they do the cleanup, which let Mom skeedaddle to work. When I offered to help, they shut me down.

"So how exactly did this happen?" I inquired.

"Your Mom stopped by the theater and enlisted my help in getting these two to join us." Nina said. "You know, she's really cool. I think it's safe to say that ours wouldn't have done this."

"Seeing as my parents don't know I'm gay, that would be a qualified no for me," Michael stated.

"They've met you, right?" Derek asked.

"And your Mom has never asked why her clothes get stretched out?" Nina asked with a chuckle.

I felt bad for Michael for not feeling comfortable enough to express who he was really for fear of rejection. I was fortunate that John had been accepting of my true identity and that Mom had really turned the corner.

"It will happen when it's right," I suggested to a forlorn Michael.

"We were just busting your balls," Derek said, detecting sadness in Michael's face.

"You know, just like the guys at the viewpoint do," Nina kidded.

"Hilarious. You should really be a stand-up comic," Michael retorted. "Your face is guaranteed to get you plenty of laughs!"

"Bitch!" Nina countered.

"The nicest bitch you'll ever meet," Michael said with a laugh.

As they dished, I pondered what they had up their sleeves for tonight.

As we headed south on the 805, they remained tight-lipped as to the birthday plans. When we merged onto the 163, it started to dawn on me that we were heading to San Diego's gay mecca, Hillcrest.

The only time I had been in its vicinity was when Mom took me to an optometrist when I was eleven.

We arrived at Corvette Diner, a place they had discussed with reverence. It was a place where the waitresses were apt to grab a seat while taking your order, then throw straws at you for your chosen beverage and sass you in general.

It was also a place with the most adorable twenty-something soda jerk. He looked as though he was moonlighting here, a side gig from his playing in a New Wave band, as he looked like a member of Echo and the Bunnymen, from his stylish haircut to the air of coolness surrounding his skinny frame.

Our waitress, Jane, took our order: four cheeseburgers and fries all around.

"Can you bring more napkins?" Nina asked seriously. "The birthday boy has a sudden drooling problem."

"Aww, it's your birthday, babe?" Jane said, smacking her Bazooka bubblegum. "You missed the Early Bird specials."

"Ooh, she clocked you!" Derek exclaimed.

"I'm like a Timex. I can take a licking but keep on ticking," I said confidently and took in the 1950's-inspired décor with paintings of musicians from decades past. Of course, I gravitated to a poster of *Rebel Without a Cause.* "I would have so misused time travel to go back in time and sleep with James Dean."

"I'm more of an Elvis kind of girl, myself," Michael declared. "He wouldn't have to keep that pelvis far from me!"

"I'm with Henry," Derek agreed.

"Marlon Brando for me," Nina said, fanning herself.

"Girl, you'd have to be on top for sure," I mocked.

"Not the fat one! When he was in his prime, you cooze!"

"STELLA!" We cried out in unison.

I looked over at the soda jerk, who had a smile on his face, and I felt a flush of embarrassment rising like a hot temporary tattoo across my face.

"Are you blushing?" Michael asked.

"Geez. Save some for the rest of us!" Derek scolded.

"I'm just window shopping, not shoplifting!" I said louder than intended.

"I'd like to give him a five-finger discount," Derek replied.

"You handing out double coupons for hand jobs again?" Nina shot back.

"Sorry. Didn't mean to copy your idea, even if yours are for free, hooker." Derek said smarmily.

"There's all kinds of ways of paying," I said solemnly.

"Way to bring it down, Henry." Michael ribbed. "Someone has gotten a lot out of Jack Handey. Such *Deep Thoughts* – what is up with that?"

It was the mention of the word "hooker" which convinced me that I could trust these friends of mine with my sordid Los Angeles backstory. I launched into it saying, "there's something I need to tell you guys." And ended it with, "and that's all of the news that's fit to print."

"Damn, dude," Nina said, not letting on that she already knew this information, lest the boys take umbrage.

"That should be a TV movie of the week!" Derek said with admiration. "But who would play you?"

"Now I remember who you remind me of!" Michael said.

"Don't keep us in suspense," I said. "Who?"

"Corey Adams," he said in a stage whisper as if his parents were standing right behind him and knew about his secret porn stash, which included *Up Your Alley*. "The resemblance is pretty uncanny, I must say."

"And I was gonna say, Dennis Quaid," Nina said with a sigh. "You know who loved him some Corey? Our dealer, Jeff. I went into his bedroom once, and he had a collage. I didn't want to ask how he stuck them on the poster board."

"Wow. You are really up on your gay porn stars," Derek said.

"As a fag hag, I feel it's my civic duty to know all things gay-related."

"What happened to Jeff?" Michael asked.

"Oh, yeah, that," I said and launched into that story.

"Well, you certainly have material for a sequel," Derek said with a whistle.

"I need to stay off of your shit list." Michael said, pushing his plate away to signal that he was done. "But you're lucky that you figured out who it was. Things could have ended very badly, and I do not want to imagine a world with Henry."

"I second that emotion." Nina agreed.

"And a taste of honey is worse than none at all." Derek sang off-key.

"Aww, are you calling me sweet?" I said with my hands clasped over my heart.

"Naw, you're just sticky a lot of the time," Derek said without missing a beat.

Before I could offer a different kind of comeback than he was insinuating, Jane returned with a vanilla milkshake with a candle atop a mountain of whipped cream.

She led the group in singing "Happy Birthday," and I blew out the candle, wishing this would be the first of many birthdays we would celebrate together. I could feel my eyes starting to well up, and they trickled down my face.

"Don't cry! You'll rust again!" Nina laughed.

"Careful, he might drop a house on you!" Michael added

"It's just nice to know I'm not dead inside!"

Jane handed me a napkin. At first, I thought it was to wipe away those happy tears. But there was a name and phone number on it.

"Courtesy of your friendly neighborhood Spider-Man over there."

I looked over, and the soda jerk, or Dash as the name on the napkin said, gave me a two-finger salute. I offered a little wave, flattered.

Jane doled out three spoons and straws to the gang, withholding mine.

"I figured you're trying to watch your girlish figure."

"That's why I'm not offering you any of this here milkshake." I shot back.

She gave me a genuine smile, indicating that she liked my moxie, then threw the straw and napkin at me. My friends grabbed the bill.

After we demolished the milkshake, with only a few instances of brain freeze, we made our way to the exit. But first, I said goodbye to Dash and told him I was Henry, in case he made a habit of giving out his phone number to customers and would save me from identifying that I was the guy whom he had given his digits to.

I stopped on the sidewalk in front of Corvette's with a sudden realization; I didn't know the last names of the people who were taking me under their wings and providing the safety of friendship, save for Nina.

"Hey, I can't thank you guys enough for doing all of this," I began. "So, unlike Michael's 'dates' - what are your last names?"

"Captain Sokolov, at your service," Nina stated with a giggle, even if her answer was unnecessary.

"Mr. Derek Stewart, esquire," he said, offering a firm handshake, and addressed Michael. "You want us to tell him, or do you want to?"

"I will since it's my cross to bear. So, um..."

While he paused, my mind raced as to what could cause him such distress over a surname, trying to land on what it could be.

"You gonna do the opposite when you give a BJ and spit it out?"

"Fine! It's Jackson."

"Oh my God, I'm such a huge fan of your work! Can I have your autograph?" I squealed.

"Sure, kick a guy when he's down!" he exclaimed haughtily, but the smile he produced told me he was immune to taunts about it.

Until Nina said something that made him bristle.

"Alright gang, let's beat it!"

As we headed home, Nina popped in a *Queen's Greatest Hits* tape she had made, and we all belted out "We Are the Champions." As "Bohemian Rhapsody" played, I informed them that was the song I wanted to play at my funeral.

"I would have guessed *The Brady Bunch* theme song," Nina kidded.

"*Ding Dong the Witch is Dead* would have been my vote," Michael offered. When Derek remained quiet, he prodded him. "Anything to add there, D?"

"I don't really think it's something to joke about."

"Duly noted, Sensitive Sally," Nina said, hoping to offset the unfunny fact that AIDS was erasing so many gay men.

The next night, I was waiting out front for Pete and just finishing a touch test to ensure my hair looked good. The reaction I got from Pete told me I was hitting all the marks, as his hands were instantly everywhere.

"Happy Birthday, mister," he said as we unlocked lips.

"Thanks," I said, resisting the temptation to ask if I could unwrap his package.

He wouldn't budge about where he was taking me, but I felt relieved when he went the opposite direction of Lavar's. We ended up at Cardiff beach, the sight of our first date. He popped the trunk and produced a picnic basket and blanket.

I luxuriated in the fact that romance was not dead. But as Pete spread out the blanket and the items in the picnic basket, he seemed nervous. Immediately, my mind thought his gift to me would be a proclamation of love, and I became empathetic with the anxious energy he was giving off.

He fumbled with a vanilla candle, then lit a cigarette shakily.

"Dig in," he said, his voice softer than usual.

"Looks great. It's nice of you to do this for me."

"No problemo." He took a long drag off his cigarette.

I didn't pile my plate with charcuterie items, as my stomach was in knots, but I took more than Pete. He was doing his best to eat like a bird impression and seemed to have a lot on his mental plate.

We finished in silence on his part. I prattled on, trying to goad him into conversation to no avail. He reached into his cigarette pack again, producing a joint.

"Better enjoy this while we can," he said mysteriously.

"Why is that?" I asked and went into my Pisces persecution complex. "Did I do something?"

"Oh no, sweet cheeks. Not at all. I did."

I thought he was going to give me some song-and-breakdance about how the guy he had slept with had "meant nothing" to him. It was the only reason I could think of for him doing something I suspected was out of character.

"Are you going to tell me, or do I guess?"

"When I lost my job, I did something I'm not proud of."

Jesus Christ! Did he star in Up Your Alley 2: Electric Bugaloo?

"And what would that be?"

"You know my dealer?"

I nodded.

"Well, I partnered up with him and we bought a pound of weed. He would sell it and we'd split the profits. But Jeff got busted the other day. I don't trust him; he could rat me out. Um, I'm going to get out of town for a while."

I decided to stay quiet. I was at fault. Sort of. I thought he'd understand the reason behind what Nina and I had concocted, but when he slammed his fist down on the blanket in anger, I quashed that notion.

"Where are you going? How long will you be gone?"

"I'm going back to the East Coast, stay with some friends." He sighed. "I really don't want to go, but you don't need a jailbird for a boyfriend."

And here I thought he was going to say those three words to me. Well, he just called me his boyfriend but …

"I'm not sure how long I'll be gone."

Despite my best efforts, I started to cry for throwing a big wrench in the plans I had hoped we would make for the future, one shared together, not on opposite coasts. Just as the candle blew out from the wind that swept across the beach, I lit up with anger at myself. Naturally, I released it onto Pete.

"Well, happy fucking birthday to me!" I yelled.

"I'm sorry!" he yelled back at me.

"You're sorry, all right! Good luck with everything!" I stormed off.

"Henry! Come back!"

I ran away from the beach and hid behind a dumpster at The Chart House. I watched Pete drive up and down the 101 a few times before he sped off out of my life.

"Another one bites the dust," I muttered to myself. "Way to go, dumb ass!"

When I reached the 7-11 up the road, I dug into my wallet for a quarter, but Nina didn't answer her phone. I sure as hell didn't want to call my Mom, so I just walked home, figuring the fresh air would do me good.

When I got to my old grammar school, Ocean Knoll, I strolled over to the chain link fence, looked at the playground, and wished I could return to a simpler time. I scaled the chain-link fence, straddling it at the top somewhere between the past and the present, unsure of what the future had in store for me.

I wandered over to the swings and sat in the leather seat designed for butts much younger than mine, kicking my shoes in the sand. Before I knew it, I was moving back and forth, higher and higher until I became one with the night, a shadow of the boy I had been, and the man I wanted to be. I jumped at the highest point possible, freefalling into nothing. I managed to land on my own two feet, no worse for wear.

If only that had been the case with Pete. I hated myself for the way that I had decided to cover my tracks with him, deciding somewhere on the trek home that if I couldn't tell him the truth, the very least I could do was apologize.

As I made my way to my room undetected, save for Shadow following me. Once I had removed the clean laundry Mom had left on my bed, I plopped down on the bedspread. Shadow jumped up and began licking my face lovingly. I knew dogs could sense earthquakes, but my girl knew my heart had experienced a seismic shift.

Rather than make her stop, I let her go on until she had properly shown me the unconditional love that only a dog could. Although my legs were tired from my unexpected walkabout, my brain simply would not shut the fuck up!

I lay under the covers, recalling the many sleepless nights that I had for over a year. I could let the manic hamster keep running on the wheel in my brain. Or I could work on my homework.

I found my book on drawing anatomy, grabbed a mix tape from my dresser drawer, and plugged my headphones into my ghetto blaster. When Katrina and the Waves began singing about "Walking on Sunshine," I knew that I hadn't chosen wisely to match my mood.

I rifled through the multitude of mix tapes until I found the one that I could keep time with. No, it wasn't labeled K-Tel presents "Songs for Sad Sacks," rather it was a compilation of Elton John songs.

And I knew firsthand why they called it the blues, how sad songs said so much, that it was time to say goodbye to the yellow brick road. But if sorry seemed to be the hardest word - why did I say it when I didn't always mean it? Then I remembered: I was still standing.

And as the light of dawn crept across the slats in my blinds, I finished my drawing and yawned. The written part could wait until later. I set my alarm for noon, and it seemed only seconds passed before it was beeping.

I was eating breakfast when the phone rang. I nearly choked on my Honey Nut Cheerios, assuming it was Pete. I wasn't awake enough yet to find just the right words to say. I decided to have the answering machine field that call. It was Mom asking to call her.

I placed her second in my queue of calls to make. Nina was first and understandably shocked by the previous night's events, saying she was sorry about our scheme. I reminded her that it was my idea and not to stress out about it. "What's done is done" was how I left it.

Mom answered the phone cheerfully, trying to pry details out of me about my date like we were girlfriends rather than mother and son. I offered a simple "It was fine" before we hung up. Then I dialed Pete's number.

"We're sorry you have reached a number that has been disconnected or is no longer in service," a robotic female voice told me. "If you feel this is in error, please check the number and dial again."

I dialed three more times. Yep, Pete had turned his phone off. I rode over to his condo, like the wind, but he was gone like it as I peered through his windows to see nothing but emptiness.

What I hadn't known was that Pete had spent my birthday packing up his belongings in a U-Haul truck, which I had missed by only ten minutes. He had once been the epitome of The Village People song, "Go West," and now he was the opposite of that musical sentiment, and it was all my fault. Howard Jones had it all wrong - someone was to blame, and it rested squarely on my shoulders.

As I drove home, it felt like my heart was dragging behind me, shooting sparks and getting road rash from the asphalt. I deserved to have a whole vat of Bactine poured into the wounds I had inflicted on myself.

Once home, I hugged Shadow tightly and then let her out in the backyard, where we played a lackluster game of soccer. Soon enough, it was time for work, and I voted against calling in heartbroken. I didn't want to do anything to jeopardize the job because I would find out in a week if I made the cut. If I got hired, I could lose myself in the flickering images on the white screen, lost in other people's lives. That might help me escape my own reality. I wasn't sure if Andrew McCarthy and Kim Cattrall in *Mannequin* would do the trick or the Dream Warriors taking on Freddy Krueger was the solution. But it couldn't hurt.

Nothing could ever hurt like this, and I had plenty of unusual experiences to base that statement on.

That night, I did my best not to bring my personal life into my professional one, which was easier tonight as Nina wasn't working. But Darren noticed a change in my usual upbeat and chatty demeanor.

"You're awfully quiet."

"Well, new meat, just not having a very good day."

"I'm a good listener if you need to get it off your chest."

"I appreciate that," I said, truly meaning it. "I really do. After work?"

"Sure thing," he smiled.

Once everything was inspected by Diane, we clocked out and then sat on the wooden bench in front of the theater. He was to my right, lit up a cigarette, and when he asked if I wanted one, I merely nodded. I took in his profile when it hit me that he was a melding of two Dicks – York and Sargent – that had played his namesake on *Bewitched,* save for a vowel difference.

His lanky frame was from Darrin #2, and his face was a better-looking Darrin #1.

"What's going on?" He caught me staring at him. But he didn't seem phased by it. I couldn't quite get a bead on him as far as straight and gay went.

"I broke up with my boyfriend," I said, wondering if he could even relate. "The messed-up part is that it's my fault."

"It takes two to tango." He said, not giving away anything about which beat he danced to. "True."

"I'm sure that he wasn't perfect, either." He said, taking a drag off the half-gone cigarette.

"No, he wasn't. I just hate the way it ended."

"Maybe this is really a beginning. There could be something better on the horizon." He patted me on the leg. "Feel better?"

"Actually, I do," I said, even though I was still wondering which team he played for. "Thanks, Darren."

"Anytime," he shrugged, then snuffed out his cigarette and threw it in the trashcan.

I took three more drags and followed suit. We made our way to our respective vehicles. His Volkswagen Scirocco was a duller red than my scooter, but our color choice made us cycle sisters or something.

"Hey. Wanna come over?" He asked.

"Sure," I said, uncertain as to why he wanted to hang out further.

"Cool. Just follow me; it's not too far away."

He led me to the Village Park area of Encinitas, off Encinitas Boulevard. He pulled into a parking lot of an apartment building across from the public pool where John and I used to jump the fence, where he would dare me to jump off the high-diving board. I never did.

I pulled up to the visitor space next to Darren's car and then followed him to his apartment. He opened the door slowly and switched on a light for the living room, which didn't illuminate any clues about his proclivities.

There were some vintage Led Zeppelin posters in frames on the wall and two black-and-white Ansel Adams wilderness shots: a winding river and snowcapped mountain and Yosemite National Park.

A beige loveseat was against the wall with a matching couch, positioned for optimum TV viewing. The entertainment unit housed a Magnavox TV, plus a record player and cassette tape- combo stereo, with an impressive number of records lining four shelves.

Perusing them could give me a hint about his sexuality.

"It doesn't look like my roomie is home. We've got the place to ourselves."

"How long have you guys lived together?" I asked, seeing if it prompted a confession.

"We met at SDSU and decided to room together about two years ago. Rents were cheaper up here."

"What's your major?"

"Psychology."

At that moment, I assumed that he had brought me here to be the subject of his thesis paper, "The Care and Feeding of the Heartbroken Homosexual."

"Make yourself at home. I need to get out of this monkey suit. Why don't you find something for us to listen to."

There were the usual college-age purchases, heavy on Tears for Fears, Kate Bush, and Thompson Twins. But no show tunes, no Babs, Madonna, Diana Ross, Cher, or Tina Turner. And then I found a well-worn copy of *The Age of Consent* by Bronski Beat. I put it on the turntable and the needle on the record. Darren re-emerged, wearing a pair of gray sweatpants and a black SDSU sweatshirt. He sat down on the couch and gave me a quizzical look.

"Hmm."

"Don't you like Bronski Beat?"

"Not really my cup of tea. It's my roommate's."

Aha! I had often heard that college was the time that some chose to experiment with members of the same sex. It sounded more like his roomie was the one apt to dabble in dick. Now I wouldn't be tempted to dip my pen in company ink.

"Something you'd rather listen to?"

"You like Van Halen?"

"Definitely."

With that, he put Jimmy Somerville and crew away and rooted through the records until he found their self-titled debut album. He opened the cabinet and came back with a handful of objects. Once he put them down, I identified a small mirror, razor blade, straw, and a small plastic bag of white powder. All the blood drained from my face and raced into my heart. I must have resembled the human embodiment of a Bugs Bunny cartoon with a heart shape extending in frantic beats from my white work shirt.

"Wanna toot?" he asked, sprinkling a generous amount of snowfall onto the mirror, then chopping it expertly with the razor blade.

"Is that meth?"

"Hell no. That shit's for hillbillies! This here is primo Bolivian Marching Powder."

"Oh."

"Is that an 'oh' as in I'll have some or an 'oh' as in I'll pass?" He was rolling the straw between his fingers.

All the disgust that I had ever felt about myself and the secret habit that I had recently just said no to flooded into my brain. Every shitty feeling also crept in. Like an axe to the bathroom door that Jack Nicholson had used to get to Shelley Duvall in *The Shining*.

Heeeere's Johnny!

"What the fuck – why not?"

He railed out four fat lines. I leaned over and inhaled. There wasn't the same burn that meth had, the drips not as prevalent, but my throat tightened like someone was choking me.

I sat back against the couch cushions as Darren snorted his two lines, then began playing with his nose as though he had an itch that he couldn't scratch. He went into the kitchen and brought back two glasses of water. He first dipped two fingers into his glass and then snorted the water.

"I find that it helps." Then he chugged the rest.

We spent the next two hours chit-chatting at a rapid pace.

"You know it's funny," I said. "When we had Career Day in junior high, they always pegged me as a psychologist."

"Really? Is it something that you wanted to pursue?"

"I don't know. I really like doing my art."

"More money in being a psychologist. Cha-ching!"

"I suppose. But art beats the other vocation they recommended."

"What was that?"

"A priest," I said, laughing.

"Yeah, I don't see that happening."

"Especially with the whole being struck by lightning thing if I walk into church."

Darren's face took on a serious look.

"Is it hard to be gay?"

"I don't know – is it hard to be straight?" I asked, sensing I was about to become a science project.

"I think it's hard to be a human. I really don't try to label people, so that was a dumb question. Let me try again. Have you had a lot of difficulties?"

"I feel like I should be lying down on the couch."

"Sorry. Occupational hazard."

"Nah, it's cool. I would say that's an understatement. The difficulties, that is."

My tongue was already loosened by the blow, so I laid it all out for him. Rather than stroking an imaginary beard and uttering "very interesting" sporadically, his response was to take off his sweatshirt.

"Sorry, man; it is hot in here! Don't you feel hot? It's just the coke; it always does that to me."

"No worries," I said, trying not to make eye contact with his skinny but muscled torso and his nipple that was at eye level. "Any thoughts on what I told you?"

"About 20 billion at once, friend. Thanks, cocaine!" He joked. "Give yourself some credit, Henry. Most people wouldn't survive like you. I'm really impressed. Sincerely. Exclamation point."

"I have been going to a psychologist to get through this. Which reminds me, I need to get my ass home. I still have homework to get done for him."

"Yeah, it's getting pretty late." He said, looking in the kitchen at the black cat clock with the eyes that moved back and forth. "You ok to drive home?"

I nodded, feeling like I wouldn't even need to have the headlight on my scooter to light my way home. Every part of me was feeling electric, a live wire casting a glow from deep inside.

"You're always welcome to spend the night."

I pushed aside remaining sexual suspicions and assured him it was a short drive home. Before I left, he gave me a small baggie of coke. When I pulled out my wallet to pay him for it, he waved his hand at me, telling me it was both a gift and our secret. I thanked him, not only for his generosity but for listening to me.

When he hugged me goodbye, his bare flesh against my crisp white shirt, my body instantly flushed.

"See? The coke makes you hot, too!"

"Yeah. Guess so. See you at the salt mines."

I got home safely, then crept up the stairs at 1:45 a.m., as my mother informed me the next morning. I had managed to sleep for a few hours but set my alarm so that I could allow myself enough time to pen the words to match my drawing for David.

"Are you feeling ok, hon?" Mom asked.

"Aces," I said with the straightest face a notorious homosexual was allowed to have.

"By the way, make sure that you empty your pockets before I do laundry. There was a bit of a mess in the dryer, like bits of paper."

I quickly realized the scraps were soda-jerk Dash's number that hadn't come out in the wash.

"Gotcha. Sorry about that." I replied, secure in the fact that I knew where he worked if and when I was ready to venture down that road.

After she left for work and I showered, I closed the door to my bedroom. Shadow was on my bed, watching my every move as I took the cocaine out of my pants pocket.

I half-expected Shadow to adopt the voice of McGruff the Crime Dog, warning me against the dangers of drugs. I chopped up the cocaine with my high school ID and rolled up a one-dollar bill.

Like Saint Nick, I was laying a finger aside my nose and snorting up my present from Darren; even though it 'twas not the night before Christmas, there was a 100% percent of snow going up my nose today.

But, like any good, tortured artist I would have to delve deep into the emotions that I was hiding behind a brick wall in order to write. I was liking the clarity cocaine was affording me; it was light years from the frenetic motion of meth. Laser-focused on my art statement, I found myself done quicker than expected.

This gave me two hours before I had to be at David's office. I kicked Shadow out of my room, then stripped and pulled out my favorite Playgirl. Naturally, it was the celebrities who had posed in the altogether issue. I knew the coke was good when Lyle Waggoner's tooth glimmered like in the opening credits of *Wonder Woman.*

However, it was a certain *American Gigolo* that caused me to release all the tension in my body. I grabbed a Kleenex from my nightstand, dabbed my sticky belly, then threw it away in the toilet so Mom didn't see it, thinking I had a cold. I had the sniffles, and my throat was numb. But that was a horse of a different color entirely.

I returned to my room, got dressed, and stashed my powdered booty in the faux treasure chest. I put my project into my backpack and left for David's office. Once there, I asked Karen for the bathroom key. That way, I could make sure it wasn't snowing from my nostrils. I gave myself the all-clear and flushed the toilet to keep up appearances two-fold.

As David listened to me read about the nature of heartbreak, he looked at my drawing, connecting the two with words meeting imagery in an outpouring of emotion.

"I'm not usually one to say, 'I told you so'" he said when I had finished my opus. "Why don't you tell me about it?"

And I did, but only the amended version, changing Pete's drug dealer exit to accepting a job back on the East Coast. In a strange way, it felt better to lie to someone else, to not have to spoon-feed myself a concoction whose recipe only called for a dash of deception. And David ate it up. Our session ended, and I returned home to further kill my appetite for food and continued that endeavor for the next few days. Each sunset melted into dawn, and although my brain buzzed along, it was as if time stood still.

Before I knew it, the night of my second birthday surprise had arrived, and I made sure to be wide awake for the evening's doings with two fat rails aiding and abetting me in that endeavor.

Adding to the mystery, Nina blindfolded me and insisted I sit in the back, which I assumed was less conspicuous than riding shotgun resembling Patty Hearst.

"Someone's a Chatty Cathy tonight." She observed as I rambled on from topic-to-topic.

"I'm just excited! Geez, give a girl a break."

"You have reason to be," Derek said with a bwa-ha-ha laugh.

"Alright, Snidely Whiplash, at least give me a hint," I pleaded.

"Never!" Michael yelled from the front passenger seat.

"Are we there yet? Are we there yet? Are we there yet?" I said rapidly, hoping it would somehow wear them down.

"I will turn this car right around, young man!" Nina faux-chastised.

"You guys are such a treasure," I said sweetly before going sour. "Somebody oughta bury you!"

The car came to a halt.

"Unmask! Unmask!' Michael squealed.

I did as instructed, rubbing my eyes, and looked out the window.

The sign above the door read "Crackers," and a ramp led to the door of the mysterious building next to the dirt parking lot Nina had pulled into. I didn't think this deserved all the hullabaloo to visit what I assumed was an after-hours Saltine factory. I decided to ask where we were exactly.

"Just follow us," Derek said.

"You'll see," Nina added.

"Where's your sense of adventure, young Mister Dodge?" Michael asked.

"Lead the way, bitches!" I exclaimed, still feeling my cocaine rush.

Nina ponied up $5 apiece to the doorman. New Order played loudly in the dark and smoky 18 and up club. Those in attendance looked like a Goth kid convention.

But once again, I felt like the invisible boy - scratch that, the invisible man. The so-called cool kids were moving to the rhythm of the music on the dance floor, grabbing at invisible spider webs above them.

The DJ booth was up on risers, high above the throng of people he was controlling through his music; there was a clipboard, pen, and paper to write down song requests. I began scribbling down song titles.

I returned to my friends, who were ordering Cokes at the bar. I began laughing to myself that the slogan "Things go better with Coke" was not false advertising.

We yelled over the din of music, with me starting by thanking them, they replied with "it's our pleasure," "no problem" and "we knew you'd be surprised" until Depeche Mode's "Just Can't Get Enough" lured us onto the dance floor.

Then the DJ played Siouxsie and the Banshees' "Spellbound." That was one of my requests, and I smiled and wondered if the DJ realized he resembled an angler, pulling the request sheet up to inspect his musical haul.

I moved over to the DJ list. I was shocked when I saw that all but two of my requests was crossed out in red.

Thankfully, Madonna had made the cut, and I flashed back to that night at Rage and how she had the knack for making people dance for inspiration. This time, it was the remix for "Open Your Heart" accompanied by the video playing on a TV screen above the bar. I replicated her stripper moves, drawing on the hundreds of times that I had watched it on MTV. Whether it was the crowd's body heat or the cocaine surging through my system, I was sweating so profusely that I decided a break was in order. I excused myself and found the bathroom. There was a small line for the women's room; I felt slightly guilty breezing by them into an empty bathroom for the opposite gender.

I toweled off with a handful of coarse brown paper towels. Then I checked my hair in the mirror, thankful that my generous use of Aqua Net had held. I positioned myself at a porcelain urinal with its cloying scent, courtesy of a pink urinal cake. The door opened, almost making me jump.

A lean-looking guy with high cheekbones came in. He had a cleft chin and spiky dyed blond hair and was wearing a Misfits T-shirt, red pants with black stripes and black and white wingtip Creepers. He selected the urinal closest to me, even though there were at least five others.

I heard his zipper go down and suppressed the desire to eyeball his junk. And then I changed my mind and fake-rubbed my chin on my shoulder, a move from Molly Ringwald in *Sixteen Candles* when she checks out her dreamboat, Jake Ryan in class.

It took me a second in my coked-out state to realize this guy was looking at me with piercing blue eyes. I returned the gaze, lowered my eyes, and saw that he had a little something extra on his average-sized unit in the form of skin that looked like a turtleneck, keeping his second head warm. As I looked, he began to stiffen.

Through the closed door, a muffled version of "To Be a Lover" by Billy Idol started in tandem with this Billy Idol look-alike turning away from the urinal to face me; his literal trouser snake was pointing in the direction of a vacant stall. Without tucking away his divining rod, he gave me a whiplash smile, and we walked into the stall.

This perfect stranger was standing at full attention, made taller by the lifts on his shoes, with his pants now down around his ankles.

My desire was eclipsing the angel on my shoulder who wanted me to turn around and keep my tarnished halo properly floating above my head. And while I did not have a hidden 666 on my scalp, I gave in to the devil I knew all too well. With a mental flick, the angel went flying without the use of his wings, bounced off the tiled walls, and landed with a resounding thud in the trashcan.

I dropped to my knees and began ministering to this dark angel. It wasn't long before the door opened, and I heard Michael call out my name, his feet making a hasty retreat, shoes echoing off the linoleum I was kneeling on. The stranger wasn't dissuaded by the interruption and pulled out of my mouth and decorated the wall with his own Silly String.

"What about you?" he asked in an English accent.

"I'm good. Happy to be of service," I said, realizing I was too coked up to cum. I stood up, facing him.

"I'm Jake, by the way."

"Nice to meet you. Henry."

"I kind of figured." He winked.

"Yeah, I should probably get back to my friends." I eyed the door.

"That wasn't your boyfriend who was looking for you?"

"Michael? No, he's more like a girlfriend. And I'm recently single."

"What twat would let a catch like you get away? I watched you on the dance floor. You know how to move."

"Thanks."

"Maybe we could hang out?"

"Perhaps," I answered casually, as "Brand New Lover" began pounding on the unlocked bathroom door we were exiting through, unsure if his proposition would be dead or alive in actuality.

Jake borrowed a pen from the bartender and wrote his number down with a room number. He was visiting and staying at a downtown hotel. With that pertinent bit of information, I returned to my trio.

I approached them sheepishly, and Nina led the teasing.

"Congratulations? When's the wedding?"

"Huh?" I said.

"You were proposing to that guy in the stall," Michael said seriously.

"How many bridesmaids are you thinking of?" Derek joked.

"Just one," I said, flipping them the bird.

"You really take the term 'bar slut' to a whole other level," Nina said in a motherly tone.

"What can I say? When you got it, you got it."

"Well, here's hoping that you don't go home with something you didn't come here with." Michael reprimanded.

"I didn't swallow," I said defensively.

"Well, spitters are quitters. I read that on a bathroom wall once. Maybe you wrote it." Derek declared.

"Y'all are a bunch of jealous bitches!" I said with real anger.

"Calm down, Mary!" Michael said. "We were just busting your balls. Just like you were doing with blondie."

"His name's Jake."

"Oh good, at least you got his name," Derek said with an eye roll.

"He's visiting from England."

"Anteater or helmet?" Nina asked, and when I looked puzzled, she added, "Uncut or cut?"

"The first one," I said, laughing.

"He didn't have any stalagmites, did he?" Derek asked. "I slept with this Mexican guy once, and his was funky. I was like, 'I didn't order cheese on this rolled taco!'"

"Jesus! That is foul!" Nina shrieked.

I saw Jake standing against a wall, watching our conversation. He produced a sweet smile, staring at me intently.

"Somebody's into you," Nina said.

"Seems like he's into S&M to me," Michael said, and before I could ask how he had reached that conclusion, he explained his assumption. "Standing and modeling, that is."

"Do you want to invite him over? Or are you boys having a staring contest?"

"As long as you're nice to him." I cautioned.

"Scout's honor," Derek promised.

"What are you still doing here? Vamanos, muchacho!" Nina commanded.

I made my way through the crush of people until I reached my intended target, whose heat-seeking love missile I was acquainted with.

"Hey you," Jake said.

"Hey, yourself. I thought you might like to join us."

"That's right kind of you, pardner," he joked in a Texas drawl.

"Impressive."

"Oh, you ain't seen nothin' yet." He answered, still in character.

"I like what I've seen so far."

As the five of us chatted, which took on more of a grilling session from my three-person vetting system, Jake utilized his sense of touch. One minute, he was rubbing my neck, then my shoulder, back, and further south to my butt, drawing lazy circles on each cheek, then squeezing the right one firmly.

He left with Michael and Derek in tow to buy us a round of Cokes.

"Otay, what do you think?" I asked Nina.

"Nice. But is it a good idea to get your panties all twisted over a guy that's leaving?"

I connected Point A to B for her, explaining that she could be describing Pete. Admittedly, I was doing it in a manipulating fashion, playing on her guilt for the ball that we put into play with getting Jeff busted.

"Besides, I could use a little fun," I admitted woefully.

"I suppose a rebound would be helpful."

"You're the best Mom ever!" I squealed.

They returned with our drinks. Jake had us huddle around as he took a flask out of his pants pocket, pouring each of us a dollop of whiskey in each.

"Bottoms up!" Jake proposed.

"Well then, here's to Henry!" And when Michael offered this tidbit up, Jake did a spit take, just missing my shoulder.

"Spitters are quitters, right Henry?" Derek smirked.

Rather than nurse our cocktails like seasoned drinkers, we chugged them and headed out to the dance floor. It was nice to have someone else's energy to bounce off of. Then Jake, dancing closer, started kissing me.

"Get a room!" Nina shouted above The Cure's "Close to Me."

"I've got one, thank you very much! If only I had a hot Yank to share it."

"What are your intentions with my friend?" Nina shouted.

"To show this hot bloke the time of his life. If that's ok with you guys."

All three nodded their heads in unison, although I saw mild annoyance from Derek.

“Well then, sounds like it’s time to blow this Popsicle stand!” I was most definitely buzzed from the alcohol and the prospect of getting naked with Jake. The cocaine was already wearing off.

“Blow being the keyword.” Derek quipped, and for a nanosecond, I thought he was on to me.

“You boys have fun,” Michael called after us as we left the dance floor.

We stood in the dirt parking lot, locking lips, and when they were unlocked, I saw another nightclub next to Crackers.

“Let’s check it out!”

There was a line of older men, meaning you had to be 21 to enter. Waiting three years to be considered of legal age seemed both a lifetime away and a bit of irony since I’d been drinking for two years now.

I wondered if the stern-looking shaved head bouncer might take pity on two underage guys. But it was highly doubtful, and I became double deflated when I heard one of my crossed-out requests, Debbie Deb’s “When I Hear Music,” lower and crescendo as the door opened and closed.

“Everything alright there, sexy?” Jake cooed.

“Yeah, just wishing I had a time machine.”

“Do you have get back to the future, Marty?”

“Just wish I was old enough to get in there.”

“All in good time. And when you are older, you’ll wish you could go back to your younger days.”

“Nah, I adhere to the James Dean philosophy of life.”

“And what would that be?”

“Live fast, die young, leave a pretty corpse.”

“Well, that’s a bit morbid.”

“Welcome to my mind,” I said with a bow. “Definitely not a street you want to walk on all alone at midnight.”

“You are an interesting person, Henry. It’s a damn shame that I’m only passing through. You are someone I’d like to get to know.”

The kiss he planted on me told me he was serious about the sweet sentiment of something that would never come to be.

“Just my luck.” I sighed. “And what brings you to town, anyway?”

“I’m a party promoter and DJ. I thought sunny Southern California might be a pleasant change from gloomy London. I’m looking at prospects to make that happen.”

“Oh really?” I said, showing a flicker of excitement.

"Yes, really. You never know."

"Nope, you never do."

"I guess that's the beauty of life. Surprises at every turn. Ok, enough with the flowery stuff. Do we stand here all night, or can I get you out of those clothes?"

"You certainly know how to woo a guy." I joked. "Yes, let's shall."

"Your rented chariot awaits." He led me to his red Mustang 5.0, our arms interlocked.

We resembled a male version of *Laverne and Shirley,* but I stifled the urge to shout out, "Schlemiel! Schlimazel! Hasenpfeffer Incorporated!"

But then he said it, so I nuzzled up to him once we were in the car, pledging to enjoy the here and now with Jake.

At his room at the Holiday Inn, it was like a kaleidoscope blur that was happening in slow motion. We attacked each other with a ferocity usually reserved for animals. Jake had already edged his way to the top of my list of best kissers, no cigarette breath like, you know who had. And once he was out of his Creepers, he was only an inch taller than me.

The passion we were swept up in was unparalleled to anything that I had experienced before, and I let myself fall into the rhythm of our horizontal dance.

Well, almost.

Our bodies were producing a volume of sweat, and the rubbing of our skin created a sound that sounded slightly like gas being passed. Despite my best efforts, I let out a little laugh, and rather than it killing the moment, Jake let out a hearty guffaw.

"Question." He said, panting. "Is it true what Michael said?"

There was no feigning innocence that I wasn't sure what he was referring to, so I nodded in the affirmative. But I did pause to ask about his HIV status and when he told me he had a minus and not a plus, then came the caveat that he would put a raincoat on his Johnson. There were no lame excuses of being allergic to latex or that it would cause his erection to cease to exist; just opening his nightstand drawer.

A package of Trojans and a bottle of lube sat on top of the hotel Bible. Soon enough, our lovemaking was hotter than the flames of eternal damnation. Rather than arriving at the Pearly gates, our climaxes left pearly trails on my torso.

We lay side-by-side in silence, both knowing what had just occurred wasn't the norm for a one-night stand. There was something more to it, yet neither one of us wanted to vocalize the thought. What was the point since he was leaving?

Jake got up from the bed and went into the bathroom. He returned with a wet washcloth, wiping away the evidence of our mind-blowing sex, even though I could still feel his fingerprints on my skin. I decided it was time to say something.

"Do you know if the maid might have left a squeegee when she cleaned your room?"

"I'm not following, mate." He eyed me suspiciously.

"I need to clean the ceiling to get my brains off of it because that was mind-blowing!"

"I concur wholeheartedly."

"I suspected as much. I'm smart like that."

"Smart, funny, and good-looking, to boot. They sure grow them good in The States."

"And that gets a qualified ditto about England."

I had a love/hate relationship with the part of me labeled "hopeless romantic," but this guy from across the pond convinced me to change it to "hopeful romantic."

"Would you like to crash here tonight?"

"Sure, that would be nice." I could tell Mom I stayed at Nina's."

"Or it could be naughty."

It was then that I saw that he was ready for a rematch, and I was game to wrestle again. And this time, it was my turn to pin him to the mat. We finally exhausted ourselves around 4 a.m., like toddlers who finally gave in to their efforts of trying to stave off a nap because they still wanted to play.

We slept until 10, then showered together, leading to going at it again. Then, it was shower number two, and I took him up on his offer of breakfast and a ride home.

We chatted about everything under the sun, except for the elephant in the backseat. As we pulled up to my house, Jake broached the subject.

"I really hope that this isn't goodbye."

"Hopefully, it's just a case of TTFN." I explained, "Ta-Ta For Now."

"I just may be back, and you're a hell of an incentive. And we can stay in touch."

He wrote down his phone number and address, he ripped the paper in half, and I wrote my information down. We exchanged them like Valentines, even though we were going to be just pen pals.

"You stay in touch, Mr. Dodge." He kissed me.

"And you better do the same, Mr..." I looked down at the surname on the paper. "Jones."

And with that, I entered the house as a textbook example of "parting is such sweet sorrow."

"Nice of you to call and let me know that you were OK," Mom greeted me sourly.

"Sorry. It got late, and I crashed at Nina's."

"And her phone didn't work this morning, either?"

"I promise it won't happen again." I offered a sheepish smile, which I had done as a kid, getting me off the hook every time I trotted it out.

"You know how I worry!"

"Sorry if I stressed you out."

"It's fine…this time. Do you want to go with me to the airport to pick up your father?"

I shook my head, explaining I needed to be at work soon.

"It's funny. Dad's never been on a business trip on a weekend before."

But she didn't take the bait. Come to think of it, I hadn't seen hide nor hair of Mrs. Woodson this week, but I hadn't been on "Check Up on Your Father's Mistress" watch.

When she left for the airport, I took Shadow for a walk. Strolling past the Woodson house as if it were the neighborhood haunted house, I saw newspapers where the paperboy had thrown them in various spots. Sure enough, they matched the number of days that my father was away.

"Motherfucker," I said under my breath.

I watched as a taxi pulled up in front of her house. Mrs. Woodson exited, red hair pulled back into a ponytail. Her usual alabaster skin was a shade darker. A guilty look crossed her face when she spotted me, and she proceeded to beat a hasty retreat to the front door, a single suitcase in her left hand.

I crossed her front lawn as she struggled to find the keys in her purse.

"You shouldn't let newspapers stack up like that. Burglars look for that, ya know."

"Thanks, I'll keep that in mind."

Shadow pulled forward on the leash, tail wagging.

"Sorry, she gets excited when she sees a whore," I said sweetly and walked away.

The rest of our walk was fueled by anger coursing through my veins. Once I was back in my bedroom, I broke out the dwindling stash from Darren.

Two rails did the trick. I took my third shower of the day and got ready for work.

Nina was just clocking in. She asked about how the night with Jake went. In my heightened state, I went into the gory details.

"I don't want to burst your bubble," she said after I had quickly rattled off the events of the evening as we descended the steps that led to the lobby. "Derek's kind of pissed at you."

"Why?"

"Probably better if you talk to him about it."

I felt a little crestfallen that, in the span of a day, I had upset both Mom and my friend. But rather than dwell on it, I let work distract me. The coke buzz didn't hurt, either.

I was in the back, attending to a sink full of suds to assist in the items that needed cleaning when Yvonne materialized next to me. I had the radio on, and Janet Jackson was singing about those nasty boys.

"I bet you're a nasty boy," she said, causing me to drop the ladle for the nacho cheese into the soapy water, its descent marked by orange tendrils.

"Jesus, you scared me!"

She pulled me to her ample bosom and stroked the back of my neck. Her breasts were firm, and pressing into the side of my face, she suddenly released me from her grasp. Nina entered the room, and Yvonne became all business instantly.

"I just wanted to let you know that we've decided to keep you on," she said as Nina stared, having seen a glimpse of what happened before turning to the cage to get candy inventory.

"Cool," I muttered. "Thanks."

"You're welcome." Then she dropped her voice to a whisper. "We should celebrate."

The party would be held in my pants. That was obvious as she grabbed my dong through my polyester slacks. Life had a funny way of throwing its fair share of curveballs at me. Unfortunately, much like my attempts at tee-ball during my stint in Little League, it was often a case of a swing and a miss. Admittedly, my curiosity was getting the better of me, especially as I got into Yvonne's gray AMC Pacer the next night.

There was a cold six-pack of Budweiser on the passenger side floorboard, which I cradled between my feet like a newborn, hoping it would help guide me in the baby steps I was taking into the unknown.

"Why don't you crack one of those bad boys open?" She queried, not looking at me, keeping her eyes on the road. "They won't stay cold forever. Some things are better warm. Beer is not one of them."

Her right hand caressed my left thigh, and I realized I was the human equivalent in that analogy. I was feeling frosty, wondering if my temperature would rise, just as a certain body part betrayed me with its ascent.

I was hoping that she hadn't noticed.

"Well, someone's glad to see me." She purred, and when I turned to look at her, she had morphed into the Eartha Kitt version of Catwoman. "Purrfect."

Holy shit! My mind screamed at me as she returned to normal, and I cursed it for all the tricks that it was playing.

The ultimate one was that I may enjoy this form of attention as much as the time spent in the hallway at Lavar's with Steve or the game of strip quarters with Craig. I wanted to punch myself in the dick, but I would have struck Yvonne's hand that was gently massaging it.

Deciding it was most definitely time for a beer, I interrupted her focus, bending forward to retrieve the first of the six beers that would do nothing to distract me that night. All they did was convince me that it would be a great idea to go back to her place. The building buzz in my brain also thought letting her undress me, like some life-sized version of a Ken doll, was a honey of a notion.

Once I was down to my dark blue Jockeys, she stripped in record time, and before I knew it, I was sitting on the edge of the bed. She wasted no time in getting to the task at hand, or rather mouth, and when I closed my eyes and employed the opposite version of thinking about baseball to slow my roll. Two months after Christmas, visions of sugar plumbs disguised as teammates celebrating their win with a group shower that evolved into an orgy danced through my head.

Before I knew it, I had reached the inevitable, popping my cork. After all was said and done, I opened my sixth and final beer. Liquid courage caused a false bravery that I was good to go for another round, this time with Yvonne being the recipient of pleasure, as my sheathed sword entered her.

Much to my surprise, no one burst into the room to haul me off to faux hetero jail as I lost my gold star status. However, as I climaxed for the second time, there was a knock at Yvonne's door.

"Hey sis, I'm home," Steve informed his sibling.

Both of us froze but for varied reasons and one common thread. Neither of us wanted to be caught in the post-coital act. Yvonne had no idea why this constituted what could only be described as an "awkward situation." My guess was that she didn't want her brother to find her with "company." I had known they were close, albeit not like he had disgustingly been with Craig, but I obviously had zero clue that they were roommates. I was also unsure as to how protective he may be.

My paranoid mind conjured up him using his kung fu skills to challenge me to a fight to maintain his sister's already tarnished virtue. Naturally, I was naked and vulnerable in every sense of the word, backed up against the wall, throwing blind punches that he predicted at every turn.

Except for one.

I rushed up and kissed him, catching him off-guard, and once his guard dropped from the weight of his secret revealed, I drove my knee forcefully into his crotch. He issued a cartoon bubble reading "oof" slinking off to his room on his hands and knees.

And just like his imaginary doppelganger, he retreated to his room, as signaled by the closing of the door across the hallway, not bothering with any further investigation. The combination of being in his presence, the beer buzz evaporating instantaneously, and the naked woman that I was climbing off all merged to the same conclusion.

"I need to get home," I whispered.

"Well, wham, bam, thank you, Ma'am." She said, clearly annoyed. "Didn't like our little science project?"

"It's not that." My brain began singing "Weird Science," and I forbade my mouth from uttering its lyrics. "Your brother and I don't get along. Like, at all. I'd rather he didn't know that we, uh."

"That you just banged his little sister?"

"Something like that."

"Fine, get dressed. I'll sneak you out of here and take you home."

I dressed in record time, putting on my shoes and tying the laces while Yvonne was still fiddling with the buttons on her blouse, pants still lying on the floor in front of the bed. I was doing my best to stop the tide of a bladder that needed emptying, refraining from doing the hot dog dance, but we had a wiener-pinching situation.

"I've gotta use your bathroom," I said.

"It's the last door down the hall."

I locked the door, as a just in case, and took a piss that lasted an eternity. And just as I was zipping up, there was a knock at the door. It wasn't a "the jig's up" pounding, it was a soft rap with a hint of urgency.

Still, I opened the door slowly in case it was Steve pulling a clever ruse. But Yvonne was standing there. A trace of the dejected look was starting to erase itself on her face.

"C'mon and make it snappy." She whispered, glancing at the fragment of light spilling out from under her sibling's door.

We made it to the front door just as his opened, and Yvonne shoved me into the hallway and called out to her brother that she'd "be back in a bit."

We made it to her car in record time, and luckily, she had parked away from the streetlight that would have illuminated who her "special guest star" was as Steve was peering through the window from behind the drawn back curtain with the hand once used to bring me to orgasm with.

I suspected if he'd known the passenger's identity in the Pacer, it would have caused his hand to clench immediately, ripping the curtain forcefully down, ready for them both to do the business of dispatching me with a one-two knockout punch.

But it was Yvonne's tongue that struck me.

"You know, that's a pretty shitty way to thank someone for a good time. But I suppose it's par for the course with *your kind.*"

I wasn't sure why she thought her vagina was transformative, able to erase the years of being too afraid to be myself, yet not wanting to conform to societal norms until I finally felt comfortable in my own skin. There was nothing disgusting about touching her. In fact, I still had not wrapped my head around the sensation of not being repulsed.

I almost put her on blast for the assumption of knowing one iota about what it's like to be part of my world. I could certainly stop her globe from spinning, throwing it off its axis, causing gravity to cease with a few choice words about her family tree with two limp branches.

The pull of my gravitational force wanted to bark out how she would know anything about it because her closet case brother and the one who would more than likely end up playing on my team hadn't confided in her. Oh, and I had slept with both of them.

Even though I was off the clock, I didn't want to make any nuclear shock waves as far as my employment was concerned when she dropped a bomb of her own.

"Listen, I'm sorry," she said quietly. "I don't know what I was thinking the outcome of this would be. I respect you for being true to yourself. Not everyone can say that. I know I can't."

"What do you mean?"

"Let's just say that I like hot dogs and tacos."

A word that Jake had said after one of our bouts of cramming a sex life into a 12-hour span jumped into my head. I was gobsmacked, as the logical conclusion to be drawn was that she was strictly dickly. But she explained that although she had a penchant for guys, Yvonne much preferred the company of women.

I silently contemplated if the secret ingredient in Lavar's BBQ sauce had turned his children gay when he was first perfecting it at home, years before he opened his popular restaurant.

It was highly doubtful that a dash, dollop, or sprinkle had resulted in all three of his offspring having same-sex attractions. Naturally, I couldn't let on that I held the key to unlock a veritable Pandora's Box of family secrets.

She must have detected that I was the purveyor of many a surreptitious notion and could be trusted in not saying a solitary word about it. When she asked me to do that very thing, I assured her that I'd take it to the grave until she was ready to dig up the bones of her sexuality and examine them 'neath the midnight sky.

"Friends?" She asked. As the car was parked, the engine idled roughly.

"Absolutely," I said, even giving her a hug.

"Cool. See you at the rat race."

"Drive safe," I said lamely.

"Absolutely."

Unlocking the front door, silently wondering if there would be any tell-tale signs for my parents to pick up that I had dabbled outside of my comfort zone. When Shadow made her usual appearance out of the ethers and kept sniffing the crotch of my pants, I figured a shower couldn't hurt.

After I was sufficiently scrubbed, I walked over to the foggy mirror, and the squeak, squeak, squeak sound of my hand revealing my face, showing no difference in it. Nope, nothing to see here, as far as they were concerned the next morning. Nina, on the other hand, was a different story altogether.

"Did you do something new with your hair?"

"No." I figured monosyllabic answers would be best in not letting the pussy, err, cat out of the bag.

"Something's off."

I simply shrugged, going about the opening duty of checking the amount of coconut oil needed to pop the corn, which was just shy of being empty. I brought a fresh mini drum out, replacing the nearly depleted one, and began opening the lid with a screwdriver. But it was Nina who was doing the lion's share of prying.

I grew tired of keeping information from my best friend, so I melted faster than the solidified butter I had put in the heated dispenser. I figured if I made her swear not to say anything about it – she wouldn't. Besides, Yvonne wasn't working today; I was going to keep it to what we had done, not what she divulged to me in the strictest of confidence.

"Well, if you were to ever have any grandkids, I'm not sure that it would be a story to tell them." She exclaimed when I finished telling her of my previous night's pit stop in Straightsville, which, I believe, is adjacent to Funky Town. "But still…I'm glad that you told me."

"And you are the only one that I will be telling. Capisce?"

"You know that I don't speak any foreign languages! But I am fluent in sassiness." She teased before giving me another assurance that mum was the word on my unexpected visit to "the other side."

"So," I said in a forlorn fashion. "Are you going to tell me what's up with Derek?"

"Oh, that."

"Yeah, *that*."

"Well, given your newfound stud status with the ladies, I suppose a little tit for tat is in order."

"Gurl."

"Sorry. I couldn't resist."

"You might want to work on your impulse issues," I said, feeling every bit the hypocrite.

"Is that a professional assessment?"

"Just a personal observation."

"Ok, I'll quit pussyfooting around it."

"Jesus."

"Well, you ain't a virgin anymore, Mary."

"You suck."

"Not as well as you."

"Project much, Edwina Murphy? I'm broke till Friday and don't have enough for the two-drink minimum. What gives?"

"He thought it was uncool that you abandoned us for your knight in shining Creepers."

"I see his point. I'll call him after work."

"Good man. I don't want any weirdness between you two."

"Aside from the usual tomfoolery."

"Exactamundo!"

When Derek answered on the third ring that night, his pleasant "hello" turned cold when he heard my voice.

"Oh, it's you."

"Hey, I wanted to apologize for the other night."

"You mean for bailing on us to pluck the petals off your English rose?"

"I really put the whore in horticulture."

"Don't be so clever."

"I'm sorry, Derek; it was amazing that you guys did that for me."

"Promise not to do it again?"

"Cross my heart." But after the events of last month, I decided not to add "and hope to die" to that assurance.

"Alright. I'll let it slide."

The downside to having friends was they were beginning to know how I operated. Yet they remained unaware of how skilled of a surgeon I really was in not exposing all my insides to them.

This was evident by sticking the straw up my left nostril, then my right the next morning – it's called balance – vaccuming up the last bit of coke. South America's version of a Band-Aid was helping me divert focus away from the open wounds of my already-scarred heart, but I was fooling myself that I could go cold turkey. I needed to replenish.

The next time I worked with Darren on Thursday, I tried to be coded in what I asked him, even though no one was in earshot.

"Hey, I heard there was a good movie playing on HBO tonight. Are you *wired* for cable?" Then I blurted out, "Do you have any blow?"

"Sure. Remember how to get to my place?"

After quitting time, I was knocking on his apartment door. Darren answered, all sweaty, brown hair matted to his forehead, almost obscuring his coffee-colored eyes, his angular face flushed with red on his cheeks.

"Did I catch you at a bad time?" I found myself trying not to eye his bare chest and his gym shorts.

"Nah. Just doing a workout. Sit-ups and push-ups. Come in, come in."

I crossed the threshold between good and bad decisions and sat down on the couch. He stood over me, his navel and treasure trail at my eye level, hypnotizing me. Then, a drop of sweat from his chest hit me squarely between the eyes. Without a word, he wiped it off with his thumb.

"I should take a shower. Make yourself at home."

"K."

My eyes were focused on the bathroom door that he had left open, his discarded shorts and jock strap on the blue bathroom rug. The water soon shut off, and I turned my gaze away from the door. A few minutes later, he plopped down next to me, still shirtless, wearing gray sweatpants.

"How much will $25 get me?" I asked.

He brought out a full mini baggie.

"You get the friend's discount."

"You don't have to do that."

"I know I don't have to. I want to. I like hanging out with you, Henry."

"Same here, Darren."

"Now, what do you say we test-drive it?"

It turned out to be the same kinetic ride for my pounding heart and throttled throat. He had turned the music up as if we were on a Sunday joyride and not approaching 9 o'clock on a Thursday. I had to steer my gaze away from his taut body, the dark hair around each nipple. He stood up briefly, and I noticed he was commando under the sweatpants.

"Say, I have an idea!" He exclaimed, bolstered by the two lines we had just done.

Jesus! Please don't let it be a game of Spin the Pickle. I prayed to my invisible friend in the sky, even though my pleas fell on deaf celestial ears.

"Oh yeah?" I asked with trepidation.

Without saying a word, he got up, turned off the music, and headed towards his bedroom.

"You comin'?"

My throat going dry, I followed, as there was no Thomas Brothers map to help me navigate this. Darren sat on the bed and patted the comforter.

"Wanna play?"

I breathed in relief; he was pointing to an Atari 2600 and a stack of video games. These would be the only joysticks to be employed that night.

Darren led me through games that required protecting cities from missiles and guiding Pac-Man on his quest to traverse mazes, avoiding Inky, Blinky, Pinky, and Clyde. The awful sound effects of his eating rectangular "pellets" caused us to laugh more than a few times.

In two hours, I had gotten killed numerous times in trying to defeat the alien bug in *Yar's Revenge*. It was time for me to go.

"You know it's weird." He began. "I was looking at you when you were sucking at *Yar's Revenge*."

I had almost made it out of his place, confident that I was in a no-sex zone despite my suspicions. Now I wasn't sure again.

He put his hand on my shoulder and gave it a squeeze, trying to figure out what base this constituted as when he offered an explanation for his assessment of what was "weird."

"You remind me of a friend when I lived in Northern California. You're the spitting image of Adam."

"Come again?" I asked, hoping he wasn't talking about Corey Adams or thought my response was a coded message about wanting to get into his sweats.

"But we lost touch after he moved to LA. He got mixed up with the wrong people and ended up getting killed. Some piece of shit got away with murder."

Well, that settled that, as my coke-addled brain became unsettled.

I managed to keep a poker face and say I was sorry for his loss.

"Sorry, didn't mean to bum you out."

"That's what friends are for."

And when he hugged me tight, there were tears in his eyes, confessing that Adam had taught him an important lesson in seeing people for what they were: just people. And he intended to carry that with him for the rest of his life,

And standing there before me was Danny, mouthing that he was sorry before he evaporated into a fine mist. I had to leave before I broke down and told him I knew what and who he had been talking about.

My mind spoke volumes, unrelenting in conjuring up things that go bump in the night as I lay in bed contemplating if I wanted to do a small one myself. I must have drifted off at some point, awakening to what I hoped was a brand-new day, not knowing what it had in store for me.

Despite a balanced breakfast of yogurt and blueberries, I still felt unbalanced. But I had an appointment with David in a few hours. And I hadn't done my homework assignment either. The former "A" student status, which I had let slip away in high school, was openly mocking my lack of preparation, a sort of belated "told you so."

Naturally, a little gun powder helped me focus. I needed to complete my project in record time. Being an expert in the art of deception, I had put my stash in a different spot in case of a possible Mom room sweep.

I went downstairs, retrieving a big glass of water from the dispenser on the white refrigerator door, light years away from the avocado green fridge of yore.Stowing away my accouterments and turning the volume on my ghetto blaster up, I boarded the "Crazy Train" with Ozzy Osbourne ten times in a row until I had my preliminary sketch. The process of finishing its shading ate up another hour, which I enhanced with poignant lyrics matching the story being told until it was time to get ready.

With the wind pressing against my dark blue Billabong shirt, I drove L'il Red. I should have felt the last lingering chill of winter in Southern California. But I felt impervious to the in-between days of cooler weather that eventually resulted in spring, focused only on a time for growth and renewal.

A pang of regret hit me right between the eyes. I was withering on the vine of poor choices again, an unending cycle if I didn't find a better footing to cope with life's disappointments.

Pulling into the parking lot, I straddled L'il Red for a moment, my heartbeat matching her low idle; I looked into the left rearview mirror, not to see wind-damaged hair but to see how I looked in the façade of having my shit together.

Once I was satisfied that David would be none-the-wiser, I made my way to the office, checked in with the always delightful Karen, and waited for my crazy doctor, as Nina and I called him.

Putting my backpack down and sitting in the usual chair in his office, I made a conscious effort to not sit bolt upright, slumping into a more relaxed position, right leg crossed over the left, hands folded daintily on my lap.

"So, how have you been?"

"Fine. Same shit, different day," I replied, quoting a popular bumper sticker.

"Well, that's an interesting way to put things," he said with a small chuckle.

"Would you expect anything less?"

"No. But I am hoping that we can dig deeper into why you do the things you do."

"Can you give a 'for example'?"

"For example: What is this need to sweep things under the carpet?"

"I can name that tune in one note. It's a very 'We are Family' trait."

Endless self-defense sentries fell like a collective row of dominoes. The dark recesses of my mind were held up underneath the fluorescent lights, on display for David to assess. When I had finished my true confessions, he offered his perspective.

"From where I'm sitting, I have a better view of the why behind it all, these masks that you wear so expertly. There is a theory about homosexuality being boiled down to a case of nature versus nurture."

"If this isn't a textbook case of irony! The thing my father hates most about me is something he helped bring about with his idea of parenting. Classic Big Ed!"

"I actually believe it's a combination of your environment and the more unconventional belief that you were simply born that way."

"Or born that gay, as it was."

"The level of denial in your family doesn't lend itself to honest conversations, does it?"

"Not. At. All. I can't really see what that would look like in our house. Like the elephant in the room being turned into a unicorn."

"But it sounds like you are making more headway with your brother and Mom."

"Let's just say that she's gone from Queen of Denial to being the Princess of it. John accepts me; I still don't feel he gets me. And Big Ed will always be the King of Beers to me."

"How do you feel?"

"I think I'm OK."

"That is not what I asked you. I have noticed that you have a problem with overthinking. Is that a fair assessment? I want you to pause occasionally and focus on your breathing. Remember, it's the first thing we do as we enter this world and the last thing we do as we exit it."

"I don't know," I said, flummoxed, that I felt more naked than with a sexual partner. "Let me *think* about it."

"Reagan should hire you as Secretary of Defense. Our time is almost up. Let's see that homework."

I handed over my under-pressure project. Then he frowned. I instantly regretted that I hadn't produced something that would keep my star pupil hopes from being dashed.

"Something wrong?" I asked sheepishly.

"Care to explain its meaning?" He asked, turning it around for me to see, even though it was fresh in my mind.

I studied the sketch of an old-fashioned steam locomotive going around a bend on the downslope of a mountain, tracks covered in snow. Beneath them, I had printed a two-sentence explanation.

"Life's a bitter shame. I'm going off the rails on a crazy train."

Dammit! Did my subconscious tell on me about my secretive behavior?

"That's the beauty of art," I offered. "It's subjective. What I've made is not necessarily what you might interpret it as."

"Spare me the Arts 101 lesson, Henry."

"I was thinking about my past," I sighed. "Probably overthinking it, as you've pointed out."

Quick, to the point, with just that signature sarcasm. It seemed to land with him, and I took my place on my observer's perch, no longer a singular lazy murder of crows gathering on the wind.

"Excellent," he said, studying it again. "If you would allow, I'd like to share these with a friend. He owns an art gallery."

And just like that, I fell off that roost of safety, feathers ruffled but still cushioning my tumble from imaginary preventative measures into the unfamiliar abyss of what my ears thought they had heard.

"I'm sorry. What?"

"Do I need to use sign language, Henry?"

I began shaking my head no and then yes.

"He's been in and out of Laguna Beach for the past few months, and it looks like that trend will continue, so it's going to take a bit. Consider this your abject lesson in patience. Sound good?"

"Seriously? Would you do that for me? I don't know what to say."

"Well, there's a first."

I wanted to skip out of his office but was convinced Karen had the men in white coats on speed dial. I figured whistling David Naughton's "Makin' It" wouldn't raise any suspicions, so I indulged myself. Straddling L'il Red, I clapped along with the song and made the little "boo, boo, boo" Disco sounds that accompanied it, vacillating between pointing my left and right fingers to the phantom sounds of yesteryear.

I felt like my head was stuck in the clouds. But I should have been paying attention to the ground underneath me. Taking the turn onto

Encinitas Boulevard at too fast a clip, I slammed into the curb, knocking me off, with my scooter sliding left and my body going in the opposite direction.

Thankfully, she came to a stop after skidding a few feet, and I did my best to stop, drop, and roll onto the sidewalk. Not so much Evel Knievel jumping across the Snake River as plain old Henry Dodge avoiding a gutter.

Orange fragments of her left rear brake light were glittering on the pavement like coagulated pieces of auburn blood. I righted my trusty companion, seeing a scrape along her left flank. It was then that I assessed my own damage, a thick stream of blood running down my right arm from a wound deeper than the one my ego had sustained. It made my brain flash briefly but powerfully on the crimson that once escaped my wrists after I put metal to flesh.

And just when I was starting to feel good about myself, too.

I cautiously rode L'il Red home, bandaged my arm, and then dialed Nina's number. Her answering machine fielded my phone call.

Perhaps it was a sign. Perhaps not, as I dialed Derek, letting him know the gallery news, and then Michael. I made them promise not to tell Nina, and each assured me it was my news to share.

I went on a few errands, which now included picking up the part I needed to fix L'il Red. I left her in the garage and walked to AMC to get my paycheck.

Neither Nina nor Darren was working, but Yvonne was behind the concession stand.

"Ouch! What happened to you?"

"I munched it on my scooter."

"You do munch things very well." The familiar and lustful glint in her eyes informed me she was hoping for a repeat visit to her bedroom. But rather than another round of being a bucking bronco that would pleasure her, I needed to convey that I was a one-trick pony in this rodeo.

"That's what all the boys saaaay." I said in a sing-song voice, changing a word in the snatch of a lyric from Madonna's "Dress You Up" to convey my point.

"And that's what all the girls saaaay." She countered.

I should have sung Jermaine Stewart's "We Don't Have to Take Our Clothes Off," because she was undressing me with her eyes.

Call it fate, happenstance, or plain old bad luck, as I noticed that Yvonne's attention was focused on a customer behind me. I turned around, fully intending to offer an "excuse me" for hogging the counter. The words escaped me, as did an audible gulp.

There she stood, all 5 feet, four inches of absolute bitch.

"Well, well, well," Nurse Wretched said.

Of all the multiplexes in all the towns, in all the world, this cooze walks into mine.

Play it cool, Dodge. There was no need to poke a sleeping bear, so I went in for a hug fit for a grizzly to give. I certainly caught her off-guard with what was akin to showing a rattlesnake affection.

"Wow! It's so great to see you! How have you been?"

She was stunned but found her voice.

"Uh, yes. Nice to see you."

"Gosh, I'd like to catch up with you, but I have a million things to do today," I said and then addressed Yvonne. "Is Erik in his office?"

Yvonne nodded and asked the dragon lady what she could get for her. Just then, it was Nurse Wretched's turn to surprise me with a hug of her own. As she clapped me on the back, whispering in my ear.

"I'm glad you're not working today," she hissed and looked directly at my fresh wound. "I wouldn't want AIDS on my popcorn. Did we have another accident?"

"Speaking of accidents, sometimes shook-up old ladies get cut."

I planted a kiss on her cheek and departed with "Toodles," leaving her behind where she belonged, a faded memory peeling itself like wallpaper from its resting place on a dilapidated wall in a haunted house.

Once I was rewarded for being gainfully employed by Erik, I returned to the lobby populated by a smattering of patrons and said goodbye to Yvonne; trying to discern if Wretched had divulged any information. But everything appeared to be on the up and up as Yvonne waved normally, denoting nothing had gone down.

I went to the bank to deposit my check, then circled back to the auto parts store.

Even though Nurse Wretched had rattled my cage, I decided during my Encinitas walkabout, I would do my damndest to keep bad thoughts under lock and key.

I saved my visit to square up with Darren for last, selfishly hoping he would be in the mood for channeling the childhood term of "sharesies."

I knocked on his door, and his usually absent roommate answered instead. To say he was a sterling example of the word "gorgeous" would be a gross understatement. Warm brown eyes offset by olive skin, a million-watt Crest smile. No stranger to the gym, his membership, an incredibly wise investment evidenced by bulging biceps and a well-defined chest stretching his lavender Le Tigre polo shirt to the limit.

He was my height, so we were standing eye to eye, although his curly brown hair made it appear he was a skosh taller.

"What can I do you for?" He asked.

I had several responses, but they all involved what I could do for him sexually. Instead, I informed him in a quavering voice I was here to see Darren.

"Well, I figured you weren't a Jehovah's Witness."

"Oh my God, they're the worst!" I said, hoping to find my footing with him. "I always tell them they caught me in the middle of sacrificing a goat and they are welcome to join in."

"Ha! Good one! He's at school," he said, glancing down at his Casio watch. "But you want to wait, Henry?"

Oh my God! He knew my name!

"I guess my reputation precedes me."

"Darren has mentioned you. Nice to put a face to the name. I'm Jason, by the way."

"That's an interesting last name – is it French?" I asked casually, although it was an old joke in my humor Rolodex.

"It's actually Papadopoulos, and that's Greek." He said amping up the wattage on that bioluminescent smile of his. "He told me you are quite the comedian. I like that."

I could have fainted dead away, knowing I would be safe in those tanned, muscular arms.

He ushered me in, clapping me on the back as I did so. When I closed the door behind me, I got a static shock, convinced it was the electricity between us that had caused it, whether he was AC or DC remained to be seen.

"Damn that doorknob has it out for me!"

Without a word, Jason grabbed my hand, informing me that he was studying to become a doctor and would offer his professional opinion.

Thankfully, he wasn't too close to my wrist as my pulse immediately went up. Even more fortunate was he not asking me to turn my head and cough.

"You'll live. Make yourself comfortable."

I walked in a daze and took a seat, shakily putting the bag with the new taillight for my scooter on the coffee table.

"What's your poison?" he asked from the kitchen.

"Vodka," I answered like Ally Sheedy in *The Breakfast Club*, feeling like a basket case myself.

"I have some chilling in the freezer. Plus, orange juice! Screwdrivers it is. Unless you just wanted your vodka straight?"

"Well, if I did, it would be the straightest thing I've done in a spell."

He laughed, asked when my comedy special would be airing on HBO, as he prepped our cocktails.

"Well, I figured if I ever did venture into that arena that I would call it *Henry Dodge: A Bridge Too Far*."

"Oh yeah?"

"The fact is, I have a warped mind."

"A warped mind is a terrible thing to waste. Care to elaborate?"

"Well, I think it's hilarious when little kids fall down."

When he chuckled, I was in the clear.

He brought our drinks over, placing them on coasters in a fastidious manner to punctuate this was their resting place and not on the coffee table, as Darren did.

With each sip of the very potent drink, my curious nature accelerated, and I asked numerous questions. He responded as I tried not to stare at his thighs that were threatening to bust through denim.

By the time our screwdrivers were drained, I discovered he was born in Greece and lived there until he was 10, his father relocated the family to San Francisco, before heading south to attend college.

I watched him raise his glass, which made his right bicep bulge. You could have drawn a chalk outline around me, because I was dead.

"You must have to beat the girls off with a stick!" I said louder than intended. "How do you have time to go to school and live in the gym?"

"My focus has been on mind, body, and soul honestly. Meaning I don't really have time for a special someone, not right now. I channel my energies into school and, yes, living in the gym as you put it."

He didn't say girlfriend. Jesus! He was like the Fort Knox of finding out his sexual preference.

"If I looked like you, I'd never get anything done."

"I am sure that you do just fine. But, if you want to put a little more meat on them bones, I'd be glad to show you how."

"Sure, that would be great," I said, just as Darren walked through the front door.

"Oh shit! This isn't an intervention, is it?" he quipped.

"It's probably too late for that," Jason responded in a deadpan manner.

"You said a mouthful," Darren said, approaching the couch, eyeing the now-empty glasses. "And that is rich coming from you drunks! It may be 5'o clock somewhere, but it is still 3:05 in the p.m. Pacific Standard Time here in America's Finest City."

He uttered a "tsk-tsk" noise, pairing it with the "for shame" finger gesture.

"Hey! How did I get roped into this?" I exclaimed.

"If the glass fits, Henry."

"Someone took his clever pills today," Jason offered up. "OK, now that I got my buzz on, I need to hit the books. Oh, what do you say about a good pump session tomorrow morning, Henry?"

I knew it was his way of asking me to join him at the gym, but it brought up a whole different visual of laying side-by-side on his bed in a round of mutual masturbation. The most rudimentary ability to respond was frozen in time and the fires of desire burning up my very core could not melt it.

I just nodded as he told me specifics about Holiday Spa, which included bringing gym clothes and a lock for the locker.

My mind immediately conjured up the scene from *Can't Stop the Music* where The Village People extolled the virtues of the "Y.M.C.A.," complete with a tour of the facilities. And while I had caught the edited version on KTLA one late night, there had been enough male flesh to spark a rigorous give myself a hand experience.

"Oh! And bring a bathing suit since they have a Jacuzzi. Meet you at 10:30."

For fuck's sake! This could very well end up being the antithesis of practicing good health, as I was sure a heart attack would be the result of soaking with this modern-day Hercules.

"You got it!" I mustered up the appropriate response but immediately regretted my lame thumb-ups salute.

When he was out of my field of vision, I slunk down into the couch becoming one with the cushions. Darren craned his neck to make sure Jason was out of earshot.

"Yo Spike, you got the Motts?"

I had nearly forgotten the reason I had come here; it hadn't been to torture myself with another imagined failed relationship. I ponied up the cash, then informed Darren I had to get home to fix up L'il Red. As I was making my hasty exit, he spoke these words to me; each syllable adding to the mystery of which team that Jason played for.

"Wear something cute tomorrow," he said and repeated my lame thumbs-up gesture, clearly mocking me.

I gave him a middle finger, my direct assessment of his comment. He batted his eyes at me, like Miss Kitty tending bar on *Gunsmoke*. I tipped an imaginary ten-gallon cowboy hat, nodded my head, and called him "ma'am" as I closed the door.

In our garage, I flashbacked to helping Big Ed in his endeavor to not have to shell out money for a new vehicle. The echoes of "lefty loosey, righty tighty" bounced around my head as I retrieved a Phillips screwdriver from his tool chest. The term had always made me giggle to myself, as I thought it sounded a tad sexual even at an early age.

And would you not know it. Just as I completed replacing the taillight all by my lonesome and was looking on the metal shelves for a can of Scratch-B-Gone, or something along those lines, the garage door opened. It was Big Ed.

Both of us shared a look of surprise, keeping our traps shut and averting eye contact.

I decided to break the silence to ask him what I could use to get rid of those pesky scratches. He explained that I had to wash and dry the patient, and the salve to help heal those wounds was Turtle Wax. I could swear that he showed genuine pleasure that I had sought his advice.

"Thanks, *Pop*." I mucked up the moment in referencing how he addressed his own Dad – and their strained relationship.

His smile instantaneously faded, as if I had taken the gooey and odd-smelling wax to his face.

"Listen, Henry, there's something I need to tell you."

"Is it that I'm adopted?" I said.

"I have stopped seeing Doreen." He said stoically, like he was telling me he had cancer.

"So, do you want me to give you a medal or something?"

"No, but I would like you to give me a break. Granted, I am not blameless. But how about ending all this hostility? Truce?"

He said this, extending his hand like we were making a high finance deal. The only thing at stake for him was in me not blowing his cover and telling my mother what I knew.

While it sounded good on paper, I went in for a hug to rattle him instead. To my surprise, he didn't recoil in disgust. He returned the gesture, followed by three claps on my back and even issued an "atta boy."

I remained in place as he left, convinced that I had entered a dimension of sound, a dimension of sight, a dimension of mind, as I had assuredly crossed over into *The Twilight Zone*. I followed my father's advice, and L'il Red looked better. Could my relationship with Big Ed undergo a similar overhaul?

I remained suspicious during dinner, but Big Ed's good mood and interactions with us felt authentic.

And when my parents "went to bed early," I retreated to my room, put my headphones on, slapping *True Blue* into my Walkman listening to "Papa Don't Preach," in part because I didn't have a mixtape with Harry Chaplin singing "Cat's in the Cradle."

I must have drifted off, because the next thing I knew the sun was up and my alarm was going off. Except it wasn't my alarm, it was the telephone.

"Hello?" I groggily answered.

"Henry. It's me, Pete."

And when it rang a second time and it was Tony and then a third with a party line featuring King George, Nick, and Danny, I yanked myself out of REM mode. As I did, untangling myself from the fine threads of sleep's lingering fabric, I heard a different type of bell ringing. Specifically, the one that alerted the Dodge household we had a visitor at the front door.

Glancing at the clock, noting that it was fifteen minutes shy of being nine. I made my way downstairs, deciding just a pair of undies would effectively remove us from the Jehovah's Witness weekly rounds.

Feeling disappointed I didn't have a pee boner to further put the fear of, well, I guess Jehovah into them. But like most things in life, it turned out to be for the greater good, as I faux-angrily opened the door, there was John, in uniform, a duffle bag at his feet.

"You shouldn't have gotten all dressed up for me. I'm touched," he said, hefting up his bag.

"You're back early – what gives?"

"That's the kind of greeting I expected from the Old Man, but you? Nah."

"Sorry, the doorbell woke me up."

"I'd ask for a hug, but I seem overdressed for that. Or you're a little underdressed. Damn, you're skinny. Is Mom feeding you?"

I was becoming more self-conscious about his comments about my weight than my attire. Out of all my family, he had once felt the need, the need for speed so he might figure out my habit.

"As long as there's Velveeta in the fridge, the Dodges shall eat like kings!" I said, making him laugh.

"And even a queen like you! And even though there appears to be less of you, it's good to see you, bro."

"You too, ya dick. And just so you know, I'm actually on the gay fat spectrum."

"Oh, you've been on the spectrum for years."

"Just a byproduct of Mom inhaling secondhand beer fumes from Big Ed during her pregnancy with me, right?" I let my mouth hang open, and my eyes glaze over to illustrate my conclusion.

"Probably what made you gay..." He grimaced, worried about crossing a line.

"Then I need to write a thank-you note to Budweiser."

"At the very least, you should go upstairs and put something on. I mean, unless it still smells like a monkey cage, and you need to let it air out."

Heading upstairs, I added, "Mom turned your room into a shrine to your old tube socks. She found a bunch under your bed when you left, and they are stuck to the wall all by themselves. Isn't that somethin'? All of them grandkids Mom and Dad could have had, they named the socks Johnny Junior, I think."

"And what about those wadded-up tissues in your trash cans?"

"Jim Henson's Kleenex Babies, naturally."

Thinking I had taken it too far with him, as he dropped his bag, bent down, placed his hands on his knees, and raised his head up, exposing a beet-red face. His lack of breathing making me fearful I had committed fratricide, or even brotricide at the very least!

I started to panic a little bit and was about to head back down to the living room when he issued a huge laugh. And the fear he was at death's door was for naught, as John laughed maniacally, unleashing more life than this house had seen in a long time.

"It's nice to have you home, John," I said.

He nodded his head in quick succession. Once upstairs, I spied my "Hey, you tried" awards for school sports. They were starting to lose the shine on their ribbons, as faded as the hopes of me being some sort of jock. And that reminded me that I had a non-date with Jason to pump some iron in about an hour and a half.

But first, I exercised my brain in formulating an impromptu welcome home gift for John. Moving with the precision of a cat sneaking up on a bird, hanging a tube sock on his wall, using a few pieces of scotch tape as an innocuous sticking method. For added effect, I grabbed a handful of tissues, placing them like a pocket square, housing them in an imaginary double-breasted suit jacket.

I showered rather than throw on yesterday's shirt and the pair of sweatpants I planned to wear to the gym. Plus, it would be another "say something hat day," lest all the physical exertion messed up my usual every-hair-in-place way I liked to present myself to the world.

Too bad it was an extension of me trying to give off the impression that I had my life as together as the gel, which held my hair in its unwavering grip of making it unmovable. The thought of doing just the tiniest bump before heading out to get physical crossed my mind, but I was able to shoo it away like an annoying fly. Not the brightest idea to raise my pulse and heartbeat prior to a workout.

I mean that factor was already a risk, given who my workout partner was. I also didn't want to embarrass myself, well, no more than usual when it came to anything that fell under the umbrella of being coordinated.

Besides, I doubted they had an area to practice my extremely specific form of pole vaulting, even if I meant I could go for the gold in '88. Local boy does good!

While I was debating strapping my private parts down with gauze so that something didn't suddenly come up, my brother's loud utterance of "Godammit," followed by more laughter, derailed that train of thought. I chuckled to myself as I layered on the fog like spray of Right Guard, and wrapped myself in a towel, opened the door, and tried and failed to ask what the matter was without laughing.

Nope. I should never play poker.

"You suck!" He said.

Rather than say something sassy, I harkened back to the days when our mother would make us watch the tortuous hour-long variety program that was *The Shields and Yarnell Show*, silently shrugging my shoulders and mouthing "Who? Me?"

Before I could wow him with my getting out-of-a-box routine, he chucked the sock at me, missing me by a country mile; tissues falling out of it like the paratrooper army men we would throw up in the air in moments of childhood brotherly connection. I responded to it by cocking an eyebrow in tandem with shaking my head.

"You throw like a girl." I teased.

"Oh, like you would have caught it!"

We fell into the familiar rhythm of being brothers. The marked difference was that we were now kidding around as adults, with no malice.

"You're really different, Henry," he said softly.

"Explains my status as a social pariah."

"Not in my eyes. I felt bad about not being here for you after, you know."

"You were there when it counted most."

"Yeah, but then you had to deal with the Old Man by yourself. Glad you aren't that scared kid anymore."

"Geez, you make it sound like I'm dying."

"Now go put some clothes on, dork."

Once in my sanctuary, I paused for a moment to relish the fact that my older brother really cared about me. Then, that moment of reverence was broken by my indecision in what would qualify as a perfect gym ensemble.

I finally landed on a ratty black Bad Boys Club t-shirt and mustard-colored sweatpants, which gave the illusion they were a carryover from high school athleticism. Today could be the day to put a positive spin on them and use them for their intended purpose rather than to keep my legs warm at home during winter months. The hat was the sticky wicket because I really didn't have one that would be event-appropriate for the gym. There were a few resting on the shelf in my closet, all purchased at Chess King after I saw *Pretty in Pink* and admired Duckie's ability to accessorize.

I'd have to rely on John's stash of trucker hats, so I went into his room. He was on the phone with Jeannie, and not wanting to interrupt the one-sided conversation of "can't wait to see you, too" and "love you too, babe," I grabbed the first one. Only after I left the room did I realize my choice read: "FBI" in large letters and "Federal Bikini Inspector" in smaller script. Ugh.

I had every intention of switching it out, but he had closed the door. I loaded my backpack with a towel and bathing suit for the gulp, after-work out soak. But I neglected to pack a very important item, as I was to discover at an inopportune time.

I had met Jason in front of the club, no tripping over my tongue or shoelaces as we stepped into alien territory for me. And the sights were out of this world, like a paradise found, as Jason signed himself and me as his guest at the front desk. My neck would definitely be getting a good workout since I couldn't help but check out the multitude of hot guys, most wearing tank tops and truly short shorts, exerting themselves on Naugahyde-covered machines and at the free weight station. I wondered if we had mistakenly wandered into Sizzler, 'cause this was some Grade A beef on display. I suddenly felt like beef jerky, scrawny, and a shadow of these guys who could have been featured in any fitness magazine.

Apparently, there was also fish on the menu with some Jane Fonda wannabes in their leotards, leg warmers, and headbands, but I didn't want to get "Physical" with them. Once was enough, thank you.

After we entered the locker room, which was disappointingly empty, I set my backpack down next to Jason on the wooden bench. The one thing I had forgotten was a lock. I realized this as I dug through my backpack for the third time in a vain attempt to somehow make it magically appear.

And when the fourth time still didn't produce the disappearing lock, I faced Jason and sighed, explaining my dilemma. The simple solution, which felt far more difficult than it should have been, was that I would share his locker. I told him I would meet him out on the gym floor, given he was changing into his gym clothes.

Trying as hard as I could, almost making it out the door without sneaking a peek. While it was fleeting, everything seemed to slow down as he peeled his polo shirt off like a second skin. The dysfunctional jukebox in my head playing The Cars' "Moving in Stereo," just as it had when Phoebe Cates emerged from the swimming pool in the pen ultimate breast-baring scene for straight guys in *Fast Times at Ridgemont High*.

Rather than wait to hear Jason tell me how cute he always thought I was, I hightailed it out of the locker room, barely missing a collision with the door frame, in what seemed an eternity, during which I could feel what felt like hundreds of pairs of eyes sizing me up judgmentally; Jason emerged from the locker room. Of course, he had opted to wear a pair of flesh-colored onion-skin gym shorts, giving the illusion he had forgotten to put on any bottoms below a skintight blue tank top.

My temperature was beginning to rise. This was going to be a trial by fire.

"What are we starting with?" I said, and the voice in my head sounded like Sissy Spacek in *Carrie* telling William Katt that they were more his crowd than hers at the prom.

"Stretching. You always want to loosen up first."

I followed him, reminding myself with each step to not salivate like one of Pavlov's dogs at the sight of his buns of steel barely cloaked underneath his shorts. He found a secluded part of the gym with a few mats spread out in a uniform manner, patting the one behind the one he'd chosen.

"Just do what I do."

It was doubtful I could match the confidence he exuded, even in the way he sat straight up. I wondered if he had been awarded a Perfect Posture award, which was actually a thing in grade school. I was a slouch in a lot of departments, having never been awarded one. He outstretched one muscular arm over his head like he was creating the Y in doing the "Y.M.C.A." Must. Not. Think. Of. *Can't Stop the Music*! The other arm went just above the waistband of his shorts, making his bicep bulge into a hardened soft ball.

Each time he switched sides, his shorts got shorter, riding up his meaty, hairy thighs. And just as he was close to indecent exposure, he folded his legs into a lotus position, causing a bloom of lust coursing through my veins. Jason took several deep breaths, each inhale inflating his flawless chest. I followed my own personal Dalai Lama as if he were leading me on a spiritual awakening. But the prospect of morning wood was beginning to take root.

"Feel good?" he asked.

"Yeah." I managed to croak, hoping he didn't see the beginnings of my chub.

"Don't worry, Henry. I won't be too hard on you. We can ease you into it."

Dammit! Was he doing this on purpose?

"Cool." I figured short and sweet was the order of the day.

"Any part of your body that you want to make bigger?"

Motherfucker! The sing-song chorus of "I must, I must, I must increase my bust" I had read in *Are You There God? It's Me, Margaret* ran through my mind.

"My chest. Or lack thereof," I answered.

"Chest day it is!" he exclaimed, surprising me with an impression of Hans and Franz from *Saturday Night Live*. "We want to pump you up!"

He put me through my paces on a series of machines obviously invented during the medieval period. He also showed me exercises to develop my biceps, even though my right one had a head start from my version of alone time.

I worked up a good sweat, wiping my forehead, then readjusting my borrowed hat.

"I thought you were gay?" Jason said.

"Huh?" I asked.

"Your hat." He replied, stating the obvious that was oblivious to me.

"Oh yeah, that," I answered. "The store was out of F.O.B.I.S. ones."

"F.O.B.I.S.?" He raised one eyebrow to emphasize his trying to understand the acronym.

"Fond of Bulges in Speedos."

"Where do you come up with this shit?"

"The dark recesses of my mind. Would you expect any less from me?"

"No, Mr. Bond, I expect you to die!"

"Too bad there isn't a gay James Bond."

"And I'm afraid to ask, but why is that?"

"My name is Dick Galore," I said, channeling my best Honor Blackman. "I expected more from you, Jason."

"Remind me not to play Trivial Pursuit with you. Damn, check out that honey!"

I followed his gaze to see what he deemed as sweet. The blonde with the huge side ponytail was cute and wasn't in any way, shape, or form what would be termed as being a dog. But it solidified that it was I who had been barking up the wrong tree where Jason's sexuality was concerned.

My good mood was spiraling downwards, crashing and burning, producing catastrophic flames designed to snuff out what could be a new friendship. All because of another one of my stupid crushes.

"Dammit!" Jason exclaimed bitterly, going through his gym bag. "I forgot my bathing suit!"

I doubted he would be descending into the water in the all-together, nixing the soaking of muscles that would undoubtedly be sore for me in the coming days. Oh well, there was my usual private soak in the spa at home.

But he came up with a solution.

"I guess I can just wear my gym shorts. Problem solved." He said with satisfaction. "See you in there."

Sure, his problem became a no problemo scenario for him. However, the thought of those flesh-colored short shorts coming out of the water, see-through and clinging tightly to him. Was it some sort of gauge to see if he could trust me to keep my hands to myself? A litmus test designed to determine if we could truly be friends, given he was as straight as an arrow.

My hands shook just a bit as I slipped out of my shirt, sweatpants, underwear, and into my blue and red board shorts. I almost left my hat on by mistake.

Arriving at the Jacuzzi, I saw his eyes were closed, head tilted back, Adam's apple protruding forward, chest half-exposed, and muscular arms resting on the concrete lip of the hot tub.

I was trying to conjure up something horrid to counterbalance the sight of a living, breathing Greek God. I entered the warm, roiling liquid. Sinking into the water as quietly as possible, I imagined Jason in *Clash of the Titans* as a fellow warrior to Harry Hamlin as Perseus.

I truly hated my brain at times, what with its innate ability to work against me, always letting me know who was truly in charge. Just as I found a seat, Jason's eyes opened, drowning the likelihood of it being a silence is golden type of soak.

"About time," he teased.

"You looked so peaceful; I didn't want to disturb your beauty rest. God knows you need it."

His response was a middle finger that emerged from the bubbly water like a periscope.

"So, does your girlfriend know that you soak in Jacuzzis with notorious homosexuals?"

Not smooth, not exactly crunchy, but if choosy mothers can choose Jif, then damn skippy, this line of questioning would have to suffice.

"Well, since she knows you, I'm sure it wouldn't be a problem for her."

"Oh, she knows me? You're not gonna just tell me?"

"Now, what fun is that?" He challenged.

"Well, Mrs. Garrett immediately jumps to mind. Witchiepoo is also a strong contender, as is Benita Bizarre. But your guys' apartment is always clean, so I'll go with Alice from *The Brady Bunch*. Am I close?"

"A big swing and a miss, friend," he said sullenly. "That's a sports reference, by the way."

"That's the one with the basket and puck, right?"

"Alright, I'll take pity on you and give you a clue. You work with her."

"Yvonne?"

"Yup. Darren introduced us, and she's a cool chick. It's still new; we're not even in boyfriend and girlfriend territory yet. Like I said, my life is pretty regimented. But this dull boy could use some fun. "

"Oh. That's. Awesome." I was worried that Yvonne had gossiped about me. She couldn't have told him about our dalliance, right?

"You ready to hit it?" he said, rising from the water, those gym shorts leaving zero to the imagination. "I'm starting to prune."

"Not from where I'm sitting," I said in what I thought was a mumble.

"Aww, flattery will get you nowhere, Henry."

"Can't blame a girl for trying."

We made small talk at the locker, drying off, retrieving clothes, and the like, all with palpable ease. I was feeling like a new man as we made our exit. But then I saw a familiar white Honda Civic pulling into the parking lot.

"You ok there, buddy?" Jason asked. "Ya look like you saw a ghost or something."

"See that guy getting out of the Honda? He's not a good person, and he has a thing for me."

"Oh yeah?" He said, taking my hand in his. "Would skipping be too much?"

"Just a tad," I replied, awestruck that he was willing to flip the script on his masculinity to protect me.

Jeff approached, eyes widening with every step until he was almost face-to-face with me.

"Jeff." I offered, deciding the fewer words spoken, the better, unaware if he might have an inkling I was behind his recent time behind bars.

"Henry." He replied coldly and turned his icy stare towards Jason. "And you are?"

"Jason. Henry's main squeeze. Nice to meet ya." He lit up a magnanimous smile akin to staring into the center of the sun.

"Charmed, I'm sure. Well, I'll see you around." And started his way past us.

"Hey, Jeff," Jason said with a quiet forcefulness. "I would recommend keeping your distance from this one."

"Oh really?" Jeff glowered. "What are you, his keeper?"

"No. But you can just consider me his bodyguard, and it's a job I take very seriously." Jason said, punctuating his statement with a slight muscle flex and a small peck on my cheek. I immediately put my hand on the spot where his soft lips had just been, mimicking Marcia Brady's proclamation that she would "never wash this cheek again" after Desi Arnaz Jr. planted one on it.

Jeff stormed off, getting a head start on his cardio.

"Ferris Bueller, you're my hero," I said to Jason.

"Tweren't nothin," he said. "Just let me know if that creep bugs you again!"

"I appreciate it. That boy ain't right."

"What's his deal anyway?" Jason pressed a bit further.

"He's the local drug dealer I used to score from. He's made it abundantly clear I would be his Michelle Pfeiffer in *Scarface*. Alas, I did not want to say hello to his little friend, so he started following me around."

"Well, that should keep him in his place. Speaking of drugs, don't think that I'm clueless; I know why you hang out with Darren."

"Yeah, yeah, yeah. My nostrils, my choice. But it's nothing I can't handle, and I can stop at any time."

I sounded like a cliché from an *ABC Afterschool Special*, but I believed some part of it to be true.

"You're a smart guy, and I don't want to see you make stupid choices."

"But then, what would I do with my time?" I joked, but his frown made me shift gears. "If it becomes a problem, I promise you will be the first person I talk to? OK? Are you done being hard on The Beaver, Ward?"

"For now." He said. "But that reminds me, I need to get going. I have a date with Yvonne."

"Nice segue way. You kids have fun. Guess I don't have to say not to do anything I wouldn't do."

And when he didn't throw out a flippant comment about that not necessarily being the case, I knew Yvonne had kept our one-night stand hush hush.

I decided to let Nina know that Jeff was back among the populace again, so I headed to her place.

"Shut the front door!" She said moments after she had ushered me through hers. "Well, that wasn't a long stint."

"But I have more news for you," I said slyly. "You got that hand on the doorknob?"

Nodding, she gulped, steeling herself for worse news.

"A certain somebody who dabbles in drawings is having his work looked over by a gallery owner!"

"Oh my God!" She squealed. "I can't believe that Michael didn't tell me himself. I'm so proud of him!"

"No dummy. I was referring to yours truly."

"Uh, duh. Who is the dummy now?" she said teasingly.

"Touché," I said sarcastically, waiting a beat. "Bitch!"

"Would you have it any other way?"

"Not for a million bucks."

We hugged, and she pressed me for details.

"Who knew our little sojourn at the nut house would lead to something good?" Nina said. "I mean, aside from the pleasure of my company."

"Hey, don't compare me to the sailors down at the docks," I teased. "Speaking of…"

"Semen?" She jumped in. "You're preggers?"

"Dammit girl, stop with the body fluids!"

"I'll come around."

"Seriously?"

"Just spill it."

"My brother is back in town," I said through laughter. "I suppose he'll want to meet the miscreants that I run with."

"Wow! A straight Dodge offspring? That should be interesting."

"He has a girlfriend, so no playing it fast and loose with him."

When I got home, Jeannie's black Toyota Celica was parked in front of the house that Big Ed had paid for and almost demolished with his duplicitous nature. Since we called a truce, I had decided not to make mention of Big Ed and the whore to John.

Meanwhile, he was taking full advantage of the fact that our parents were out of the house. Since he knew that I was apt to show up, ever the annoying little brother with horrible timing, he had hung the formerly balled-up tube sock on his doorknob. I heeded his makeshift version of a do not disturb sign and headed back downstairs, succumbing to Shadow's desire to play soccer.

Just as I was contemplating how else I was going to occupy my time, John came out into the backyard.

"So, does your job have any fringe benefits?"

"But of course. Otherwise, what's the point?"

"We should go see a movie then."

As we sat in the dark, myself on his left and Jeannie on his right, watching the return of Nancy Thompson taking on Freddy Krueger in the third *Nightmare on Elm Street* installment, I began to feel like that numeric equivalent of a wheel. Jeannie would push her face into John's shoulder whenever she got scared, and John would put his arm around her shoulder and pull her closer to protect her from a cinematic boogeyman.

Where was my protector when things got scary? Admittedly, I was desensitized to horror movies. But still, it would be nice. Another sore point to watching The Dream Warriors was the mental hospital setting; I felt a sharp stab of shame that cut deeper than Freddy's finger knives on his glove.

I forced the negative thoughts from my mind, but as the credits began to roll, they returned with a vengeance. As John and I walked home, since Jeannie had to work at Crown Books and had been our ride, it turned out to be a trek along the path not usually taken in the direction of honesty. After I told John about what had transpired and braced myself for some sort of backlash for being weak, he chuckled.

"You know it's funny," he said. Although I thought my suicide attempt was devoid of humor, I let him continue. "On the ship, they showed *Rebel Without a Cause*, and there's the part where he yells, 'You're tearing me apart!' And I totally thought of you. I felt bad that I wasn't here to help keep you together."

I nodded.

"But don't feel guilty. I learned how to take care of myself. I've even taken on the old man a time or two in your absence."

"He must have loved that!"

"Yeah, not so much. But we have reached some sort of understanding lately, so it's all good. So am I. Honestly, I even, gasp, have friends. And I want you to meet them."

"Sounds good." He said. "You know, if I can fit it into my busy social calendar and all."

That night, Mom and Dad told us about a weekend motorcycle trip to their favorite destination of Idyllwild. I figured that was the perfect, and quite fortuitous, time for a small gathering of friends to celebrate John's return.

When Saturday evening arrived, so did the crowds. Nina thought it was an open invite and told some of the people from her own house party. She even brought Jeremy and Joshua the Doublemint Twins. There was a sullen blond guy who was squiring Nina to the soiree and two girls that Nina had been chummy with in high school, Traci and Maria.

The AMC crowd that wasn't working the night shift was in attendance, specifically Darren, who arrived ala carte, and Yvonne showed up with Jason. In a weird way, I felt a pang, low and strong, of jealousy.

I declared the occasion as B.Y.O.B. so people wouldn't raid Big Ed's bar or drain the keg in the garage. I had the requisite orange-flavored California Cooler in hand.

I got the skinny on Nina's mystery man, who she had met at Lou's Records and was named Gary. What she had failed to mention was that he had taken a tab of acid prior to the party. But as the evening wore on, it became evident that he was on a different wavelength. Hell, he was on another planet in a galaxy far, far away. He asked if he could watch TV in the den, and I gladly obliged. But as it turned out, Darren had followed me in my endeavor to have the TV watch Gary as his electronic babysitter.

"Hey, wanna bump this party up a notch?" Darren asked. When he ran his index finger under his nostrils, I got the gist.

We snuck out to the garage, as I figured the two of us coming out of the bathroom was the way rumors got started, and I had a reputation to uphold. Once we were behind the metal shelves, I pulled out a Dutch Masters cigar box, where Big Ed now stored spark plugs and the like.

Darren drew up four generous lines, then rolled up a twenty-dollar bill, and we imitated Hoover vacuums. My alcohol haze was replaced with a heightened alertness and a desire to turn the living room into a makeshift dance floor.

I pulled Nina by the hand, and we led the charge in getting others to follow suit in the pursuit of getting our collective groove on. I pretended the living room was Studio 54 as I danced to "Le Freak."

The giant moon with the coke spoon descended, and instead of dancing with Nina, I was bumping with Liza Minnelli, wearing a Halston creation. Just as she began to compliment my rhythmic prowess, I was returned to the present day, and Nina was staring suspiciously at me.

"Ok Travolta, let's take a breather. You are sweating more than a, well, me in church."

"Yes, I could stand to replenish my fluids," I said, trying to casually wipe an ocean of sweat from my forehead.

Once in the kitchen, I used several paper towels to wipe away the coke sweat, and then filled a glass once, twice, three times a lady from the refrigerator water dispenser, being serenaded by The Commodores from the living room as I did so.

"Damn, dude!" Nina said with a slight slur. "You part camel?"

"Nah, but I sure love to hump!"

John and Jeannie entered the kitchen, and I made my demeanor take on a nonchalant air. Derek and Michael entered from the dining room to join the conversations. I was stoked; this is how I had imagined the night going.

"What was Henry like as a kid?" Michael asked.

"A complete and utter spaz," John answered.

"I can see that." Derek offered.

"Basically, nothing has changed then?" Nina joked.

"Yeah, not really." John chuckled.

I fought the desire to make a drunk proclamation of "I love you, man." But it wouldn't have been a lie; far from it. I did love my brother, although the insecure part of me still believed that he would receive the statement as being "too gay."

"Sorry to break up this little chat," Nina announced, "but I better check on my date." She retreated to the den while the rest of us returned to the living room.

Darren was having a very animated conversation with Traci on the couch while Maria was napping in Big Ed's chair. Yvonne and Jason were slow dancing to Janet Jackson's "Let's Wait Awhile" as if in junior high, complete with keeping a space between their bodies. The distance made me wonder if they had adhered to the lyrics in their dating life. If she were, I should offer to take her to see David because that fell into the clinical term of being "bat shit crazy."

Jeremy and Joshua were sharing a Jolt Cola, their third one, based on the empty bottles on the coffee table, making it a variation of the soda company's slogan being rebranded as "all the sugar and six times the caffeine."

Surveying our living room, peopled with individuals having a good time, I saw it could also double as Noah's Ark. Everyone, well except for Maria, was paired up. As always, I was the odd man out. I decided against insinuating myself into anyone's conversation and went to check on Nina. She was sitting with Gary, who resembled an extra in *Night of the Living Dead*. His eyes were glassy, his jaw slack, mouth open, and a fine strand of drool dangled from his bottom lip, demonstrating his total commitment to the role.

"Jesus! Is he alive?" I said, concerned about how I was going to explain to my parents why the coroner had been at our house.

"Well, he has a pulse."

"Ah, just the way you like 'em."

"You're such a caution. You should throw yourself to the wind." Her voice took on a more serious tone. "Seriously, what in the actual fuck am I going to do with him? He met me at my house. Obviously, he can't drive. This sucks!"

"I didn't realize I was throwing a pity party. What about Traci and Maria? Can't they take him home?"

"I'll go corral Traci. Keep an eye on Timothy Leary."

"Absotootley," I said happily. Then, as it had done so many times before in my life, the pull of the TV screen caught my eye and what viewing choice Gary had landed on.

An episode of *Lancelot Link, Secret Chimp*, was in progress. Lancelot and his partner Mata Hari were involved in some sort of spy shenanigan. Gary was transfixed. I snapped my fingers in front of Gary's eyes. To my surprise, this simple gesture proved effective. He blinked, turning his head, looking at me with unfocused eyes, and wiped the drool from his mouth.

"You alright there, Gar?"

"Uh-huh." He responded slowly.

Looking into the living room, Nina had been drawn into whatever subject Darren was going on about and was now sitting next to him. I had time to do what I felt needed to be done as a jury of one in Gary's trial by fire.

"Just to be sure, let's check your reflexes."

"K." He murmured.

"Can you cross your legs for me?"

It took him two tries to complete my request.

"Very good!" I said, giving my best example of having an impeccable bedside manner. "Now, take your right hand and grab your left ankle."

This task took him four times to get right, and I wished I had a Twister mat to really mess with him. Right hand red, ya burnout!

"There you go. Now, see if you can twist it all the way around."

He looked at me puzzled but started to give it a go.

"I believe in you," I said enthusiastically, but he could only get it a quarter of the way from his goal. "Hey, you tried. Let's try something else. Tell me what you see on the TV."

He furrowed his brow, trying to discern if what was being televised was real or a byproduct of his acid trip.

"Uh. There's two monkeys talking?" he said cautiously, looking at me quizzically.

"You mean like the monkeys that are in the backyard? The ones that are looking at you through the sliding door, wanting to come in. You see them, right?"

He stared at the glass while I excused myself, claiming that my back teeth were floating. Going out to the garage, unlocking the side door, making my way to the gate, and reaching over it to unlatch it.

Stepping into the dark backyard, Shadow, who had been banished to her doghouse until the party ended, came running up to me. She stayed at my side as I snuck up to the glass and gave it a short series of raps with my knuckles, doing my best impression of an angry chimpanzee.

By the widening of Gary's eyes, I knew it was doing the trick. Bending down and putting my right arm around Shadow's torso, lifting her up a bit, taking her left paw and putting it on the door, her needed-to-be-trimmed nails making a perfect scratching sound. Gary was pushing himself back into the throw pillow on the couch, a look of panic and terror merging into one telltale sign that I had him on the hook.

Raising Shadow up and making her stand on her hind legs, I opened the door a crack while pushing her left paw through and began making George more furious than curious. Gary looked like he wanted to run, but instead grabbed his legs and began hugging them. He slowly rocked back and forth, protecting himself with the simple mantra of, "Not the monkeys! Not the monkeys!"

Shadow wanted to go inside, so there was no further need to control her paw, and I took the opportunity to raise her gums up and expose her teeth. This set Gary over the edge as he grabbed the throw pillow and tried to use it as a makeshift shield. After I closed the door, I patted Shadow on the head, told her she was a good girl, and retraced my steps back into the house.

I sat down by Gary, consoling him until Nina and Traci approached.

Nina had an exasperated look on her face, and I simply shrugged. When Gary took the throw pillow away from his face and his unmuffled whimper of "not the monkeys!" was audible, she approached him cautiously.

"What are you talking about, loser?" She hissed.

He merely pointed towards the door, but Nina caught a glimpse of the TV.

"I guess it's a good thing that he wasn't watching *King Kong*," I said.

"Or *Planet of the Apes*." Traci sighed. "I told him dropping acid was a bad idea. Sorry Nina."

"Thanks for taking out the trash for me. I mean, for making sure he gets home. I am half-tempted to have you drop him off at the viewpoint."

"Oh, don't do that to my people," I fake-pleaded.

"Fine. I'm not a total bitch; just a girl with shitty taste in men."

"Join the club, sister."

Gary was walked-dragged out, propping himself against Traci's more petite frame. Shadow began scratching at the door, which was all the motivation he needed to disengage from Traci, hightailing it to the front door.

Darren was making his exit to chaperone Traci. Yvonne and Jason also left, offering their thanks for having us. This left my usual crew, plus the twins, who had an idea that made them the embodiment of the phrase double trouble. All jacked up on caffeine, they began stair-diving, using the couch cushion to soften their landings. The look on Michael and Derek's faces told me they had grown tired of the shenanigans. They said their goodbyes. The twins finally gave up and exited.

When all was said and done, and all evidence was bagged up in trash bags, clearing the living room of having been the scene of the crime, and with John squiring Jeannie home, I plopped down on the stairs.

Then I let out a sigh, ghostly echoes of the revelers still filling the living room. But I was sitting here all by my lonesome, and rather than burst into the song "All By Myself," I made my way to my fortress of solitude.

Fine, I was humming the Eric Carmen hit from over a decade ago. And even though I had been surrounded by people that had wanted to hang out with me. Now I decided to throw an impromptu pity party.

And what was a get-together without party favors? I drew up two smallish lines, fully prepared to suck them up into my nostrils, like gravity in the dead vacuum of space, where no one could hear you scream. But then the house began to shake with the rolling motion of an earthquake. At first, I thought it was a hallucination, some phantom karmic retribution for messing with Gary.

But the blinds were swaying back and forth – an indicator that I was of sound mind. As it abated, I wondered if it was a heavenly intervention to prevent me from letting my inner demons come out and play with gleeful abandon. And in that moment of having my world physically shaken up came a mental plate tectonic shifting, its fault line running deep beneath the memories shallowly buried, cutting a path between my head and heart.

As the fissures broke open, so did the truth. If I kept on this course of using the real numbing agent of doing cocaine on a frequent basis, it could irrevocably change the trajectory of my life once the dust had settled, and I was free to wander away from the destruction of the past.

The typical Henry Dodge modus operandi of shirking deep thoughts for my chosen armor, pop culture, came into play.

"There's always tomorrow for dreams to come true," I said, quoting Clarice from *Rudolph the Red-Nosed Reindeer*. "Yeah, if you don't fuck it up first."

This skillset was most definitely in my wheelhouse, so I gave in to my addictive nature.

"Whatcha doin'?" a voice asked from the doorway. It was John.

Fortunately, I was sitting on my beanbag chair with my back to the door. John's view was obscured by the bed. For all he knew, I was tying my shoes or taking a closer inspection at a spider bite. Still, my already elevated heart rate jumped through the roof just as my heart found a resting place in my throat.

"Nothin,'" I answered with a believable air of nonchalance. "What are you up to, bro?"

"Did you feel that earthquake?"

"Why yes. I felt the earth move under my feet. However, I also saw the sky tumbling down."

"Well, Carole King doesn't have anything to worry about, that's for sure. But perhaps there's a one-man show of *Chicken Little* in your future."

"Don't hold back, Doc." I faux pleaded. "Give it to me straight."

"There's an oxymoron; you and straight in the same sentence." He smirked.

"True. I can't even think straight."

"Alright, enough with this foolishness. We have a mission to accomplish."

He meant dumping the trash bags filled with the party evidence: bottles and cans, once vessels for both alcoholic and mega caffeinated beverages.

"So, what's the plan, Stan? Drive out to the desert and bury them; maybe figure out where Jimmy Hoffa took his final nap and pin it on him?"

"I had something easier in mind."

"Do tell, brother. I'm on the edge of my beanbag chair!" I said with all the hammy aspects of being the lead in a school play.

"Calm down, spaz. You're awfully, uh, animated for this time of night."

Oh shit - was he onto my drug-induced burst of energy? I lied that I had sucked down a Jolt Cola.

"Enough jibber jabbing, Agent double zero," John said. "Operation Hefty is officially on. Let's motor…spaz."

"You couldn't resist, could ya?" I admonished him playfully. "Perhaps we'll switch this to a military operation because you are being a major dick."

"Whatever floats your aircraft carrier, dork."

We both laughed, then loaded up two trash bags, clinking musically from the bottles hitting one another, into the trunk of The Green Bomb. We agreed that the Dumpster behind AMC seemed a fitting burial site. Our mission possible was done in a matter of seconds, not exactly covert, with the dumpster empty and the shattering of glass in a plastic sarcophagus echoing down the alleyway.

When we spied a pair of headlights illuminating the far end of the alleyway, we ran to the car with John bringing it to life, even though it felt like we had been caught in the act of getting rid of a dismembered body. Instinctively ducking down in the passenger seat, fixing my eyes on the rearview mirror, I saw two sets of car headlights.

Jeff!

A familiar white vehicle seemed to glow with a spectral quality, coming to a full stop and extinguished its lights. The headlights of the second car were still on, and as we rounded the corner, making it difficult to discern who was foolishly following Jeff.

I didn't know if I should open the door and re-enact some half-assed version of a stunt Colt Seavers would perform on *The Fall Guy*. Rather, I embraced the reality of the moment, one in which I was curious as to why Jeff had a rendezvous in an alleyway. What was it about me and alleyways anyway?

"Hey, can we stop?" I asked John, pretending I owned the world's tiniest bladder. "I've got a wiener-pinching situation happening."

"Is this some kind of gay thing?"

"Nope, it is an I have to pee like a racehorse situation. And don't pull a Mom and tell me that I should have gone before we left the house."

"Well…" he said with a feigned air of me being chastised like I was a four-year-old.

"Save it, Kate!" I replied urgently. "Be back in two shakes of a lamb's tail."

"More than two, and you're playing with it."

"Gross-a-rama."

I headed to the corner of the building to peek around in the hopes that I wouldn't be spotted by Jeff and his mystery guest.

Standing face-to-face with Jeff was none other than my own dealer and friend, Darren. He was taking a paper bag that raised the hairs on my arms. He opened it up and peered inside. It was logical he got his endless supply of cocaine from this particular someone.

Still, it left me with an uneasy feeling that these two twains had met as a third figure emerged from Jeff's car.

It was Danny!

He approached Jeff with familiarity, casually, and without the trepidation of a shocked stranger who had witnessed a drug deal. He lit a cigarette, the flickering from the match highlighting his face. But as the cherry on his cigarette burned red, my hatred became an inferno, feeling as though no amount of water could ever put it out.

"What in the actual fuck?" I muttered.

But this was no dream. Danny didn't evaporate like the cigarette smoke he blew into the night. He was here in the flesh, and it was making my skin crawl. As he put his hand on Jeff's, the first thought was that it saved two other people from unhappiness. But when Jeff swatted it away and raised his voice, it became a case of misery loving company.

Danny gripped Jeff's right hand tightly, and what I assumed was a lover's spat became something more twisted. I clearly heard Jeff say Corey's name, to which Danny spat back my name ferociously from his once-kissable lips. Their heated exchange escalated, and then Danny pushed Jeff to the ground with orders to "stay away from him."

That had to be meant for me, since Corey was no longer in the picture.

I felt a hand on my shoulder.

"Jesus! You scared the piss out of me!" I told John in a whisper tone, not wanting to give up my vantage point among the shadows.

"Glad something did! You've been over here for a long time, little brother."

I didn't want John to see the trio, but he was already peeking around the corner, and I followed suit, ever the follower of his lead. Just then, we saw the Honda tear off. The sound of screeching tires reverberated down the alleyway; the smell of burned rubber filled my nostrils as the cocaine Darren sold me had. But all this was leaving a bad taste in my mouth. Darren exited the scene in less of a hurry than Jeff had, leaving only Danny, who was fortunately walking away at a fast clip with his back turned to an audience of two.

"What was that all about?" he said.

"Just some drama," I replied with strained frivolity. "You know how the gays love that!"

"Can we go home now?"

"I don't know, can we? I know we certainly may." I said snidely.

"Grammar Nazi!"

Malcolm McLaren's "Buffalo Gals" serenaded the short drive home as I tried to make sense of what I had seen and heard.

"All that scratching's making me itch" encapsulated the feeling of dread in my brain.

I needed to figure it out. That would take time. The way I thought, it would take hours. And the only way to make the night last? My dwindling baggie of nose candy. It was my duty, and I was nothing if not dedicated to getting to the bottom of this.

The emerging dawn sliced through the darkness, releasing shades of orange, yellow, and crimson in its wake. How many more sunrises until I had the answers to the questions that ran marathons in my brain all night?

I did manage to grab a quick catnap. I wouldn't say I awoke as fresh as a daisy, more like a withered stink weed. The combination of my body odor and breath could fell an elephant. I twisted the blinds open and immediately regretted that decision due to slices of sunlight stabbing my eyeballs with daggers. And I returned fire, shooting my own across the street where *he* undoubtedly dwelled at his mother's house.

As if I had manifested him into existence, Danny's VW Microbus could be partially viewed through the pepper tree in our front yard, fragmented, spectral, but no figment of my overactive imagination.

"Good riddance to bad rubbish," I said with a faux British accent, which acted as a harbinger of what the day had in store for me. As the mail arrived, I tore into an envelope with a London return address.

Jake's letter was equal parts sweet and salty, saying how he wanted to see me again, both in and out of clothes, and that he was thinking of heading back here in the future for DJ gigs.

While it was a vague date for a visit, I wrote him back straight away and included a small drawing. I hoped it spoke volumes. It was a tree trunk carved with our initials.

Hope was not something I relied on in life, always putting it into the hands of others so that when the inevitable disappointments came, I could lay the blame on them for building false hope.

I hated that I was so jaded at my age. But my record of accomplishment wasn't an accolade for The Guinness Book of World Records unless they started highlighting the uncanny knack of picking the wrong men. Then I would be a shoo-in! It all seemed like wishful thinking I'd end up happy and fulfilled as a "we" and not just a "me." The Pet Shop Boys had informed me that sometimes "Love Comes Quickly," so I decided to throw caution to the wind, adding a separate message to the letter to let Jake know it was actually an "I care" package.

The poem read:

Some romantic notion travels across the sea,
knowing no boundaries
and only sees endless horizons
for you and me.

Would that sentiment come to pass? Who knew? But it felt good to write it down. I sealed the envelope, adding what I hoped was the proper postage, dropped it in the mailbox, and put the little red flag up to alert the mailman there was outgoing mail.

And then the waiting game would begin. Tom Petty had lamented that "the waiting is the hardest part."

I watched 1987 turn into 1988 with no word that this year could be the one where I would find true love. I turned 19 with no response and spent all my spare time with the friends that were becoming more like family, cracking each other by reciting lines from *Hairspray* and *Beetlejuice*. All that time, no word from Jake. I briefly thought about saying his name three times in succession to make him materialize out of thin air. But by then, if he had shown up, I would have told him to fuck off as the year edged toward being halfway over.

Eventually, I pushed the thought of him, of what could have been, to the back of my mind. Before I knew it, I had moved from behind the counter at AMC to the position of usher, and my time with David ended with no word from his gallery owner friend.

I didn't let it detract from my artistic endeavors, as rejection and I were the best of friends. The biggest surprise turned out that I had not stuck a straw up my nose in quite some time, altering that dangerous landscape of behavior that was as comfortable as a pair of well-worn tennis shoes. Unfortunately, the same could not be said about my father and his secretive behavior.

I was having a soak-your-cares-away afternoon in the Jacuzzi, even though the interior of the greenhouse, as we called it, was nearing unhealthy heat levels, given that it was July. Good idea on the solar panels to heat the Jacuzzi water there, Big Ed!

Soaking was a tried-and-true tradition that still fit as snugly as Cinderella's glass slipper. Alas, there would be no Prince Charming to slip a slipper onto feet that resembled Fred Flintstone's. The irony that Debbie Gibson was lamenting about love being "Only in my Dreams" through my ghetto blaster's speakers was not lost on me. But I still hadn't given up on finding romance. For now, immediate gratification would suffice by calling 976-MEET in the hopes of meeting Mr. Right Now, at the very least, in the hopes it could be parlayed into a lasting connection.

So far, that had not happened, just disembodied voices asking what I was looking for. And that depended upon my mood and usually ended in a hot and heavy phone sex session. Luckily, I was blessed with a healthy imagination, conjuring up the image of what the anonymous caller wanted to do to me. But I was also cursed with a sense of reality, knowing that a true bond wasn't to be found on the sex lines. It was something that momentarily filled a void.

I turned down my tunes, then walked my wet body over to the phone we had in the spa. I waited for the pre-recorded, incorporeal voice to inform me that I was, in fact, connected to a possible dream, accompanied by the sound of a doorbell to let someone through the door of my wounded heart.

But as I picked up the receiver, fingers at the ready to punch in the well-used numbers, there was already a voice on the other line. My father was engaged in a conversation with a woman who wasn't my mother but was the parent to one Daniel Woodson.

"I want to see you, too," he said in a conspirator's tone. "But we need to be careful, Doreen."

"I know, Ed. I know. But it's so hard to be so close to you and not be able to get close to you - if that makes sense."

The conversation was straight out of the Danielle Steele novels Mom devoured and was making me sick to my stomach. It also made my blood boil, and my breathing became as laborious as an asthmatic running in a marathon. I placed my hand over the receiver, not wanting to give away that I was eavesdropping on the destruction of my parents' marriage.

This is what really cheesed my whiz. Sure, this was an established behavioral pattern that Big Ed had exhibited throughout his marriage. But I had called him out on it. And he told me that he had dropped the whore like a bad habit. And here we were, back at square one, the past and present, dancing a tango that would only bring heartache to my Mom.

The question wasn't when he and Doreen could practice their clandestine ways as they were discussing - but should I barge into the house and confront him yet again? It certainly hadn't been taken seriously before; I'd merely be carrying out a conversation with a human brick wall.

As their chat became static in the background, my overthinking brain began ticking away with scenarios to hasten their downfall. Lighting Mrs. Woodson's house on fire seemed a bit extreme and wouldn't let me keep a close eye on her if she had to move. Besides, if I got caught, there would undoubtedly be jail time, and a jumpsuit in orange was not my color!

Think, think, think, my mind commanded, just as Pooh Bear uttered when faced with a problem. Granted, an adulterer in the Hundred Acre Wood wasn't the cause of his dilemma. But my father had his hand in another woman's honey pot and was in store for a blustery day of epic proportions. But how?

I snapped myself out of childhood solutions to a very grown-up problem. Maybe the answer lay in the soap operas I loved. What would Sue Ellen Ewing, or better yet, Alexis Morell Carrington Colby Dexter Rowan do? She would have proof of the infidelity as a back-up rather than have someone take her word on it.

I ran over, grabbed my ghetto blaster, and hit record to document the rest of their heart-to-heart.

Even if I never played it for anyone, it was a better insurance policy than the one from State Farm my parents had for their vehicles.

Given that the weight of the ghetto blaster made it impossible to also put my ear up to the receiver, I would have to listen to the recording to see if it was intelligible and anything I could use against my father. Once I heard the busy signal going off, I turned down the volume and listened as intently as frightened Americans during Orson Welles' *War of the Worlds* radio broadcast.

But the fear I hadn't gotten anything of note, merely a harmless conversation about the weather, was vanquished by him agreeing to attend a barbeque that Whoreen was throwing that weekend.

Big Ed offered to come over before the guests arrived so she could show him her special meat rub technique, and her response that she could show him again sealed the deal. Then I heard Big Ed sign off with "I love you," a rare phrase he had never said to me. Yet he offered it so freely to Doreen. That was the nail in the coffin for him. I was prepared as the lone pallbearer to inform the grieving widow as to the cause of death to her wedding vows.

If the truth hurts and sets you free, Mom will suffer majorly until she realizes it would be for the best. As she would say before doling out any punishments in my younger years, it was for my own good, hers in this case.

I wouldn't miss Big Ed once he was thrown out. If I never laid eyes on him again, it would be fine by me. I had longed for the day when they would announce they were getting a divorce. It almost happened when I was in third grade when Big Ed asked who John and I would like to live with. Mom explained she would be moving back East to her mother's house. John and I said "with Mom" in unison, rather than He Who Drinks A Sixpack Every Night.

Unfortunately, the next morning came, and Big Ed had convinced her to stay, that he'd change and be a better man. I had to unpack my clothes and Disney records from my suitcase.

And here we were years later, ones that could have been different for everyone, had the broken record played a different song, one whose lyrics hadn't been warped by my father's false promises. For better or worse, indeed.

I had a few days to broach the topic before the barbeque. I was tempted to fuck with Big Ed until then, just enough to make him paranoid. It could potentially force his hand, cards on the table time, with nary an ace up his sleeve.

I turned off the Jacuzzi, the roiling bubbles fading away like the footsteps my mother had taken down the aisle in her wedding dress.

I put the cover back on the Jacuzzi gently as if I were lowering the lid of a coffin, resolute in delivering the death knell to Big Ed's duplicity. I dried myself, dressed, and welcomed the afternoon sunlight in by raising the shades, letting the light caress my face, drawing on its warmth. I gathered up the incriminating evidence housed in the ghetto blaster and exited my happy place.

Upon entering the house, I found the philanderer sitting in "his chair," a beige recliner made for a poor substitute for the throne he felt he deserved. The living room was filled with the music of The Kingston Trio singing about "A Worried Man," even though he didn't seem to have a care in the world. An ever-present Budweiser was in hand that knew the route up to his lips by memory, a mental map drafted years ago with peaks and valleys.

"I didn't know you were home."

Both of us knew my whereabouts weren't a priority for him.

"Yup. Hey, did the phone ring a little while ago?"

"Not since I've been home." He answered after swallowing a gulp of beer that was dangerously close to becoming a spit take.

"Hmm." I let the word hang in the air.

I began ascending the stairs, looking back.

"Interesting choice in music," I said, looking pointedly over my shoulder.

"Huh?"

"I would have expected you to be listening to Hank Williams's 'Your Cheating Heart.' You love that song!"

"Why do you say that?" The electricity in his eyes suddenly reflected an overloaded brain, close to short-circuiting.

"No reason. Such a classic tune is all. Good chat, *Pop*."

When I was alone in my room, a giggle escaped from me, like Muttley on *Wacky Races*. I was resolute to win the race, mindful to go slow and steady so that Big Ed couldn't worm his way out of this one.

I sat at my drafting table to exercise my creative muscles when Mom pulled into the driveway later than her usual arrival from work. She didn't exit the car, and from my vantage point, I watched her stretch her arms out, using the steering wheel to hold them rigidly in place. The force made it appear as if she might snap the wheel in half until she removed her hands from it and gingerly covered her face with them in an impromptu game of Peek-a-boo. Then I saw her wiping away tears, the other digging through her purse with its endless supply of Certs, instead producing a tissue and dabbing each eye. She went about brushing her hair, putting on some lipstick, and smoothing out her blouse. She got out of her vehicle and looked at our house with a momentary grimace before changing it into her usual smile. As I descended the stairs, she brushed past me silently, and determined to retire to her boudoir for the evening. She broke her vow of silence to inform us that she wasn't feeling well, and we were left to our own devices for dinner, prompting a puzzled expression on Big Ed's face.

He decided on a liquid diet for the evening, downing one Budweiser and cracking open one after another. I opened a can of Hormel beef tamales, drained out the oily sauce in the sink, removed them from the wrappers, covered them with Velveeta, and nuked them.

I retreated to my room with Shadow hot on my trail in the hopes I might share my food with her. Sitting on the bean bag chair, she was edging closer and closer, solely transfixed on what was passing for dinner tonight.

When I was down to the last gut bomb morsel, she licked her lips and, upon spearing the last bite, brought the fork up to my mouth, a whimper and a small string of drool was her plea that she deserved having people food.

"I don't know," I said to her, hypnotizing her with the motion of the fork going back and forth between midair and my mouth. "Have you been a good girl? Tamales don't grow on trees, ya know."

Wanting the growing volume of her whining to subside, I caved, which was inevitable anyway. She was a good girl, and it struck me as both sad and humorous that I had a better parent/child relationship with my dog than Big Ed and I would ever have. As I circumvented my desire to tap into my imagination for some TV watching, half-listening to a rerun of *Soap*, I began wondering about Mom's out-of-character behavior. Had she discovered Big Ed's unfaithful ways?

Like any good detective worth his salt, I'd have to put the clues together by interrogating Mom, barraging her with questions disguised as normal conversation born out of the curiosity that I still clung onto like the security blanket they made me abandon at age seven.

Well, if curiosity killed the cat, then Big Ed may have used up his nine lives.

The next morning, I found my mother still ditching her usual chipper demeanor in favor of a steelier façade. It was not your typical Friday morning at the Dodge homestead, with no offer to cook me breakfast. But she wouldn't deprive herself of nourishment after not eating last night. Mom began cracking an egg to be scrambled, then put her hand over her mouth and ran to the half-bathroom in the den.

I could hear retching signs emanating from downstairs, which put me off breakfast. When she re-emerged, I saw that she had refreshed her face with a splash of water. However, the dark circles under her eyes belied the fresh-faced appearance.

"You alright there, Mom?"

"What do you think?" She said with bitterness and a look that conveyed there were, in fact, stupid questions, even when asked by not-so-stupid people.

Ducking the rhetorical question, I left the kitchen to give her space. She appeared as pale as a vampire, hanging back in the threshold of my bedroom, reticent to enter without an invitation, looking instead to exit. There was no mistaking that she wasn't experiencing her monthly visitor. It was the only conclusion I could draw without the aid of her words providing the shading to fill in the blank canvas of her demeanor.

Was it a chauvinistic assumption? Absolutely. But the situation called for a solo round of our "What If?" game. Since Aunt Flo was off the table, the next natural conclusion was she knew about Big Ed and Whoreen.

As she crossed into my room, it was I who was treading lightly as to how to broach the subject.

"I'm sorry, hon."

Her apologetic words trickling out of her mouth were followed by a torrent of tears staining her cheeks.

"It's nothing you've done. I just wanted you to know that." She said, on the verge of hiccupping from trying to keep her breathing steady and losing the battle of trying not to sob at the same time.

"Let me guess. Is it something Big Ed did?"

I expected her to answer with, "Elementary, my dear Watson!" But it was my turn to don a deerstalker cap, holding up her marriage underneath a magnifying glass as effectively as Sherlock Holmes.

She nodded with a bizarre look on her face and liquid anger in her eyes.

"You don't think he's cheating on you again?" I asked directly, but her unyielding expression showed I had missed the mark by a country mile.

"Why would you assume that?"

"Well, it is Big Ed we're talking about. So…"

"He has something to do with my mood. But not for that. He has been unusually nice and, uh, attentive lately."

I caught her drift and let the not-so-hard-code-to-crack and suppressed a shudder.

"Well, isn't that special?" I said as Enid Strict, better known as TV's The Church Lady.

She sensed my discomfort in broaching a subject I didn't want to study, informing me she would take a drive.

I hit play on my ghetto blaster, listening to Johnny Hates Jazz explaining how someone had given him "Shattered Dreams." *Join the club, sister*. My mind drifting into a jet stream of memory, forming my own band called Henry Hates Danny. I allowed his image into my mind for a few seconds before banishing it, knowing full well it would always be lurking.

"Johnny. Why do you hate jazz so?" I asked into thin air, knowing my query was merely a distraction from the bigger question at hand and a way of diffusing the Danny bomb lying in wait, threatening to explode, wishing I could turn all thoughts of him into dust with a megaton force, eradicating him from memory for all time.

The following day, I was still no closer to how to delicately strike up the conversation of Big Ed's infidelity with Mom without blowing it all sky high. This all seemed above my pay grade. So, I called my favorite fellow conspirator, punching in the numbers I'd committed to memory and to heart.

"You got me. Now, what do you want to do with me?" Nina asked seductively, clearly not expecting me to be on the other end of the line.

"Braid your hair and talk about boys." I shot back teasingly but with a smidgen of lust in my voice, which I deepened to give it the proper effect.

"Oh, hey. What's up?"

"Three guesses, girl," I said, fully enjoying catching her off-guard.

"Not in the mood for 20 Questions. So, what can I do you for?" The cajoling timber was beginning to leave her voice, steering towards her becoming annoyed.

"I was wondering if we could meet up. I wanted to talk to you unless you had other plans. And by other plans, I mean someone being balls deep in you."

"Well, let me put it this way. It could be a possibility, but I'm guessing the guy I met last night is so flaky that he needs to be baptized in Head & Shoulders."

"Just call me back if your latest victim falls through."

"Roger, roger."

There was a clicking sound, indicating that Nina had a potential booty call.

"Hold please." She said excitedly, but when she got back to our phone call, her demeanor was defeated. "He can't meet up today. But *maybe* sometime this weekend. Whatever. So where do we meet up?"

We agreed on the Pannikin, which seemed apropos given it was the scene of our last scheme. An hour later, with coffee in hand, we managed to secure a table among the weekend crowd of caffeine junkies.

"What's wrong, poodle? Man trouble? Not feeling so fresh? Thinking about a life of celibacy?"

"None of the above. But you certainly get an e for effort."

"Spill. I'm on pins and needles."

"Probably your anal herpes flaring up again," I said too loudly, given the glowering looks from the couple at the table next to us. "No, it's a parental issue."

"Did they find your crusty tube sock collection?" She said just as loudly, causing the couple to collect their beverages and angrily vacate the patio area. "Ah, they finally told you that you were adopted."

"Now that would be cause for a stronger drink!" I answered, as a caffeine buzz began to sting my brain and I detailed my dilemma.

"She really needs to know."

"She seems super fragile lately."

"But the sooner the hurt happens, the sooner the healing can start."

"Damn, how much Oprah have you been watching?"

"How dare you! I'm much more of a Geraldo Rivera type of girl." She said with feigned horror at such a slight. "But seriously, I watched how hard it was on Mom when Dad left and how long it took for her to get over it. I still don't think she is, in all honesty."

Her misty eyes conveyed that she may not have been quite over it herself, every failed relationship a direct result of the dissolution of her parents' marriage. But I wasn't going to pry, since I was no Phil Donahue.

"Yeah, you're right," I said resolutely, even if the prospect caused my stomach to churn.

"Do you want me to be there for moral support?"

"She would be mortified and pissed that I broke the family code of denial being 9/10ths of the law. But I appreciate it. You're the best friend a girl never had."

"Never had it, never will."

"Great! Now I want a 7-Up!"

"Crisp and clean, no caffeine."

"This jet fuel will definitely help me get the words out."

Naturally, this made us bust into a chorus of "The Words Get Stuck in my Throat" from the kaiju slugfest *War of the Gargantuas*. We finished our coffees, and I gave her a big hug and kiss on the cheek.

"What was that for?" she asked.

"Just because you're you."

"That's what friends are for dummy."

"Takes one to know one," I said in a childlike tone.

We laughed, hugged again and I promised to give her a status report.

Thanks to the caffeine, I was practically vibrating as I pulled into the driveway. But it subsided when I saw Mom's car in the driveway and Big Ed's motorcycle in its spot.

I'd have to postpone the chat I wanted to have with her, which ran the risk that I might wuss out altogether. Nina's warning that Mom needed to know, whatever the consequences of that knowledge would mean, pinballed in my brain.

Mom was alone in the kitchen, sipping coffee, the familiar faraway look in her eyes present and accounted for.

"Hi, hon." She said, also letting caffeine change her earlier mood.

"How was your drive?" I asked, scanning the house with my ears, listening for where Big Ed may be lurking.

"Good, good."

"Where's Pop?" I asked casually.

"Oh, Mrs. Woodson asked for help with the BBQ."

I bet he was lending her a hand, but it was probably a case of vice versa. Grossed out at the thought, I felt my anger rising. Since they were both invited, Mom was making her famous German potato salad, unaware that Big Ed and Whoreen probably thought they were awfully clever in their charade.

She rose from the kitchen table, while I sat down at it, watching her gather her ingredients and begin filling a large pot with water, then grab a knife to cut the potatoes.

"Can we chat before you…" I started.

"Make it quick; I'm running behind."

"So yesterday, I asked if you thought Dad might be cheating."

"Henry, I really don't have time for this!" She emphasized the point by turning towards the stove, looking at the time on the stove's clock.

"What if I told you that I know he is?" I pushed gently. "I even have it on tape."

"What are you, some kind of detective now?" She sighed heavily. "I should never have told you about any of that business, it's all in the past where it belongs!"

"But it's not and I'll prove it."

Almost knocking over the chair, I ran to get my ghetto blaster. Plopping it down on the table, I hit the play button and we both heard the incriminating conversation between Big Ed and Mrs. Woodson.

"Shut it off!" she yelled. "I don't want to hear that!"

I turned it off, ever the dutiful son, hating that I had to do it, telling her so and she left the room, slamming her bedroom door. I knew there was no point in knocking on the closed door. Instead, I headed out to Mrs. Woodson's house. Hellbent on confronting Big Ed, I might have noticed that the license plate holder on the white VW Scirocco indicated it was purchased at Volkswagen Santa Monica parked next to Mrs. Woodson's in the driveway. Perhaps if I had been aware of that, I wouldn't have banged on the door.

When it opened, I was mere inches from Danny.

REUNION

I could not move, nor breathe. The more he looked at me with that stupid puppy dog look, the more I wanted to call animal control, reporting a vicious stray dog on Arroyo Street. But words did not escape me. Nothing. Nada. Zip.

Yet, I could not take my eyes off him, as if I had been lost in the desert for God knows how long and was suddenly confronted with an endless ocean. However, an ocean with a dangerous riptide underneath that was deadly and most assuredly had the power to drown me.

But dammit, he looked good. His skin was summertime-brown, highlighted by a white polo shirt. His torso clearly still benefiting from a diligent workout routine. His legs looked toned, covered by light blond hair, kissed by the sun. The pistachio colored Stussy shorts now seemed to be expanding, like some grotesque version of a kids' pop-up book. At this exact moment, I hated my brain so much and wanted to gouge my eyes out.

Yes, he was hot, but he was nothing more than a hot murderer.

I tried averting my gaze because it was as dangerous as staring straight into the sun. He had once been my sun, the moon, the stars I wished upon. It seemed like an eternity ago I had even been that version of Henry Dodge. Just as long ago as when I had first walked into this house and made my first real friend.

I hadn't been standing in this spot for nearly a decade, and though the interior of the house was vastly updated, I could visual the very spot where I would lie on my stomach on the floor, hands under my chin, and watch The *Hardy Boys/Nancy Drew Mysteries*.

Somehow, I think that Parker Stevenson, Pamela Sue Martin and Shaun Cassidy would have declined to investigate the mysteries at the palace, as they would have deemed them too dangerous.

At that moment, the name Shaun Cassidy was equivalent to the Prince Matchabelli perfume ad; his Windsong was staying on my mind. Letting my imagination wander past Danny and up the staircase to his right, making its way down the hallway to Kelley's old room, the door creaking open. A disco ball was affixed to her bedroom ceiling, the lights were all dimmed sweet darling, and it spun recklessly fast; refractions of light bouncing off Teen Beat posters of Leif Garrett and Shaun Cassidy, giving them an otherworldly glow. Two enormous speakers burst through the shag carpet coming out of the floor, reaching their pinnacle just before they could explode through the ceiling.

I was surrounded by sound, both deafening and soothing, as Shaun sang of the time he met a girl named Jill on a Monday. His heart wasn't the only one that stood still, and surreal didn't begin to describe what was transpiring.

"Da doo ron-ron" echoed ghostly, reverbing all around me and as I looked down, I was sporting John Travolta's white suit from *Saturday Night Fever*. A burst of smoke crept slowly across the floor, dissipating and revealing I was now standing upon the multicolored dance floor from said movie.

Suddenly I was confronted with the visage of Kelley, not as she had been, but as she was now. And in the imagined visage, she was beautiful with shoulder length chestnut colored hair, wearing an off the shoulder red dress that displayed a dancer's body. She beckoned me forward with one finger and it was all I could do to not run over to her and hug her with all my might. As it was, I strutted like Travolta had in the opening sequence of the movie, all cool and cock assured.

"Night Fever" enveloped me, wrapping me in the safety blanket of its warm memory. I struck the ultimate disco pose with my right arm up at a slight angle, index finger pointing at the disco ball. I had the fever, and it wasn't for the flavor of a Pringle!

Kelley smiled in the warmest of ways, nose crinkling just so as if this was the most delightful sight that she had ever laid eyes on. And we were off, putting into play the very moves we had practiced diligently in this room, lo those many years ago, and we were magnificent. She began spinning endlessly, a ballerina set on high, until she stopped suddenly and began snapping her fingers right in my face.

Only it wasn't Kelley who was doing the snapping, it was Danny trying to bring me out of my reverie.

"Earth to Henry." He sounded concerned. "You alright?"

But I knew better. He only cared about one person and that was himself, all the window dressings of his golden boy good looks harbored something much darker. And it was a darkness I knew all too well.

"I've never been better, old bean," I answered with false confidence.

"You kinda zoned out there for a minute," he said.

"'Nam flashback," I countered. "Is your mother home?"

I asked this as Reverend Kane had queried of Carol Anne in *Poltergeist II: The Other Side*. Hopefully, I wouldn't break into a rousing chorus of "God Is in His Holy Temple."

"No, she's out with your Dad. They're running errands for the BBQ."

"Thanks ever so much. I will call on her later." I said, trying to channel my inner Southern belle. More than likely, I sounded like the sharp edges and clipped tones of Julia Sugarbaker from *Designing Women*.

"Listen Henry, I'm probably the last person you want to see right now…" Danny began.

"Just about," I interrupted. "But that's only because Hitler had other plans today. I think he was going to the mall. Big sale at Chess King."

I turned to leave, unwilling to put myself in his orbit again, as the crash and burn factor upon re-entry was equal to visiting the seventh layer of Hell with an already existing third-degree burn. But then I felt his hand clamp down on my right shoulder. I swung around and clocked him hard against his right temple. Danny stumbled back, lost his footing, splayed out on the tasteful beige carpeting. He looked at me with those godammned brown puppy dog eyes and I could only imagine what he was seeing. More than likely, I had sprouted devil horns with flames jutting up behind me, a plastic pitchfork from one of my old Halloween costumes in one hand while the other one was being used to point a finger at him, as laughter poured out of me.

"Honey, you're not the one that got away," I said. "You're the one that needs to stay away!"

I wanted to be the bigger person, to not sink to his level and rise above it all. However, as much as I didn't want to admit it, the view from up here was pretty fucking awesome. For the first time in an exceedingly long time, I felt like I was in complete and utter control of a situation.

Danny didn't make any attempts to pounce and beat the living crap out of me. He just laid there, a lesson in abject stillness, and positioned his body so that he was mimicking Hippolyte Flandrin's painting *Young Male Nude Seated beside the Sea*, although he was fully clothed.

And in three, two, one, the waterworks started.

A funny thing happened at that exact moment; I realized that I wasn't entirely dead inside and cast off the rigor Mortis that had gathered like moss around my heart.

I walked across imaginary broken glass, shards puncturing the soles of my shoes and into my feet, to where he was slightly rocking back and forth, hugging himself because no one else would. I touched his shoulder as gently as a butterfly had landed on it; he looked up at me in utter defeat.

In that split second, I remembered what had made me pine away for him

The soulfulness in his eyes had always drawn me in, and the water pouring from them made me want to swim in them. Because he had always seen something in me I never could in myself; he had loved me for me. And now he was a broken man sitting shattered on the floor.

I realized if this were a horror movie, say, *A Nightmare on Arroyo Street*, this would be the part where moviegoers would shout out, "Look out! Don't go in there!" But like an atypical horror movie character, I would blindly stumble inevitably into harm's way, a casualty of common sense.

Still, I kneeled next to him and threw my arms around him with such abandon that I was worried for a split second they were going to become unattached from my body. His whole being tightened up, thinking I was going to wallop him again. I put my hand under his chin, tilting his head upwards, then our lips touched softly at first and then with a ferocity of passion. Together, as we should have always been and perhaps as the two of us would always be.

I offered a hand and pulled him up to a standing position. He grabbed my hand and tugged me upstairs to his bedroom, just as I had imagined for so long, putting our encounter in his van in LA out of sight and out of mind. He lit a candle and put on music, Echo and the Bunnymen serenading us with "Lips Like Sugar." Our clothes came off with sheer abandon and hitting parts unknown on the floor, a fevered exploration of one another's bodies propelled along with tongues and hands, tugging and sucking. In one frenetic moment, Danny ransacked his backpack for a condom. Not having any lube, he substituted hair gel and inflicted the sweetest of pains.

Afterwards, we lay wrapped in each other's arms, my head on his heaving chest. I inhaled deeply, taking in the scent of the Drakkar Noir. His hand was stroking my back when he decided it was time to speak.

"There's something I really need to tell you."

My heart sank like King Kong toppling off the Empire State Building onto the sidewalks of New York City. Splat!

Oh, sweet Jesus...was he going to tell me he had AIDS?

It recalled a memory of L.A. and our other post-coital moment when he said, "I have something to tell you. And you have to promise not to get mad." So much for out of sight, out of mind.

I just nodded, my head bouncing against his chest, as I had no words. I inhaled deeply, taking in the scent of the tropical smell of the candle, which had notes of coconut and pineapple. Maybe he wanted to tell me he was moving to Hawaii and wanted me to come with him. If I shut my fucking head up for once, the answer would come quicker.

"So..." he started, then stopped. "Dammit. This is a rough one, bro."

Oh shit! He trotted out bro; I could be in big trouble.

"It's ok, just tell me what's on your mind," I said reassuringly, a bit like Dr. Joyce Brothers.

"I didn't kill Corey," Danny stated.

"What?!" I shouted.

"It was Nick, and I took the fall for it."

I tilted my head upwards. I had to look him in the eyes to see if this was mere subterfuge or the truth.

Ding, ding, ding. We had a winner on the latter, as the tears springing from his eyes were holy water used in his absolution, washing away the sins of his past.

I listened, enraptured by the words, sentences and syllables coming from his mouth and painting a vastly different picture than the one employed with broad strokes by Nick. The candlelight was now capturing just half his face and mouth, yet I knew he was not speaking out of both sides of it. The flickering of the candle would bring images, brief flashes of his room with its surf posters, and mental pictures of what he was telling me. Nick standing over Corey's body in his apartment with Danny by his side. He explained that Corey was threatening to leave him for someone else and "things had gotten out of hand," as was evident by his unmoving body and the shattered glass coffee table. His duffle bag was packed and next to the wicker table, filled with belongings he would not need anymore.

Danny had looked at Nick incredulously when he explained why exactly he had asked him to dispose of the body of the boy he had grown obsessed with. There was one of Danny's co-stars that was not of age and Nick threatened to take the evidence to the police. How they would react to getting an anonymous copy of *Pickle Learns a Lesson* with a handwritten note implicating that what had happened onscreen was nothing short of statutory rape was not something he wanted to comprehend.

When Nick threatened Danny about what would happen unless he complied with Nick's request of disposing of "the body," he caved in faster than a coal mine in Kentucky.

However, unbeknownst to Nick, Danny began hearing a knocking sound from the back of the Microbus. At first, he thought it might be a flat rear tire, but then Corey's duffle bag popped up and began banging around his makeshift body bag.

He quickly pulled over to the side of the road on Mullholland Drive at The Groves Overlook, which afforded Angelinos panoramic city, mountain, and ocean views. At present, it was offering Danny a different vantage point of where his life was heading.

Among the fairy lights of the city, which made it appear both mammoth in scope and miniscule at the same time, Danny unzipped the duffel bag and sprang Corey from his canvas sarcophagus. There was fresh blood coming from the wound Nick had caused.

Danny grabbed a beach towel, and made sure to shake it out first, to not add painful sand granules to the wound, and applied pressure to the gaping gash and then wrapped it around Corey's head, making him resemble some sort of cut-rate swami.

He was barely coherent, but he asked Danny to help him. Now that he was thinking more clearly, Danny knew one gentleman caller, a doctor, who lived nearby in Bel Air.

He laid Corey gently down on the backseat and reassured him that he would be fine, and drove fast, but not recklessly, on the notoriously winding road, until he arrived at the front gate of Dr. Matthew Danvers. He frantically pressed the call box until a sleepy voice responded. Danny looked at his Swatch watch; he hadn't realized that it was well past midnight and informed the good doctor with a penchant for leather it was Miles O'Toole - his screen and escort name.

Dr. Danvers sighed as Danny explained there had been an accident and his friend was hurt. The gates electronically swung open. He drove up the wide driveway until he was parked in front of the magnificent house, consisting of eight bedrooms and 20 bathrooms in its expansive 36,000 square feet.

Danny walked up six concrete steps to a wrought iron gate that separated the outside world from the belly of the mammoth white structure. The doctor, who hid behind the veneer of being a mild-mannered man in his late fifties, opened the door.

"Exactly what happened?" he said, taking in the sight of Corey whom Danny was carrying in his arms, striking an immediate resemblance to a Universal Studios monster of yore who had made off a damsel-in-distress.

"Well, uh…" Danny stammered, "We were doing a little night surfing and the board hit him."

The doctor said nothing, but there was a look that registered his bullshit detector was on.

"Looks like a nasty wound. Take him out back and put him in one of the chaise lounges. I'll get my bag."

As was often the case in this house, Danny did as he was told. However, the humiliation he was feeling right now was an albeit different kind than what he felt after exiting the palatial home after turning a trick. Sometimes he'd return to the apartment he could barely afford and found bruises that would yellow and fade away, even if the act that caused them wouldn't fade from memory so easily.

In the pursuit of pleasure through the conduit of pain, Dr. Danvers was apt to cross boundaries, attempting to put salve on the wounds he inflicted by explaining there was extra cash involved in submitting to his will. Danny wasn't sure if he could trust him. But this was a literal any port in the storm situation.

Besides, his gut told him that his on-the-fly story for Dr. Danvers would not survive a police interrogation, and he be good and goddamned if he could think of another one. Not right now, not with Corey in the condition he was in.

And the doctor, with a dark bedside manner, returned with his 1950s-style doctor's bag and remained calm and utterly professional in his assessment of Corey's injury.

"He needs to go to a hospital for x-rays and sutures to close this wound," he said.

"You have to help me," Danny squeaked. "A very bad man did this, and he wants to blame me for it. He thinks Corey is dead."

The bubble of snot that grew in his nose told Dr. Danvers that Danny was not only in real trouble, but immensely frightened at the situation he had found himself in. And that he could exploit that fact to his advantage.

"Listen, there's no reason this man has to think otherwise," Danvers explained. "I will take care of it for you, but I need you to stay strong and make sure you act like you have taken care of the, uh, situation."

Dr. Danvers said he would take Corey to County/USC Hospital, where he was the Chief of Staff. And another wave of sadness washed over Danny. This was the very hospital that appears in the opening sequence of *General Hospital* and Danny considered this as the initial badge of failure. By not getting a role on the popular daytime drama had crushed him and helped in deciding to adopt his Miles O'Toole moniker.

The yarn the doctor told was one of simply happening upon the young man on Mullholland Drive, a victim of a hit-and-run accident. When Danny called him the next day, he was informed that Corey was in a coma. And he would be picking up the bill. He did ask Danny if Corey had any immediate next of kin. Danny knew Corey had been Adam Cornelius from Sacramento and had lived with his mother prior to his sojourn south. A downward trajectory into a life he figured would be better for him than living with the shrew of a woman he called mother.

He instructed the doctor to look up Mary Lou Cornelius in Sacramento and told him he could not thank him enough for taking care of this mess as effectively a Bounty paper towel. Dr. Danvers was the human version of being the quicker picker upper.

However, he explained to Danny there would be many a free of charge job to be had in his immediate future, to attempt to pay the doctor back. The pit of his stomach opened to the size of a cavern; his fragile mind told him it was the least he could do for pulling him into his charade of a life.

What it ended up being was showing Dr. Danvers just how much he could take, in both terms of physical pain, endurance and humiliation.

Not knowing the reason for his sadism being ratcheted-up, Danny endured every slap, punch, kick and being subjected to any number of sexual-based tortures the doctor could concoct. Danny was surprised that an iron maiden-themed glory hole hadn't been installed in the playroom.

But over the span of a few months' time, the not-so-good doctor had kept the intel close to his chest, letting a secret fester inside of him, one that had caused the violent escalation in their overly aggressive playtime. He had been tied up, beaten severely, and robbed at gunpoint by another rent boy, who had grown tired of his abusive ways, paid for or not.

Since he couldn't phone the police, given the circumstances, and for fear it would ruin his reputation at the hospital if he did admit the truth; he let anger grow inside of him like cancer. And Danny, indebted to the practitioner, was the one to pay the price.

The umpteenth time this occurred, Danny had reached the end of his proverbial rope after being left tied nude to a tree all day in Dr. Danvers's yard while he would be working well into the night. The sunburn he was getting wasn't the only thing that was making his skin red; it was also from the anger bubbling underneath his flesh like hot molten lava.

Somehow, Danny had managed to wriggle free from the ropes that bound his wrists to a low branch on an old oak tree. He was seething and concocted a backup plan to keep the doctor in check and hedge his bets should he have a change of heart – if he truly had one - regarding Corey's care and the nature of how he really came to be in a coma.

He made his way to the bedroom, quickly put on his clothes, and started to vacate Matthew de Sade's home, vowing never to return to what would make George's interpretation of what living in a palace meant, like existing in a shoe box by comparison.

As soon as Danny opened the front door, the doctor was standing there with the discarded nylon shackles in his hands.

"Going somewhere?" he queried. "You're still on the clock."

Danny struck Dr. Danvers hard across the nose, then hard in the stomach; the noises escaping him were akin to the opening of *Batman*, with its cartoon balloons of Pow! Bam! When Dr. Danvers elicited an "oof," he slumped forward. Danny then dragged the semi-conscious man to his little shop of horrors, tied his hands behind him and kissed him on the lips.

"Don't ever call me again if you know what's good for you!" He was very forceful in that proclamation, but inside he hated himself for what he had just done. But Dr. Danvers was a villain in a rogue's gallery of the type of men he had fallen into favor with in Los Angeles.

Danny explained this was why he had issued the "Not again, oh my god, not again" after our last sexual encounter. He was sickened by that part of him that hadn't come to terms with his post-traumatic stress disorder and caused him to turn a frightening shade of red and then green at his brand of Hulking out and striking out at me. Danny smash Henry's dreams!

He held me tight at that moment, and while I wanted to halt the memories this session was bringing forth, I did not doubt the sincerity. It was far more believable than the people behind *Grease 2* thinking that movie was actually a good idea.

"And what happened to Corey?" I asked him earnestly.

"I went by the hospital a few days later," Danny responded. "And he was gone. The nurses told me his mother had taken him home. I never heard from him again."

We sat in silence; I wasn't sure what more there was to say.

"Let me get a joint," he said. "You're going to need it for this next part."

We passed the joint back and forth a few times, but I could not inhale too deeply as my breath was shortened in anticipation of Danny's story. He snubbed it out in the ashtray on his nightstand. If it had it been made of wicker, I would have tried to pull the Danny mask off Nick's face, ala a Scooby-Doo villain, Ruh roh! I desperately wished I had a Scooby Snack, as the munchies were eating away my stomach lining. I was feeling more than loopy, like the time that Troy and I had smoked the pot with something extra years back.

Before Danny began the next portion of his *Tales of Terror*, sponsored in part by deception and Maui Wowie, he pulled me on top of him and gave me a huge kiss. I reciprocated and we played tonsil hockey for a few minutes, until both of us had no more spit from two bad cases of cotton mouth. He went into the bathroom and filled a plastic cup that usually held his toothbrush and was now an oasis in the desert of our mouths.

"Ok," I said dreamily, feeling incredibly mellow and very much a space cadet from the strong pot. "What's the rest of the story?"

Danny began patting down the bed, like he had misplaced something, and he caught the "what the fuck?" look I was giving him.

"I was checking for seatbelts. You're gonna need one," he said with a giggle and was all at once the guy I had fallen for years ago.

A smile marched across my mouth, and I gave in to the levity of the moment and pulled him in for another kiss. The radio was now playing "I Could Be Happy" by Altered Images and I let the lyrics seep into my ears.

In one of those moments fashioned by fate, the lyrics seemed written with me in mind, or so it felt in that hormonally charged moment, until the next verse set the record straight, in a manner of singing. All of the things I had done to get away, to escape from the memory of Danny had been for naught.

As we unlocked our lips, and before he let the story tumble out of his, "The Stand" by The Alarm came leaking out of the stereo. It took me back to three eternal summers ago, when a shellshocked version of myself had read about the world being divided into camps of good and evil. It was all too familiar a tale in the evil that men could do thanks to my time in Los Angeles and could pen a magnum opus that would rival Stephen King's.

And one of the villains had been Danny.

I recalled how my first crush had meant to put me under his thumb and keep pushing down until I existed no more as the boy I had been. Or until I existed no more. What I suspected about the how of three years ago was being supplanted by the why behind it all.

His story had made more sense by the word. I mean if Nick had merely helped Danny, then why was there a shrine for Corey in his closet? Why wouldn't he have discarded his belongings in a dumpster, given it to Goodwill or…

"What's going on in there, baby?" Danny said, absently tapped a finger on my forehead.

"Tell me about it, stud," I said, channeling Sandy as we lay ensconced in the room across the hall from where Kelley had found religion in vinyl gods, whose task for us was to spread the gospel that *Grease* was the good word.

A sly smile illuminated Danny's handsome face and his mouth began to form words I wasn't sure I was ready to hear, the candlelight acting like a campfire as he began telling a ghost story with players I had known. Or thought I had known.

"Do you remember when you guys came up to visit me?"

I nodded silently.

"Well, so did Nick," he murmured.

And with that, he launched into his story. About how when John, Jeannie and I were walking down the stairs and across the deadened lawn of Danny's apartment building none of us noticed Nick's Cadillac parked behind Danny's Microbus. I vaguely remember him stopping dead in his tracks, a momentary look of worry crossing his face, before returning to being jovial.

He worried that Nick would approach us and disclose information about Danny's identity as Miles O'Toole, among other things.

And those other things were all Corey-based.

In fact, Nick told Danny that he thought I was Corey after we pulled away in the Green Bomb, and Nick bounded out of his car. Well, bounded as best he could, given his ample frame.

"You have some explaining to do, Daniel! What was Corey doing here?!" He kept his rage to harsh whispers.

"Huh?" Danny sputtered. "That wasn't Corey!"

"Really? How stupid do you think I am?"

"I don't think you're stupid at all," he said in a shaky voice. "Just mistaken."

"Then exactly who the fuck was that?"

"Come inside," Danny commanded, fearful Nick would make a scene.

In the apartment, Danny began rooting around his bookshelf and pulled out a photo album, as Nick went to sit down on the couch. Before Danny could issue a warning, Nick had fallen through the middle. The crappy couch belonged to his roommate Jeff, who was out doing one of his many "odd jobs," as he called them.

My mind was reeling, screaming *Jeff! That Jeff?* The coincidence was just too great to not be. But I kept mum, so I didn't sidetrack his story. I would broach the topic afterwards.

"Godammit!!" Nick yelled and he hit the couch with such force that the James Harrill print *Monastery Near Salonika* came dangerously close to falling off the wall.

On the inside, Danny was laughing quietly in front of this man, this creature. He knew the length of his duplicity and did not want to end up in a duffel bag for his transgression.

Danny hauled Nick's fat ass out of the hole in the couch. It took almost two minutes to get him up and out; Danny had inwardly wondered if he should call for a tow truck. Or a crane. He almost lost his composure at that visual, but Nick was pressed up on him in a reverse Heimlich Maneuver position and would have felt the rippling of the inside laughter.

Like the world's biggest toddler, Danny gently placed Nick on another cushion next to the one that had momentarily humanized him. Then he brought over the photo album.

The faded cover featured a green tropical scene, resplendent with palm trees and the pages inside were browning with age, memories of a paradise lost. Danny skipped past his school pictures until he came upon a cluster of photos from Encinitas.

"See, that's not Corey," Danny pointed to the 12-year-old version of myself next to my brother swimming in Danny's pool twenty million emotions ago. He then directed Nick's attention to the one next to it with us standing in front of our house, in the middle of our street.

Nick took the photo album away from Danny, as if grabbing a piece of cheesecake. He lifted his glasses, held the photo album closer to his face and squinted.

"No, it's not. But damn, he's close." He slyly inquired, "Who is he?"

"My friend's little brother," Danny answered, not wanting to give any names to protect the innocent.

"I see," Nick answered casually, but clearly analyzing the matter.

He put the photo album down on the coffee table, began feeling around in his front pocket for his cigarettes and lighter. He moved the abalone shell ashtray closer, lit his cigarette, inhaled, and produced a massive cloud of smoke. He then grabbed the TV remote, and the Zenith sprang open with one eye, until it was fully awake. Nick settled on *Elvira's Movie Macabre* but had little interest in *Dynasty*'s Joan Collins being tormented in *Empire of the Ants*.

But much like the onscreen giant insects, Nick had latched onto the crumb of an idea he wanted to bring back to his queen. Or in this case, his king. He put his feet up on the coffee table and leaned back in deep thought.

"Make yourself at home, Nick," Danny grumbled.

Nick ignored him and Elvira's pithy comments about how the special effects in the movie weren't really all that special; just real ants superimposed to make them seem bigger than life. Somewhere in his reverie, Nick registered what The Mistress of the Dark had said, and the morsel was starting to be consumed into something that would become all-consuming over the next few days.

The lesson he gleaned was that things which are faked can be made to seem realistic, albeit through the magic of the camera lens.

And if it appeared that Corey Adams' time away from the spotlight elicited a return to home video, then so be it.

But if Danny had suspected this was the rabid hamster running endlessly on the rusty wheel in the cage of Nick's mind, it seemed doubtful he would have sold me down the river. What neither of us knew was that Nick was tailing me for a good week, monitoring my schedule, making plans to kidnap me and do his bidding as Corey Adams prior to my running away from home.

He had gleaned enough information in his dealings with Danny to know where to find me. But when I decided it was time to be gone from my surroundings was when Nick had to construct another plan. A plan that consisted of befriending me, of being my confidant, of using that weird holding power he seemed to have over the younger set.

And around the second or third week of my tenure at the palace was when Nick showed Danny the fake documentation that upped my age, much like I had done in my reinvention as Billy Collins. However, the name on my new forms of ID all read the same. I was to be known henceforth as Corey Adams and to pick up the mantle of being a shining star who had previously fallen from the sky.

"I knew that would be nothing but bad news." Danny's solemn look, captured by candlelight, was made more morose, the haze of the marijuana through bloodshot eyes made him appear to be something out of a German expressionistic film. I was sliding into feeling way more than fucked up territory and made myself concentrate on what was verbally unfolding.

"My plan was to go to the police."

For whatever reason –maybe it was remorse or to serve as a reminder of how out-of-control his life had gotten – Danny had held on to the duffel bag Corey had been placed in.

All that he needed to get his idea in motion was to plant it in Nick's car and place an anonymous tip to the police. What he got was nothing at all like that. There was never a way to get alone with Nick long enough to spike his drink or whatnot, as he was spending all his free time at the palace. Late one night, Danny was wide awake in dreamland and could not stop thinking about how his actions were about to ruin my life, too.

He vehemently resolved he would go to the police the next day, tell them everything, even if the category of "everything" fell under the umbrella of implicating himself. He fell asleep, albeit fitfully, and was awakened by the shrill ringing of his phone.

My brother was on the other end, fresh from his West Pac, asking if he had heard from me. Before he realized what he was saying in his half-asleep stupor, Danny said he had an idea of where I might be. He paused in his storytelling momentarily and I couldn't quite make out what was going on behind the blank expression on his face.

"Where was I?" He said, but it sounded more like his present location than his place in the story.

On the radio, Bronski Beat was commanding Danny to "Hit That Perfect Beat," because he was shutting down somehow; swallowing hard and moving away from me, not uttering a word.

"What's wrong?" I asked, not really wanting an answer.

He didn't respond immediately, and I gathered the sheets up around my torso, detecting a sharp drop in temperature in the room. I wanted to stroke his back but was afraid of frostbite. Taking a very deep breath and holding it for a moment, and then he exhaled dramatically. I was about to make a joke about him not bogarting all the air in the room when he finally broke the icy silence.

"I hate the person I was," he began. "I put you in harm's way and for what? So that I could continue to live under those motherfuckers' control? I let Nick get away with murder. I was going to do his bidding, like some flunky! What if Corey hadn't woken up in the van? Would I have buried him alive?! Jesus!!!"

"You are not that same person you were," I said to placate him.

"Fuck! I hope not." He said this with a little laugh that morphed into a residual cough from inhaling the smoke from the devil's lettuce.

"Listen, we all have things in our past. The trick is to remember where you are at now." I said after his fit subsided and if it was my life's mantra; it was always so much easier for me to give advice than listening to my own.

He turned to face me, rivulets running down his cheeks, becoming rivers of sorrow.

"Do you remember what I said to you in the van?" he asked, grimacing at what being in the van had entailed on that night.

"That you had feelings for me?" I asked directly, and whether it was from information overload or the effects of the pot, the world went dark.

Suddenly, I wasn't in the bedroom anymore. Hell, I wasn't even inside the house, as I was standing on a football field. Glancing to my right, I saw a young girl kneeling with an object in her right hand, which was spinning around at a very rapid clip. I approached with trepidation, seeing she was holding a football with a picture of Danny on it. Lifting her head she gave me, well, the queerest of smiles, nodding towards the ball.

I backed up and ran as fast as I could towards the pigskin, and before that little bitch could pull the ball away from me as she had for so many years with Charlie Brown, I kicked Lucy in the side of the head. She went down faster than a drunk girl on prom night. Scooping up the ball and running down the field, I came to a carnival-like setting.

Making my way towards an attraction called The Shake Shack, boys in leather jackets and Levis and girls in angora sweaters and poodle skirts moved out of my way on either side, a parting of the sea on this strange tide I was riding.

It was becoming difficult to walk and upon looking down, I could see why. I was wearing a skintight leather catsuit. I brought my eyes upwards; they landed on Danny standing on the stairs leading up to The Shake Shack.

He broke into "You're The One That I Want" and I began tearing at my leather pants until they were nothing more than leather Daisy Dukes, running up to him, jumping into his arms and straddling him. We both turned around as Greased Lighting came driving up without anyone at the wheel.

A disembodied and melancholy chorus began, informing us that we belonged together, as assuredly as rama lama lama did. Let's give it up for The Valium Singers!

With Danny in the driver's seat and me happily riding shotgun, we were both amazed and delighted as the car raised itself into the air, next stop heaven. I turned back to give a toothy grin and wave goodbye to all the hep cats and cool chicks. But there was no one standing there except Nick, just like Michael Myers had been when Laurie Strode saw him in Mr. Riddle's yard on that fateful *Halloween*. He was eerily still with white sheets billowing next to him, until they reached out and enveloped me.

I awoke from my little cat nap, staring into the sheets, while Danny was looking at me aghast.

"Really?" he asked, his usual huffiness replaced by laughter.

"Sorry 'bout that," I giggled. "You were saying?"

This brought forth even more peals of laughter from the both of us. I moved closer to him and gave him the biggest of hugs and he returned the gesture in kind, harder than I had hugged him, in fact.

"I love you," he said. "You booger."

And there it was. Words I had been longing to hear for years. And I, too, had feelings for him over the course of the past few years. Primarily they were revulsion, loathing, and hate. Up until a few hours ago, I didn't ever want to ever see that handsome face of his again. I certainly never suspected this strange turn of events.

And I certainly didn't expect to be feeling funkier than a *Soul Train* dancer.

"Man, what is in that pot?"

"I was wondering that myself," he stated. "Fucking Jeff! He gave me a laced joint and didn't tell me. Typical. Fucking asshole."

"Does the Jeff you know drive a white Honda?" I asked, suddenly paranoid if he would follow this proclamation of love with another bout of anger.

"Yeah," he sighed. "I know you know him, Henry. He called me once after you scored from him, and he was convinced you were really Corey. I just hung up on him."

"Well, I saw your little late-night rendezvous behind AMC last year. What was that all about?"

"About me almost making a big mistake in being one of his distributors. I came to my senses, and he got really pissed. Haven't spoken to the guy since. But on the subject of Corey. Well, um..."

Before he could continue, there was a sudden and jarring crash from outside, coupled with raised voices drowning out Level 42's "Something About You."

We both dressed hurriedly, well, as hurriedly as possible with the disregard we had for the clothes we had taken off with wild abandon, unable to find our shoes in a timely fashion.

A ghostly lyric came floating out of the air as I spied Kelley's old room.

"*I wanna put on my-my-my boogie shoes*."

Despite this mind fuck, I was feeling sobered up as we raced down the stairs. The voices were growing more prominent by the moment.

They were both female and each belonged to a woman who had given birth to Danny and me.

We reached the screen door that led out to the backyard as I heard "You goddamn bitch!"

The speaker was Kate Dodge, the woman who usually substituted cuss words with less impactful versions. Shit was "sugar," and an old person driving too slowly was an old "faygart," as the word fart was even too much for her to say.

I stopped dead in my tracks. Not from the words roaring out of Kate Dodge, but the sight of what she was currently in the process of doing. She resembled a member of The Gorgeous Ladies of Wrestling (G.L.O.W.), as she fended off Doreen Woodson's punches and slaps by whirling her around by her sleek ponytail.

Doreen was flung into a card table, knocking off the red-and-white checkered tablecloth. Chex mix, pretzels and dry roasted peanuts sprayed out in a fan in the air before hitting the ground. Doreen managed to right herself as the table took a nosedive into the grass, landing with its four legs up in the air and awaiting a chalk outline to chart its demise.

Doreen spun to her right, red hair swinging out behind her, like the tail of a red Betta fish and picked up a glass punch bowl, raising it over her head and hurling it at my mother. She miscalculated and it missed by a country mile, shattering into a million pieces like my parents' marriage on the concrete.

I suddenly noticed Big Ed standing by the BBQ, prepping the charcoal briquettes for the yet-to-arrive guests. He was sucking down a beer and watching two broads fighting over him with a drunken grin.

"You're going to pay for that!" Doreen howled at the loss of her family heirloom.

"I'm quite sure K-mart has more," Mom said calmly, although she was huffing and puffing a bit. "Isn't that where you buy your wardrobe?"

"Don't you have something to make with Velveeta, Kate?" Doreen retorted. "Or did you have something else in mind that will keep your husband equally dissatisfied?"

I couldn't believe it. Our mothers were staging a catfight right out of *Dynasty*! All that was missing was a tussle in a lily pond.

And it looked like I had that thought too soon, as my mother lunged forward and put a death grip on Doreen's peasant blouse, turning her around toward the pool, kicking her hard on the butt which sent her flailing into the pool. And she jumped in right after her.

The men finally woke up. Danny rushed towards the pool and then my father. My mother began holding Doreen underwater, who in turn was smacking her face, but it was as if Kate Dodge was built out of steel, impervious, The Mominator.

"Kate! Stop it, she's pregnant!" Big Ed announced, looking as sheepish as I had ever seen him.

Mom let Doreen up and turned to look at her husband and what she said caused the man who said it stop dead in his tracks with her response.

"So am I Ed, so am I."

My mother began making her way to the shallow end of the pool, ascending the stairs. I rushed to her side, as Danny waded in and helped his gasping mother. My father remained still, and surprisingly silent, shocked by the revelation that both his wife and mistress were pregnant.

Much like Mom's waterlogged outfit, I was trying to soak it all in myself.

If my parents divorced and he married Doreen, that would make Danny and I stepbrothers. I shuddered at that very prospect; talk about a family affair! This absolutely could not be happening. Not. At. All.

As much as I wanted to make this about me, I really needed to shift my focus onto my mother. I would have said my poor mother, but after seeing the way she dug her claws into Doreen, I felt that I may have underestimated her.

But not as much as my father did.

She rushed over to where Big Ed was standing, slapping him so hard that his glasses went flying off into the hedges.

"You fucker!" she yelled at maximum velocity; had his glasses still been on they surely would have shattered at the tenacity inherent in her primal cry.

It was a red-letter day, well in the sense of Big Ed having to sew a letter A on his white shirt, like Hester Prynne. Not only did I hear my mother cuss, but I saw my father waste a beer. It dropped from his hand and bled out on the grass, dying a foamy death.

She fled the murder scene, leaving my father to do his Velma from *Scooby-Doo* impression, arms outstretched in front of him as he tried to relocate his missing spectacles. I wanted to laugh, had the situation not been the definition of dysfunctional, I would have. Danny was attending to Doreen, aka The Whore of Babylon, and I decided that I should check on mine. It wasn't difficult to figure out which way she went, wet footprints that were already beginning to dry led the way through the house and out the front door, which stood open.

She was making her soppy way across the street to our house, and I ran to catch up with her.

"Mom. What the hell?" Asking if she was ok seemed trite.

Her look was one of anger and sadness. She kept walking hurriedly, flinging open the front door, then slamming the one to her bedroom closed. She did it so forcefully that the silhouette pictures of John and me fell from the wall, cracking the glass in both frames. The fracturing of our never-happy family solidified.

"Where is she?" Big Ed barked from the doorway

I clamped down hard on his shoulder, feeling the live wire of anger swelling in me, an orchestra of hatred I'd felt towards him over the years reaching its crescendo. I may have been an inch smaller than him, but in that moment, I felt gigantic.

"Don't even think about it!"

"Fuck off faggot!" he screamed in my face.

And there it was. The never talking about what I was to him laid out in three hateful words.

"Eat shit breeder," I said, pushing him back from the stairs, shoving him hard into the living room. "And that's Mister Faggot to you!"

He righted himself in front of *his* chair and lunged at me. However, given his physical prowess, all it took was a quick sidestep on my part to avoid him, all that was missing was a red cape. Ole!

Grabbing him by the scruff of his white t-shirt, letting go before shoving him into that goddamn cut-rate throne. Hulk Hogan, eat your heart out! He turned to face me, and the smoldering look of contempt was what I attempted to wipe off his smug mug, taking Mom's cue, supplanting her slap for a full-force punch in the face. It knocked him back into his throne.

And the thing was, I didn't want to be angry, to fight his fire with my fire, stoked by a long-simmering hatred. It put me on the same level as him, and I didn't want to sink that low. I was about to voice a cease-fire when he hurled a lamp at my head. It missed by inches, smashing into pieces on the terrazzo.

I raced towards Big Ed and delivered a well-placed kick in the balls. He went down with a groan but grabbed my ankle and pulled me to the ground. Then, my father started wailing on me.

But he and his weight were off me as Danny appeared and hauled him off me.

"Get off him, you son of a bitch!" Danny said with the ferocity of a lion protecting its cub from, well, a hippopotamus seemed an appropriate comparison.

I was doing fine in fighting for myself and didn't need to be saved. My damsel in distress days were behind me, not needing him or John sticking up for me anymore. Somewhere in the mess I had made of my life in an abbreviated time, I had become oddly self-sufficient.

To paraphrase Jon Lovitz's impression of Harvey Fierstein on *Saturday Night Live*, he just wanted to love me – was that so wrong?

No, it wasn't, but somehow it felt like it should have been. However, I chose to believe his story and the fact that he loved this human form of dried mucus.

"ENOUGH!!!" This came from the top of the stairs, bellowing from Mom's mouth.

Three heads swung in unison to where my mother had an armful of her cheating husband's clothes, and began throwing them at Big Ed, making it rain tighty whiteys, white t-shirts and work attire, reiterating the point that it's not nice to fool Mother Nature!

A stray pair of tighty whitey underwear landed squarely on Big Ed's face. He removed them as if he had walked into the snare of a spider's web and they dropped to the floor as more of his clothes dotted the area around him.

For once Oz the Great and Powerful remained silent, but you could not ignore the fact the man behind the curtain was nothing more than a sham. He began picking up his clothes, heading out to the garage where his Goldwing motorcycle was housed while Mom kept up her impromptu spring cleaning.

Danny gave me an awkward look, and I returned it, feeling strange that he was witnessing this slice of drama between my parents. Everything was out in the open for once. And while that should have been liberating, it had the opposite effect, as she was wounded.

I made a beeline for the kitchen, bringing back his beloved owl mug. It made an impressive sound when smashing against the garage wall. Now, I had solidified to never again have to fetch him a cup of coffee. But he had done that with his actions. Surprisingly, he didn't come for me. He focused on the task at hand, packing up his belongings in the side compartments of his escape vehicle.

He hopped on the motorcycle, pushing it back with his feet, embarking into the night. And just like the man himself, the roar of the motorcycle faded away.

Detecting a presence behind me, assuming it was Mom, watching in faded reverie as her husband fled into the night, wanting to join me in a rousing chorus of *Ding Dong! The Witch is Dead.* Danny was pressing himself against me with arms encircling me. I wanted to stay this way and in this exact moment, now, tomorrow, forever.

Turning to face him, I was as good as a melted pool of ice cream on this sultry summer night. He leaned in to kiss me and I gladly reciprocated, feeling it was the two of us against the world.

Except there was an unexpected plus one, well, more of a plus two.

"Get out of my house and go back to your whore mother!" Kate bellowed at Danny with veracity and hatred oozing venom with each syllable.

Well, this was quite the pickle. Am I supposed to defend my man or rush to my wounded mother's side? Yeah, thanks a lot, life. I was stuck in hesitation's molasses grasp when Danny made the decision for me, releasing himself and disappearing through the open garage door. Only this time, I wanted to stop this man from walking out of my life. I looked back at Mom, but she had already retreated inside the house.

Danny was halfway across the street. I could tell by how he was walking, which was extremely focused, that he was upset.

"Danny!" I yelled after him, surprisingly not choking on the vapor trail from his speedy exit.

He stopped in the middle of the street and turned around. He wasn't mad; he looked dejected as I ran over to him.

A split second before I could reclaim my place in those muscular arms, his eyes turning very round, mouth forming a silent O. The next thing I knew, he pushed me hard to the right. So hard, in fact, I ended up landing on my back on the sidewalk. So hard that I narrowly missed being hit by the car that plowed into him. He flew up over the hood, along its roof, and then rolled off its trunk, all in slow motion.

"DANNY!!" I screamed as the headlights turned into taillights and the car sped off.

He laid silently on the ground, unmoving, bloody, with a very deep gash on his forehead and legs crumpled underneath him at what can only be described as "an unbelievably bad angle." I got up, ran over to him and immediately was overcome with déjà vu; this scene was reminiscent of when Bobby Ewing was had been struck with a car and killed by Katherine Wentworth on *Dallas*. Oh fuck, oh shit, please don't let him be... *dead*. This was the mantra I said internally as I made my way over to him.

Mr. Michaels came running out of his house to say he had already called 911. I was in a dream state that was unfolding into a nightmare.

Standing over Danny, I could not discern if he was breathing, knowing not to move him in case of an injury to his head or neck. I am not sure why I was able to latch onto this tidbit of information or where it even came from because the word numb did not even begin to cover what was happening.

Danny's eyes fluttered slightly. I got down on my knees and whispered that it was going to be fine, that he was going to be fine. But from my vantage point, it didn't seem like a very good likelihood. He opened his eyes, and they appeared glassy and unfocused. But then he said something that made me know he was aware of my presence.

"Booger," he said in a semi-gurgle.

I leaned down closer to his mouth, so he wouldn't have to exert himself. He began to whisper things into my ear that I would have to file away for later, the information cut short by the sound of sirens and the arrival of both the police and an ambulance.

Leave it to Doreen to make a dramatic entrance, flying out of her house, caterwauling at the top of her voice. She reached the EMTs and let out an ear-splitting cry. The officer ordered for her to be held back, putting her right next to me.

"This is all your goddamn fault!" she screamed right into my left ear.

Without hesitation, I slapped her incredibly hard across the face.

"Calm down, Doreen," I said this as calmly as a Stepford Wife who would just die if she didn't get that recipe.

She put her nails up like claws as if to scratch my eyes out, and I robotically seized her wrist, looking her straight in her eyes, and in my best Schwarzenegger voice, uttered a single word.

"Don't."

Then, as I'd expected her to do, she returned her focus to Danny, no longer laying the blame at my feet. Something about her words really got under my skin, but it was the words her son had whispered to me that were swimming around in my brain.

Was what he said true, or some byproduct of a traumatic head injury?

"We need to stabilize him," one EMT barked to another before I had a chance to ask him his professional opinion of my medical query.

Danny's eyes fluttered, as if in the throes of a deep R.E.M. sleep. From what I could tell, it was looking closer to being a permanent case of goodnight, sweet prince.

The tears jettisoned themselves from their ducts, leaving no room for error that I was coming out of the fog I'd been in.

The mantra of "Please don't let him be dead" began again in my mind until I was repeating it aloud. But, like much of my life had gone, no one was paying attention to me. The bigger fish to fry were whale-sized portions. As was evidenced by the hurried way the EMTs hustled Danny into the ambulance, allowing Doreen to get into the back with him. As the doors were being shut, she shot me the iciest look I'd ever seen.

One of the police officers approached me, and for a split second, I thought he was going to handcuff me, repeating Doreen's accusation that this was, indeed, my goddamn fault.

Yet he adopted a very soothing voice, the volume instantly setting me at ease.

"Tell me exactly what happened, as much as you can remember."

"Well…" I began, stopping as I almost told him that Corey Adams was really my half-brother.

I told him everything I knew. Well, almost everything, except what Danny had whispered to me. I wasn't really much help, in all honesty; I didn't know the car's make or model and certainly didn't have the wherewithal to get a license plate number. It had happened so fast, like how, in an instant, life can be altered. I wanted to remain hopeful this was just a huge pothole in the road to Danny and I might traverse in a life together.

But as it stood, it was a life falling apart.

Officer Diaz asked me to contact him if I remembered "anything, anything at all," as he phrased it.

"Sometimes, after a trauma wears off, you may remember something. Even if it's something small, call me." He headed to his squad car.

And when he left, it looked as if nothing amiss had happened on Arroyo Street.

I wanted to go to the hospital to be with Danny. However, I needed to avoid his slag, err, mother. I was torn by my sense of duty and not wanting to haul off and slap a bitch. Well, slap a bitch again.

I walked into a completely silent house; the door to my mother's room was as closed as her heart must be. The sound of an ambulance and police car was not enough to make her care about what was happening in the outside world.

I went upstairs to the bathroom, half-expecting Danny to be in the shower, signaling that what had just transpired was nothing more than a dream…a horrible, horrible dream.

Nothing was as it seemed, and my world had been turned upside down.

Taking a shower and letting the water pummel over me, beads of water mixing with the tears pouring out of my eyes, provided a momentary release. An emotional waterfall was cascading out of me, and I let it take me over, setting free the feelings I had been suppressing. Each tear was for specific people: Tony, my mother, Danny, Corey, and myself. Tiny watery apparitions, their faces looking up at me as they plummeted to the shower floor, splashing apart upon contact, scrambling to not be sucked into the void of the drain.

I had heard of the term "circling the drain," and it suddenly clicked as I watched my visage explode from a water droplet, remaining intact as he tried to fight against the tides that were forcing him back.

He put up a very valiant fight; alas, he was no match for the weight of water and was sucked into the abyss. Staring at the drain, I witnessed one tiny hand and then another grasping the edge, followed by a tiny head, torso, and legs. I squished him under my foot in my reverie; it was a kinder death.

This absolutely made me lose my shit, including deep and soulful sobs. I had made a mess out of my life, failed at what it meant to be a real man, nothing more than an extended version of that scared child, afraid of letting himself feel he could be loved or even love in return.

"I love you, you booger."

Those five words brought me out of the pity party I was throwing for myself.

Danny could be near death in a hospital, more than likely at Scripps Memorial, which housed the special wing I had been sent to after my suicide attempt. I didn't die and didn't want him to. I needed to see him and didn't care if his mother made a scene. This was about him, not even him and me, just him. And I'd be good and goddamned if I was going to let that bitch stand in my way, especially if there was the very real chance I would be saying goodbye. Ok, so I made it about me, too. Shocker!

Shutting off the water, I grabbed a towel hanging on the bar on the front of the shower door. I started drying off when I heard a sharp, rhythmic – almost seismic - sound. Thinking I was knee-deep in another, well, delusion, I was relieved when it stopped.

But the sigh of relief was cut short, not fully escaping from my mouth, when the noise started again. Wrapping the towel around me and leaving the foggy bathroom beyond for the harsh reality of what my mother was doing, as Dorothy had left her black and white farmhouse life for the Technicolor splendor of Oz.

However, my scene would have been filmed as the antithesis of that movie's moment of discovery, as I went out in the hall and saw my mother swinging a hammer and smashing holes into the wall. Jack Nicholson in *The Shining* would have been a more fitting analogy.

"Heeeeeeere's Kate!"

"Mom! Stop it!" I yelled.

The look in her eyes, part hurt and part gleeful rage, scared the shit out of me, honestly. She paid no attention to me, and I certainly wasn't going to go up to her to take the hammer from her hand. She needed to tear her playhouse down, knocking out the deception within its walls that she was subscribed had to come tumbling down, when the walls come crumbling, crumbling, as John Cougar Mellencamp had sung because we knew a person who was no damn good.

She began to assault the walls that lined the stairs when she miscalculated a swing, sending her reeling down the stairs, landing with a very audible thud on the marble terrazzo.

"Holy shit!" I didn't realize that I was saying this aloud; yelling it aloud was more like it.

Rushing down to the bottom of the steps, I carefully made my way around to where she lay unconscious but breathing. Running over to the kitchen, silently cursing my father for still thinking having a rotary dial phone was better than a push button one, making every number difficult in reaching its destination. It was like the phone had been coated with glue, and I had to fight to dial three simple numbers, the clicking of the dial stretching itself out to infinity.

The 911 operator answered, and I explained the situation, including the breaking news that my mother was pregnant. Within minutes, and for the second time that day, the sound of an ambulance siren sliced through our calm suburban neighborhood; a banshee's wail not often heard and sure to bring the neighbors out of their cocoons.

The red of the siren's lights pulsed through our curtains, giving the room a very disturbing blood hue. My mother's face was tattooed with it one moment, and seconds later, she appeared serene, dreaming the sleep of the unencumbered.

I opened the door, and two paramedics were making quick work of getting to our front door. There was also a remarkably familiar-looking lawman, one Officer Diaz, who must have thought he was having the strangest case of déjà vu.

As I was apt to do when nervous or worried, I blurted out the first thing that came to my mind.

"Officer Diaz, we must stop meeting like this. People will talk."

A blush bloomed across his face. It registered as a tepid blip on my gaydar, but that obviously wasn't my focus at the moment.

The two paramedics looked at each other. One shrugged at the other and turned their attention to my mother. Her vital signs were off, according to the shorter EMT, and I heard the information through some sort of tunnel. The information was being formed in their mouths but was synchronized like one of the Godzilla movies I had obsessed over as a kid. The kid who was now a man in terms of age only.

They needed to take her to the hospital, and given all the time that we had spent watching *General Hospital*, I really hoped that Rick Springfield, as Dr. Noah Drake, would be the one to take care of Kate Dodge.

They loaded her onto the gurney, took her down the stairs and the slope of the driveway with ease, and put her in the ambulance. I was going to ride along, but Office Diaz offered me a one instead.

His hand fell onto my shoulder; a tinge of electricity was being conducted from its owner into my body.

"I can drive you to the hospital," Officer Diaz said kindly.

"I should be with her," I pleaded.

"They need room to do their thing," he said. "Besides, I need to ask you a few questions."

I didn't like the sound of that. Cops and questions went together like the banana and peanut butter sandwiches my father was fond of. Or, they went together like Henry Dodge and authority figures, not a good combination.

But there was something different about him. He seemed invested in helping me; the feeling was uncomfortable, like wearing a new pair of jeans for the first time. I decided to put a little faith in humanity, even if it was just one person. Given all that had gone down that day, he might even prove to be a friendly ear.

I followed him to his police car, noticing the faces of neighbors peering out of their windows as though watching me being carted off to jail. Officer Diaz explained it was "just procedure" that I had to sit in the back, behind the caged window.

Oh great! The neighbors were most likely drinking in the scene, drunk on the drama of it all. Yet not a single solitary one came outside to ask what was wrong or what happened.

Hopefully, they were being observant and noticed I was not placed in handcuffs, nor did Officer Diaz hit the noise and the cherries, and that his patrol car was driving off at a moderate speed.

"So…" Officer Diaz began and trailed off before I chimed in.

"Yes, *Knott's Landing* has nothing on our street," I said glibly.

A slight smile spread across his face as soon as the "oh fuck" look on his face subsided. He was really handsome. No, he isn't. Oh, who was I kidding? But I had much bigger fish to fry right now. Like *Jaws* sized.

"Sorry," I said, hating my pop culture defense mechanism.

"I want to make sure how you're holding up," he said and waited for me to answer in the affirmative, which I did quietly. "Now, what happened with your mother?"

"You have a scorecard handy?" I asked before detailing all that had transpired.

By the time we entered the hospital parking lot, Officer Diaz was well-versed in what had gone down that evening. He let me out of the back of the car and held the squad car door open for me. What a gentleman, I thought, and then squashed the sentiment like a fly under a swatter.

"Listen, Henry, I know you are right in the thick of it, and it will be overwhelming to deal with. But I'm here for you if you need a sympathetic ear or remember any more details."

He handed me a card on which he had written his home number on the back. I shoved it in my pocket, out of sight, out of mind.

"I appreciate it."

"No problem whatsoever," he said before adding. "And call me Antonio."

Really, fate? Another Tony? I said nothing, then began walking into the hospital, where I had my wrists stitched up and now had accrued a new batch of scars.

It was like walking into a haunted house, the ghosts of memories keeping time with me as I approached the nurse's station to inquire about both Danny and my mother. Naturally, Danny's mother had left specific instructions not to give out any information unless it was to immediate family.

It was smoother sailing with finding out about my mother until what the nurse told me was akin to striking an iceberg.

"Your mother will be fine," she began as all business, and then her tone quickly changed to concern. "However, she lost the baby."

I simply turned away and did not utter a word, fading into the scenery, a ghost, minus the clanking of chains and otherworldly groans and shrieks.

I immediately started on the “why was this happening to me?” train and just as swiftly derailed the thought. This was not about me; it was about my mother and Danny. The spotlight was not shining solely on me.

I plopped down in a chair in the lobby, wishing that John was here to perform his brotherly duty of rescuing me from the slings and arrows of the world. But he was on his delayed honeymoon with Jeannie in Hawaii. I didn’t want to call his hotel in Oahu, casting a pall on their wedded bliss.

Yet, I didn’t want him to return home to all this sad news without something like a warning shot. Oh yeah, and there was little detail that we have a half-brother. And there was even more to that, but I couldn’t even deal with that right now.

Wouldn’t someone throw me a life preserver in the sea of information I was starting to drown in?

The visual for NBC’s *One to Grow On* appeared before my eyes, as did Nancy McKeon, television’s Jo on *The Facts of Life*, and she began a monologue about overcoming adversity.

“Meet Henry Dodge, oh the things his eyes have seen and the things he’s done. You may suspect that Henry is gay, and you’d be right! While not a flaming homosexual, he does enjoy the company of men. In the past 24 hours, ’Ol Henry has been thrown into a tailspin. His mother and father are splitting up because his father got another woman pregnant and impregnated Henry’s Mom, too! Oh, and his could-be-boyfriend may be dying, and his mother is the other woman that Big Ed got preggers. Let’s see how Henry handles a rather sticky situation!”

Fade to black, and Nancy was gone before I could even fan girl out on her and tell her how much I loved *The Facts of Life,* even though Mrs. G. was gone this season, as was her sage advice. If only I could conjure up the visage of Charlotte Rae, my myriad of problems and how to deftly handle this situation would become clear as a sunny Southern California day.

As it was, this was going to be a case of stay tuned.

As I slogged through the numerous mindfucks of the past day, I looked up and saw Ms. Doreen Woodson striding purposely over to where I was sitting. I stood up, not in the act of being a gentleman, but so that I could look her dead in the eyes; a poor choice of words given that I wasn’t sure what Danny’s prognosis was.

“Don’t start with me, Henry,” she hissed.

“I’m not the one that strutted over here, Doreen.”

"I'm sure you've been informed that you will not be finding out anything about…" she paused and then said his name in a melancholy tone. "Danny. I blame you for this, if he hadn't become entangled in your bullshit, he might still…"

"Still what?" A rush of dread moved my heart to my throat.

That's when the waterworks started, and she began striking out at me, just as Tippi Hedren had done to the titular avians in *The Birds* at the end of my second favorite Alfred Hitchcock movie after the one detailing the strange relationship between a boy and his mother.

"You killed him! You killed my boy!"

The nurse who had been so kind to me now had a disapproving scowl on her puss as if I were standing over a dead body with a bloody knife and zero remorse showing on my face.

"What?" It was all that I could muster as shock began to infiltrate every fiber of my being.

I grabbed her by the wrist, halting her physical assault.

"No, I didn't. You know that is not true!"

"Well, here's what I know is true. Your father never loved you and he's going to give my baby all that love he could never give a loser faggot like you!"

I held back from delivering her second slap of the day and offered a verbal assault.

"Is there anything else you have in your bucket from your little well of knowledge?"

I would always have sarcasm as my steady companion. But what I would never have Danny again. I was too shocked to cry. And I wasn't going to cry in front of this bitch.

"Don't even think about coming to his funeral," she said. "I'll make sure you're not in attendance."

She bowed her head, making her way out the doors that slid open as if they were afraid of what she might say to them, too. They closed with a whoosh, as if their breath could not be exhaled until Doreen had left the building.

I was left to my own devices, all alone with no one to turn to.

Walking over to a bank of phone booths, I pulled the door closed behind me and remembered an oft-dialed number from my memory bank. I got out my wallet and siphoned through it until I found two dimes. My

Mom had always taught me to never leave home without at least enough to make a phone call that was answered after two ringie-dingies.

"I need to see you," I said.

We both sat there, not saying word one. When I was in his presence there was always some type of unspoken tension, and I now knew exactly where it came from. And I was here to confront it head on.

"I'm sorry, David, that I always ignored what you had to say. I didn't want to face the truth, about my life, about myself."

"And why do you think that is, Henry?"

I had to take a moment to pause. I wanted to tell him what he wanted to hear, when in fact, I really didn't know. I had an inkling as to why, but I was in the frame of mind to have it spoon-fed to me. I simply shrugged, but it summed up everything I was feeling.

"You have many escape routes. TV, movies, reading, music, sex," he paused. "I suspect that there's drug use, too."

I didn't know how to answer that last part. So, I just clammed up, having smoked a joint with…with Danny a few hours ago. But, as far as the cocaine I was taking during our previous sessions went, I had wanted it to be gone and had banished it from my life.

I wanted to get some perspective on the current round of revelations and be as clear-headed as possible, my mellow had long since been harshed. For the first time in a while, I thought of Candy and her sage advice she had imparted to me in her makeshift office at Rage, wondering how she was doing; resolute to reach out sooner rather than later.

"Yes," I simply answered, wanting to tell him about making the healthier choice to see him instead of a garden variety drug dealer. But this felt false, harkening back to my school days of wanting to get a gold star for good behavior.

"You are stronger than you think, Henry. There is a lot of strength in all that you have been through, of making mistakes in trying to discover yourself and a tribe to call your own," he said in a gentle manner. "And now you are faced with more than you can handle. I want to help you, but you need to be completely honest with me and yourself."

And therein lay the problem in facing myself and taking a good hard look at myself. While I was free of the dirty and treacherous grip of meth and cocaine, I had almost gone to score whichever one would quell the raging storms inside me. While I had made the better choice of talking to David Chan, I still had to come clean about my feelings. I slouched down in the leather chair, hoping to blend in with its black exterior and use it as camouflage.

I immediately conjured up Rodin's statue of The Thinker. I knew this had always been an issue for me; thinking, or more appropriately overthinking situations, rather than feeling, as he had pointed out previously. And I began my conversation with David, covering all that had happened on Arroyo Street over the past few years and today.

I was most definitely telling it like it was and not how I wanted it to be, to be seen as a shining star in the dim vacuum of space that was my heart. He would interject sporadically and two hours later called our session to a halt, as it was nearing 11 o'clock.

But there was one thing I kept to myself: that Danny had told me, the fact that I had another sibling. I needed to figure out what it meant before I attempted to explain it to someone else.

He didn't pronounce me cured, nor did he want to have me committed. Instead, he asked me to meet with him next week. I agreed to a set time and day and was on my not-so-merry way.

And that way was a two-mile trek home, just me and my feet, without my usual musical accompaniment, except for the dysfunctional jukebox in my head, and my mental finger pushed the D2 button, flooding my head with music.

But I was feeling like the living embodiment for the lyrics to Whitesnake's "Here I Go," as I too was going down the only road I'd ever known. And until recently, it had been alone. But this wasn't the case anymore, I had people I could count on and trust. Something I thought was forever broken. I wasn't sure how to give them the details of all that had transpired; either as a group or solo. The former seemed a better choice than relaying the story three times over.

Hell, I didn't know how to process the information myself.

Now all I needed to distract my mind was to find a Jaguar to straddle with a nearby fog machine adding a misty effect to my video and I was all set. Eat your heart out, Tawny Kitaen; there's a new sheriff in town! I almost laughed but did not. And I was right back in the moment of moving my feet in a forward motion, trudging into an unknown future.

I walked up Santa Fe Drive and the evening felt unnaturally quiet. A slight wind pressed at my back, pushing me forward. Off to my left, like a monolith to my failures, was San Dieguito High. It loomed there, as spooky in the dark as a gothic castle in a Universal Studios monster picture. The place where the torch wielding villagers had dwelled, pushing me to come out. I heard ghostly echoes of my contemporaries between classes, laughing, almost mocking me. Well, from past experiences there among the student body, most assuredly mocking me.

But I had taken a stand there and had made peace with who I was. And those ghosts couldn't haunt me anymore. Could they?

But now I had a new fleet of phantoms tearing me up inside.

I suppose I could have called Michael or Derek to ask for a ride home. But then I'd have to rehash all that had gone down tonight. I remembered there was a payphone at school and debated calling either one for a ride home. And since it was Saturday night, they were with Nina at *The Rocky Horror Picture Show* at the La Paloma Theatre, where I had wanted to walk out during the rain scene during a viewing where I was extremely intoxicated, imagining the water from the squirt guns was the patrons spitting on me. Sticking around seemed to be something of a problem for me.

"*No shit, Sherlock*!"

All of this had come from some deep seated need to grow up faster than I was ready to do, but I was willing to go through it to find out what it meant to grow up. And I still didn't have a fucking clue.

"They wanted charade," I said this aloud, just as Danny had mere hours ago.

And exactly who were "they"? Did "they" want to play a party game? It didn't make sense at all, and I was feeling mentally spent with no logical withdrawals to be had. It could have just been some jibber jabber nonsense, due to his being clobbered by the car.

As I was trying to remember anything about its make and model, coming up with a blank, lost in reverie, I may have noticed the car that was behind me. The same one that had plowed into Danny. It was driving slowly, lights off, edging up to where I was walking slowly, a predator hunting its prey.

Suddenly I was bathed in bright light, otherworldly and all-encompassing, casting an elongated shadow of myself that turned around in tandem when I did. I held my right hand up to block the glare which was blinding me. The car merely idled, visions of Stephen King's *Christine* danced through my head. The vehicle didn't rev its engines, nor peel out to run me down, pulling off the main road into the dirt, staying still. And just as I began to think there was indeed no one driving the car, that it was a spectral mode of transportation, the door swung open slowly and one foot touched the ground, followed by a second.

My gaze followed the shoes, up to the legs, the extended belly, until it caught sight of the glasses and mustache. Christ on a cracker! It was Nick! I felt my heart stop beating, while my brain was still functioning, urging my feet to run. But they were not complying whatsoever. For the second time in as many years, it was time to make a stand in this location.

I needed to play it cool, like I didn't see the big dent on the hood, or what appeared to be rust running up it. How the fuck did I not recognize this land yacht plowing into Danny? I vowed to remain calm.

I may have pulled that off like a master thespian if I hadn't seen the gun in his hand.

"Get into the car, Henry." Nick practically growled.

I had two choices; I could test the theory of Superman being faster than a speeding bullet or I could do as I was told. It clicked in the back of my mind that Nick may just know something about "they" and "charade."

I quickly affected my best hangdog expression, even going as far as to kick a bit of gravel underneath my feet, all but defeated. It wasn't 1.21 gigawatts, but hopefully my performance convinced Nick that he was transported back three years ago from the present.

Although my feet were moving towards him, they were resolutely standing still in 1988 and I'd be damned if someone was going to drag me back to being the person I once was in 1985, the same year *Back to the Future* was released. I mean it wasn't like someone was pointing a gun to my head in making me go ahead with this on-the-Marty McFly plan to extract information from him.

Oh wait.

Nick pointed the gun as a directional device, which saw me scoot me into the seat. In the time it took him to get his ample portions into the car, I could have easily wrestled the gun out of his hands. I wanted to think Nick wouldn't hurt me; he had acted as a sort of protector in LA. But I was sitting in the exact vehicle that he had used to kill Danny.

I wanted to break down and sob, but that would be so 1985 of me. I decided pleasantries and directness would make for strange bedfellows that may I heard the voice of Jim Backus as Thurston Howell, III on *Gilligan's Island*, as he informed me to "Keep a stiff upper lip, old chap."

"And what brings you to town, Nick? What's up with the gun?"

He just stared at me, an incredulous look on his face, somewhere between remorse and lust, eerily lit by the glow of the dashboard. He was reserving his right to remain silent, looking down at the gun, seeming as if he was having a telepathic conversation with it, furrowing his brow, looking away from it, breathing a heavy sigh.

Perhaps Nick wasn't going to be the fount of information I hoped he was going to be, and now I was stuck in the car with him and his Colt 45, and although it wasn't of the beer variety, I detected alcohol on his breath.

His shaky left hand reached into his pocket for a pack of cigarettes. He came up empty for a lighter and then patted down the car seat. Sighing, he opened the car's ashtray, finding a matchbook among the discarded cancer sticks.

He lit the cigarette and placed the matchbook on the seat. The streetlight outside caught it in its watchful view, illuminating the venue he had gotten it from, a little place he had visited in Los Angeles, a little place called Charade.

Although I was more of an UNO aficionado, I did my best to keep a poker face. The car was diffused in tendrils of smoke, reaching out and wrapping themselves around my face. I tried to keep my eyes from looking too long at the innocuous-looking black matchbook with the blood-red lettering and Mardi Gras mask logo. There was no address on the front, not particularly good advertising there. But I now had a bead on part of the puzzle, the where of it - now it boiled down to whom, or rather, who "they" were.

"Can I have one of those?" I asked.

"Sure thing kid," he answered in a monotone fashion, lighting one from his cigarette, something that always appeared as sexy in classic movies. But Derek had informed me the terminology for what he'd done was called "a monkey fuck."

I wasn't a seasoned smoker, but I managed not to cough, hoping this spark of commonality might keep him from hurting me.

He turned on the radio and the George Michael and Aretha Franklin duet "I Knew You Were Waiting (For Me)" came on mid-song. It sounded like a comment on our meeting. My mind drifted back to Danny's story of how Nick wanted me to be the new Corey, and I was trying to figure out how to use that information.

"I need your help," he blurted out. "I'm in some trouble."

Sure, let me help the man who had just killed Danny in the frigid waters of murder, with glaciers clogging his veins. Not to mention the fact that he had, ahem, been keeping a watchful eye on me. Oh, and let's not forget that he had nearly murdered my half-brother.

Where can I sign up? I just sat in stunned silence.

The song rotation switched into Rick Astley's "Never Gonna Give You Up." Damn, was B100 taking song requests from stalkers tonight or what? All they needed next was Animotion's "Obsession."

As it was, the next song was "(I Just) Died in Your Arms" by Cutting Crew and I knew I would never hear this song the same way again. And that was because of Nick.

I wanted to have him drive to Doreen's house, knock on the door, and fess up to the fact that it had been his fault and not mine. But what did it matter? Danny was gone and never coming back. I would never know what could have been with us, only what it had been and could never be again.

Nick snapped off the radio, awaiting an answer.

"Does the trouble have anything to do with that gun?" I queried. "Can you please put it away?"

He answered by tightening his grip on its handle. Jesus, I had even added a please in there for good measure. Rude!

"Alright," I said resolutely. "What do you need me to do?"

And what he wanted me to do was to impersonate my half-brother, as he had been questioned about his disappearance. Granted, the disappearance happened a few years back, but it was only last week that Danny had finally gotten up the nerve to place that call to the police.

I was going on that assumption, as it made sense of the senseless violence that Danny had faced at hands, or wheels rather, of Nick's hit-and-run.

I was to go to Los Angeles, march myself into the police station with the ID Nick had faked and tell them that I, err, Corey was just fine and or dandy. Nothing to see here. Just the ghost of my doppelganger, a person left to rot in the ground, in a duffel bag for the worms to fight over. A person, who, until a few hours ago, was just a name and face to me - and now my half-brother. And the man next to me who believed that he'd had gotten away with killing him.

The man to my left that was still holding the gun, who fired off a name I was happy to never hear again.

"None of this would be happening if I'd never met George," he said assertively, as if saying it could make it true somehow. "And now they are in control of everything and he's on life support. I'd like to be there when they decide to finally pull the plug."

I knew the only way to get out of this was to play along and try to ferret out the information I still needed to find out regarding "they." A plan was starting to form, the basis was born from how cozy Nick and I once were, biblically speaking.

Hell, it was based on how I used to be in general in using my sexual wiles to get what I wanted. Now, it was something that Nick wouldn't even have clue one about regarding my true intent. But I knew. I knew what a sick man he was, and I felt the anger welling up in me, ready to burst forth in an angry spray of verbal gun fire.

"OK, I'll do it," I muttered, wanting to scream it in his fat fucking face.

"Good," he said, and I expected Nick to rub his murderous hands together. "Most excellent. I am also going to need you to stay with me for a while."

"I'll do it," I said again in a straightforward manner, before adding an addendum. "But there's something I want to do before we leave town."

"And what would that be?" The annoyance was clearly evident in his voice.

"Let's go watch the sunrise at my favorite spot," I added with a cooing inflection. Unlike how I enjoyed my waffles with every square saturated with syrup; I tried not to pour it on too thick.

He pondered it, looking at my face for any tell-tale signs of deception. Like one of my drawings at inception, I was a blank canvas.

"Is it far from here?"

"No, it's only about a 15-minute drive," I said. "It's the Torrey Pines Glider Port."

We soon arrived at the entrance to what I had considered my little slice of paradise. I figured I could somehow make an escape down the hill and Nick would be unable to follow me. All I had to do was get that damn gun away from him. I had a few hours to do so, but the clicking of a clock was ticking away in my mind. Just like Genesis had sung about an "Invisible Touch," the night reached out with its dark grasp, slices of the bumpy parking lot irradiated by the Cadillac's headlights.

"Drive over to the right," I instructed, being the seasoned pro and all.

He pulled into a spot nearest the beginning of the downward slope of the slightly treacherous cliff leading down to the beach.

"Can I have another cigarette?" I asked, making sure my hand was steady taking it from him.

He shut the car off, the ticking of the cooling engine marking time with the hidden clock in my head. He turned the key forward, so we could listen to the radio. I felt as though I should give a subtle cue that may remind him of Danny, making him confess to me. This was the plan, to take him to this isolated locale and make him sing like a bird, before he kidnaped me, returning to Los Angeles. All so he wouldn't be locked up in a cage.

I switched the station from B100 to 91X, hoping that change may trigger something in Nick. Granted, I had no idea if he knew the type of music Danny had listened to, but it was worth a shot. And World Party was summing up my very thoughts that he and the other people I had encountered in LA – except for Candy and Angel – had been steering their "Ship of Fools" right into a rocky shore. As I stared out into the darkness, the cherry of the cigarette lit my face in a fiery hue.

I looked over at Nick, trying to gauge a reaction. He was sitting still, his blank face revealing nothing. I was scared to think about what might be going on in his mind, a slight shiver ran down my spine.

"You cold, kid?" Nick inquired.

In response, I slid closer to him and gave him a kiss. I didn't want to resort to this, but a seed of an idea was germinating in my brain.

"Wanna warm me up?" I asked innocently.

He looked perplexed for a nanosecond before he was all over me like the proverbial cheap suit. I held the cigarette off to my right, letting it smolder, just as my feelings for Nick had been snuffed out.

As he moved towards me, the gun slid along the seat until it was poking me in the thigh. At least, I thought it was the gun. I reached down innocuously and touched the cool tip of the barrel, gently caressing it as Nick was doing the opposite to me. Inch by inch, I brought the gun closer, and soon enough, it was there in my hand.

Nick was done assaulting my neck with his tongue and looked up with eager eyes as he started heading south. I took a huge drag off the cigarette and plunged its cherry into his neck.

He yowled like a kicked dog. I pushed him off me and pointed the gun at him. I was hellbent to make things right. For myself. For Corey. For Danny.

"Get out of the car, Nick." He was out the door in no time flat. If I had been staring into a mirror, the person staring back would have been a stranger, devoid of emotion, some unearthly creature hell bent on an eye for an eye.

I followed suit, emerging from the car, channeling Arnold Schwarzenegger as *The Terminator*. I thought I was hearing the ocean roar, but it was the sound of blood rushing like an unbridled torrent in my ears.

Nick backed away from me. As I made my way around his car, he tripped on one of the many fissures running along the expanse of the Torrey Pines Glider Port. My natural instinct was to ask if he was all right, but frankly my dear, I did not give a fuck. He scuttled like a crab away from me.

"You're going to answer a few questions," I said. I cocked back the trigger to add an exclamation point to my statement.

He just nodded up and down, his head taking on a bobblehead quality, as if to say, "I'll tell you anything!"

"What is Charade?"

"How do you know about that?" He lobbied back.

I released the trigger, and the bullet slammed into the earth a foot from him.

"I'm asking the questions here, Nick."

"George owns it and Troy runs it."

"AND?" I roared.

"He's using it as a drug front," he said. "And he's up to his father's old tricks."

Nick laid out the story of how he had moved away from Los Angeles, hoping for a fresh start in Phoenix. Apparently that clean slate was born from old habits that would die hard. He had picked up a 16-year-old street hustler and taken him back to his apartment.

More than likely, a whole new batch of wicker furniture was purchased for this place. He didn't include that detail in his story, so I filled in that blank myself. I really wanted to laugh at that visual, but it would go against my tough exterior that was riddled with the church giggles on the interior.

He continued his tale and I let him talk, although I wasn't sure how germane it was to what I needed to find out.

"I fell asleep, and the little bastard rifled through my pockets, stole four hundred dollars out of my wallet and took my car keys," he said, anger evident in his voice. "The next thing I knew, the cops were banging at my door. The kid smashed into cars in the parking lot of my apartment building."

He was pointing in the direction of the Caddy, as if I could not put two and two together.

"When my neighbors came out to see what the noise was, he told them he was going to get his Dad and took off.

"The cops began nosing into me too much, so I went back to LA, and had to deal with more cops asking questions. If I ever get my hands on that little bastard…"

"Let me guess, he was blond? About my height?" I asked, even though I knew the answer. "You have a real thing for blonds. Me, Troy…Adam."

I watched his face for any recognition, hoping that using Corey's real name would illicit any reaction, then I decided to force his hand.

"Well, that kid was lucky he didn't end up in a duffel bag. Like Adam did."

His face went slack, as though he was having a stroke and for all I knew, he was. And that was his problem for all I cared. Oh wait, I didn't. I moved in closer, so that he could glean how much disgust I had for him.

His eyes were filling up with water and his chin began to quiver. A slight feeling of pity entered and left the building of my mind in a flash. I needed to board up my heart and declare the area unsafe. But as was the case for me all my life, there were cracks in the foundation.

My mind was engaging in a tug of war, on each side was Nick and he was getting pulled back and forth between the man who had helped me three years ago and the Nick who had killed Danny.

"Godammit!" I shouted to the sky.

It was all too much, this day, this night, this life. Even though it was clear as a bell outside, a lightning bolt blinded my vision, followed by a clap of thunder echoing in my mind. I was the problem because I didn't know what the fuck I was going to do. What I wasn't going to do was sink to levels that would make it all but impossible for me to slink out of the primordial ooze of hatred.

I supposed it was natural to hate Nick, to make him suffer, but I could never take someone's life.

Just as I was about to let him off the hook, he took off in a run towards the cliffs.

"Nick! Stop!" I did not say this in some off-shoot fashion of Schwarzenegger, Eastwood, or Stallone, it was in my own voice; a voice I was still finding.

I could see him running for his life, certain I was going take the coward's route and shoot him in the back. I looked at the gun in disgust and threw it to the ground. Unfortunately, I didn't put the safety on, and it went off.

I saw Nick's shadowy figure one minute and the next it was gone, an apparition that made me wonder if he was even there at all. I ran towards the cliff, calling out his name, tripping in a fissure, practically landing face first in the dirt. Much like I had done for my entire life, I picked myself up and dusted myself off.

Nick was nowhere to be seen and it began to feel fruitless to continue calling out a name that may belong to a dead man. I couldn't tell if his body was lying lifeless on the beach. Everything was blurry, due to tears. I had felt so devoid of feeling until today, but I wasn't sure that this was the way I wanted them to be brought on. I was instrumental in the death of this man, whether I had a moment of clarity before I may have just shot him point blank; I was guilty, nonetheless.

There was no rush of redemption for what Nick had done to Danny; justification and rationalization were nowhere to be found. There was only me, kneeling underneath the full moon, and although I was illuminated, I was entirely in the dark about what to do next. I decided the best route to take was to leave the keys in Nick's car in the parking lot, to make it seem as though he had gone for an early-morning swim.

I contemplated an anonymous call to the police about an abandoned car at the Torrey Pines Glider Port parking lot, but quickly figured it may only arouse suspicion. I began wiping my fingerprints from the interior of the car and I grabbed the keys out of the ignition and put them in my pocket.

I retraced my steps and found the gun, picking it up between my thumb and index finger, taking it back to the car as if it had stunk to high heaven. In a sense, it reeked of deception and death, and I didn't want that foul odor anywhere near me again.

But this would not be the case. I couldn't let anyone, innocent or not, suffer under the oppressive thumb of what King George had created and what Troy was now carrying on with, an heir to the throne of flesh and ruination for personal gain.

I reached the car again, fumbling for the keys while trying to balance the gun. Not wanting another shot in the dark type of situation, I gently placed it on the ground and opened the trunk, I was expecting to have a Geraldo Rivera "The Mystery of Al Capone's Vault" moment of there being nothing to see.

However, what I saw took my breath away.

There was a duffel bag, and I could only assume that it had once held the thought-to-be corpse of my half-brother. It looked to be full, and I hoped that it wasn't another victim inside.

Poking it with a finger, nothing registered of there being anything resembling flesh and bone in it. I breathed a heavy sigh of relief. Then I gathered up the courage to unzip it. I found a roll of duct tape and zip ties, coupled with a sense of déjà vu. Among the other items were recent Polaroids of myself and my house.

And then I uncovered my long-missing underwear, hiding a tape recorder and an assortment of cassette tapes, some of them still in their wrappers and none of which were labeled as mixtapes.

There were also some rolled up objects that appeared to be blueprints and I suspected that they weren't for something that Mr. Brady had designed as an architect. Sitting between them were a bottle of poppers, a package of Benadryl and a jar of Vaseline. A pen and its mate, a notepad. Next to those were a bundle of envelopes rubber-banded together, with a return address in London.

I was filled with dread and fascination as I peered into this makeshift shrine that someone could go to this extent to have me in his life.

"Cheese and rice!" I exclaimed.

Just then, Nick's meaty paw clamped down on my mouth.

I bit it as viciously as I could, and he let out a guttural yowling sound. He released me and I instantaneously knew I needed to get the gun before he did. I wasn't even sure if he had seen it at all. But I couldn't afford to take that chance. I had seen enough *Friday the 13th* movies to know that it was kill or be killed, as there was no reasoning with someone with bloodlust in their heart and hate in their eyes.

I reached the gun, with Nick right on my tail, and swung around and clicked the hammer back and then moved it back into position. I was no killer. But as I struck him with the barrel of the gun in the temple, I realized that I could most definitely cold cock someone in self-defense. No fuss, no muss. He went down like a 250-pound sack of potatoes, and I was surprised additional fissures weren't added to the Glider Port from his impact. He stayed motionless. Breaking the final girl rule of not going near the body, I put two fingers around his neck and found a pulse. Now what was I supposed to do with him?

Rather than try to lug him back to the car, I circumvented my usual ass backwards train of thought, backing the car up to where he was and hauled his ample ass up into the passenger seat. Grabbing two zip ties from his kidnapper kit, I pulled his hands behind his back, repeating the motions to his ankles, so that he ended up looking like a pig ready for roasting. All he needed was an apple in his mouth. Feeling inspired, I took one of my missing pairs of underwear and put it in that orifice.

Next, I retrieved the tape recorder, unwrapped a virgin cassette, then grabbed the pen and notebook. I awakened him with the amber bottle of poppers underneath his nose. He awoke after a moment disoriented and a tad horny, looking around in confusion, trying to move his hindered extremities and began shouting. The sound was muffled by my tighty-whities.

"Now, now Nick," I said soothingly. "It's not going to do you any good to make a scene. Especially when I'm the only one here to see it. The good news is that you are now in the position to do me a favor."

He stopped thrashing and shouting, bug eyes staring. All I could think of was David Hedison and Patricia Owens in the original version of *The Fly*. He was seeing things in multiples, as Hedison's insect scientist had, but rather than seeing Owens screaming, I remained the face of calm. Blasé to it all on the surface, but my knotted stomach begged to differ.

I immediately thought of my mother, all alone in a hospital room. She had been the one to who introduced that classic to me. And when the new one came out on VHS, I thought I would return the favor and rent it. Unfortunately, we were eating her famous Chicken Cacciatore, and the scene where the baboon is split apart by Jeff Goldblum's teleporting machine ended that viewing for her. Ok, now where was I? Oh yes, Nick.

I asked Nick if he would behave. He nodded. I removed my underwear from his mouth.

"Now, tell me about your little kit in the trunk. I'm also curious about those blueprints."

"Floor plans for Charade," he answered tersely.

"Go on; don't be stingy with details."

"Well, I was planning on taking it over," he confessed. "I should be running that place, not Troy. George promised it to me long ago and then must have changed his mind after Corey…"

"Oh, you mean Adam, my half-brother?"

His mouth dropped open, then closed, then opened again.

"Close your mouth, you don't want to attract flies now, do ya? Yes, my half-brother. Didn't you ever find it strange that he and I looked so much alike? It makes just boatloads of sense that you fixated on me, just like you did with him. I guess you figured you had killed one, so why not kidnap the other?"

"How do you…" He said and gulped at the same time.

"Well, you can thank Danny, another one of your victims, for that bit of pertinent info." I was trying not to tear up, so as not to rust my steely façade.

"I didn't do it," he said. "I swear!"

"I think the dent on your hood says otherwise, chief. Or did you mean Corey? Of course, you did. Now here's the corker. He didn't die. He is still out there somewhere, maybe he's even out there in the dark spying on you right now."

He peered out the window, the dashboard lights illuminating his face like a campfire for this spooky story he'd just been told.

"You want to take over George's little hobby, eh? Let me guess; Troy would have a nasty accident?"

"Well, no. It's not really Troy I'm after."

"Go on, spill it."

"Let's just say that every King needs a Queen," He let the statement hang there.

"And?" I didn't want him to start getting the better of me.

"And Ellen Niles is the Queen of Charade."

He laid out the story of how George had given in to his ex-wife's complaints that he was living in the lap of luxury, while she had to toil away in retail to put food on the table for his son. He relented, upping her alimony, and cutting her in on the profits from the club and its extracurricular activities. She must have thought that his apartment's nickname of the palace really lived it to its moniker. Well, it was just one of George's real estate holdings within the city of Los Angeles and he had others elsewhere.

"I need to get that bitch out before I can even focus on Troy," he spat out. "He's next in line in George's will. I'm just some kind of afterthought. And after all I did for him!"

"Yeah, it's a regular love story for the ages," I said sarcastically. "What's the problem with getting her out? Afraid she has another frying pan?"

"She's a shifty type; all the money has gone right to her head! And it should be my money, not hers!" He was sounding like Veruca Salt before I cut him off.

"What were you planning on doing?"

He stared out the passenger window, looking for Corey/Adam approaching, wearing a hockey mask and carrying a machete.

To paraphrase a popular song of the day, he didn't need no water, he wanted to let it burn. Burn. Motherfucker. Burn. While it wasn't going to be the roof that was on fire, Nick detailed how he had stowed explosives in the boiler room at Charade, connected to a timer, and a bang. He would eradicate both who stood in the way of him collecting what he felt was owed to him on this coming Saturday.

Of course, if other people were injured or killed in the process, it didn't matter to him whatsoever. I could detect a blankness, the place where emotion should be, behind his eyes.

Despite the fortuitous nature of what he told me; it meant there was even more for me to process, I had a new wrinkle to iron out in the dirty laundry of Nick's tale.

I pulled two Benadryl from their packet.

"You're gonna take two of these and don't call me in the morning," I said.

He looked leery but did as instructed, choking on them without water.

"Now, you're going to write a little To Whom It May Concern note."

Soon Nick was snoring in the passenger seat, as I piloted the vehicle towards Encinitas as the sun was coming up, signaling a new dawn. I parked on Via Molena, which was in proximity to AMC and the sheriff's station. I began wiping my prints from the car for a second time. I cut his wrists and ankles free, put all the items I had used to get my confession out of him, save for one.

When Nick was in the driver's seat again, I stuck the note in his shirt pocket, put the gun in his lap, and spread some Benadryl around for added effect and removed the duffel bag. But I left the zip ties, duct tape, my clothes, and the photos.

I had initially wanted to remove all evidence of myself from the scene of the crime. But, if I learned anything today, I am one hell of a great actor and could easily feign horror at the news of this from the police. Should I practice my shocked face in the mirror when I get home? Nah, it would look too rehearsed.

I walked down to Alpha Beta and sought out a pay phone, and put in an anonymous tip to the police about a man passed out behind the wheel of a parked car.

I waited for a patrol car to appear before I left Nick and the scene of his alleged crime against himself.

I lay in my bed, going over all the details that Nick had given me. I had the where, why, how, and when. I was racking my brain and it was only 7 am. Sleep was as elusive as when I was dating Tina. Hell, we had been in a full-blown committed relationship for a spell.

And now that spell was as broken as my heart. My thoughts turned to Danny. He was gone and never coming back. I was about to turn into a blubbering mess when Shadow nudged the door open.

Damn, I had forgotten to feed her. She leapt up on the bed, slobbering me with kisses.

“Ok, ok. C’mon Speck let’s go get some breakfast!” I said in my finest Pee-wee Herman voice.

As we headed downstairs, I surveyed the holes my mother had made in the wall. I needed to check on her after Shadow was satiated. I practically ran into the kitchen and got her bowl and kibble out in no time flat. She was jumping up and down, as if possessed.

“Calm down, Linda Blair, before your head does a 360-degree turn!” I said setting her bowl down; she greedily attended to its contents, finishing them in no time flat, and then immediately flipped over on her back for belly scritches, which I happily obliged. My eye fixated on the avocado green phone in the kitchen and I gave Shadow a hard pat and walked over towards it.

She repositioned herself and was living up to her name, sitting at my feet, waiting for me to take her on a walk.

I reached for the phone when it sprang to life with a ring so jarring, I thought I was going to jump out of my skin.

“Hello?” I said in my best faking staying home from school voice.

"Henry? It's Officer Diaz. Sorry to call so early. But we have a break in the case." He said with politeness mixed with urgency.

When I didn't respond, he asked if I was there. And there was the big question. I felt present and accounted for, more so than I had been in what seemed like an eternity.

"Yes, I'm here," I replied.

"Can you come down to the station?" He inquired.

"Yes, of course. I just woke up, so give me about a half hour and I'll be there." I didn't add "with bells on," although the phrase turned up in my mind's eye.

"Good enough, see you then." And then there was nothing but a dial tone.

I got the phone book out and looked up the number for the hospital and dialed. And on the third ring, a very no-nonsense, slightly harried voice answered. I told the switchboard lady I was looking for Kate Dodge. Without a word, she put me on hold and then connected me.

"Hello?" She answered with vagueness and skepticism.

"Hi Mom, it's me, Henry." I didn't know what tact to take, so I opted for 'just a regular chat between mother and son.' "How are you?"

"Oh Henry." I heard her "bubbling" and that was reassuring.

"Mom, everything is going to be fine. Better in fact!" I said this as if I believed it. The funny thing was I did. Big Ed the oppressor was out of the picture, as I could not imagine my mother taking him back.

She didn't answer with words, just sobbing. I told her to rest, and I would be by later to see her and hung up. Even though we had started forging a better relationship and she was more accepting of who I was, I was a bit unnerved when I saw the human being behind the mother figure.

She needed me and I was going to be there for her.

But right now, I needed to get my ass in the shower and head down to the police station. As the water was cascading over me, washing away the sins of yesterday down the drain; a thought struck me. What if Nick told them all about my little "we-have-ways-of-making-you-talk" experiment last night?

Well, at this point he would be better served to keep his big yapper shut and I was hoping that would be the case. However, it was my word against that of a murderer and would-be kidnapper.

I made my way out in front of the house. Two neighborhood ladies were walking by. Upon seeing me, they began whispering.

"Oh, fuck off!" I said loudly. This was just a little Peyton Place, and they were just a bunch of Harper Valley hypocrites! They scurried along before I could elaborate that sentiment vocally.

The small-minded set not realizing there were bigger problems behind the idle gossip really cheesed my whiz. Then again, the past 24 hours would be fodder for neighborhood lore for years to come. So, I guess I couldn't blame them. Just like it had been for most of my life, I only wanted people to understand. I realized that this wasn't the time to get in the middle of the street on a megaphone and chastise them. Some sort of offshoot of Sally Field as *Norma Rae*, just some pale version…Henry Dodge as *Norma Gay*.

I had to get my head in the game as I turned the scooter around in the driveway, started her up and pointed myself in the direction of the police station.

I drove with a purpose I had not felt in quite some time, what with the clock ticking away as to what was going to take place in Los Angeles. I was feeling conflicted as to how to proceed. If I were too late, lives could be lost, and I wasn't doing this to be some sort of hero. I felt a duty to be the one to stop it, to end the hateful legacy that George had created and that had spread like a cancer to others.

The seeds of a plan were planting themselves in the soil of my mind, as to how I was going to pull this off. A quote that, according to my teacher Miss Alley, inspired the book *Of Mice and Men* by John Steinbeck that I had to read for English class in 9th grade bloomed as red as a rose, all thorns.

"The best-laid plans of mice and men often go awry."

It punctured at the reverie I was in, leaving me to question if it would be my plans or those of Nick that would go amiss. This thought wrapped itself around my mind, growing to the size of Audrey II in *Little Shop of Horrors*, insisting that I feed it with my fear.

I arrived at the police station. Officer Diaz came out to greet me with a surreptitious smile. Keep your gun in your holster, there Antonio! I had more to worry about than a cop with the hots for me. It was time to mine from the talents that I had seen over the years on the silver screen. A montage of different women I admired danced behind my eyes, Meryl

Streep in *Silkwood*, Cher in *Moonstruck*, Goldie Hawn in *Protocol* and Sally Field on *Gidget*, to get this delicate ballet into motion.

"Officer Diaz," I said calmly.

"Henry, thanks for coming in." I watched him eye me up and down, leaving me unsure if it was born of concern or lust.

As I'd been doing since I was a child, my response was to simply nod. I was shell-shocked, given all that had gone around me in the past day! And now, he was going to "tell me" about this latest wrinkle involving Nick. Would pretending to faint be too, well, too gay? Would tears be enough to drown out any connection as to why Nick was discovered passed out behind the wheel of his car, an apparent suicide that didn't quite take.

Well, I could relate to that scenario a little too well. A new thought struck me with its cold open palm and at full force, minus Lisa Lisa and her Cult Jam. Nick wouldn't be here at the sheriff's substation, he would have been taken to the hospital and placed under a 72-hour hold at the psych hospital. And if he decided to turn stool pigeon, this bought me some time, so I had to make this snappy.

It would have helped if I hadn't stopped dead in my tracks when I realized that Nick was handcuffed to a hospital gurney. Antonio, strong and silent, gently grabbed my hand and enveloped it inside of the warmth of his and tilted his head. For the shortest of moments, I thought he was going to lean in to kiss me. And when he did begin to lean towards me, my mind raced with how to thoughtfully decline. But it was for naught, and I stopped the soundtrack of Debbie Harry singing "French Kissin'(In the USA)" as he whispered, "Let's go, cutie."

I sat in a chair in front of Sergeant Gaines's desk, in close enough proximity to discern he'd had something with garlic for dinner last night. Antonio detailed what they discovered in Nick's possession.

Why. I. Was. Shocked.

I'm so lucky that people can't hear what I'm thinking. But outwardly I was giving this performance the Academy Award treatment. Biting on my thumb nail, affixing what I hoped conveyed a look of abject terror on my face, and a slight rocking back and forth to my upper torso. I didn't want to over or underdo it, finding a steady middle ground was my lot in life.

"Do you know this man?" Gaines asked, holding up a Polaroid of an unconscious Nick.

"Nick?!" I said it as both a question and as a statement.

I gave them both a brief rundown of how we knew each other, giving it the three-dot version after that summer three years ago. As in, I knew him in LA…I haven't seen him since…what is he doing here...omitting any current knowledge of his whereabouts and why he might want to kidnap me.

"We have reason to believe he may have been involved with the hit-and-run accident involving Daniel Woodson," Gaines said without an ounce of emotion, an automaton that didn't give three licks for a dead gay man, a potential gay kidnappee, or the gay man who wanted to squire him away.

Meanwhile, one of his officers was holding my hand out of his sightline behind the desk. It was nice to have someone in my corner. The warmth of his meaty mitt was comforting.

I took a very deep and audible sigh, which either man could read however they wanted. Ol' Sarge Garlic Breath as "Thank goodness that didn't happen" and Antonio as "Oh yeah. He's into me!"

Whatever the case, it was just a temporary respite that I was, to quote Simple Minds, "Alive And Kicking." I could have very easily been bound and gagged in the back of Nick's car, being returned to the place I never wanted to go again, in every sense of the word. Or I could be on a slab next to Danny, lovers intertwined in the afterlife, toe tag to toe tag in the here and now.

I really should get a job creating the morbid version of a Hallmark Card.

"Well, I have a feeling that he won't be bothering you again," Gaines continued breaking the tangible silence. "He should be going away for quite a stretch. But that is where we are going to need your help, son. Are you willing to testify?"

"Fucking A I will," I said with strength and conviction. "Just tell me where and when."

A smile broke out across Gaines's face, and he nodded.

"We'll be in touch," Antonio added, and as if to emphasis the point, gave my hand a squeeze and then removed it from mine, all business as usual. "I'll walk you out."

As we stood by my scooter, Antonio's demeanor seemed to change slightly, like a light breeze on a scorching day. He looked less like a cop and more like a person. That's the funny thing about labels: we place them on ourselves without realizing that they are visible on whatever uniform we decide to wear in life and are entirely unnecessary. We are who we are.

"So, uh," he began. "I was wondering if, well, you might go to dinner with me."

I stood frozen, a queer stuck in the headlights, not so much blindsided as I was extremely frustrated at life's timing. Antonio was someone I could see going on more than a date with.

However, there was not only the fact that I had just lost Danny, but I also had a plot to foil. And with him sitting there awaiting my answer was a different kind of torture than I'd had ever known. And that was saying a lot. What was the shelf life of sorrow and grieving? Certainly, it was not less than 24 hours.

"I can't, not right now," I said, staring at something infinitely more fascinating on my scooter. "You understand, right?"

I looked up to meet what I suspected would be the hurt in his eyes. But he was gone and walking away. Well, so much for that. Ever the people pleaser, I was tempted to call out after him and say yes, even though it wasn't the right thing to do. And just like that a small bubble sprang up from the cauldron of anger. Fuck him for not understanding. He just saw me as some piece of ass.

Or he saw me as something completely different, something that I didn't see myself as yet, or perhaps never would.

And if I hadn't been zoned out and in my own head, I would have noticed that Antonio had said, "Hold that thought," as a call came in over his radio, and that is why he was off and running.

Well, I didn't have time to sit here and have this form of mental masturbation right now. I had shit to do.

I hopped on my scooter, put the keys in the ignition, and made it roar to life, more kitten than lion, but it still had the desired effect of making me feel one with the machine, like the opening strains of Depeche Mode's "Never Let Me Down Again." While just a scooter, I strangely counted L'il Red as something to depend upon, a vehicular best friend as it were, and I was going to be taking a ride with her into the unknown. For the first time, I did not want to run away like I always had before; I was running towards some pre-destined date with destiny.

A sense of purpose, and I had not always been the steadiest of acquaintances, but we were starting to become familiar with one another.

Hopefully, it would become a case of being fast friends, or at the very least, like lesbians on a first date who move in together too quickly.

Before I knew it, I was parking my scooter at the hospital in a space next to a big elm tree. Talk about being on autopilot! I turned the key off and the handlebars to the left and locked the steering, so that no one could steal my sweet, sweet ride.

A car pulling in nearby caught my attention by the sun glaring off its windshield, which nearly blinded me. When my vision came back into complete focus, I saw a familiar-looking red Mercedes and its striking driver, dressed to the nines in a red dress with black lapels, a red and black hat, and even red leather gloves on what promised to be a sweltering summer day. She did have one accessory that made it impossible for me to tell if she was looking at me, a black pair of Ray-Bans.

Deciding to fault on the side of caution, I began slinking over to the elm tree, watching her from a distance. She was fumbling with something in her purse which ended up spilling all over the asphalt, conducting herself ever the lady that she purported herself to be visually, I watched and listened as she put all the items back with nary a cuss word issued.

From my vantage point, I saw a case of one of these things is not like the others, one of these things just doesn't belong. A hypodermic needle didn't seem like something that this well-to-do woman would be carrying in her purse. She calmly put it in her pocketbook with the reversed and interlocking Cs on its clasp, and the two remaining items left were a pack of Nat Sherman cigarettes and a gold lighter with a visible design. It was a black spider with a red hourglass. I was done playing *Win, Lose or Draw* sans host Bert Convy. I knew who this mystery woman was. Why, it had to be none other than Ellen Niles!

I watched her making her way into the hospital after lighting a cigarette, the sliding doors closing behind her, cutting the exhaled smoke in half where it lingered for a moment and disappeared, a ghostly apparition that could only be the harbinger of Nick's doom.

I hung back for a moment to collect my thoughts and formulate some sort of scheme that could give me the clarity of what in the actual fuck that I was going to do next.

Well, I was here to see my mother. Who said that it had to be Kate Dodge?

I strode to the hospital with a confidence that I did not know I had when a pebble in my shoe entered my train of thought. What if the nurse who was there last night is still on duty? Surely, someone being accused of killing a grieving mother's son doesn't happen all the time, which would make my face familiar and not in a good way.

And just like that, the jig would be up, and I'd have to figure out another way to track Ellen Niles aside from following her smoke signals. Leave it to me to make a pebble into a boulder, always gaining momentum by being pushed down that hill by doubt.

Happily, a new nurse was on duty. An older red-haired nurse who resembled Bobbie Spencer of *General Hospital*. She looked up from her crossword puzzle, having been interrupted on a 9-letter across for being deceitful in speech or conduct for the second time in less than five minutes. A sigh escaped before she changed her tone and greeted me with a "Help you, hon?"

"I'm here with my mother," I lied. "She came in a minute ago. Did you see her?"

She checked her registry and looked at me as I plastered a saccharine smile on my mug.

"Yes, sweetie. She went to Room 222," She leaned forward and then said in a conspirator's tone, "Sure hope your Dad will be better. Go straight down the hall and take your first right. You cannot miss it."

"Oh yes, we were quite a happy family," was what I hoped my nod conveyed.

But something was troubling me on the inside…

Given my own visit to this hospital after my suicide attempt, I knew that they would have taken Nick to San Luis Rey on a 72-hour hold, as he was a harm to himself and most definitely to others. At least that's what I shared in the note I had him write, which included his confession to killing Danny. Maybe they were going to take him off to jail when he was cognizant enough to know what I had done to him, what he had done to himself, really.

I found a police officer sitting on a folding chair outside of Room 222. Well, wasn't this a little bit of fuckery? He was reading Stephen King's *It*, and I literally knew it chapter and verse, having devoured its content as surely as Pennywise the Dancing Clown had fed upon children. I began to make my approach, the hollow sound of my tennis shoes reverberated off the linoleum. The door to the room was closed, and the young officer was engrossed in the doings in Derry, Maine.

"We all float down here," I said in a creepy voice. "You'll float, too."

The officer sat straight up in his chair, and reactively, his hand went to his holster, and he stopped himself shy of pulling his gun out.

"Sorry, sorry," I said in quick succession of each other. "That's my favorite Stephen King book." He didn't reply, as he was catching his breath, so I went the direct route. "Did my Mom go in there?"

He gulped visibly and gave me the shittiest of looks, figuring I was some trust fund brat whose Dad was in hot water for insider trading or something. It did not seem that he truly knew what was going on and was what was known affectionately known as "being wet behind the ears."

"I'll just let them have a minute together," I said, and then Deputy Dipshit shrugged and went back to reading.

I was about to go to the pay phone to call Antonio for help. But the longer I waited, the greater the chance of Ellen pulling out that hypodermic needle and jabbing it into any number of fleshy parts on Nick.

I spun around just as Ellen emerged, purse tucked snugly against her tall frame as if she were protecting it. She was, as it could be, holding a murder weapon. We locked eyes, well, I assumed we did, as she was still wearing those damn Ray-Bans. But the cocking of her head told me a few things. One was that she was looking at me, and two was she had some sort of recognition upon doing so. I wanted to break eye, or sunglasses, contact with her, but there was something both mesmerizing and frightening about her.

Then a sly smile crossed her face, and she made a self-assured exit, lighting another cigarette and not giving any form of fucks as she strode down the hall.

I was half-tempted to run after her, tackling her from behind while yelling for Deputy Dipshit to call for backup. But she and I would be seeing each other soon enough, whether she knew it or not. My suspicion was that she did not know about the powder keg that was ready to go bang, bang, bang, bang at Charade.

And if she had put Nick down, for lack of a better term, and had he not confessed his plan to me like a Bond villain who thought 007 wouldn't get out of his nefarious trap, then the circumstances may have been different. As it stood, and to quote the worst theme song in the series; the building and innocent people would be at an "All Time High," as far as being above the skyline of Los Angeles went.

And I didn't have anyone with a sexual moniker to help me foil that plot, like a Rod Cocksure or Danny's old porn name Miles O'Toole. The grieving process immediately went to anger, directed at Nick, and suddenly, I did not care if he was taking his last breaths.

For all I cared, he could be turning blue, eyes rolling up into the back of his head, ready to see nothing but darkness evermore. But I had to know. And I hated myself for not being the uncaring and heartless bitch who lived inside me sometimes. Still, it didn't mean I was going to help him.

Deputy Dipshit ushered me into the room with a swift motion of his left hand, not knowing who was really entering the room. Or who had exited the room, as the window was open, and a gentle summer breeze was blowing the curtains forward, expecting Michael Myers to be standing on the lawn, staring at me from behind his blank mask.

I rushed to the first-floor window to see if Nick had landed with a splat lying in the bushes with his limbs askew. Alas, it turned out that would be a hard no. He was being hoisted up and dragged away by someone familiar. It was Jeff, my old drug dealer.

I made great concessions to not be seen by him as he attempted to make what he was doing not look like a kidnapping. It looked like last call with your handsy Uncle, who had been overserved while wearing a hospital gown. Nothing out of the ordinary there. And who better to help with this situation than his friend in the red Mercedes to take Nick for a joyless ride.

Ellen was pulling the car up to where staggering Nick and struggling Jeff were, when I realized something. I could not walk back out the door, even if Deputy Dipshit wasn't the best and brightest law enforcement had to offer, he was still 5-0. So, this also meant the reason I had come here, to visit my mother, would be a wash.

A kernel of anger exploded in my brain, and like popcorn being heated by a nuclear bomb, I latched onto that feeling in a symbiotic fashion. I let that anger propel me out of the window with the precision that Lee Majors displayed as stuntman Colt Seavers on *The Fall Guy*. Alright, truth be told, it was more on par with a cautious leap that either Cagney and or Lacey would have taken, but as George Michael sang on my current cassette obsession, "*You gotta have Faith.*"

I stood up straight, well as straight as I could. I still had to stay unobtrusive to Jeff and Ellen. They were betting that with Nick out of the way, there would be no correlation between him and them. There was something more at stake here than real estate holdings and who was favored by King George.

And there was the Jeff connection that I didn't have time to dissect like a bug held in place by pins at this moment. I found a tree to hide behind while watching Jeff put Nick into the passenger seat and place the seat belt across his ample portions.

Buckle up or you fuckle up, the made-up PSA in my mind shouted.

Jeff closed the door, and Ellen sped off. Then he walked over to Danny's old microbus.

I was expecting him to get in on the passenger side, as Danny's always tan arm emerged, and its hand motioned for me to join them from the driver's side window.

You'll float, too, Henry, you'll float too!

As it was, I slid down the bark of the tree until my butt was firmly on the ground. I needed to feel something solid, as all of this was beginning to feel like something out of a dream. I readied myself for the roots of the tree to emerge from their subterranean confines and wrap themselves around me, pulling me into the earth. At this juncture, I was more subscribed to let that happen and to not get involved any further. But I couldn't let these people ruin the lives of others.

To quote Nu Shooz, "*I'm at the Point of No Return*."

So it was up off my ass, standing on two legs, crossed the parking lot to my scooter in seconds flat. There was still time to see where the Queen of the Niles was heading. I gunned L'il Red and sped off towards Encinitas Boulevard, as Ellen had to be heading towards 5 North. Sure enough, I saw her merge onto the freeway, flicking a cigarette out of the window. Since her vehicle had more horsepower than mine, I could just follow a trail of discarded cigarettes in some twisted variation of the breadcrumbs in *Hansel and Gretel*.

I knew where this witch's lair was already and the dangers that were inherent within its walls. What was I going to do? Play chicken with her on the freeway? Yeah, that didn't seem like the most solid of plans. However, I could further my burgeoning detective skills here by paying a visit to Jeff and seeing how he figured into all of this.

First, I had some loose ends to tie up before I went off to thwart an explosive situation.

I hung up the phone, surprised by what I had just accomplished. I had convinced Grandmother Christine to be with her daughter duringher time of need. She had always been something of an enigma to me, who lived back East, hated my father, and was still disappointed in her daughter's poor choice of spouse all these years later. Therefore, I had only seen her a handful of times in my short lifetime.

Something in her voice changed, as if she were trying on the fit of what it meant to be maternal when I asked for her help. I didn't want my mother to be alone in case things kept me away longer than anticipated. And she agreed to get on a flight and come to sunny SoCal, not to enjoy the beaches and sunshine, but to help her child in her darkest hour. I was to call her back in an hour to get the flight details.

The next dialing of the blue princess phone in my room that was fit for a queen, really, went to Nina to see if she could take Shadow on for a few days, if necessary. I didn't want Grandmother to have to be saddled with a dog on top of an on-the-mend daughter. Besides, I figured two bitches under one roof might make for less rest for my mother.

As it was, I could most assuredly predict more accurately than Dionne Warwick and her Psychic Friends Network that my mother was going to be none too pleased that her own mother was coming for an indefinite stay.

"This is Nina," the voice on the other end informed me as if I didn't know who I had just called. "Talk to me."

"Hey girl, it's Henry," I responded in kind to her non-demand.

"What's up, boooooyyyyyyyy?" She said in her best Beastie Boys voice.

Despite myself, I laughed, and it felt good to release some tension as I was wound tighter than a marching band worth of drums.

"I have a favor to ask," I said, mindful to keep the conversation light and not to tip my hat in telling her the whole story. "I need to get out of town for a few days. Too much has happened, and I need to sort it out."

As I spoke these words, I realized that she had no idea of what had happened at all, so I gave Nina a rushed and abridged story about Danny, Mom, Nick and Ellen Niles.

"Holy shitbuckets!" she yelled when I finished. "Oh my God, of course, I'll take her."

"Thanks girl, I owe you one," I replied. "I'll call you when I'm ret to go."

I figured I didn't need to call my other friends; Nina would spread the word. I felt momentarily guilty for not letting these people I considered the best friends I'd ever had in, but they would want to help me stop this plot. And I couldn't risk anyone getting hurt on my account, especially since I could call the police in Los Angeles and put a quick stop to what was going to go down, or rather, what could go up.

As the poster for *Jaws: The Revenge* had informed me: "This time it's personal."

This mission was for Danny, Adam, and the countless others who had tasted the brand of poison served up by King George. It was time for this monarchy to be thrown out of the palace.

The next call was to Mom; I had to deliver the bombshell that good 'Ol Christine was coming. Clearly, she was going to think that I was insane.

"Are you insane!?" she practically shouted, although it came out more like a very harsh whisper. "I cannot have her here. What were you thinking, Henry? Call her and tell her not to come."

"Too late Mom," I said, standing my ground and wouldn't let my footing slip into quicksand. "She will be here tomorrow. There's something that I need to do, and I don't want you by yourself."

"Well, sitting in a room with that woman is pretty much the same thing," she muttered and then trained her mothering skills back onto me. "Now, what exactly is it that you need to do?"

From somewhere in the back of my mind, I conjured up the smell of Tollhouse cookies, and they came wafting into the room, reaching out to get into my nostrils and up into my brain for me to tell her what, indeed, I was going to be doing. I figured the obligatory "nothing" wouldn't really cut the mustard this time. But I obviously couldn't tell her exactly what I was going to do, so I figured I would keep my story consistent.

"I need to figure some things out," I said, doing a delicate dance to spare her fragile feelings.

"Is it because of Danny?" I am so sorry you're going through this. I've known how you felt about him for a long time."

"Wait, what?" I sputtered. "You knew I was gay before I told you?"

I was waiting for her answer to be something along the lines of "Yes, I've met you," but instead, she spoke these words to me.

"Henry, you've always been so special to me. So fragile, always in your own little world." She paused. "I noticed early on that you were not like your brother and, thankfully, not like your father. I wanted to protect you so I wasn't always so supportive of your, uh, lifestyle. I just want you to be happy and never have to suffer. But that's not very realistic, is it?"

The last question could be applicable to her, as well.

"I love you, Mom."

She responded by bubbling, and the tears slid down my face in tandem. I wanted to remain strong in the face of the adversity to come, but godammit, it felt good to cry in the now. When Kate Dodge told me she also loved me with a gurgled voice, I was cooked, and we both decided it was time to hang up.

I slumped down into my beanbag, almost becoming one with the small balls of foam residing within. Fear ran through me, a live wire I gladly latched onto in times of trouble, but this time felt different. I didn't want it consuming me, drawing me into its endless maw. Instead, I did as David often said and focused on my breathing.

With each inhale and exhale, I drew myself back from the mouth of madness, or at the very least from the tonsils of troubles, knowing I had it in me to stop what Nick had started. All I had to do was check my to-do list and then leave for Los Angeles on L'il Red.

I was a cowboy on a steel horse I ride, and there was going to be a showdown with a wanted man. Hopefully, I emerged alive and not dead.

I glanced at the digital alarm clock, the one who used to mock me as night turned to dawn when Tina and I were officially a thing, deciding the time might be right to call the man who had introduced us.

I was nervous as I would have been calling up someone and asking them out on a date, given the fact that I hoped Jeff hadn't seen me earlier. But I had to find out what additional information he could give me. I stared at the poster on my wall of Sigourney Weaver in *Aliens*, holding Newt in one arm and her M41A Pulse Rifle in the other. I let my mind travel to the scene where she fights her fear by confronting the Alien Queen and cocks her head ever so slightly and then burns down the Queen's lair with a flamethrower.

I had my own evil queen to burn down. Hopefully, this flamer could vanquish a monster in human form.

The phone just rang and rang, and when his disembodied voice informed me he was unavailable to come to the phone. I decided against leaving a message. I needed the element of surprise.

Besides, this way I could concoct a solid plan for getting the info I needed out of Jeff, and I already knew his Achilles heel was located in his crotch region.

And whatever that plan was to be, I needed to figure it out in a hurry, as the fine grains of sand were collecting in the bottom of an imaginary hourglass bit by bit.

I shut my eyes for a nap before calling my grandmother again. But when I opened them again, an hour had passed, and I was nowhere nearer to a solution.

And somewhere during my slight slumber, Shadow had nuzzled her head up on my shoulder. She began licking my face upon my awakening, and something about that loving action triggered in my brain. Here was this supposed "killer breed" of dog often on the news for doing harm to humans, and yet my girl was as sweet as could be. And why was that?

Training. I had shown her love so that she knew to give it back.

Yet it was I who needed to rewire my own brain. Not a stay, sit situation, but a forward motion to carry out what needed to be done, to not be a damsel-in-distress, but the hero of the story, not reliant on anyone but myself. A rebel with a cause.

And there it was; if I had to spin the situation, it would be spun out of control in no time flat. I could not drag anyone else into this. Maybe getting info out of Jeff wasn't the solution. Neither was whoring myself out for info, even if it were in the name of truth, justice, and the American gay.

I was aware of the players, even if I wasn't entirely sure what game they were playing. It sure as hell wasn't Parcheesi! More than likely, Charade was acting as a living pop-o-matic, the dice being rolled in its confines as the players in this game moved their pegs around, hoping not to land in Trouble.

Like it or not, there was to be no help from Brother John, as I was on my own, and it felt right; I should be doing this by myself.

I called my grandmother to find out her flight details. We chatted very briefly as if making pleasantries with a stranger about the weather we were having. Instead of that steady Southern California sunshine that San Diego was famous for, there were dark skies ahead, and the promise of thunderstorms hung in the air, Cumulus clouds pregnant with damaging storm conditions.

She would take a taxi to the house, as I would be well on my way to Los Angeles. I would leave the key under the mat and write down Mom's hospital room number.

I grabbed the backpack used for Black's Beach and shoved in clothing, toiletries, and tapes to feed my Walkman's insatiable appetite. I added Big Ed's pair of binoculars, just in case. I was indeed ret to go, so I called Nina to say Shadow's food and favorite toy were in a bag in the kitchen, with the same instructions as I gave grandmother, keys were under the mat, and I'll leave a light on for you, just like Motel 6 commercials told us they'd do.

I gave Shadow a long hug and told her to be a good girl for Nina. She licked my face as if to confirm she would do my bidding.

I called work and debated telling them I had the flu but assumed word may have gotten out about what had happened on our street. So, I told Erik a version of the truth.

"A friend of mine died, and I have to go to LA for the funeral."

I headed out to the garage, brought L'il Red to life, and headed out onto the blackest and most unknown stretch of highway I had ever traversed in my life.

RETURN

The highway unfurled before me, and even though I was surrounded by cars, I felt isolated in my music and sense of purpose. Much like the last time I had struck out in search of intelligent life in Los Angeles, a series of questions nagged at me.

Would I be able to stop Nick's deadly plot? What had Ellen done to him? How could I get in undetected, given that Troy and Angel were likely going to be at Charade? And finally, the big question - what in the actual fuck was I doing?

The *Pretty in Pink* soundtrack, which was the third version I owned because the first two tapes I had of it were played so much I had to replace them due to wear and tear, was currently on "Shellshock" by New Order. Bernard Sumner was narrating my love/hate relationship with the city I had sworn off, like a lover you discover is no good for you, but you can't resist one more hop in the sack.

I had changed dramatically since the last time around, stumbling my way through what it meant to be a man. The measure of a man was marked not only by miles but by the unstoppable force of time. And I could hear the internal ticking *60 Minutes* stopwatch inside of me, saying that I was on the cusp of something more than I thought I could handle.

And there was patented Henry Dodge art of the underscore, never giving myself any sort of credit as to what I was capable of. I had my fair share of adversity over my short 19 years on Earth, and I had come through it, not necessarily unscathed, but had at least come out the other side of it. Jesus, the past 24 hours alone would have put even the strongest man to the test. And I was still taking an onward-and-upward approach to the task at hand. In part, this deadly situation was a distraction from what had gone down. If I stopped long enough to think about it, I may sink into a morass of sorrow.

Much like *The Terminator*, I needed to be singular in nature and have my eyes on the mission. And although I had vowed to do the opposite of

Arnold Schwarzenegger's signature catchphrase of "I'll be back" in relation to returning to Los Angeles, I was nearing my destination, none-the-less.

I was now on the 101, heading to West Hollywood via Santa Monica Boulevard.

As I made my exit, I pulled into a Chevron station. At first, I didn't realize I was having a case of gayja vu, and then it hit me. I had been here once before. This was the same gas station I had gussied up at before heading off to my first Gay Pride. I spied the phone booth, sitting as silently as an obelisk that marked a specific time and place in my life where I had called to check on Angel.

There was no need to make that call today, as he was doing just dandy with his involvement with both Troy and Charade.

The thought of the two of them made me grip the throttle even harder on my scooter, and my hand was already aching from keeping up my all-steam-ahead determination to get here. And now that I was here…what was the next course of action?

Well, a sloshing bladder was the first thing to be dealt with.

I went into the bathroom, expecting it to be covered in cobwebs, a haunted place with creepy crawlers. While it did house a ghost from my past, the harsh fluorescent light quickly dispelled any such dark fantasies about things that go bump in the night.

I made my way to the urinal in record time, as it felt like I was going to explode, and relished the sweet relief of dispelling liquid from my body.

As I approached the sink, I caught my reflection in the mirror and realized I wasn't too far removed from the 16-year-old version of myself who had stood here three years ago, pondering a future that remained elusive and a quest to find a tribe to call my own.

And now that I had, I had to stop and wonder why I held onto my loner ways. Was I afraid people would reject me if I got too real with them? Or was I being proactive in heading off heartbreak at the pass? Naturally, it was an off shoot of my self-deprecating humor. Saying it about myself before someone else could was a mantra in my life. Well, I could continue this psych session with David later; I reiterated to myself that I had shit to do.

First, I had to check in with Nina.

"This is Nina, talk to me." She said as if it were the first time she had uttered it with a fresh lilt in her voice.

"Hey girl, it's me," I said. "I got here all right. How's Shadow? She's not being a pain in the ass, is she?"

I asked the last part, knowing full well the answer would be a resounding "no," as all she needed was human companionship to keep her happy.

"She's being a good doggie. Yes, she is - who's a good doggie?" I asked as Shadow was in the process of licking Nina's face. Still, I couldn't resist a little smart-ass response.

"I'd like Who's a Good Doggie for $100, Alex," I said, and without missing a beat, Nina chimed in with the clue.

"This good doggie had a super annoying nephew and a cousin that was technically sloooooow."

"Who is Scooby-Doo?" I said, stifling a giggle.

"Correct," Nina said stoically.

"Good Doggie for $200."

"The Brady Bunch had not one, but two dogs, Name them."

"Who are Tiger and Mop Top."

"You are on fire, well at least flaming. Pick again."

"Good Doggie for $300."

"Ah, The Daily Double..."

"I'd like to risk it all, Alex." As I spoke these words, they seemed fitting to my current situation. I wanted to tell her about it but was enjoying the levity reprieve.

"This Good Doggie was good, until he got rabies and was shot."

Oh hell, there were two choices to go with, either Cujo or Old Yeller. Well, I suspected Nina might be going with Cujo, given my penchant for reading Stephen King. But she might think I would think that also. My decision became rushed after she began whistling the *Jeopardy* theme.

"Who is Old Yeller?"

"Oh, I'm sorry homosexual contestant," She chided. "The answer was Cujo. Really bitch? With all the Stephen King that you read, I thought you'd be a shoo-in to win. Alas, you lost. But you are not going home empty handed! You're getting a three-month supply of Rice-A-Roni because it's the San Francisco treat and you're gay. So, you should like that."

Despite myself, I laughed, and it felt much more cleansing than the tears I felt should be shed.

"I need to tell you something," I said after the belly ache subsided and proceeded to explain why I was really in LA.

"Holy shit Batman!" she screamed into the receiver. "You shouldn't do this by yourself! Do you want us to come up? There's strength in numbers and all that."

"Just wanted to let you know, in case..." I let that thought trail off into the ether. "Listen, let me check out some stuff, and I will report back. Sound good?"

"Yeah, I guess so. But dude, be careful in the meantime."

Before I could say that I promised I would, the operator demanded another 50 cents to continue the call. I dug into my pocket and came up empty, so I hung up.

I went into the store to get a snack and a Pepsi, which would give me some change, so I wouldn't come up short for the next phone call. The clerk barely spoke and eyed me warily, figuring I was just some fresh off the scooter type trying to make it big in the city of dreams.

"Thanks," I said tersely.

"Don't mention it," he volleyed back before he delivered a word I hated since childhood. "Queer."

"Sorry the only job you could get was ringing up queers on Santa Monica Boulevard, dumb ass."

I thought he might jump over the counter, but he just glared at me. And with that, I made my exit, grabbed a new tape out of my backpack, put on my headphones and let Elton John inform myself, and the rest of Los Angeles, that "The Bitch is Back." I let this musical proclamation guide me off into the sunset.

As darkness enveloped me, I headed west down the boulevard of so many broken dreams, passing the French Market Place where George had attempted to teach me about what it was to be gay. This wasn't a case of the student who has now become the teacher, far from it. But I had a better understanding of what it meant in the here and now.

I pulled off the main drag and onto Hilldale Avenue and parked, figuring it was better to hoof it on foot to stakeout Charade. I made my way down Santa Monica Boulevard, carrying a backpack lighter than the contents in my head weighing me down.

I spotted a familiar bar. Rage seemed quiet compared to the last time I had been there during Gay Pride eons ago. Well, it made scads of sense given that Pride had already come and gone, and that fact was akin to the song that was audible over my headphones.

The girl group Exposé was enticing me with an invite to "Come Go with Me." I had a sneaking suspicion gaining entrance two years shy of the legal drinking age would prove fruitless with the smattering of people to camouflage my actual age. I couldn't blend with the Thursday night drunks as I had at Pride.

Where were Manny, Moe and Jack when you really needed them?

They were probably drunk as skunks somewhere or performing as The Fushia Debs...or both. I could really go for a cocktail myself; it would quiet my mind and calm my nerves. But I had to stay alert, letting the memory of my first Gay Pride pass by me like the refreshing breeze that had sprung up.

If it had been of a hurricane magnitude, then it would push my feet along at the fastest of clips and plopped me in front of Charade, which would be helpful as they currently felt stuck in wet cement. I didn't know if I could do this. Suddenly I thought I might break down right there on the sidewalk and wail for the confused boy I had once been.

Here I was again, on a quest. But I had met someone back then, who had, for lack of a better word, set me straight on what it could be like to accept who I was and gave me much-needed insights. I hoped Candy was magically in Rage and would rescue me again, my knight in shining pumps. I scanned a dozen people through the window. No sign of her. Perhaps she was out performing more acts of good will to confused gays, lesbians, transgender types and even the oft-forgotten bisexuals.

I approached the crosswalk on North Robertson Boulevard with trepidation, making a conscious effort to make my leaden feet move when the little green man told me it was time to cross the street.

I positioned myself across from Charade but hid behind a car. I'm not so sure how covert I looked whenI pulled out the binoculars for a closer look at the warehouse-like structure, or if it looked like I was trying to boost a car for that matter.

It seemed innocuous enough, just another dance club; a nothing to see here, move along type of situation. However, Ellen's red Mercedes came into a closer proximity through the lenses than I cared to see, nestled in a parking spot at the side of the building. I heard myself take a sharp breath.

I moved the magnification to the left; it didn't look like there was anyone inside. And then repeated the sweeping motion back to the right to make sure there was no one in Ellen's car, mainly the lady herself.

I saw a flutter of movement out of the corner of my eye and there in my sightline was her son Troy, standing in the shadows. He was moving his mouth, which told me that he was addressing someone else not viewable among pockets of light and dark.

That is until I saw a shock of peroxided hair came into sharp focus. It belonged to Rocky, one of the show ponies in King George's once thriving stable. I repositioned myself to get a better view and saw Troy hand over a package to him.

Rocky tore into it like a greedy child on Christmas morning. He dipped his finger into it and snorted the powdery substance into his hungry nostrils. Why, if it wasn't my old nemesis, Tina! I hadn't figured on her being in attendance. I chastised myself inwardly for not packing a scorecard.

And like a thief, or rather a dealer, in the night he was gone after getting a silent directive from Troy, who made his way into a side entrance. A warm breeze moved my hair off my forehead and then placed it gently back into position.

I stared at the front of Charade and saw a poster advertising a weekly event. A weekly event that was held on Saturdays. A weekly event that starred Candy. The kind eyes and inviting smile on the poster were so close that I felt that I could reach out and grab Candy's attention with the news of the prodigal son's return. I did have a momentary fear of her reaction would be to my darkening Los Angeles' doorway again. Obviously, I sucked, and not in a good way, in keeping up corresponding with her. Not so much as a card attached to say, "Thank you for being a friend" was ever mailed her way, or better yet, dropped off in person.

The breeze once again seized control of my hair, I patted it back down and out of my left eye, putting the binoculars down, wondering what to do now. I turned my head to the left and saw a shadowy figure coming towards me, as it drew near, one shadow stepped out from behind the other, becoming two.

Now, had I been doing what Rocky had been doing, well, then I would have a perfect out as to why my eyes were playing tricks on me. And as they drew nearer with each double sound of footfalls on the sidewalk, my chances lessened for looking less conspicuous.

I removed the binoculars and stowed them away in the backpack, deciding if I looked like I was tying my shoe, it would arouse less suspicion from my mystery guests.

And from the reception I received, I guess I needn't worry about them noticing anything about me, save for one physical attribute.

"That is one fine ass," a slurred voice said. "Lookit Percy, like a ripe little peach."

"Jesus, Terrance…you are cut off!" the other voice said, before issuing me an apology. "I'm so sorry, I'm going to get him a shorter leash."

This was one case where silence is golden applied; watching their shadows from the streetlights elongate and shrink, until I saw them fully realized as human beings and not something from the netherworld. Well, one wanted to visit my nether regions, but that was neither here nor there.

As the shorter one pulled the taller one past me. The sweater wrapped around their shoulders immediately labeled them as yuppies. I wondered what their story was. They seemed like they'd been together for years and I wondered what it would be like to grow old with someone. Hell, I wondered what it would be like to make it past a one-night stand or see it beyond a few weeks max. And before I could let my mind drift off to Danny or lament the horrible timing of meeting Antonio, a hand clamped down on my shoulder.

I didn't think Terrance had gotten off-leash and could see them staggering down the street away from me, so this was a horse of a different color altogether. I turned in slow motion, as if a tarantula had mistakenly wandered onto my shoulder, careful not to startle it, lest it force its venom into me. I couldn't miss the hot pink fingernails which dug into my skin, as a voice broke the tension.

"Are you messin' with my ride, sweet thing?"

I had only heard the female equivalent of it before, but there was no mistaking the inflection was all Candy, even as a male. Also, the nails should have been my first clue.

"No ma'am," I said, with my head still looking down.

"That's Miss to you," he chastised and then continued. "Is there somethin' I can help you with? If not, kindly get the fuck out of here."

"My, my, my, that's not very ladylike," I said, turning my face upwards.

"Shut the front door!" Candy exclaimed.

I took in the sight of her, sans a wig and make-up, sparkly dress or high heels. In their place were a flat top, a pair of camouflage pants, a black t-shirt with a paint splatter motif – pink naturally - and a well-loved looking pair of monkey boots.

"Dammit son, I was just 'bout ready to clock you! What are you doing here?" Candy enthusiastically inquired.

"Well, as always, that's a long story," I stated.

"Come into my home away from home, I am just about to start my shift, so you can tell 'Ol Candy all about it."

"Honestly, that wouldn't be the best of ideas. Let me give you the Cliffs Notes version."

And that is just what I did, as her face went from having a smile on it to one where Candy appeared to be physically ill.

"I think I'mma gonna be sick!" she proclaimed, before arching an eyebrow and hitting me with a question. "Are you absolutely sure? This wasn't the best week to quit smoking. I sure could use a ciggie about now."

"Witches Honor," I assured her, affecting the sign for it from *Bewitched*.

Candy simply folded her two muscular arms onto each other and blinked with a nod of her head.

"I was more of an *I Dream of Jeannie* girl myself, but I hear what you're sayin'" Candy laughed. She paused, took a deep breath, and nodded towards Charade. "And I believe you, hon. If I had half a mind, I'd march right in there and quit. But since I have a full brain in this noggin, I know it's important to stay and help you."

"I know it's riskier to wait, but I have to do this, I need to do this." I hoped it came off as sincere and not as selfish. "Besides, there's always the chance this is where they are holding Nick and he'd turn rat fink on himself quicker than MacGayver here could diffuse that bomb."

She looked me dead in the eyes and squeezed my shoulder.

"Now, since you know all of the key players and they know you – how exactly am I gonna sneak you in?"

I turned my attention to the poster that featured the full-drag realization of who was standing in front of me.

"Are you strictly a solo act?" I queried.

She pursed her lips together, cocked her head to the side and half-lidded her eyelids before replying.

"I've been known to have backup from time to time. Why?"

"Room for one more on Saturday?"

"Only for a very special guest star, baby." A beauteous smile spread across her face and then she dug into her pocket and produced a key ring. She took off a silver and gold key for me.

"I assume you'll need a place to crash," she stated. "Besides, we're going to need to practice, I know you can dance, but in heels is another story."

She gave me directions to her apartment, made me repeat them several times and then just said.

"Oh hell, just call me here if you get lost," She handed me a familiar looking matchbook. And as I took it into my hand, I began to feel like this was going to work.

If only I had noticed a pair of eyes in the shadows across the street watching what was happening, perhaps then I would have changed my mind.

Candy crossed the street and I stayed on my side, not wanting to get too close to Charade, and headed North. I felt a little extra spring in my step, a buoyancy that had felt like it had been missing from my life as late. I changed out tapes in my Walkman and slid the headphones over my ears and let The Jets tell me a story about a crush they had.

If I hadn't been lost once again in musical reverie, I may have heard footfalls behind me. And I would have also heard them stop, as I headed onto Santa Monica Boulevard. The same pair of eyes had been watching the exchange between Candy and myself were now watching me making my way into the night and then returned their focus onto Charade.

I walked down Santa Monica Boulevard, letting lightness carry me along the small tide of people out for a night of fun. TGIT was apparently a thing in West Hollywood and why wouldn't it be?

To borrow a title from TV's *That Girl* Marlo Thomas, this town was very indicative of her children's television special *Free to Be, You and Me*. I came here two years ago seeking out a place to call home, with people to claim as my own, when in fact I had ended up finding at the other end of the rainbow, was the familiar quote "There's no place like home."

Trust me, *The Wizard of Oz* parable of my life was not lost on me. But rather than seeking out a way to return home, or a brain, a heart, or courage; I'd asked the Wizard for an overabundance of cock to help mend my broken heart, to shut my brain up in the hopes I would eventually have the wherewithal to find a solid relationship.

And wouldn't you know it? A twister's worth of emotions began swirling around inside me. I had been running on complete and total shock for the past day, way too much had happened for me to take it all in. I felt lightheaded, close to asking for a mint julip, while swooning away into my own private summer.

I leaned against the nearest building and took a breather, as I watched two shirtless and hirsute men approach, wearing leather harnesses, making them resembling flying monkeys. I supposed I looked like I had one too many and was trying to control the spins, and or was going to unleash a technicolor yawn. I took off my headphones and rested my head against the outside wall of the Mineshaft.

That meant that my "ripe little peach" was facing towards the street, and I counted no less than five grabs of it while I collected myself. Not once did anyone ask if I was ok, needed anything. Hell, I would have settled for a wolf whistle.

But there was only silence, save for the screaming in my head, the voice telling me to whirl around and tell everyone to fuck off. Call it instinct, the good witch versus the wicked witch on either shoulder, one a sage advice dispenser and the other suggesting I lose control. But I was not listening to either right now.

Would anyone hear me anyway? Well, there was only one way to be sure.

"Buy a lady a drink first!" The words came flying out of my mouth as a random person attempted to put his hand down my underwear. And it retracted just as quickly, as if it had touched a burner on a hot stove. "You have no power here. Be gone before somebody drops a house on you, too!"

I began laughing, looking to the outside world like a loon, but to the inside one it was a welcome relief. Whoever coined the phrase that "laughter was the best medicine" had it right; it felt cathartic and empowering at the same time.

I was tempted to share my very newly found sunny disposition at the bar, but as with Rage, me being underage would impede me in spreading the news that the Wicked Old Witch at last was finally dead. Ding Dong, bitch. Ding. Dong.

This may prove to be a fleeting moment anyway. So, on went the headphones, feet pointed eastward, and I was off down The Yellow Brick Road on my little red scooter.

Amazingly, I remembered Candy's directions to her apartment off Hollywood Boulevard, mostly in part because of the landmark she gave me in relation to where to turn. Frederick's of Hollywood loomed large, as I made my way onto Whitley Avenue and pulled up kitty corner from her apartment building, named Dalton Heights, according to its awning over the front door. It was French inspired in design, small, recessed windows, surrounded by cement on every side, overlooked the street and were behind a parapet. The way the bricks were interlocked with each other over the windows gave the building an Art deco feel, even if the illusion was broken on the ones that had fire escapes in front of them.

I immediately had visions of Bette Davis, lit cigarette in her right hand, on the fire escape welcoming me, before a mannish laugh, born of too much whiskey and countless cigarettes, ruined the sentiment. Imagine how nonplussed I was when the lobby door opened and an older lady, mid-60s, emerged. While not a *Dead Ringer* to Bette, she appeared to be cut from the same cloth.

She had a paisley scarf tied around her coiffed hair, as if it were the dead of winter and not the stillness of a summer night. From my vantage point across the street, always the silent observer, I could tell she was overdressed to be going to the market. She was wearing a smart-looking tweed skirt and jacket, with a maroon top that had a collar which reminded me of Olive Oyl's, looking a bit like a flower petal cut in an interesting pattern. But her rose still appeared to be in bloom with a noticeable spring in her step. And without speaking word one to her, I would most definitely describe her to people as a "character."

She strode down the sidewalk, a sense of purpose and a quiet determination moving her feet along at a quick pace. After she was around the corner, I used one of the two keys that Candy had lent me and inserted the silver key into the lock for the door to the lobby. Even though if one were to assume and, as Benny Hill had taught me, that made an ass out of you and me, the silver key slid effortlessly into the lock and turned.

I walked into the lobby, which I imagined was grander at some point in its past. As it was presently, a bland looking yellow tiled floor carried my footfalls on it, and matching yellowing walls closed in around me on either side, a sporadic placement of pots led to a fountain in the middle of the room. Drawing my attention, like a moth to a flame, were the spectral reflections from the swimming pool light, dancing off the glass door leading out to it and refracting on the wall in front of me. It was hypnotic, soothing, and otherworldly. The last adjective could sum up the surrealness of being back in The City of Angels.

"Toto, I have a feeling we're not in Kansas anymore."

I had the option of taking the stairs or an elevator to Candy's third floor apartment. As I was not a huge fan of elevators and given that I guessed this one may be more of the rickety variety, I chose the stairs.

The apartment number for Candy was easy to remember, as it was only a few years ago the 3D craze, popular in the '50s, had resurfaced with *Friday the 13th* and *Jaws* in three-dimensional terror.

The only terror in the latter is that I had plopped down my hard-earned allowance to see it. The only redeeming quality was a particularly good-looking usher who was exiting patrons from the movie made mention of how I resembled its star, Dennis Quaid. If my gaydar had been honed a bit better, I would have realized he was coming on to me. As I was an awkward 14-year-old at the time I had nary a clue as to how to spot my kind, but now I was a seasoned pro.

In fact, a punk rock-looking guy was walking out of one apartment, his Cramps sleeveless t-shirt hanging off him in a very sexy way, as opposed to his tight pair of many zippered red and black plaid pants, a requisite pair of Doc Martens boots and a short Mohawk dyed purple completed his look. He had a skateboard under one skinny, tattooed arm. I could feel his chocolate eyes boring into me, like Superman trying to see through lead.

My brain was shouting at me, "Put me in coach, I'm ready to play" upon realizing he was a member of the same team. Timing was proving to be a bitch again. That is not to say I didn't eye fuck him as I sauntered past, making sure to peer over my shoulder as I reached Candy's door.

Amid the death surrounding me, both real and possible, it felt great in this instance to feel alive. But that's all it could be, as tempting as he was, and given the smile he had spread across his face, like butter on bread.

I took the other key out, gave him one more look, unlocked the door and closed it, pressing my back against it to keep temptation at bay. I had work to do, and I wanted to make short measure of it.

I put my backpack down next to the couch and then plopped onto it with a bigger sigh than I had intended to make. And before I could succumb to the temptation of the welcoming maw of the plush velvet couch, I hopped up as if spring loaded.

I surveyed my temporary domain, taking in the mix of both feminine and masculine décor. A vase housed dyed pussy willows, blood red, while the table they sat upon was a wooden World War II era munitions box with a glass top.

There were colorful watercolor paintings of flowers, with framed posters of singers such as Grace Jones wearing an open blazer with a cigarette dangling precariously out of her mouth; while Billie Holiday had a soulful look on her face, her mouth captured mid-song from the side, sharing an unlikely duet with Wendy O. Williams from The Plasmatics in the frame to her right, decked out in a unicorn horn headband and her signature tits out approach to fashion. Punk god Sid Vicious sneered, guitar in hand to her right. The dichotomy of the two lives Candy led were the impetus in the apartment's décor. Which led me to wonder, what was Candy's name as a man? My female persona was that of Nosey Nancy, as I became determined there had to be some physical evidence of it around the apartment.

I shuffled across the innocuous tan carpeting towards the kitchen, to see if there were some bills on the kitchen counter. Nope. Maybe they were on the kitchen table? Negative. I felt like the bedroom and rifling through drawers would be something of an invasion of privacy and suspected there wouldn't be any evidence of his moniker in the bathroom.

So much for that. I rationalized it was a suitable time to look through her record collection and see if there was some material to practice with. Besides, looking through her vinyl versus scouring the underwear drawer for clues was the safer choice. You didn't want to get on the bad side of a drag queen! And it was a fortuitous decision, as splashed across the bottom of the hot pink Supremes A' Go-Go album was the proclamation stating it was The Property of Marvin Jones.

I thought this discovery needed a soundtrack and why not go with the album that given me her birth name? In pulling the album out, something fell out of its sleeve. There, face up on the carpet, was the grinning face of Danny. Alongside him was Candy. They were leaning against a vehicle. A VW van.

He had his arm around Candy, they certainly were chummy in the moment taken for posterity. In her appropriately named Candies shoes with their elevated wedged cork heels and wig teased so much that it bordered on bullying, made her tower over him. Her hands were clasped on his shoulder, one leg off the ground and bent at the knee, head tilted back, a radiant and genuine smile illustrated they were having the time of their lives. Danny was leaning back into her slightly causing his half-shirt to hug his defined chest tightly, his treasure trail leading my eyes onto the unmistakable bulge hidden within the denim of his Daisy Dukes.

Although he was smiling, his eyes told a different story; they looked dark, stormy and lost at sea. I turned the photo over, but there was no date on it. But his feathered hair led me to place it close to the time he'd moved away to find fame and fortune, on the precipice of realizing it might not be the case. And that road taken had led him back to the street where he'd moved to as a teenager; the same one where he was run down on.

I had tried to keep him from pushing his way into my mind, like he had shoved me out of harm's way, paying for that act with his life, cutting our reunion short, putting the brakes on the possibility it may have gone somewhere.

I put the album on the turntable, turned the volume down to a respectable level, not noticing I had started crying during "Come and Get These Memories." That would be all I'd ever have of him now, the good, the bad and the ugly of it all battling for supremacy. But I'd never have him; maybe I was never supposed to.

I stared at the image of two people through blurry eyes, never realizing they had known one another, absently wiping away a trickle of snot trying to make its way down to upper lip. If only the pain of the past day could be vanquished as easily.

"I love you, you booger" came out of my mouth, just like it had been said to me in what felt like a lifetime ago, right before a life was snuffed out. The rational side of my brain – yes, I have the capacity to be rational – told me that it wouldn't have panned out. How could it with all that he'd put me through? The romantic side begged to differ, offering me a glimpse into a future which would never be, one of living happily ever after with the man I'd fallen for years ago.

Now I was falling in a different sense, right into a rabbit hole of nostalgia dancing alongside depression of what would never be and anxiety about what I had to do. I flipped the switch on wallowing in misery and illuminated the need to find a song to present to Candy.

As I rifled through the vinyl choices, I glanced at the photo sporadically, not wanting to put it away in part because I did not want to. Not yet. So, I didn't. Also, I wanted to ask Candy, or Marvin, about it.

I was glad to have something to occupy my mind, but as the record collection began reaching the back of the yellow chipped painted wooden box they lived in, my selection to make my stage debut began to dwindle. None of the album covers were inspiring me, I didn't know if I could pull any of this off with only two days to do so.

I had spent so much of my life being a follower that the concept of being a leader seemed like a foreign one. Call it kismet, fate, or plain dumb luck, but the record I reached for next was the Shangri-Las *Leader of the Pack.* Bingo! I had a greatest hits compilation of the 60's girl group in my vast cassette collection and would entertain myself by lip- synching it in front of the bathroom mirror when no one was home.

And I was doing that in the full-length mirror in the corner of the living room for the umpteenth time when Candy surprised me.

"Somebody is gettin' their practice on. Don't let me interrupt your little one-man show now. It's lookin' good, real real good. But it will look great with a little assist from your sis. Now scooch over, you're hogging the mirror."

Its reflection caught us perfecting our choreography and miming the words seamlessly. I knew it was an odd choice, given the nature of the lyrics, but it brought some type of strange humor to the situation. Each time Candy pantomimed, "Look out, look out, look out!" I had to suppress laughter – then fight back tears over Danny. Eventually, I lost the battle and Candy became my comrade in arms as I told her about the portion of the story I had omitted earlier, not wanting to talk about it.

"Shit, you've been through it!" she said with a whistle.

"Amen sister!" I said. "And you knew him. I found a picture of the two of you. It fell out of a record."

"Where is this picture, sweetie? Bring it to your Mama, I mean your slightly older big sister."

I fetched it and her mouth immediately formed a capital o, retracted to a lowercase o, eventually producing pursed lips.

"Do you remember him?"

"Do I remember Miles?" she said, shaking her head up and down vigorously. "You better believe it."

"His name is… was… Danny." It felt weird to put him in the past tense.

"I didn't know him socially, only professionally."

"You did porn, too?" I asked incredulously.

"Hell no! I mean I could have, but my talents were needed elsewhere, on the stage to be exact."

"Then how did you know him?"

"He was a go-go dancer at Charade," Candy said. "With that big 'ol piece of meat of his, you better believe he got lots of tips. Then he got into all sorts of shady shit: dealin' drugs and hookin.' Sorry hon, I don't mean to speak ill of the, well, you know."

"No harm, no foul. I knew about it."

"He was nice, until he wasn't. But you'd know more about that than I would. I'm sorry, baby. Given the circumstances, a cheerier song is in order. But let's tackle that tomorrow, I need to get my happy ass to bed. I'll make up the couch for you. Sound good?"

It did, even if I wasn't sure how much shut eye I'd be getting tonight. As it turned out, I woke up with a trickle of drool running from my mouth onto the pillow, which meant that I had slept soundly.

In fact, a little too soundly, as the clock on the living room wall read 9:45. After I relieved my bladder and splashed cold water on my face, I stumbled to the kitchen to see if there might be a cup of ambition to be had. Candy took a sip of hers and stopped reading the paper to greet me with a wide grin.

"Somebody got his beauty sleep," she said sweetly. "Coffee?"

"Yes, please."

As the caffeine made its way through my veins, Candy outlined the plans for the day. She had to be at work at 3pm for the start of happy hour. This gave us a few hours to figure out a new song and routine in partial drag, which involved us perusing a local thrift store for a dress and shoes that would fit me, since I would drown in one of her dresses and fall out of her enormous heels.

I knew I had big shoes to fill in the possibility of pulling all of this off. After we landed on Bananarama's "Venus" as the song to orchestrate my debut, appropriating the trio's choreography from memory and adding our own flourishes, I began to shuck off my impression of a horse foal learning to walk.

I was grateful Candy decided a kitten heel was the way to go, so as to not have me break my ankle in a full heel. The thrift store had a mini version of the black fringe dress and matching gloves she had hanging in her vintage wardrobe. It fit perfectly and was the definitive uniform for our '60s inspired take on the song, incorporating elements of the hip sway from the Frug, the semi-spastic Jerk and arms-in-motion Swim.

The steps were simple, rudimentary even, like a beginner's guide to drag, as was the toned-down blonde flip wig that Candy selected for me. It was less likely to go flying off my head and was a stark contrast to the purple beehive she was styling on a Styrofoam head and was spraying generously with Aqua Net.

When she was satisfied with it, Candy instructed me to take a seat in front of her vanity to do a makeup test run, applying foundation, blue eyeshadow and a matching hue to my lips that made it appear as if I had snacked on a Smurf.

"I don't need to add fake eyelashes. You have flawless natural ones that any queen would give her eye teeth for! Bitch!"

"Don't hate, appreciate!"

"Save the sassiness for the stage, Missy!" She instructed in a chiding manner.

"Yes, Mommie Dearest."

"Did you scrub the bathroom floor today? Do you think it's clean? DO YOU?"

"Mrs. Jenkins said it was clean!"

"Well, that bitch is so fired!"

We laughed at our impromptu re-enactment of the much-maligned Faye Dunaway portrayal as Joan Crawford. Once the guffaws subsided, she performed a touch-up on my closed eyelids, and I was instructed to open them. I had never fallen into the pretty boy category, so it came as no surprise I wouldn't be transformed into a pretty girl. Still, I was a far cry from Dustin Hoffman in *Tootsie*. Candy had done her best with what she had to work with, and I was passable enough for a one-night-only gig.

"Not bad. Not bad at all." She proclaimed, inspecting her work. "Now what to name you? Any ideas?"

I was stymied, racking my brain for the perfect moniker, coming up blank. I went through my diva Rolodex, determining I was more Mandonna than Madonna and couldn't be the boss like Miss Ross. I could be like Janet, Ms Jackson, in attitude and that I had been known to get nasty, but appearance-wise, not-so-much.

"How did you come up with your name?"

"Easy, I'm sweet as candy." She said and a light bulb went off in my brain, bringing the answer into the light.

"Well, let me introduce you to Lolli Pop."

"Is that because you're an all-day sucker?"

"It takes more than three licks to get to my chewy insides."

"That ain't what I heard."

Again, we fell into peals of laughter. Then we got down to the serious business of studying the blueprints of Charade, trying to pinpoint where Nick could plant a bomb.

"This section right here," Candy pointed to with her painted fingernail. "It's not used for the club and there's a door that is always locked leading to it. And only two people have the key."

"Let me guess, a mother-and-son duo?"

"And bingo was his name oh." Candy joked and then looked at her watch. "Shit, I'm gonna be late!"

After a quick change into gold lame pants, sparkly silver tank top, cowboy hat and boots, she was off with her parting words of "keep practicing" following her out the door.

I dropped the needle on the redo of the Shocking Blue song that was as old as I was a good dozen times, until I was interrupted by a knock at the door. I peered through the peephole and saw a smaller, distorted version of the skate punk who had checked me out yesterday. I was surprised to see him, but not as much as he was when I opened the door.

"Hey," I said, keeping it simple.

"I was just wondering if there are any other songs you like, little lady?" He asked smoothly, his composure regained.

For a minute I had almost forgotten I was trying to nail tomorrow night's choreography and hoping my painted face was hiding the blush which felt as though it was burning my skin.

"Oh my God, sorry about that. We have a show tomorrow night and I was rehearsing. I'll turn it down."

"You and Candy are 'we,' eh? That's too bad."

"No, not like that. We are just friends. Sorry to have bothered you." I was flustered in a million separate ways.

"For the record, you're a lot cuter as a guy." He extended his hand through the door I had started to close. "I'm Deke."

Of course he was.

"Henry," I answered, feeling an electrical surge as my Lee Press On nailed fingers enclosed his hand. If it was possible to die from embarrassment; I seemed like a good test case to prove its validity.

"That's an interesting name for a drag queen."

"Oh. Yeah. I. Guess." I sputtered. "It's my first time doing it."

"I never would have you pegged as a virgin."

I was waiting for *The Twilight Zone* theme to start as an accompaniment to the bizarre fact he was flirting with me, despite the drag. If Candy had put false eyelashes on me, they certainly would have been batting at him to indicate he was hitting a home run rather than experiencing a strike out.

That is until the mental umpire called him out, but not with a cry to denote that; Danny's spectral proclamation that he loved me took me out of the ballgame, effectively benching me from giving into Deke's advances.

"Ok, then. Gotta get going." I shut the door on him getting to third base, hoping he hadn't noticed that the protrusion in the crotch region of my dress was a batter up situation.

"I'm next door if you need anything, anything at all." He said through the door, not getting the point I didn't want what he was peddling, a sexual surrogate of a Jehovah Witness that wouldn't take no for an answer.

"K. Thanks. Bye now."

I took the needle off the record, returned it to its resting place and turned off the stereo. There was always tomorrow to get it right. The thought of what the next day entailed caused a shiver to run through me, its cold diffusing the leftover charge from Deke's electricity. I took a hot shower, scrubbing away the second identity I'd taken on in LA, hoping I had some of the bravery of Billy Collins under my skin. I emerged from the steam as Henry Dodge, and mama needed a cocktail to calm his nerves and quiet his mind, a liquid bandage to cover fresh wounds.

After the third screwdriver, all it had done was make me melancholy and the poster boy for being a sad sack, a satchel of emotions I didn't want to unpack for fear they would make me abandon my crucial mission.

I debated knocking on Deke's door, knowing that a bit of carnal pleasure would distract me momentarily. I even stumbled to the door, hand on the knob, instead of opening it, I engaged the lock, shutting out temptation in favor of making good choices. And that's what I wanted to make going forward, good choices or at least smart ones. Not wanting the usual distractions of casual sex or drugs to dull the anger I needed to latch onto a life preserver, as to not drown in a sea of fear.

I figured in the meantime that one more drink couldn't hurt.

And it didn't until the following day when I awoke with a hangover headache of epic proportions and a vampire-like hatred of the sun pouring into the apartment, signaling another scorcher would mark the slow burn hours until it showtime. As the day wore on like a jar of molasses being dragged by a turtle, the pain in my head was supplanted by a butterfly the size of Mothra in my stomach.

"It's just nerves, honey," Candy said kindly as we were putting ourselves through the final paces of dress rehearsal. Well, it was technically, a dress, wig, and heels rehearsal. Despite feeling like a steaming pile of shite, I was surprised at how I was still managing to remember the routine, even in heels, I was showing off my fancy heel work. John Travolta, eat your heart out! Even if my case of *Saturday Night Fever* resulted in a trip to the hospital from exhaustion, I would put my best foot forward in making sure my plan would go off without a hitch.

I sat patiently on the closed lid of the toilet as Candy applied what felt like a heavy dose of makeup. I kept my mind from getting clogged with thoughts of tonight going to shit, complete with me stinking up the stage at Charade with mistakes, the dancing equivalent of not noticing you have toilet paper on your shoe.

"There," she said. "Not the Mona Lisa, but good enough for government work. Go take yourself a gander."

And what I saw was nothing short of a miracle, staring back at me was the daughter that Mom had always wanted. Well, one that wasn't painted to the nines with blue eye shadow, matching Day Glo blue lips, a healthy application of rouge and a generous helping of foundation that erased the 5 0'clock shadow I got right after a fresh shave. My nose was shaded, or contoured, as Candy had explained while setting about to make me look the part I was playing tonight.

It was a hugely different off-shoot of the moniker of Billy Collins from three summers ago. As Lolli Pop, I looked like I'd traveled to the future from the 1960's by way of Willy Wonka's Chocolate Factory. But I needed to keep on target while the bittersweet ran through my veins.

As we headed down to Candy's car, Deke was making his way home from points unknown. The scarlet telltale sign of a blush ignited underneath my heavily made-up face, making the rouge seem applied heavier than it was.

"Lookin' good, ladies," he said.

"Thank you kindly," I answered with a Southern accent, dripping with honey so sweet, it could cause me to instantaneously become a diabetic. It was also reminiscent of Rue McClanahan's Blanche Devereaux.

"Not so bad yourself, hot stuff," Candy added.

"Thanks. Where you off to?"

"A boxing match," I said demurely. "Where do you think we're going?"

"My guess would be to lay 'em out cold at Charade, since you're both a couple of knockouts."

"I've always depended on the compliments of strangers," I said with a return to the less shady side of the street.

"Well, would you look at the time?" Candy said, checking a non-existent watch, sensing the chemistry between myself and the guy whose mode of transportation was nestled in the crook of his heavily tattooed right arm. "Later, skater."

"Lates," he replied. "See you around, I hope."

"You never know," I said, pulling myself back into my body and mindset of getting this show on the road.

Once we were in the car and heading into the great unknown of how the evening would play out, Candy asked the question many people have asked throughout my lifetime. The one that inquired if I was ok.

It was not so easily answerable with certainty, as this did not come near where I wanted to be, reluctantly back to the scene of so many crimes and people who haunted my dreams seemed to be surreal. A dream within a dream, an inescapable nightmare, something conjured by Stephen King.

"I'm fine." It was the only answer to truthfully land on.

"So, you're fucked up, insecure, neurotic and emotional, then?" she said to break the tension mounting with each click of the odometer.

"How much do I owe ya, doc?"

"Only the truth, Ruth." Her voice did a 180 degree turn with her next sentence. "It's not too late to back out, ya know. We can leave it to the experts."

"I've come this far," I said with a steely resolve which had a marshmallow center. "I need to do this for myself and for Danny."

"For Danny," Candy said and wrapped her index finger around mine, a drag queen pinky swear to not let him have die in vain.

We drove the rest of the way in silence, no music to create a diversion of what was to come. Soon enough, we found what George had once referred to as Doris Day parking, across the street from Charade, which resembled the haunted castles in Roger Corman's Edgar Allan Poe movies through the burning anger in my eyes. I was relieved to not see Vincent Price as the doorman; the one who stood guard was a regular cookie cutter Angelino muscular guy in a white t-shirt, blue jeans and white Nikes who greeted Candy warmly with a hug.

"Who's your friend?" He asked when they untethered from one another.

"This here is Lolli Pop, my friend visiting from the southern portion of these here United States." She said, giving my newly adopted, and hopefully passable, accent more credibility.

"Oh yeah? Whereabouts are you from, sweet thing?"

It was a valid question, one that should not have taken me what felt like an eternity to answer.

"Georgia. Why, you gonna come visit me?"

"Don't you want to get his name first?" Candy asked.

"Not necessarily," I said slyly, a cat in heat, or one on a hot tin roof.

"It's Jack, for the record." And then said with raised eyebrows. "You're a bad girl, eh?"

"Oh honey, you have no idea," I purred. "Don't let appearances fool you, sugar."

It was strange to flirt in full drag regalia, there was an unexpected freedom in pretending to be someone else, light years from the persona I'd created for myself as Billy Collins.

"Duly noted." He turned his attention back to Candy. "Boss is looking for you."

"That right? Well then, we better shake a tailfeather and get inside."

"Bye ladies," he called after us. "Knock 'em dead."

This caused us to momentarily stop in our pumps, until the centrifugal force of the situation finally made our get-up-and-go has got up and went; I wasn't hankering fer a hunk o' cheese. It was time for Timer, or rather diffusing a bomb, if we could even find it. I felt nauseous immediately after crossing the threshold to this duplicitous business.

As soon as we rounded the corner to the bar area, I saw the ghost of summer's past. Troy stood with his back against the bar, arms crossed, a scowl spread across his brow, eyes squinting as if he was working on his Clint Eastwood impression. I didn't think I'd make his day by any stretch and the sight of him wasn't doing too much to ensure a pleasant evening.

"You're late," he said, not paying any attention to me, all his asshole energy trained on Candy.

"Correction." She said with a forced smile. "I am on drag queen time. There is a difference."

"You're just lucky Mom isn't here yet. She would rip you a new asshole. Then again, you might enjoy that."

"Doubtful."

"And who is this?" he asked, eyeing me up and down.

"My friend Lolli Pop from Georgia."

"Oh yeah, is that so? What brings you here?"

Oh, if only you knew, fuckface.

"Just seeing how the West Coast agrees with my southern sensibilities." He merely shrugged, like he had other things on his mind. Could Nick be one of them? Then he looked at me.

"You look familiar. Have we met?"

My heart skipped twenty beats, and my mouth went drier than the Sahara.

"Probably not since it's her first time visiting here," Candy intervened.

"That's right," I said as though I had just stuck a spoonful of peanut butter into my mouth. "I am a bit parched. I need a refreshment. Lovely to meet you."

"Charmed, I'm sure," Troy said with minimal effort, and it took a maximum one for me to stand up against the bar as though I wasn't shaking.

Candy was speaking to him from 20,000 leagues under the sea, as my head was swimming and the roar of my blood sounding like the pounding of the surf during high tide. Well, the tide was certainly high, and I needed to hold onto the reason I had hatched this scheme.

When she motioned to me, I surfaced back to reality and heard her inform Troy her solo act would be a duo tonight.

He shrugged again, not giving a shit either way. He walked away, his brisk mannerisms as cold as the air conditioner pumping evaporated freon into the room, to keep patrons comfortable on this balmy summer night. And before he disappeared towards a dimly lit hallway, he stopped once more to give me a twice over. I couldn't detect if it had registered as to when he had met and hoped it would be a no sale, as far as putting two and two together.

"Let's get you that drink," Candy said from behind me. "It will help those nerves. But just one shot, we've got a show to do. Two tequilas, Maureen."

"Wait, what are you having then?" I said as gentile as if I were asking about the weather.

"You gonna have a busted lip if you sass me one more time."

The fire of the tequila became the epitome of liquid courage.

Candy produced a can of Aqua Net from her enormous purse, while she sprayed her wig within an inch of its non-existent life, I saw a pack of smokes among the clutter of makeup and the like.

"I thought you quit?"

"My Mama didn't raise no quitter. Besides, I allow myself one after each performance, you know, like being in the afterglow. If a show goes right, it's better than sex."

"And if it goes bad?"

"Then darlin,' you should have stayed home and played with yoself."

The sentiment fit perfectly with the self-abuse nature of mental masturbation dominating my brain, lubed to perfection in reaching the climax to the question if I could succeed.

If *we* could.

For once I wasn't in this alone and for that I was grateful beyond measure. The pendulum swung back to being nervous about including Candy in my plan. What if she got hurt? I let my brain dwell on the prospect for a few seconds before I dismissed it, a wadded-up Kleenex in the trash can of negative thinking.

It was going to work. It had to work.

We waited for our cue from the emcee who introduced us as "Candy and her sister from another mister, Lollipop."

The opening strains of "Venus" came roaring out of the speakers behind us on the medium-sized stage and the fear of forgetting our choreography blipped on my radar and disappeared just as quickly. Soon, I was in lip-sync with Candy, the dancing and miming version of cycle sisters in a blur of black fringe. And the crowd was eating it up.

But what caught my eye mid-twirl cut like a knife. Cheering us on were Nina, Derek, and Michael, I cussed inwardly that I kept my word to keep

Nina in the loop. More potential harm to worry about, and three times over to boot.

I almost stumbled, but kept time with Candy, hyper focused on nailing our performance, unable to question why my three amigos were here. The lights went out, allowing our Day-Glo lips to conclude the whirlwind routine with me retreating to the back of the stage, fading away nonchalantly, drawing the curtain back to aid in my disappearing act which allowed me access to the route Candy had detailed.

Unfortunately, I immediately encountered an unexpected roadblock by running into Ellen Niles with such force that my wig fell to the floor. I sucked in my breath, unable to turn my forward motion into one of a backwards nature. I looked down to see if the floor was made of quicksand rather than concrete.

"Hello Corey. We've been expecting you."

I began to back away from her case of mistaken identity and was strong-armed from behind with a right arm against my windpipe and the left one using all its might in pressing the cold steel of a gun barrel into the small of my back.

A sense of déjà vu as to who was behind me, but for a different reason this time around, became evident when Troy told me I better not try to fight. And that might be a tough piece of advice to heed, as I was worried I was on the verge of Hulking out, leaving nothing of my former self, save for a shredded black dress with fringe modestly covering my privates. I could feel the anger welling up, a hot flame tempered by cold steel, a juxtaposition of thought versus action. The eternal flame of self-doubt sparked yet again, as had the cooling of my feet. But my brain was firing on all cylinders, telling me to give into that command and embrace my inner chicken, otherwise my goose was cooked.

And for once, I decided to take my own advice because submitting could lead me to the place that I needed to be in being resolute in seeing this all the way through, despite the odds being against me currently.

And while I didn't necessarily have an ace up my sleeve, there was a queen in my corner. I caught a blip of Candy on my radar just before Troy shoved me forward, sandwiching me between himself and his mother.

I was forced forward, dragging my kitten heels, until we reached the door at the end of the corridor that separated the club from whatever nefarious goings-on were on the other side. Ellen produced a key, slid it into the lock, and what lay beyond the threshold lay a more industrial-looking setting; pipes lined the wall and ceiling. Ellen stopped with her back to me, arachnid-like arms stretched onto a metal railing and looked out into the black expanse beyond the platform, a set of stairs led down into the darkness to her right.

She strode over to the landing at the top of the stairs and turned on a light switch, the dark of the room was flooded with the deceptive warmth of a series of fluorescent lights, with only the top of them visible in my sightline.

"Let's put a little light on the situation, as my dearly departed father used to say." She said without humor or any trace of a smile.

"I didn't know Satan had any children," I muttered under my breath, she didn't hear me, but Troy did. Rather than laughing, he kicked me in the back of my right knee, which drove me to the floor.

"Are you hungry?" Ellen inquired with genuine motherly concern.

"Not really," I said, confused by her line of questioning.

"Then why are you trying to get a piece of the pie? Any way you slice it, none of this was meant for you to profit from."

"And it wasn't for you, either." An ethereal voice said, ascending the staircase, a rotund body following its course.

It was Nick's voice.

"I thought I smelled something," Troy said before doing an overexaggerated sniff. "Smells like desperation to me."

"And what cologne are you wearing?" Nick asked. "Calvin Klein's Failure?"

I wanted to chuckle, but I knew it was no laughing matter, since my inappropriate giggle could result in being shot. Troy pushed the barrel of the gun harder into my upper back now, and given my submissive position, it felt like it might pop out the other side, a metallic version of the Chestburster in *Alien.*

"I would like to interject with look what the cat dragged in," Ellen sniped. "But you aren't a fan of pussy."

"Yeah, neither was George," Nick snapped.

Ellen pounced and pushed Nick down the stairs, where he landed with a thud.

"What an inappropriate time to take a nap," she quipped. "But what can you expect from such a fat, lazy bastard?"

Her slam revealed Nick was indeed knocked out, cold metal a poor substitute for a mattress.

"Well, that's one down," she said, turning her steely gaze onto me. "And one to go."

"Room for one more?" Candy asked sweetly, as if crashing a ladies who lunch get together.

"What is this, an episode of *The Love Boat*?" Ellen mused sarcastically. "So many special guest stars. Who is going to show up next, Charo?"

Candy silently illustrated it was a former star of *Charlie's Angels*, as she kicked the gun out of Troy's hand and it flew out into the brightly lit abyss, clanging off a light fixture, causing it to sway, casting shadows across Ellen's face. But even the momentary darkness couldn't hide the anger that she wore on her face like makeup.

Candy followed up her surprise attack by swinging her purse like a shotput wind-up until it connected with Troy's nose, which immediately began to spray blood like a Rainbird sprinkler. The contents of her purse were also a causality of her method of attack, spilled like guts all over the floor.

I used the commotion to pop up and drive my elbow as hard as I could into Troy's ribcage. And he assumed my former position, he issued an "oof," and took his hands away from his bloody nose to cradle his ribs. His white button-down shirt resembled a napkin used to sop up spaghetti sauce.

"Bad day to wear white, buddy," I observed before targeting the small of his back with my right foot.

"Wow! Who knew you were such a bad ass!" Nina exclaimed from behind me, as the distant strains of LA Dream Team's "The Dream Team is in The House," accompanied her assessment of the situation.

"I had to take something away from watching all those *Charlie's Angels* episodes."

"Damn not-so-straight," Derek said.

Michael stayed back, almost fading into the woodwork, taking in what was happening until his bellow of "look out" brought us back to reality. Ellen was doing her best impression of a charging bull, aiming for Candy. But the impromptu matador laid her out flat, clocking her in the windpipe with her forearm.

"Don't get any funny ideas, pretty boy," Candy snarled at Troy, who was trying to land on which painful body part to attend to. "You doin' ok there, Boo-Boo?"

I nodded, really at a loss for words, as my friends took turns clapping me on the back. But we were not out of the woods yet and the chance to see the forest through the trees diminished, as Ellen stood up, rigid and unmoving as a mighty oak.

But she uprooted herself from her solitary game of freeze tag and pounced on Candy, panther-like and ready to go for the jugular, which was where she was struggling to keep Candy still, her arm wrapped around her throat. She was regaining the upper hand, or arm rather, as Candy's hitting at her freakishly strong arm was slowing down to a series of half-hearted slaps.

"None of you can stop me. Not. A. Single. One. Of. You. Freaks!" She declared triumphantly, and it was all I needed to hear.

I dashed over to the discarded items from Candy's purse, snatched up the hairspray and lighter and moved closer to Ellen, who backed up towards the railing in response. My hatred must have been written all over my face, and she sensed it could spell her doom.

"Get away from her, you cunt!" I said, channeling my inner Ripley, paraphrasing her crowd-pleasing line from *Aliens*.

"You don't have the guts!" she said snidely.

"Oh, really? Try me." I said, pressing down the nozzle on the bottle of hairspray with my index finger on my left hand, while the thumb on my right one brought the flame to life, deftly and with precision. "How about a little fire, scarecrow?!"

A flame shot out at her, which caused her to back up further and loosen her death-grip on Candy, who slumped to the ground as I stood mine. I approached her languidly, in a surprisingly calm manner, focusing solely on scaring the absolute shit out of her.

Just for added effect, I brought my impromptu flame thrower back to life and completely miscalculated how close I intended to get it to her. The combination of flaming hairspray mixed with the hairspray she had applied to keep her tresses in place sparked a fire on top of her head.

She immediately began flailing, beating her head as if she were Joan Crawford showing her displeasure with Christina for having wire hangers in her closet. She did a half-pirouette, tripped over her feet, and went careening over the railing, leaving only the smell of singed hair in her wake.

My friends all yelled my name in unison, and I turned around just in time to see Troy bum-rushing me. If it hadn't been for Candy sticking her leg out as an obstacle, I may have suffered the same fate as Ellen. As it was, his trajectory changed course, and he struck his head with an audible thud on the railing, which rendered him unconscious.

"Thanks," I said breathlessly.

"That's what friends are for," Candy said. "Can someone call the cops?"

Derek and Michael decided this was a two-man job and vacated so quickly that I was surprised they didn't leave a vapor trail behind them. And just as they were out of sight, a new one was ascending the steps. Jeff had found both the gun and Nick, who was being marched like a prisoner of war, hands above his head.

"Well, well, well," Jeff said snidely. "Hello, Corey. Not sure that's a good look for you. You're a cute boy, but as a girl, not so much."

I had almost forgotten I was in partial drag regalia, minus my wig, which lay like a slumbering cat in the hallway. But I still had my heels on, as my mind stepped forward with an impromptu plan to distract Jeff long enough for Nick to grab the gun from him.

"I know; these heels are killing me," I said calmly. "I need to take them off. Do you mind?"

"No need to stop there," he leered.

I took off one shoe, rubbed my foot for added emphasis, removing its twin, keeping it in my hand until I lobbed it like a kitten heel grenade. It smacked him above the right temple, and this was all Nick needed to try to wrestle the weapon away from his captor. He pushed him to the floor, channeling his inner Hulk Hogan.

But for once, it was his bulk that came in handy, landing directly on Jeff's back, appearing to be giving him a horizontal version of the Heimlich Maneuver. But rather than it being a lifesaving method, Nick grabbed Jeff around his throat and was choking the life out of him. He only stopped when Jeff released the gun from what could be a death grip; he took it and rose from his current position with the look of a lover unsatisfied with the physical act he had just partaken in.

But he put his foot against the back of Jeff's neck to keep him put, for good measure, cocking the hammer of the gun as another added precaution, lest Jeff get any funny ideas.

The look of abject terror on his face told an entire story, as I wondered what Nick's was. Only days ago, Nick had murdered Danny in the coldest of blood and was now playing savior.

"I want you to tell them what you told me!" he bellowed at Jeff. "And make it snappy!"

"I was the one that planted the stuff I stole from your house in Nick's car. Let's see, now, how did your poem go? 'Some Romantic Notion Travels Across The Sea, Knowing No Boundaries And Only Sees Endless Horizons For You And Me." He performed quietly, not looking me in the eye, but I knew who he was addressing. "I had time to read it after I ran Danny over."

"You motherfucker!" It flew out of my mouth immediately and drove my body forward, even though my brain was trying to process the information. I began punching at him in a blind rage, my eyes open to the fact he had not only killed what could have been between Danny and me but had tried to pin his nefarious act on Nick, a man who had proved to have my back in the past.

And I had turned mine on him, going as far as to make karmic retribution instantaneous. But why had he pulled a gun on me? I stopped punching Jeff long enough to direct that very question at Nick.

"He told me you two were working together." He said. "That you were going to be playing the part of Corey for the police and to tell them I had tried to kill you, of how you went into hiding for fear I would really end your life. He used it as leverage to carry out his little plan with the bomb."

"You mean this bomb?" Ellen said from the shadows, now awake, but looking disheveled and in a now dirty outfit, one shoulder of her blazer was ripped, exposing a wanting-to-escape pad. The gleam glowing in her eyes matched my impromptu flamethrower which had not thwarted her as previously suspected. She was a little worse for wear, but her newfound accessory was intact with little red and blue wires.

"Oh, for fuck's sake with this bitch!" Candy commented.

"The feeling is mutual." Ellen countered, just as Nick took a rapid step away from Jeff and me with his elbow raised high enough to clock her in the nose, showing that spraying blood must be a hereditary trait.

She cradled the bomb like a baby while trying to suppress the blood pouring out of her nasal cavity. She divided her focus between the two, causing her to not see Nick run at her, sending her over the railing for the second time that night.

I'll give the bitch props; she knew how to make an exit.

As did Nick, as it turned out to be his inaugural turn to try to stake his landing, judging from the in tandem sound of breaking glass below made it appear and they had both missed the mark by a country mile.

I ran over and peered below to see where the police would draw the chalk outlines of them both. They looked as if they were in repose but could only be sleeping like the dead, given their bodies were displaying necks that were not what one would call being in "a natural position."

Ellen's especially because there was some sort of glass shard from the beakers that once held the dangerous chemicals, pooling together, of what had been the meth lab which had proved to be a lucrative side business for the Niles family. And it was now going up in flames, just like their dreams of becoming drug kingpins. In the middle of the burgeoning fire sat the bomb, and while I was no expert, it didn't take Einstein to see that this place was gonna blow!

I issued a command of "run!" My pleas were followed by the first explosion, which roused Troy from his semi-unconscious state. By the time he had gotten to his feet and the rest of us were using ours to flee, a second explosion thundered, sending up a plume of smoke.

It was all the motivation he needed to act as though he had bought a new pair of shoes, holding the promise of jumping higher and running faster. Troy sped past us and into Angel, who was waiting in the wings, an understudy and not a featured player for what had unfolded on the makeshift stage rife with drama and revelations.

No, he had quietly subscribed to staying in the background, an observer of the inner workings of Charade's drug front. But he had found his voice tonight, finally calling the police who were on their way, one of two they had received regarding the nightclub that evening. He had silently planted six kilos of meth in Troy's car. It was his insurance policy that Troy would do some time for his crime of hooking more restless souls on a drug that had stolen his innocence.

His many pleas to Troy to stop what he was doing over the past few years had fallen on deaf ears; a seismic shift from the nice guy he had once loved caused him to concoct his plan, choosing tonight after spying on Candy and me a few nights back. Angel knew if I was on the scene, something was about to go down, and he had to move his disdain for Troy further away from him.

Angel feigned concern, taking on the role of the scene stealer, leading Troy down the hallway and into the throng of police and firefighters that were swimming upstream as a unified tide. And oh, how they were going to turn for Troy. One of the police officers stopped and turned his attention to Troy.

"Are you Troy Fraser?" He asked.

Angel, who had given the police a description of his boyfriend, remained silent until Troy was in handcuffs and being led outside to an awaiting patrol car. But it was for himself and out of earshot of a pleading Troy, insisting it was all a mistake and for Angel to call his lawyer.

"I hate what this did to you, to us." He said, a hair above a whisper. "I hope you rot in jail, puto."

He made his exit into the night, sultry with humidity, lit up like a fireworks display with the various sirens from law enforcement and rescue vehicles, taking a deep breath at what turned out to be his Independence Day. Freedom was his for the taking, even if he didn't know what he wanted to do with his future, as he looked at a face from the past. Mine, to be exact.

I was standing just outside of the door to Charade, its cover literally blown, as Angel walked up. He offered his condolences about my recent loss with a "Sorry about Danny, mijo," turned around, and walked up the street, a shroud of smoke from the fire enveloping him as he disappeared into the dark.

I stood with my tribe, each of us making sure the other one was intact when two random thoughts entered my mind and exited through my mouth.

"Say, what did you do with Shadow?" I asked resolutely. "And, how did you guys get in, anyway?"

"Really? That is your takeaway?" Nina said with a hearty chuckle. "First, your baby is safe and sound at my house. It is amazing what Dimitri will do for 10 bucks, but you'd know all about that, wouldn't you? Second, we promised the doorman you'd blow him. And third, their rum and Cokes are to die for."

"Yeah, tell that to Ellen." I giggled. "Too soon?"

"Not for that one. I always hated her." Candy mused as an officer of the law began approaching her. "You kids should scram. You don't need to get involved in this nonsense. Besides, I don't need the three of you gettin' popped for underage drinking on my watch. Now scat! You keep in touch, mister."

"I promise," I said resolutely, not wanting to only call upon her in times of trouble.

As we beat a conspicuous yet hasty retreat, I knew Nina had been telling the truth as to her method of entering the establishment. The doorman was looking at me longingly.

"Next time," I said and blew him. I mean, blew him a kiss.

"I hope so," he replied.

And there it was, that word, hope. It's such a funny expression of emotion. You could be hopeful one day, hopeless the next, even hopelessly devoted to someone. And I felt it for the first time in what seemed like a lifetime. Hope.

And I could see it reflected in my eyes as I looked at myself in the bathroom mirror of my first apartment three months later.

But if I had known that two different pairs of eyes had recently fluttered open, unfamiliar with their hospital surroundings, I am not sure the feeling of being hopeful for a drama-free future would have remained intact. Nor was I aware that I had an unscheduled date with destiny tonight.

Epilogue

I entered the familiar stomping grounds of Crackers minus a costume on All Hallow's Eve, which served as the inaugural launch of Michael and Derek's new specialty night called Fisher-Price.

But it was also a special night for me.

They had requested a representation of my works of art, and I caught my breath at the sight of people studying the three I had created, taking in their meaning with the accompanying text on a non-descript white piece of paper, typed out on an old Underwood typewriter Mom had in her bedroom closet.

The summations below each work had been taken from song lyrics mostly and one of the journal entries I had made over the past few months, a healthy tool for getting thoughts out of my head, to not let the wheels of my brain spin out of control.

I positioned myself next to a girl dressed as Debbie Harry in *Hairspray,* a huge beehive that hopefully didn't contain a bomb; I'd had enough of that experience at a club, thank you very much.

She turned to me and said she found the work fascinating and was thinking about the piece in front of her. The one simply titled "Red." The caption read: "Red is the color of anger, red is the color of passion, red is the color of fear."

"Do you know the artist?" she asked.

"I'd like to think so," I said mysteriously and moved onto the next painting I had put my blood, sweat, and tears into until I deemed it fit for public consumption.

It was the likeness of Nina as Lydia Dietz from *Beetlejuice*, wearing the red wedding dress, throwing a bouquet of dead red roses into a black pit. The inscription read: "I am alone. I am utterly alone."

As if the painting had come to life, Nina materialized next to me, dressed as my muse, red wedding dress and all.

"You couldn't have picked a better quote for me?" she said, smacking me on the arm.

"Who said that's you?" I answered in all seriousness.

The next painting to its right detailed a singular hand reaching up towards the sunlight. The italicized typed letters cribbed from the opening line of Crowded House's "Don't Dream It's Over" was the hopeful message of where she was now. Of where I was now.

"*There is freedom within.*"

"What's up with you not wearing a costume? I thought tonight was gay Christmas to you, homos."

"I've been enough people for a while; it's time to be myself," I proclaimed, and her silence indicated she understood completely.

I had wished Mom would have been in attendance for my artistic debut, but she had plans with grandmother, as the two had buried the decades-long feud. Besides, as ok as she was with who I was, this wasn't really her scene. But it was now mine, and I relished the friendships I had made and being able to show off my sweet moves on the dance floor.

"Would you care to dance?" I asked gallantly.

"I thought you'd never ask," Nina answered demurely before adopting her regular speaking voice. "Move it, bitch!"

"Yes, ma'am."

As soon as we were out among the sea of people pretending to be someone they were not, I had the feeling that I was being watched. I turned around to see Freddy Krueger staring at me up and down. He took off his fedora with his clawed hand, then bowed with an arm flourish, silently asking me to dance.

The juxtaposition of the cinematic boogeyman acting as a gentleman instead was unnerving, but I went with it. Nina joined us in giving it our all to New Order's "Blue Monday," which I had choreographed for an audience of one in my bathroom mirror.

Right before the lyric "I see a ship in the harbor," I did a pelvic thrust that made Freddy put his clawed fingers to his mouth as if to say, "oh my" behind his rubber mask. But he didn't speak, merely laid the weirdest kiss on me that I'd ever had.

And when it was over, he started to remove the mask just as the power went out from an overloaded fuse box. Leaving me to wonder who was that masked man and question what would happen when the lights came back on? Would he still be there or vanished into thin air, returned to his nightmare realm, a figment of my imagination

My questions were answered when the lights came back on. Standing in front of me was Jake.

"What are you doing here?" I asked breathlessly.

"I never heard back from you," he replied. "And I couldn't stop thinking about you. So...I came back for you."

"Aww," Nina exclaimed and turned away with feigned disgust. "That's so sweet, it's sickening."

During the momentary blackout, the DJ had bumped into the turntable, and the song was now in the middle of New Order's "The Perfect Kiss," and he drew me in for one, minus the Freddy mask clutched in his hand. Even though his face was slick, given that he was sweating like a whore in church, I didn't care, happy to know he was made of solid matter.

But I'll be good and goddamned if it wasn't the embodiment of the song providing the soundtrack for our reunion.

Nina, caught up in the spirit of the moment, tossed her rose-red bouquet over her shoulder. With no head's up given, it bounced off the back of mine, landing at my feet.

I immediately thought of it as a bad omen. But only time would tell if he would be the man of my dreams or the stuff of nightmares.

That's the funny thing about life; you never know what's going to happen next. And shit was going to go down.

Acknowledgements

I've always wanted to do an Academy Award-type speech. Yes, I know the names don't mean as much to you as they do to me. But it's my book and I'll do what I want, thank you very much!

First, I need to thank the chosen family I am lucky to have found: Brett Card, Jennafer Grace Carter and Jack Conca, Gail Fellows, Kevin and MaryAnn Fitzgerald, Shannan Martinez, Tanya McAnear, Lisa Parish Moynahan, Mackenzie Moynahan, Deb and Mike Morrison, Carol Parish, Jeffrey Parish, Tina Fellows-Reinhardt, Chris Reinhardt, Cameron Reinhardt and Abby Reinhardt, James Swank, Miss Judy Taylor, Rebecca Woolston, and Cari'ssa Burnett Writer. Thanks for the support and hi to all of their pets that make my heart happy.

And to my family family. Tommy Parks, Fred Parks, Andy Parks, Mike and Juliana Parks (John and Jeannie). Sharon Baker, Fred Kramer, Starr Lanto, Julie Liles, Ricky Liles, Ethan Liles, Angela Mellors, Allyson Mogelnicki Alex, Courtney, David, Emily, Joey, and Paige Parks, thanks for putting up with my shenanigans, lo these many years.

I wouldn't be anywhere without teachers who fostered my creativity. A humungous thank you to Elaine Treadwell, Ramona Nevett**,** Terra Harris, Steve Grant, and Lynn Alley.

But I owe the biggest debt of gratitude to two women, my late mother Mary Parks and Willie Ginaven, who ran The Media Center at Ocean Knoll Elementary. She encouraged me to submit a short story I wrote in sixth grade, "The Basketball Star," to Stone Soup Magazine, which they published. Much in the vein of Henry Dodge, it was merely a thinly veiled plea for a puppy. Sorry I never got to meet you, Rusty. Not yet, anyway.

And the authors who have inspired me to put pen to paper and fingers to keyboards: Clive Barker, Judy Blume, Beverly Cleary, Michael Cunningham, Nick Hornsby, John Irving, Stephen King, Wally Lamb, and Armistead Maupin, who instilled in me during my twenties that my story had merit.

To the friends that let me be me back in the '80s and Beyond: Kurt Boyd, Joe and Caitlyn "Kitty Cat" Carvalho, Tyler "Squirrel Monkey" Dennis and Shelli Anderson, Carolyn "Tangina" Derrough, Ian Grove, Scott Hadden (Kevin), Dave Merino (Michael) and Brent Seward (Derek) – my first two gay friends and two of my dearest ones now, Todd Klein and Mike Rosensteel. Cheerleaders for my first novel, Mari Axiala, who saw the potential for *The Scheme of Things* to become a TV series. Kathleen Phaneuf-Lorraine and Kirk Lorraine. Sophia and John Hall – I still don't know what my motivation is. Henry Tran for letting me use his photo for *The Scheme of Thing*'s cover. Christy Savage Jaynes and Joseph De Vico. Lisa Vella and Donna Walker for selling the book at South Bark Dog Wash. Helen Erickson Barker, an angel among mortals. Ryan Young and Sean-Robert DYoung. Sorry, I made you lose sleep on copyedits on the first book because you couldn't put it down, Sharon Worth.

To my Palm Springs crew: William Klausing, Carsten Bertz, Rusty Best, Mark White, and Tim Livingston – thanks for reading Scheme aloud while in the hot tub and for all of your encouragement.

And Sharon Phillips (Sharon), who counts among favorite hag status, as does Kristin Stiles-Hall and her hubby Ayres and their children Henry and Ella - tiny giants in their own way.

Big gratitude to all the people who loved the first book, the independent brick and mortars that carried *The Scheme of Things*, and all those who attended my signings at Warwick's in La Jolla, Ca. Book Soup in Los Angeles and Dog-Eared Castro (now Fabulosa) in San Francisco. Support your local bookstores! And local libraries while you're at it!

OMG, I almost forgot my dog Simon, you are a constant source of entertainment, even when you're being an asshole. But you sure are cute.

And to my cancer doctor, Dr. Reza Shirazi, whose care made it possible for me to continue to be able to do what I love. Male readers over 45, get yourself checked out for prostate cancer, and God forbid you do have it, look into Cyberknife!

Sounds like the music is starting to play me off!

Wait, wait! To the guys who bullied me in high school; I have seen your Facebook profiles. Sorry you peaked in high school.

Henry Dodge will return in *The Fear of Heights*

Printed in the USA
CPSIA information can be obtained
at www.ICGtesting.com
LVHW041141130224
771667LV00005B/18